Stories Untold

By

Enitan J. Rotimi

In Memory of Professor Ola Rotimi
And
Dedicated to those who returned.

Acknowledgements

The idea for this book was sparked from a conversation with my father (Ola Rotimi) as he researched material for the Pidgin English Dictionary. I asked why Pidgin, a Krio dialect is only spoken in West Africa and not in former British Colonies in South, East, or North Africa. He responded that the slaves who escaped from Jamaica, USA and Brazil settled along the Coast of West Africa spoke a mixture of slave English, Jamaican Patios, and other languages of their former masters.

Krio is an African mispronunciation of American "Creole" referring to the "Slave English" they spoke. They came in batches between 1792 up until 1844. Escaping slavery and returning to the motherland did not guarantee their safety. The slave trade was in full bloom and slavers targeted returnees because they fetched more on the auction block than first generation Africans. As a matter of fact, the first settlement of returnees was decimated. More on this in the book.

The seed for the story was planted that day. The first draft would not be written until 2011. I had written 11 stories but was reluctant to publish afraid of failure and afraid of success. Failure because if it failed, I would disappoint him much like the children of many great men whose sons try to walk in their father's footsteps. Society compares them. Fear of success – What if I beat him in his field? So, I focused on making my mark elsewhere just as he had made his own mark elsewhere from his own father Enitan Samuel Rotimi – Founding member of the NLC. Fought the British for equal pay for African Engineers and their British counterparts. First black VP of the first college of Technology and later, the director of the Ports Authority where he had started out as a steam launch engineer. Rather than follow in his father's foot steps Ola Rotimi made his mark in Dramatic literature. I believed that I too should make my mark else where rather than walk in his footsteps despite the writing talent deposited in me.

Despite a successful career in Information technology, the urge to write increased over the years and I completed eleven novels unknown to most people who knew me. During Saturday prayer vigil Pastor Trevon Gross came to me and said: "I have a message for you from the Holy Spirit"

" Me? Am I going to win the lottery? Because that's what I'm praying for right now." I replied

"No. Gambling is a sin." He replied

"Today's Jackpot is $260 million; I will pay $26 million tithes. Think what it will do to advance his kingdom on earth." I said feigning religious piety.

"God gave you a talent and you have hidden it much like the wicked servant in the parable of the talents. He wants you to utilize that talent and he will bless the works of your hands." He said.

I have some "Doubting Thomas tendencies". While I follow Christ, I like to see proof.

The proof came when Pastor Gross said: God wants you to write books. He gave you the talent and expects you to use it."

How did he know? I wondered.

The next thing he said silenced the doubter in me: "You let fear paralyze you all these years. It is the desire of your father that you and all his children surpass him. That's why he invested so much time and money in your education and pushed you to be your best version of yourself fully utilizing your God given talents".

That night I decided to write something outside my comfort zone – Crime Thrillers. I will write a love novel instead. Initially it was hard especially as I don't read these types of books or even watch such movies.

Two hours into the struggle I got into "The Zone" . This is the phase in writing where the story plays like a movie in my head and my fingers type out the movie. Later I would fact check and research what I typed only to discover the character names may be fictional but their story weaves around verifiable historical facts and sites like Fort Tangiers built by former slaves turned soldiers fighting against the US government for their freedom. The Naval Dockyard in Bermuda where the former slaves split into two groups. One to Trinidad to establish their own independent community of free blacks – The Merikins and the other to West Africa – The Krio. The fortress in Nova Scotia built by the Cudjoe town Maroons on their journey from Jamaica back to Africa. The 400+ year old cotton tree still standing in Freetown where returnees did their thanksgiving prayers upon reaching the shores of Africa.

While I would like to take all the credit for writing this book, I must acknowledge that Stories Untold told itself as a series of visions that I merely typed out. I thank Pastor Trevon Gross for the message that freed me from illogical but paralyzing fear and allowing me to be a conduit through which the story got told.

Typing fast to keep up with the vision is bound to produce typo's misspelled words and right spelled words in the wrong context like "There" instead of "Their". Something my father if alive would catch easily. In came Gina Billups a schoolteacher who can catch errors in professionally edited NY times best sellers. She edited the early manuscripts for free because she loved the plot and thinks it should be required reading in schools especially during black history month.

The novel would go through several reviews before publication.

- Historical - History Professor Emeritus E.J Alagoa P.H.D. An award-winning author of 18 historical books.
- Theological - Dr, Pastor Trevon Gross, P.H.D, and Rev . Dr. Kunbi Merriman Johnson
- Developmental editor - Orakay, Author of <u>Big Girls don't Cry</u>, <u>Compton Collections</u>, <u>The Daughter and Woman of Vengeance.</u>

- Copy Editor - Enuma Chigbo. Executive producer of My Creek town Adventure film. Author, Letters from the wilderness, Joggling in Jamaica, and Children of Destiny amongst others.

Though a love story, I avoided rated X material because my children often come to mind my business when I write. Princess is eight, the twin boys are seven and they read everything on my computer, ask lots of questions and I don't want to explain certain things to them at this age. They helped with the cover design. Princess chose the colorful fonts. "To make it pretty" she said. The lion on the back is the symbol of the Kapora Empire. Dandan put it there. Little Daddy chose the background.

Contents

Prologue

Stories Untold is a riveting story of love, intrigue, and triumph over insurmountable odds.

1809 West Africa: Crown prince Macati son of King Zaki of Kapora falls in love with princess Awat of Wagombe. As the young couple plan the most spectacular wedding ceremony ever, beautiful Nyoka, Zaki's second wife has other plans for them.

Weeks to the fabulous wedding ceremony, prince Macati, princess Awat and most of their wedding party are chained on separate slave ships bound for Brazil and USA. Never to become King and Queen of Kapora, but to spend the rest of their lives separated from those who love them and toiling for those who love them not.

King Zaki dies in a desperate attempt to save the young couple. With Zaki dead and his crown prince Macati enslaved in Brazil, Nyoka's son Ika becomes king, with his domineering mother as the real power behind the throne. Sometimes, pretty faces come with ugly hearts.

Anyone considered a threat to their power end up on slave ships bound for the Americas and Caribbean islands. That includes Macati's mother and his baby brother. The new King becomes the regional ***Pombeiros***. A term Portuguese slave trader use to describe an African who sells other Africans into slavery.

Macati must escape slavery, reunite with Awat in Virginia USA, and return to regain his throne and save his people from tyranny.

Stories Untold by Enitan J Rotimi, a descendant of returnees maneuvers his characters around actual events of those who escaped slavery in Brazil, USA and Jamaica and returned to West Africa between 1816 and 1844. A time when Pombeiros targeted recent returnees for sale back into slavery because a returnee fetched more money on the auction block than a first generation African. The returnee already understands the language of the task master and the rules of the plantation while the first-generation African captive must first be broken then forced to learn the language of the new overlord.

How they escaped slavery, returned to Africa, outmaneuvered the Pombeiros and rose to political and economic prominence in West Africa is one of many stories untold in history class.

Chapter One

Love At First Dance

The shortest path to success is through troubles.

Ola Rotimi, *Ovonramwen Nogbaisi*

The Wagombe delegation walks carefully, yet confidently through a narrow footpath in the forest towards the Kapora capital. Concealed in the bushes, are armed young men watching. Nandi, an elder of the Wagombe tribe knows these men have been observing them for quite a while.

The narrow footpath opens into a wide clearing in the forest. It looks like an old farm left to fallow. Her long and sharp fingernails dig into her husband's biceps as she observes a dozen armed men join the group. The newcomers make no effort to conceal themselves. Unable to contain her anxiety any further, Nandi whispers to her husband Kebede an elderly Wagombe Herdsman, trying not to alarm the other members of the delegation.

"Those men have been following us for some time. We have come for peace, and they are battle dressed. They have surrounded us in the bushes, our sides, and in front."

Kebede gently unclenches her fingers from his biceps as he speaks in an even tone and closely locks his eyes with hers, inches apart from each other.

"We are not in danger. Those are Kapora scouts, not warriors."

Nandi raises her voice in disbelief, as her husband towers her height.

"Scouts with weapons? Look at them! Do they look like they are here to welcome us?"

She turns from her husband to the other members of the delegation to see if they see the same things she is seeing. Makuak, the leader of the delegation, and the others seem unconcerned.

"This is crazy!" Nandi blurts out, frustrated at their lack of concern.

Kebede shoots a look at her.

"Will you please keep your voice down?" He says.

Members of the delegation notice the edge in his voice. They look away from the bickering couple and continue walking.

Judgmental looks will not deter Nandi from following her instincts.

She glances about, assessing their strength, looking for weapons and possible escape routes. Four elders with wooden staves; her teenage niece unarmed, two young porters leading the donkeys laden with supplies, and four Parapouls, Wagombe Warriors, with spears and one in training — her last-born son Jabulani.

Nandi believes that she needs to protect him, but not him protecting her. How he got this far in the Parapoul training, without her assistance still amazes her. The family went through a period of hardship. It was like everything went bad at the same time. His birth brought the series of multiple hardships to a sudden halt, so they called him Jabulani – meaning "Rejoice". Added to being the baby of the family, they see him as their "good luck child" and fondly call him Jabu. She now wishes she had not pressured her brother, the tribal leader, to order him to come on this trip.

"We have four spears between the twelve of us. What good are they against thirty armed warriors? We cannot defend ourselves if they attack. Look up front to the right. One of them is demonstrating his fighting skills to intimidate us!"

Her husband smiles and then puts his arm around her waist. He admires the colorful multi-strand tribal choker necklace on her neck made from cotton rope wrapped in maroon embroidery threads, as he traces a light pattern across her soft neck with his thumb. To him, she looks like a goddess, and he admires her flawless dark skin, matching his skin tone.

Her gold earrings glisten together with the gold gemstones in her flattering goddess braids, as she tilts her head and leans back. His finger redirects its way to her defined face, as he locks eyes with her and reads the worry hidden in her dark brown eyes.

Nandi worries too much, and as always, he took the opportunity to assure her with a soft and comforting touch.

"My love, there you go, over-analyzing things again. That is a teenage scout dancing. The Kapora people are a warrior kingdom. Everything about their culture is militaristic. Even their dances involve kicks, swipes, summersaults, and jabs as if they are fighting. They train their boys in the art of war very early in life; the same way we train our boys to herd cattle. That teenager is showing off his dance moves to his friends. You know how teenage boys behave; they tend to show off their dance moves to their friends."

Nandi's brother, Makuak, leader of the Wagombe tribe, joins the conversation.

"I do not think he is showing off to his friends. He is demonstrating his dancing skills to someone in our group."

Makuak's eyes flash in the direction of his beautiful teenage daughter, Awat, who is oblivious to the conversation going on around her.

She is engrossed watching the scout's strange dance. The teenage dancer notices she is watching him and dances even harder. She laughs, playfully imitating some of his moves as her white and traditional umbhaco skirt featuring rows of black strips that follow the curve of the hem bordered by white rows, sways from side to side. The gold choker necklace glistens in the sun as she twirls.

He is in his own world, admiring the young lady. She was the most beautiful girl he had ever seen - tall, straight strong muscular legs, and a slim figure. Her hair looked as soft as cotton, in a big and thick brushed out afro, with a few twists wrapped in gold metal cuffs and woolen strings. Her smooth shiny black skin accentuates the bright colors of her jewelry.

Her big and dark brown eyes had his full attention.

His friends notice and start displaying their own moves. Soon all the scouts are somersaulting, kicking, jabbing, and swirling.

Nandi, realizing what is happening, nudges her favorite niece to stop looking and flirting with the scouts. It is not fitting for a lady of noble birth to gawk at young men and entertain them. "And how do you know they are scouts and not warriors? She asks, straightening her red umbhaco dress, in her attempt to steer the conversation away from Awat.

"Kapora warriors wear armbands and dashiki made of animal skin while scouts wear ankle-length baggy pants," Makuak says, pointing at the distinctive differences in the young men's' appearance.

"As part of their initiation into manhood, the Kapora boy must go through solo survival in the wild. That is to live off the earth with his weapons and return with the skin of a dangerous animal he killed unassisted He will wear this skin to important festivities, meetings, and battles for the rest of his life. The more dangerous the animal, the greater the status he has in his community. Until he goes through this rite of passage, he remains a scout, lives in his father's house, and is ineligible for marriage,"

The delegation's translator, a Maasai herdsman, interrupts the conversation by pointing at three men riding towards them. The rider in front is wearing an agbada, a flowing African robe of many bright colors, and a matching cloth cap with two parrot feathers stuck to the side.

The two men riding behind him are dressed in full warrior garb; one with a dashiki made of crocodile skin and matching armbands, and the other in a similar style made of leopard skin.

"Up ahead, riding towards us is Uzaza, Kasuku to the grand council. He is here to welcome us and lead us to the palace."

The Maasai refers to the rider in the agbada with red and grey parrot feathers in his cap.

"What is Kasuku?" Nandi asks.

"It means parrot because he is expected to always speak the truth, even when others are reluctant to say anything. His duty in the grand council is to present a counterargument to anything the King says lest the King is misled by "*yes men*," praise singers and sycophants who agree with everything he says or keeps silent in the face of a bad decision that will cause injustice or hardship to the Kapora people. It is through the Kasuku that people with a dissenting voice air their opinions at the grand council. Anyone who is too shy or powerless to make their petitions before the King in person will air it through the Kasuku. This includes citizens who want to make known a matter to the grand council but wish to remain anonymous."

"I see, so the Kasuku, like a parrot, repeats what he hears, good or bad?" Nandi asks, folding her arms.

"He doesn't just talk; the Kasuku's vote is equal to five votes in the grand council. For this reason, I asked my in-law to persuade him to present our case to the grand council." The interpreter replies.

"What if he says something the King or nobles don't like?"

It's typical of Nandi to ask that type of question.

"His person, office, property, and members of his family are immune to reprisal, even from the King. The person who holds that title must be a person of great integrity, wisdom, courage, and widely known for honesty and fairness. It's an earned title, not inherited. Uzaza, like those before him, has demonstrated these values on so many occasions that he has earned the trust and respect of the elderly King despite his age."

The teenage boys stand in order the minute the Uzaza rides into full view. They greet him and scurry off in different directions. He stares at the teen that started the spontaneous dance fest; the teenager is visibly uncomfortable.

He quickens his pace to the nearest exit in the clearing. Uzaza holds his gaze until the teenager disappears into the bushes.

Uzaza slowly turns to the Wagombe delegation, looking directly at Makuak.

"You are welcome; I am Uzaza, Kasuku to the grand council," he says in Kapora.

The Maasai translator translates into Wagombe.

Makuak stands erect, chest out and shoulders square; he greets Uzaza in Wagombe.

He glares back at the young Uzaza, about the same age as his first-born son. Both men stare at each other as though they were trying to stare each other down. Who would back down first? This makes Nandi uneasy.

"Why must men behave like animals trying to establish pecking order the moment they meet? This will ruin the purpose of our visit before we even start."

Nandi exhales when Uzaza looks down, then dismounts his horse and walks up to Makuak.

"Men, like every other animal that hunts in packs, instinctively seek to establish hierarchy. Dogs, wolves, lions, and men need a hierarchical order to coordinate prey's tracking and attack. Be it another animal, essential resources to sustain the pack, or, in the case of humans, economic activities for the benefit of the community or war to take by force from another or to prevent another from plundering them. Establishing the Alpha leader is instinctively embedded in the male psyche. It appears my big brother is the Alpha."

Nandi smiles.

Makuak is head and shoulders taller than Uzaza. It is no surprise considering the Wagombe are Nilotic — slim built and, on average, seven feet tall with smooth shiny black skin — whereas Uzaza is a Kapora Bantu from the Niger-Congo region. The Kapora, like their Bantu cousins, are generally thickset and grow between five feet and six feet five maximum. There are three Aboriginal groups in Africa from which every tribe branches or is mixed with other ethnic groups: the Nilotes, Bantu, and the Khoisan. Typical Nilotic features include very dark smooth skin and slender, tall bodies. They often possess exceptionally long limbs, particularly vis-a-vis the distal segments – forearms, calves. Those of southern Sudan are the tallest people in the world, averaging seven feet or more. Nilotes are also known for great stamina and well-known long-distance runners compared to the

Bantu's short bursts of energy. Over the centuries, many have intermarried with other ethnic groups producing children with mixed features. Khoisan features are short — between three and four feet tall. For example, the pygmies, Twa's and Negritos which means Little black people.

"I will walk with you and introduce you to the grand council. We have a lot to talk about between here and the council hall," says Uzaza.

The warrior in crocodile skin takes the reins of Uzaza's horse and rides to the back of the delegation. The warrior in leopard skin gallops out of sight, in the direction of the capital.

The delegation continues their trek towards the Kapora grand council hall. Makuak and Uzaza discuss, and the Maasai herdsman interprets. Uzaza asks what took them so long and why they are traveling on foot. The interpreter explains that they tried to take a shortcut through a tropical rainforest, but Tsetse flies bit the horses, and they died. The two donkeys survived.

"It's a good thing no one in your delegation got the sleeping sickness from those flies. They are the reason forest and coastal people do not ride horses, and our mounted horsemen cannot protect that region. I will request replacement horses for your trip to the grasslands. This time, no shortcuts," says Uzaza.

Nandi is relieved when they finally walk into the massive hall of the grand council. Her ankles hurt after walking for several hours. She wastes no time finding a place to sit in the benches reserved for the delegation. From her seat, she notices that the dynamics between Uzaza and her brother have changed significantly. It's as if Uzaza is a thirsty puppy lapping up everything Makuak has to say.

Their conversation is interrupted by the sound of loud royal drums. Elderly chiefs of the land walk into the hall. They arrange themselves in order of seniority. The drumming picks up tempo as servants' troop in, carrying the royal stool.

Palace guards position themselves on either side of the stool. The Royal bard walks in, announcing the arrival of King Zaki of Kapora.

"The great warrior like a lion whose enemies flee upon his appearance. The wise King who brings health and prosperity to his people, may your reign be long," the bard yells.

The gathered crowd answers in unison.

"ISE," exclaiming *amen.*

The women kneel, the young men lay prostrate, and the elderly bow their heads in greeting, as bearers of the royal "*Asa,*" the sacred, red twin staves, the shape of a caret, forming a big red inverted letter V appear, followed closely by the imposing figure of King Zaki himself. His right hand is upon the left shoulder of his youngest son, Ikwunga, who is named after his ancestor, the great Ikwunga.

On Zaki's wrist is a wide gold wrist cuff with a lion's face. Who so ever wears the cuff on his right hand has the mandate of the Orishas to rule.

Young Ikwunga is carrying a decorated gold scimitar. A gold sword representing the power of the Kapora was handed to the great Ikwunga, Zaki's ancestor, by the Orishas and passed on from generation to generation.

Ikwunga means "*My raised right arm.*"

It is believed that the Orishas saw the waywardness and wickedness of the nations of the earth, each one acting like animals, lacking discipline and morals, so they created the great Ikwunga for the very purpose of subduing the nations and bringing order on earth. They imbued him with great strength and matchless fighting skills that manifested in every aspect of his life, including how he danced.

When great Ikwunga came of age, they handed him the gold cuff with the lion's face and scimitar with the mandate to subdue all the nations of the earth and bring order out of anarchy. The Orishas gave him a mandate, a promise of victory, and a warning never to practice the wickedness and lack of morality of the nations he conquers lest he too will be subdued and will remain subservient to another.

His descendants will be scattered across the face of the world to be oppressed and exploited at home and abroad. They will create great wealth and buildings yet stand as outcasts amongst the wonders they have made.

The cup of adversity will not turn from them until they return to the ancient's disciplined lifestyle and moral laws.

Great Ikwunga had a band of twelve with whom he went out with to achieve the Orishas' mandate. To avoid the trap of power, drunkenness and the wickedness that stumbles out of it, he swore an oath to an honest, wise old man, to always tell him the truth and no matter how ugly it is. Hence, the first Kasuku came into being.

The band of twelve became the ancestors of the present-day warrior chiefs of the grand council who command thousands of Calvary men, archers, spearmen, and swordsmen.

The Kasuku title is given to anyone with the same virtues as the first Kasuku.

Nandi kneels in respect to the King like the other women present.

She observes King Zaki scanning the room and then disengaging from his son, young Ikwunga. Zaki walks over to the royal stool unrushed. The page takes his position in front of the King. Bearers of the royal "Asa" stand behind him.

The bard tells everyone to sit.

Uzaza stands up and addresses the council.

"Great one, may your reign be long."

The crowd answers.

"ISE."

Uzaza continues.

"It is said that a child cannot see standing, what an elder sees while seated. Elders of our land, it is you I greet. We seek your wise counsel in this negotiation with the Wagombe."

The elders nod in acknowledgment.

Uzaza swirls as he yells.

"Warriors of Kapora!"

All the warriors in the hall raise their spears and chant in unison.

"HUH!"

"You will never run from the battle!" Uzaza bounces as he speaks.

"The kingdom of Kapora did not taste defeat in the times of our fathers. Is it in your time that we will see shame?"

All Kapora in the hall respond, "*Ewo!* The Orishas forbid such a sight to cross the eyes of the living."

The royal drums erupt. The crowd burst into war songs. Even the elders join in singing, reminiscing about their youthful days as warriors. Testosterone fills the air. Minutes later, the singing and drumming subside, and Uzaza continues.

"Today, we have gathered to discuss the request of the Wagombe to become a vassal of the Kapora."

Nandi turns to the Maasai interpreter.

"What is vassal state?" She whispers.

The interpreter explains that the Kapora kingdom has expanded through military conquest and subjugated their neighbors. However, in recent years, the elderly King Zaki, a great warrior in his youth, has resorted to less violent methods of expanding and maintaining his empire. Zaki made non-aggression pacts with his powerful neighbors like the Wiley Wayo and the Kongo, while turning less powerful kingdoms into Vassal states in return for protection.

Leaders of less powerful kingdoms renounce their status as sovereign Kings but take on the lesser title of vassal chief, equivalent to a governor in a modern-day federal government. They continue to govern their territories but pay an annual tribute, a form of tax, to the King of Kapora.

In return, they become a Kapora protectorate. They have a representative in the central government and are guaranteed military protection from other powerful kingdoms that could easily overthrow them.

It is better to retain some power as a Kapora Vassal state than to be annihilated by another Kingdom.

Everyone dreads the Kapora warrior with his lion mane-looking dreadlocks and matchless fighting skills. No king in his right mind will attack a Kapora vassal state.

"What is the reason for this change?" Nandi asks.

The Maasai interpreter explains.

"King Zaki does not want to overstretch his army. He would rather grow it during peacetime and use it to serve a swift and crushing blow on anyone who encroaches on his territory. The quick and overwhelming destruction of an encroaching kingdom will send a powerful message to anyone who doubts the strength of the Kapora."

Unknown to anyone but Uzaza, there is another reason King Zaki broke from tradition and adopted this approach.

"Are you sure that we, Wagombe people, will fare well as a vassal state to the Kapora?" Nandi asks

"We discussed this before traveling hundreds of miles for this meeting; why bring it up here and now?" Her husband interjects.

"Just double-checking." Nandi lowers her voice.

He smiles and gives her the *eye*.

She knows what he thinks when he gives her that look.

"My love, must you over-analyze everything?"

The interpreter answers her question anyway.

"Other Vassal states have thrived under Zaki. As long as you pay your tributes, all will go well with you."

Nandi notices the oldest chief getting up.

He has a very hairy armband.

He must have killed a lion for his rite of passage into manhood.

The elder speaks.

"In my youth as a warrior in this land, I have seen great men fight to death to maintain their sovereignty. I was skeptical when our great King introduced the policy of voluntary vassal statehood without a battle. I thought; why would any self-respecting man, much less a leader of men, agree to become subservient to another man without a fight or the threat of total annihilation snarling at him?"

Nandi agrees with his logic, also wondering.

He continues.

"However, it has worked quite well for everyone, especially those Kingdoms about to be devoured by other kingdoms. But I don't understand why the Wagombe would leave their homeland and travel hundreds of miles to become our vassal state when they are not under attack. Our warriors didn't even know they exist, talk less about intending to subjugate them."

Uzaza responds.

"Wise one, I thought the same thing myself. When our scouts sent word that they were approaching our capital, I rode out to them, expecting to meet a cowardly bunch. I was wrong. So, I walked with them and spoke with their leader all the way here, and this is what I learned."

"The Wagombe are a pastoral people of Nilotic ancestry. They average seven feet tall and originate from the upper Nile region. They roam the grasslands with their cattle in small groups and built small, isolated settlements, making them easy targets for slave raiders from the North and Middle East."

There is silence in the hall as the Kapora in the room observe their visitors.

"Nilotes have been attacked and captured as slaves for centuries dating back to ancient Egypt through to the present day. The boys are pressed into military service, manual laborers, or turned to eunuchs to serve in Kings' and rich men's harems. The women are sold as domestic servants and child-bearers to rich short men seeking tall offspring. The offspring of such unions belong to the father. The Nilotic mother just produces and nurses the babies. The demand for Nilotic women is higher than for their men. Centuries ago, it was the Egyptians, then the Babylonians, next the Persians, then Arab Islamist expansionists. *Arabizing* and Islamizing the African continent from the Northeast, spreading southwards. For this reason, different Nilotic groups have migrated from the southern Nile regions in successive waves to various parts of the continent, mixed with the locals, and morphed into groups like the Dinka, Dix, Maasai, and Luo amongst others."

"The Wagombe, if threatened by a large, organized army, have on several occasions been able to unite to fend off the invader. Only to return to their segmented and pastoral lifestyle once the threat is over. However, in the recent past, the enemy today has taken a different form that has cost many people and cattle. They come in marauding bands to attack and kidnap isolated cattle herders and small Wagombe settlements and quickly disappear with people and cattle."

Uzaza narrates.

"To stem the loss of their people, the Wagombe have traveled hundreds of miles southwards into Kapora territory in the sub-Saharan grasslands, far beyond the reach of marauding Arab slave raiders and cattle rustlers, seeking a place to build a settlement and raise their cattle safely under Zaki's protection. In return, they want to pay us a thousand head of cattle annually."

After stating their case, Uzaza sits and lets the interpreter, Makuak, and the Kapora elders haggle prices and terms of the agreement.

Both sides haggle back and forth. The interpreter struggles to interpret between the Wagombe and Kapora.

Macati, King Zaki's teenage son, on the other hand, is communicating effectively with the tall and beautiful Wagombe princess with his eyes.

She recognizes him as the scout who was dancing earlier as they approached the Kapora capital.

She, too, responds in the same language with her eyes.

Uzaza abruptly interrupts this communication with a quick backhand slap to the side of Macati's head.

"These are important matters of state. Pay attention and stop making eyes at the girl," he says in hushed tones, not to disrupt the important deliberations.

Those who notice this exchange try hard not to laugh.

A settlement is reached; the Wagombe will have a parcel of land by the great river in the hinterlands for their town and graze in the Savanna. They will pay a thousand bags of cowries every year for grazing rights and an annual tribute of a thousand cattle as a vassal state.

Tonight, they will have a feast. Tomorrow morning, King Zaki will send them off with a contingent of mounted horse riders and donkeys to their new homeland.

As the guests settle in after the meeting, Macati sneaks out of the grand council hall to a narrow backway towards his friend Waggy's house. Waggy, son of the cattle trader and butcher speaks Maasai, a language similar to Wagombe. His father is Kapora, and his mother from one of the prominent Maasai cattle holding families.

She is the sister of the interpreter.

Waggy will interpret for the Wagombe girl and me. I want to know everything about her, he thinks to himself.

Macati turns the corner of a hut and runs into Uzaza.

"And where do you think you are going, young man?"

"Oh, just going to see a friend," Macati smiles wide to hide his surprise.

"*Ehem…* and would that friend happen to be Waggy by any chance?" Uzaza peers into Macati's eyes.

Macati takes a deep breath, contemplating whether to lie or tell Uzaza the truth. It is as if Uzaza can read his mind.

Uzaza continues speaking without waiting for Macati's response.

"Just like your father, when it comes to love, you think back to front."

Only Uzaza can make a statement like that and not have his tongue fed to vultures. As Kasuku, he can say anything he likes.

Uzaza has a good reason for being on Macati's case often. King Zaki has confided in Uzaza something that he has not told anyone else. Not the wisest elder in the land, not even his first wife Halima; the one who holds his heart.

"Walk with me. I have a few things to discuss with you."

Uzaza tugs Macati's arm before he can respond, leading him to a secluded area.

Uzaza informs him that there is another reason Zaki averted war and adopted the peaceful vassal statehood policy.

"King Zaki intends to live long enough and hold onto power until you, as his younger son, Macati can effectively take over the royal stool. Additionally, he wants you to be strong enough to counter a palace coup or fend off powerful neighboring kings that might seek to take advantage of an inexperienced young king. Zaki knows that political transitions are the best times to destabilize and overthrow a government, especially if the new leader is young, weak, and yet to establish personal and direct loyalties with the heads of parastatals." Uzaza says.

Macati is taken aback.

"Me, King? What of Ika? He is the first-born son oh!"

Uzaza looks about to make sure no one is within an earshot of their conversation. He motions for Macati to keep his voice down.

"I talk, you listen, and you will come to fully understand why you must be King instead of your older brother Ika. While Ika is the first-born son and nine years older than you, you are the son of the first wife Halima, and Ika is the second wife's son."

"Your mother Halima had difficulty giving birth for the first ten years of their marriage. She suffered multiple miscarriages and stillbirths that most people thought she would never have a living child."

Uzaza opens up.

"Your father married Nyoka, the Wayo princess, to cement diplomatic ties between the Kapora and the Wayo people. Like you, he was smitten by Nyoka's good looks and light skinned caramel complexion. She also had light brown eyes and the longest hair in an afro that made her hard to miss and resist. Unfortunately, pretty faces sometimes come with ugly hearts, and such is the case with Nyoka, pretty face, but very wicked and narcissistic. Nyoka had a son Ika, shortly after marriage. Being the mother of the only prince gave her the impetus to bare her fangs. Just as the Gaboon viper passes on her venom to her offspring, so did Nyoka. She passed her wicked ways to her son Ika. Those of us close to the throne danced for joy when your mother gave birth to you. Hence your name, Macati, *one who gives us cause to dance for joy.* While the first son usually assumes the royal stool, the stool can go to any of the sitting King's sons or a member of any of the ruling houses that trace their bloodlines to the kingdom's founding ancestor. Great Ikwunga, the raised right arm of the Orishas. Any of Ikwunga's descendants can mount the royal stool. That includes you and young Ikwunga."

"Zaki is determined that his first-born son Ika, son of Nyoka cannot succeed him as King and young Ikwunga is way too young to hold the office if enthroned in the near future. Zaki is getting old." Uzaza continued.

"That's what I want to know. Why the change in plans?" Macati interjects.

"Less talk, listen more," Uzaza responds.

"Ika is a hot-tempered bully, arrogant, and headstrong. A head full of pride leaves no room for wisdom. Even when his mistake is becomes apparent, his pride will not let him acknowledge it, much less try to correct it. He will do anything to prove a point. Far be it for him to listen to reason or opinions that differ from his. Ika's recent despicable action at last month's grand council meeting further reinforces Zaki's fear that as King, Ika might tear the kingdom into pieces. Alternatively, cause a mutiny by powerful warrior chiefs within the grand council." Uzaza answers.

"I heard about it; he violated the age-old oath and physically attacked you when you presented a logical counter-argument to his," says Macati.

Uzaza nods then continues.

"The concern is Ika, as King could become power-drunk, immoral and violate the covenant between the Orishas and our people, thereby invoking the curse of dispersal to strange lands, servitude to others, and the perpetual backwardness of our people.

Haven't you noticed that recently, your father makes you attend every council meeting, diplomatic meeting, and non-aggression pact agreement?"

"Yes, I wondered what that was all about," Macati replies.

Uzaza nods again.

"Your father is feeling his age and wants to coronate you while he is still alive. But first, you must prove yourself ready to take over the kingdom. The kingmakers will resist your coronation if you still run around acting like a child. That is why I get on you every time I see you acting like a child. It is not fair to set standards for someone and not tell them; that is why I am having this conversation with you now. It is time you started acting like a King and not like a teen because your father is getting old. The sooner you prove yourself worthy of the royal stool, the better it is for everyone."

Macati straightens up.

He puts on a somber face and says, "I will act like a King from now on."

He attempts to speak in the deepest voice possible, but Uzaza laughs.

"The shortest path to success is through troubles. The greater the success, the greater the troubles. Sometimes just the mere perception of success invokes the demons of envy in those close to you, bringing upon you a multitude of troubles ranging from gossip through sabotage to murder. Those who stand to lose if Ika does not become King will try to eliminate you. Especially Nyoka, as your coronation prevents her lifelong ambition of becoming the power behind the throne."

"How?" Macati demands.

Uzaza shakes his head.

For a moment, he second-guesses himself for giving this youth information that might be too big for him to handle.

"There are many ways they can do it. Poison is the preferred weapon of choice in situations like this. A hunting accident, juju to make you mad, or they can send a Kwagoso spirit after you. That is the weapon of choice of the wily Wayo."

"What is that?" Macati demands, frightened.

Uzaza is slow and deliberate in his words.

"The Kwagoso spirit creates distractions and hurdles to waste your time, energy, youth, and talents on fruitless endeavors and keep you from your predestined greatness. So, while others with fewer talents and less intelligence get further ahead in life, the victim meanders through life from one incomplete project to failure, to another near success, but never quite accomplishing anything worthy. The victim embarks on many great endeavors, but Kwagoso brings major distractions to block him from completing any successfully. He or she will toil for something, only to watch other people achieve and enjoy it for less than half the effort put into that endeavor. Over time you are viewed as a good for nothing, and never do well -an *efuleefu* to be shunned by friends and family. Your children will grow to despise you for the life of multiple failures, incompletes, and the embarrassment you bring them." Uzaza pauses.

"That is worse than death," Macati says.

Uzaza nods then continues speaking.

"The sad thing is, unlike poison or madness, which are overt, and people can quickly seek a resolution, the *Kwagoso* spirit starts out so subtly. Usually, in your teen years, and increases its activities over time that everyone, including its target, blames the victim. Many victims kill themselves out of frustration, while the sender takes delight in watching the victim and their descendants suffer."

"Descendants too?" Macati is alarmed.

"Apart from the direct consequence of the victim's failures, this spirit will follow its victim's bloodline for generations until it is exorcized or returned to the sender or the sender's living descendants," Uzaza replies.

"So, you think this is what makes me dance and chase after the Wagombe princess?" Macati stares at Uzaza with disbelief.

Uzaza laughs.

"No, Kwagoso isn't following you, the last time your father and I checked. You are just living up to the meaning of your name — Macati. The circumstances of a child's birth determine the name we give him or her. In your case, your birth brought great joy and dancing to the royal household, except for Nyoka, of course. Her special status as the mother to the only prince and her hold over the King ended that day. She did try to lay a curse on your placenta tree but was stopped, and she was summarily sent out of the main building."

Uzaza is referring to the Kapora custom of burying a newborn's placenta under a tree. As the tree flourishes, so does the child. Those seeking the good for the child will tend the tree and make prayers of blessings under it whereas, someone seeking to harm the child of an opponent could find the tree and lay a curse at its root that will impact the child's progress in life.

"Is that why she lives in a separate building at the far end of the palace compound?"

"Yes. She lived in the main building and was given high esteem as the crown prince's mother. Then shortly after your birth and your placenta buried under a tree, she snuck out there at night to lay curses on the tree so terrible things could happen to you. Unfortunately for her, one of the palace guards apprehended her, first thinking she was an intruder. She denies trying to curse you, but no one believes her. Your father and I checked your future to ensure she hasn't done anything to block your star."

"My father checked my future?"

Uzaza shrugs his shoulders in the typical African body expression, as if to say *what do you expect?*

"*Ehen* now! We never make a great decision without first consulting the ancestors and the oracle of Ifa, the all-seeing god."

"And what did they say?" Macati asks.

"They confirmed your father's concern that Ika as King, will at his mother's behest, violate the covenant between the Orishas and the great Ikwunga, thereby bringing our great civilization to ruin and servitude. The Kapora will taste defeat at the hands of the most ruthless coalition of nations, and the land will be filled with the slain. Evil men will plunder our wealth, and the hands of foreigners will be filled with our treasures. No longer will there be peace, and fear will spread over the land until you, Macati restore us to our proper position, giving us cause to dance for joy again. While you will make a good king, there are powerful forces at work to prevent you and your descendants from sitting on the royal stool."

"And this force at work is Kwagoso?" Macati peers at him, looking for any facial signs that will tell him if Uzaza is holding back anything.

Uzaza's facial expression is frank as he speaks.

"We were concerned that she might have sent a Kwagoso spirit, for that is the spiritual weapon of choice for the wily Wayo. Then again, she might have found another way to cover your star, thus prevent you from shining bright in your preordained place in history. However, the Oracle said, it is a physical barrier that will be used to prevent you, not spiritual. Nevertheless, we must be cautious."

"What is this physical barrier?" Macati demands.

"The Oracle of Ifa did not elaborate. Therefore, we have to investigate further through our human intellect. Is it sickness, injury, blindness? We do not know. Between now and when we find out what it is, your father will not say anything to scare you until he is certain. I am telling you this, so you, too, are cautious and stop being so open. This brings me to my next point."

Uzaza looks around before speaking.

"I have a plan that will endear you to the kingmakers and remove all objections when your father presents you for coronation before his death. It is important you do your solo survival rite of passage into manhood. Ika killed a Hyena; you must kill a more dangerous animal, preferably a lion."

Uzaza instructs Macati to act normal but at the same time, to not do anything that will endanger his life.

Most of Uzaza's words fade into the distance as Macati's mind races to figure out what physical barrier will prevent him from becoming King.

"Will I die young?" Macati blurts out.

Uzaza realizes the teen has not been listening to him for the last few minutes.

"We asked the same question, and they said you will live a very long life. What the oracle of Ifa would not say is in what condition. That is why I say don't do something that will expose you to permanent disability."

"The Orishas forbid! Long-life as an invalid is a fate worse than death," says Macati.

Chapter Two

Smoldering Embers

"A stick already touched by fire is not hard to set ablaze".

Ola Rotimi –*Kurunmi*

Later that evening, at the welcome feast, Macati joins the dance troupe to entertain the Wagombe. Participants form a half-circle and take turns sparring in pairs at the center. Fluid acrobatic play feints, takedowns, leg sweeps, kicks, mock jabs, head spins, swirls, summersaults, and footwork to the drums' rhythm and stringed instruments that look like a longbow with a gourd at the end. Macati is the best dancer in the kingdom. He devised his acrobatic stunts and blends them in with the traditional kicks so effectively that everyone gathers around to watch him anytime he dances. The only person in the kingdom that comes close, is his best friend, Waggy. They practice together; choreograph their mock fights that wow the crowd every time. Waggy will not be sparring with him today.

Waggy is decked out in a colorful dashiki and plants himself in the audience near Awat, the Wagombe princess.

On the pretext of explaining the meaning of the dance moves to the Wagombe royal family, he is talking up Macati to the Wagombe and observing Awat's reaction.

He later discreetly arranges a meeting between Macati and Awat after the feast. So discreet that no one, especially Makuak and Uzaza, won't notice.

But Nyoka observes their secret rendezvous from behind a cluster of banana trees.

Minutes later, Nyoka marches straight to her son's compound; her daughter-in-law, Jumo, greets her at the compound entrance.

"Mama, welcome." She curtseys in respect to Nyoka.

Nyoka sucks her teeth, then spits.

"Who is your mother, me? Do I look like a Hippopotamus? I beg, please where is my son Ika?" She yells, fastening the *duku* headwrap on her head.

The way your family treats your spouse reflects their opinion of you. If they do not respect you or your feelings, they will disrespect your spouse. Failure to protect your spouse enables the likes of Nyoka to attack that spouse and your children with impunity. Appeasement in response to their insolence encourages them even further. Your spouse and kids grow to resent you for your chicken-livered response to their tormentors.

Nyoka barges past and marches straight to the biggest building in the compound. She walks in without knocking and sees Ika drinking palm wine and laughing with his drinking buddy, Ayilara, a hilarious storyteller whose mouth spews even funnier jokes when his head is filled with wine.

"You bloody waste of space! I spent my sweat and time trying to raise you into a great man, but you insist on making a public disgrace of yourself and those who love you!"

Nyoka stands in her usual combative stance, with her hands on her hips as wrinkles form around her mouth in a frown. Her hands travel to the duku on her head before she brings them together in a dramatic clap, expressing her disappointment. Her hips wiggle as she mocks his drunkard friend.

The kitenge fabric covering her waist and the lower bottom of her dress loses its tight grip as she circles her son.

"I didn't do anything," Ika blinks hard, stammering his response.

Ayilara sneaks out.

He knows what happens whenever Nyoka barges in with her dramatic antics. She is no respecter of persons when angry, except the King. She will say and do anything hurtful to any and everyone around; witnesses and passerby, anyone, not just the object of her wrath.

Nyoka opens fire.

"That is the problem, idiot! You don't do anything worthy of praise or admiration. Macati, son of a commoner, has successfully wooed the pretty Wagombe princess despite the language barrier, swept her off her feet, and she is now madly in love with him. Soon they will be married and have tall, beautiful children!"

Nyoka tends to present whatever's in her imagination as facts in the most histrionic and inflammatory way.

"What is wrong with tha-that?" Ika protests.

Nyoka will string together disjointed insults, accusations, and hurtful words to dumbfound and depress her victim in this state.

"Are you so stupid that I should explain everything to you like a little child? Use your brain, moron!" Nyoka shakes her head like someone in deep lament.

She looks at her son with fire in her eyes, tears stream down her cheeks. Nyoka can conjure tears anytime she wants to manipulate through guilt.

"Oh! And I was glad when the midwife said you have a son. Little did I know that my enemies sent you into my womb to disgrace me for the rest of my life!"

Nyoka will play the victim while abusing you.

"Normal people marry spouses worthy of their status or the status they hope to attain in the future. You, the product of two royal bloodlines, lowered your standards and married something that looks like a pregnant hippopotamus!"

"My wife is a pri…pri… princess too. I married her at your behest."

There is a quake in Ika's voice.

Nyoka puts both hands over her head and sinks to the ground in an over-dramatized display of lamentation.

"*Eeeyi!* See the nonsense I have to put up with!"

She looks around as though searching for someone to bear witness to a great injustice being done to her.

"You blame me for your failures in life! Real men make sound decisions; stretch their hands to grab from life the things they like. You loaf about until life hands you what nobody likes. I have to step in every time to save you from failure! Be glad you have a loving mother like me who thinks for you and clears the paths to make your life better."

Nyoka shakes her finger in Ika's face.

"I said, marry a Kongo princess, so the kingmakers will deem you most qualified amongst your brothers to assume the royal stool after your father dies. Because they will say that when you march the Kapora army out to battle, the Wayos, your mother's people, and the Kongos, your wife's people, will march alongside you. The Mani Kongo, King of Kongo has several daughters you could have married. You settled for the ugliest one nobody else wants."

Nyoka adds a base to her voice for effect.

"Bottom feeder; now I have piglets and tiny Hippos calling me grandma while Halima will have beautiful tall grandchildren. Look at… look at!"

She points at Ika's chubby first-born son playing outside.

"Useless, fat, and stupid like his mother. And I say I have a grandson. What an embarrassment."

She raises her voice again.

"The popular Macati is closing the distance you had over him. You further closed the gap by your despicable act at the grand council last month. All muscle, no brains; like a gorilla, you physically attacked the Kasuku rather than counter his points with logical reasons for your position. The only advantage you have now is age, and that diminishes as your father lives longer and Macati grows into full adulthood. Keep on drinking, and one day, you, the product of two royal bloodlines, will bow without shame before your younger half-brother, son of a common woman."

Sweat runs down Ika's face. He looks around to see if anyone heard his mother talk to him as if he is a stupid little boy. He hates the way she has forced him into a war by proxy against Halima. Ika learned very early in life not to do anything that can be construed as disobedience to his mother. He dreads her.

"So, w-what are you s- saying, mama?" He asks, half hoping she does not tell him because he dreads the diabolical machinations of her mind.

"You are too stupid to understand even if I explained it to you. But I will rather die than be ruled by Halima's son. I would leave you to your folly and watch you grovel in mud while the son of that commoner sits on the throne that should be yours."

Nyoka hisses and walks out.

Ika stands at the door perplexed, watching his mother shove his firstborn out of the way as she walks out of the compound.

"Get out of my way!" She yells at the chubby lad.

"So sorry, grandma I wasn't paying attention," he forces a broad smile to hide his feelings.

Nyoka pauses then mutters under her breath, loud enough for the lad to hear.

"Kinyonga," She insults him with a word in Wayo meaning chameleon.

Nyoka uses it as a verbal cut to the boy. She knows he is hurt from how she treats his parents. He hides his true feelings and does anything to appease her, including accepting the blame for her wrongful treatment of him with a forced smile. His ego is dying the death of a thousand cuts, and she enjoys slicing him verbally and watching him grin and bear the pain.

Satisfied with the impact of her statement on the boy, she turns to Ika and says, "Don't worry, we shall see."

She laughs and walks out of the compound, leaving Ika even more confused.

"See what?" He wonders.

She does that often. She flies into a rage, then a barrage of accusations and hurtful words strung together by tenuous logic, then ends with something disconnected from all that just happened; this often leaves him depressed and confused.

Will she kill dad or Macati to ensure I ascend the throne? Is she doing this for me, or is she doing it for herself? She tried ruling through dad and failed now she thinks she can do it through me.

Chapter Three

Smallpox, Big Trouble

"Joy has a slender body that breaks too soon."

Ola Rotimi, The Gods are not to Blame

It has been a year since the Wagombe settled in their new homeland. Life in the new land is safer than their original home; their cattle grow fat and healthy. Wagombe have learned farming from their agrarian neighbors, and to everyone's surprise, they have a bumper harvest.

The Wagombe elders decide to invite the neighboring tribes to a festival marking their first anniversary in their new homeland. To open the week of festivities, Jabu and the other Parapoul trainees will go through their final rites of passage into manhood. They will be the first set of Parapouls initiated in the new homeland. Every tribe has its own rites of passage into manhood.

The Parapoul Initiation marks a young Wagombe boy's passage from boyhood to adulthood. *Parapoul* means one who has stopped milking, for he no longer does a boy's work of milking, tethering the cattle, and carting dung.

On that day, he will receive several parallel straight lines scarified onto his forehead with a sharp knife. The straight lines identify him as a camp guardian against predators like lions, leopards, and cattle raiders. He must not flinch in pain when the Benny spins a sharp blade across his forehead lest it cause a kink in the lines on his forehead, permanently identifying him as a weakling and a coward. A scar you wear for life.

Finding a wife with the mark of a coward on your forehead is very difficult. Such men end up with the women no one else wants to marry or, worse, forever remain single; never to have offspring, and therefore never become an ancestor to be venerated by your descendants after you pass on.

The relationship between Macati and Awat blossoms. He visits often and begins to speak their language, thanks to the help of his friend Waggy.

Awat also starts learning the Kapora language and customs.

Early one morning, as Macati prepares his horse to travel to the Wagombe settlement, palace guards inform him that his parents have summoned him. Macati goes to the throne room.

Seated in the room is his mother Halima, Uzaza the Kasuku, Obya, the medicine man, and on the royal stool, the imposing figure of King Zaki himself in royal robes.

This must be serious; he thinks to himself.

They inform him that there is a plague in the Wagombe settlement and that the planned anniversary celebration and Parapoul initiation has been postponed until the plague passes.

Obya explains further.

"Smallpox is ravaging the Wagombe community and nearby villages. The victim suffers high fevers, headaches severe abdominal and back pain. They become weak, and pimple-sized lesions appear all over their body, with high concentrations around the eyes, mouth, and throat. At that point, it's highly contagious. Breathing in droplets from the victim's sneeze or cough can cause infection. Unlike its lesser cousin, chickenpox, smallpox can cause delirium, set off psychotic episodes, blindness, and in many cases, a slow and painful death. The disease has decimated the Wagombe settlement. Among the dead are Awat's Mother and oldest brother, Nandi's husband, and all but one of her children, Jabu."

King Zaki orders Macati that under no circumstances must he go to the Wagombe settlement until the plague is completely gone.

Halima uses a softer approach. She begs her son not to go there lest he too catches the disease. If he survives it, he could have pockmarks for life if lucky. If not so lucky, he could be permanently blinded by the disease.

"Imagine spending the rest of your life in darkness, unable to do anything for yourself. Dependent on others and led around by the hand," she says with tears in her eyes.

Macati scans the room, noting the expressions on the faces of those present. His eyes and Uzaza lock.

The look in Uzaza's eyes reminds Macati of their conversation a year ago.

Could this be the physical barrier to my ascension to the throne the Oracle spoke about? He thinks to himself.

Macati remembers his response to Uzaza on that day.

"*The Orishas forbid! Long-life as an invalid is a fate worse than death.*"

That was before his love for Awat came to full bloom. Now he feels differently.

Life as King without Awat as my queen is a fate worse than death.

Chapter Four

A Message Of Hope In The Valley Of Despair

In a grassy valley next to the Wagombe settlement called the "*Valley of Dry Bones*," Nandi smears oxblood and fat on Kebede's dead body. She is trying to make him appetizing to scavengers.

The Wagombe are one of the few African tribes that don't celebrate the end of life or bury their dead. The body is left out for scavengers to "complete the cycle of life" and maintain the earth's natural balance.

Like most African groups, they are monotheistic; they believe in one Supreme Being — The Wagombe call that being *Engai*. Engai is a single deity with two natures, *Engai Narok* and *Engai Nanyokie*.

Engai Narok, the Black God is benevolent like the black clouds that bring showers on earth to make plants grow, fill up streams, rivers and provide water for man, plants, and beasts alike. On the other hand, Engai Nanyokie, the Red God like an all-consuming fire in the dry season, is vengeful, sending plagues, drought, and famine to those who he is angry with. Because no mortal is worthy of approaching Engai directly, the Wagombe appeals to lesser deities to ask Engai Narok to shower them with blessings or appease his polar opposite nature Engai Nanyokie when he is angry with them, much like Catholics praying through patron saints to almighty Jehovah.

The Wagombe believe Engai created a natural balance in the earth, whereby all his creatures eat other creatures to live and are in turn eaten by other creatures. Plants, creeping things, insects, fish, land animals, and humans play a part in the delicate balance. Engai provides rain to feed the grass, herbivores eat the grass, and carnivores eat the herbivores.

Omnivores, like human beings, eat both plants and animals, and in turn, get eaten by scavenger's insects and worms upon death. Whatever is left fertilizes the earth for plants to grow and the cycle continues. Burying a body breaks the cycle of life and soils the earth.

A body rejected by scavengers, mainly spotted hyenas, is seen as having something wrong and liable to cause social disgrace to the deceased's living relatives. The Spotted Hyena eats everything, living or dead, hair, bones, and flesh. If it rejects you in death, then you must have been a terrible person in life, an evil sorcerer, a wicked witch, or warlock. Whatever great achievements you made in life is attributed to wickedness, be it open or done in secret like evil sorcery, causing pain and suffering on other people to get ahead.

Scavengers will reject you in death for your wickedness while alive. Scavengers have rejected several bodies of those killed by the evil disease. Some say it's because Engai Nanyokie is punishing the Wagombe for leaving their original homeland. Others say the dead are just too many for the scavengers to keep up. Regardless of the reason for these rejections, Nandi isn't taking chances.

She smears oxblood and fat on her husband's corpse to cover the pockmarks caused by smallpox. The scent of the oxblood and fat will make him more attractive to hyenas, thereby averting the added shame associated with rejection to her already painful loss.

The valley of dry bones feels like trudging through the valley of despair. All around her is the evidence of decomposing corpses of people she loved in recent times past. Every day the dead bodies increase.

When will it stop?

There's nothing bright about the future.

Who's next?

It would have been better if death took her instead of her sons and husband. To outlive your spouse is a bad thing. To outlive all your children minus one is a curse. In her grief, Nandi does not notice the eyes watching her from the cluster of bushes behind her.

Several minutes later, they slowly move towards her from behind.

Nandi hears twigs snap under their feet. Through her tears, she notices their shadows moving slowly towards her. She hopes it's a pack of wild animals that have come to end her misery; the shadows stop moving.

They remain motionless for a while. She turns to see who or what is standing behind her.

Two human forms in strange clothes stand with their hands raised high. Nandi lets out a deathly scream at the top of her voice. *Evil spirits!*

The black one speaks.

"Fear not, we are not evil spirits but an angel of the Most High God and his prophet. We have come to comfort you in your time of grief," he says with a smile.

Nandi scrutinizes them closely.

One is a black man in long white robes with a black waistband, wearing lots of gold jewelry and a tall gilded miter that glitters in the sun. The second one is dressed in a similar fashion with a red waistband but not as much jewelry. His skin is pinkish white, like an albino or a man suffering from vitiligo. His hair is straight, his nose is long, his lips are thin, and his eyes are crystal blue.

They carry a black book, in one hand and a strange-looking stick with a hollow metal in the other.

The black one speaks with a strange accent.

"Fear not, God Almighty heard your wailing and sent us to help you."

Nandi peers at him with distrust in her eyes.

"Who is this God that sent you, and why did He not send you earlier to save my family from death?"

The black man introduces himself as Bishop Matthew, a prophet from God, and the European as Angel Gabriel, the special messenger of God in Heaven.

Nandi notices that Angel's eyes are blue like the sky.

Only a messenger from Engai could look like this strange being standing before me, she thinks to herself.

Nandi has never seen a white man before.

The North African Arab is the closest thing to white people that this generation of Wagombe have seen, and they are brown skinned with wooly black hair and brown eyes.

Bishop Mathew tells her about Heaven. He describes it as a beautiful place where good people go after they die. The streets are paved with gold. There is no sickness, suffering, or hunger but lots of wonderful things to enjoy for all eternity.

Bishop Mathew shows her some beautiful trinkets and western manufactured goods. He tells her that they are gifts from God in Heaven. Nandi says she doesn't want heavenly gifts but for the angel to tell God to bring her family back to the land of the living if he is real and all-powerful.

Back in the settlement, Jabu and several Parapoul trainees heard Nandi scream when she first saw Bishop Matthew and his companion.

He grabs a spear and jumps on a horse.

Barack, Awat's younger brother, and several other Parapoul trainees grab the nearest available weapon and run after him; some on horseback and others on foot. They head to the Valley of Dry Bones where Nandi was preparing her husband for the scavengers.

At the valley of dry bones, Bishop Matthew informs Nandi that there is a big river separating the land of the living and the land of the dead. People on each side are not permitted to return once they pass through the "*door of no return.*"

However, they can send messages to each other through mediums like the Arch Angel here.

Bishop Mathew points at the white man.

Only high-ranking angels like Angel Gabriel can carry things through the "door of no return" and travel between Heaven and earth. He likens the door of no return to the birth canal during delivery, just as the baby spends all of its fetal life in the womb for nine months and comes through the birth canal into the world to spend decades in our new world, never return to the womb via the birth canal.

"So, it is when we spend just a small portion of eternity in our present environment, earth, and pass on to the next phase of life in a different form. That phase of eternity is spent in Heaven if you are good, purgatory for some time if you were bad but redeemable, then taken to Heaven or become a permanent resident of Hell if you were irredeemably terrible."

Bishop Matthew explains.

"Occasionally, God would make exceptions and rapture people up to Heaven while still alive. But that is entirely up to His discretion, and it's very rare."

Bishop Mathew knows that the Wagombe, like many Nilotic groups, have embedded in their folklore, stories of Enoch the Ethiopian, who God so loved that he was taken up into Heaven while still alive — this is the first in a series of syncretic lies Bishop Mathew will tell the Wagombe.

Bishop Mathew believes it is easy to convert people when you mix biblical facts with their own religious beliefs, folklore, fear, and personal greed.

As they speak, Jabu arrives on a galloping horse, and a spear in hand.

Jabu, like other Wagombe, has not seen a white man before. He figures the white man with the red waistband is the wickeder of the two evil spirits his mother screamed about earlier. He charges at the white Catholic priest with a spear in his hand to thrust him through. Nandi shouts at him to stop, but it was too late.

The white priest raises the unusual-looking stick and points it in Jabu's direction, and the stick shouts with the voice of thunder, spitting fire, and death to the horse beneath him.

The horse drops to the ground, taking Jabu down with it. His spear falls out of his hand. The loud bang spooks the other horses behind Jabu. They shriek and run away, some dropping their riders to the ground.

The Parapoul trainees on foot stand transfixed in fear and confusion.

Jabu scampers to grab his fallen spear, and the priest reloads his musket, while Bishop Mathew cocks his gun.

Pointing it at Jabu, he shouts, "*don't move or we will strike you dead like we did to your horse.*"

Nandi jumps between her son and the strangers.

She thinks, *if the fire stick with the voice of thunder speaks fire and death again, let it take me instead of my only surviving child.*

"Do as they say, do as they say! I can't lose you too. They have come to help us!" She shrieks.

Jabu stands up slowly, leaving his spear on the ground.

Nandi explains to Jabu and the Parapoul trainees that a god sent these people in strange clothes and fire sticks with the voice of thunder to help them.

Slowly, a crowd gathers, and one by one, they come cautiously into the Valley of Dry Bones to see the strange-looking messenger from Heaven and his prophet.

Bishop Mathew tells them that their belief in a dual-natured Engai is wrong — there is only one God.

"He is white with blue eyes like Angel Gabriel," he points at the white man.

"Not black or red. He is the creator of the universe, and He is benevolent. However, He has a wicked enemy called Satan. God loves the Wagombe and has prospered them in their new land. However, Satan sent this disease to decimate those whom God loves since he can't attack God directly."

"Think of it this way, a man who can't effectively harm his opponent will try to harm his *song bull.* You the Wagombe are God's *song bull*, and Satan has decided to harm you since he can't harm God directly."

Bishop Mathew uses the cattle analogy to make his point, knowing that the Wagombe are cattle herders and place a very high value on cattle.

Every Wagombe man, on initiation to manhood, gets a bull they call his "Song bull." He starts his herd with this bull, raises it, sings to it, shapes its horn, and gives it a name by which he himself will be addressed.

Similar to how parents in other cultures are called by their favorite child's name. For example, Johnny's mom or Michael's dad, Wagombe men are called by their "Song Bull's" name.

"I see," says Nandi.

"So, God sent you and this Angel to save us from His enemy?"

"Correct," says Bishop Mathew.

Some in the crowd like Nandi believe, because a heart in pain is malleable to comforting words of hope, even if that hope is rooted in lies. Nandi wants to believe that her husband and children are in a better place and there is hope for reunification. Some, like the local Shaman, do not. Many others like Jabu and Awat are confused.

Bishop Mathew explains further that God created us with free will. We can choose to obey Him or try to make it on our own, like stray sheep in the wild.

Those who obey are like sheep under the guidance and protection of a shepherd. The shepherd leads them to green pastures and still waters. He guides them with His rod and with His curved staff, pulls them up should they fall into a ditch. Those who choose not to obey are like stray sheep with no protector. They are easy prey for wild animals.

Sooner or later, they will starve to death because they know not where to find green pasture, especially in times of drought. They have no help if they fall into a pit and live in constant fear because they have no protector.

In the spiritual realm, humans are powerless like sheep when confronted by Satan and other wicked spirits. The wicked spirits are like the lions, leopards, and hyenas.

"Just as you mark your cattle, goats, and sheep, God wants us to mark His people. So that He can easily identify those He will prosper and protect from pestilence. When the angel of death sees the mark of God on your arm, it will pass over you and move on to someone else without the mark."

He explains.

Unknown to the Wagombe, what Bishop Mathew calls "receiving the mark of God on your arm" is actually a smallpox vaccination that prevents the disease even if you were exposed a few days to an infected person but have not yet started showing symptoms. If you get the disease by chance, it won't be as severe as one who was never vaccinated.

Your survival chances go up 100 percent as opposed to 30 percent if you were never vaccinated, and even at 30 percent, you could have permanent effects like blindness.

With the vaccination, the disease doesn't get to the point of blindness. While effective, the smallpox inoculation methods used in 1809 leave a permanent mark on your arm. That mark is what he calls the "mark of God."

The believers line up and receive the "mark of God" on their arms.

Unbelievers like the local Shaman do not receive the mark. Several others, undecided like Jabu and Awat, remain; they watch to see if any strange thing happens to the believers with the mark of God while taking the preventative herbs prescribed by the local medicine man.

Three weeks later, the Shaman catches the disease from one of his patients. None of the believers with the mark of God catch it. That day, many undecided Wagombe convert to Bishop Mathew's brand of Christianity and receive the mark. Awat is among the new converts. Jabu and Barack remain skeptical.

The Wagombe being a pastoral community, interact with peoples from other tribes far away from their homeland. They take with them stories of Bishop Mathew's miracles and his religion. Word of Bishop Mathew's miracles spread across the region fast. Over the next few months, Bishop Mathew's congregation grows rapidly, taking in people from neighboring tribes.

At times, Bishop Mathew would show up at a village with the angel, but he often comes alone, every time bringing western manufactured goods like umbrellas, iron pots, and mirrors he calls *Heavenly Gifts.*

Many people come to hear him preach about prosperity, good health, and happiness and watch him perform miracles and wonders. Some join in hopes of getting 'Heavenly Gifts,' while many join out of fear of the evil spirit spreading agonizing death, the smallpox.

Mathew's church is designed to feed fat on the fears, greed, and despondency of its congregants. After the local Shaman caught and died from smallpox from one of his patients, everyone who believed in his healing powers abandoned their traditional beliefs and ran to Bishop Mathew to receive the "mark of God."

With the whole community inoculated, the disease stopped spreading.

Modern medicine refers to this as "herd immunity."

Word of how Bishop Mathew banished an evil disease from the land spread rapidly. People suffering from all sorts of conditions travel great distances to meet this miracle worker in hopes that he can rid them of their ailment.

Bishop Mathew starts demanding payment for prayers. Some get healed due to the placebo effect, while some get recovered due to modern medicine. Mathew grinds the modern medicine and mixes it with water. He and gives them to drink, claiming it's miracle water that chases out the wicked spirits that cause sickness.

With an ever-increasing congregation, Bishop Mathew's message gradually changes to one of self-promotion, personal aggrandizement, and demands for a "Seed."

His solution to every problem is, "Sow a seed," meaning, give the man of God, the Bishop, something.

Every time you turn around, there is a request to fund a new project. The first project was to build a massive church and a house for the man of God. Just as the first project was winding down, another came up.

The demand for people's time and resources increased, yet fewer heavenly gifts came from the Bishop and the Angel of God – the white man with blue eyes.

Instead, he gave them a promise of a better life and great treasures in Heaven after death. Soon, church attendance gradually decreases, starting with the religious prostitute.

A religious prostitute is a person who is affiliated with religion for personal gain, and not their love for the deity being worshiped. They come around only to get something — wealth, health, business opportunities, or seeking a spouse.

The list is endless.

The moment someone or something else offers to "Give them this day their daily bread," they are gone. Only those who truly love, stay for better or worse, or till death do they part from their religion.

As the threat of the dreaded disease fades into distant memory, the young people return to their daily lives of farming, hunting, fishing, and herding cattle. Jabu busies himself with taking care of his late father's cattle; on the other hand, Nandi gets more involved in Bishop Mathew's ministry to fill the nothingness of her empty hut, devoid of a husband and children.

Rather than spend her days brooding, she passes time in church; a place of hope, singing, and dancing. Something they do a lot of in Bishop Mathew's church.

He says it invites the Holy Spirit from the heavenly realm to move amongst the living congregants. A formula that resonates well with most traditional African religions. Adherents sing and dance themselves into a frenzy. The spirits of the ancestors and deities join the living in dance, sometimes possessing them and making them speak mysteries, see visions, speak gibberish, and sometimes act drunk.

The Kapora call these spirits the *Eguns.*

Bishop Mathew replaced the activities and manic manifestations of the *Eguns* with signs of Holy Spirit manifestation. His congregants don't know how to read the bible, otherwise, they would realize that these manic manifestations are not biblical but taken out of African traditional beliefs in *Egun* manifestation when they come to possess their adherents in worship.

Another syncretic lie by the bishop to get his message across to Africans.

The conga drums, metal gongs, and other musical instruments used in calling down the *Eguns* from the spirit world in African traditional religions are the same instruments used to usher the Holy Spirit's presence in Mathew's church.

He swaps out the symbols of the Orishas painted on the musical instruments with crosses and paintings of Jesus and the saints. All of whom look like his white collaborator; they call Angel Gabriel.

Bishop Mathew said that through good works, one could earn their way to Heaven. Nandi goes over and beyond the duties of a "good Christian," so she could be amongst those going to Heaven.

As abundant harvests near, and cattle increase, the Sunday service crowd starts thinning again. To stem the increasing number of backsliders, Bishop Mathew talks about a terrible place called hell — fire and brimstone for any unrighteous person who hears the gospel but refuses to convert.

There is an even hotter place in hell for those who converted to Christianity and later returned to their old ways after God protected them from Satan and his terrible disease. Just as people hate to be used and discarded, so does God.

If you come to Him only when you want something, then discard Him after He has blessed you, He will remove His protective cover from you and your descendants. As soon as Satan or any of his minion evil spirits notice you are unprotected, they will strike you with the very things you fear most. Your punishment does not end with death but continues for all eternity after you die.

The plan works for a while, and membership gradually increases again.

Many attend out of fear, some because of the prosperity messages, others because of the pseudo-miracles he performs, and Nandi, for the music and promise of a good life after death.

Mathew occasionally has open-air crusades where he performs miraculous healings. Sometimes people get so revved up by the music that they feel good for a while and believe they are truly healed. Attention seekers will stand in front of the large crowds and make outlandish testimonies of miracles to feel important before large audiences. Soon Bishop Mathew starts demanding payment for special prayers.

"Special anointing," as he calls it.

"A bull-sized offering gives you a bull-sized blessing from God. If you are a farmer, you will get a bigger harvest, if a fisherman, greater catch and if a cattle herder, no wild beast will kill your cattle; they will be free of disease and will have multiple calves."

He would say these things to thunderous cheers from the crowd, punctuating his sentences with *Amen!*

Much to Jabu's annoyance, Nandi starts handing over the prized family bulls to Bishop Mathew. He complains to Makuak that Bishop Mathew is robbing him of his inheritance with this false religion that demands bull-sized offerings from hungry people to give an already rich God who does not need beef to sustain Himself.

He believes Bishop Mathew is a fraud. Nandi counters that she is sowing a seed that will yield a harvest of success and prosperity in her son's life that will ripple to the fourth generation.

An intense argument ensues in Makuak's compound between those who believe in Bishop Mathew's message and those who think he is a fraud. Nandi points out that all who received the mark did not die of the strange disease sent by the Devil. Jabu points out that he and several of his colleagues in the Parapoul training did not receive the mark, yet they did not get the disease either. The same goes for most of the children of "milking age."

He points out further that Nandi took care of his dad and his brothers while they were sick and did not get the disease even before Bishop Mathew gave her "the mark of God." (Vacine)

Nandi didn't notice the pattern until Jabu pointed it out.

She looks at Makuak, and the others gathered for the meeting. It is as if Jabu is making her look like a gullible old woman.

Shame and anger start boiling up within her.

Awat knows that terrible things fly out of Nandi's mouth when anger fills her head, displacing logic and objectivity. Nandi will say anything to cause the other person as much pain and embarrassment as she feels. Even if it's something, she will regret after the anger has subsided.

Awat notices Nandi's voice getting sharper as it becomes increasingly apparent that the family is leaning in Jabu's favor. Nandi hates to lose an argument; especially with her husband and, worse with her children, whom she has made great personal sacrifices for.

Nandi knows something that will bar Jabu from the final initiation rites of passage into manhood if divulged. Awat knows it too.

Quarrels end, and bruises heal, but hurtful words never die. Awat must prevent Nandi from blurting out hurtful words that will cause lifelong damage years after everyone has forgotten what the argument was about.

Awat jumps in the middle of everyone and suggests that the family cattle be divided in two. Nandi can do whatever she feels best with her half, and Jabu does what he likes with the other half.

Everyone agrees with Awat's suggestion, and peace prevails.

Something that is unknown to anyone at the meeting, is that anyone who comes in contact with a cow with cowpox develops immunity to the human smallpox variant. Wagombe adults don't milk cows unless their life depends on it.

It's the job of the children of milking age and Parapouls in training until they complete their initiation. Jabu, the milking age children and the Parapouls in training had developed immunity from milking cows with cowpox.

A Parapoul in training can lose his position if he fails to perform his duty and his mother helps him. Nandi helped Jabu milk the cows on several occasions when he was overwhelmed. Unknowingly, this act of assisting Jabu gave her immunity to smallpox. She would never have gotten the disease, even without the "mark of God."

Awat leaves the family compound feeling triumphant that she just saved Jabu from major embarrassment and also Nandi from saying something she would regret for life.

From a cluster of bushes, she hears someone call her name. She recognizes the voice. She ignores it and keeps on walking. But the voice calls her again, this time louder. She turns around and responds sternly.

"Where were you when my mother and older brother died? You did not stand by me in my time of grief, yet you profess your love to me. Now that the crisis is over, you come around, hiding behind the bushes. Your words of love count for nothing if I can't count on you in time of trouble. I now count you out of my life! Go back to Kapora and don't return ever again."

"Come here, and I will explain everything to you."

Macati responds in hushed tones from the bushes.

"You come out of the bushes and show your face like a man. I thought the Kapora men were brave; why are you hiding like a coward?"

Awat demands.

Macati responds. "Because nobody must know that I am here. The Palace guards are after me. Once they know that I escaped, they will come here. If they discover that I was here, they will force you and your family to give me up. If you don't, they will burn your settlement."

Awat is visibly worried.

"Are you in some kind of trouble?"

"Yes," Macati replies.

"Come here quick before people see you talking to a bush and think that you have gone mad. It won't be long before the Kapora warriors arrive."

Awat goes into the bushes and Macati takes her deep into the forest, where he is certain the Kapora palace guards won't find them.

Macati explains that he was about to visit her several months ago, when his parents summoned him to the palace and informed him of the smallpox epidemic in the Wagombe settlement.

He agreed not to visit, but that night, he tried sneaking out of the capital to visit her. But Uzaza, Obya, and several palace guards had set up an ambush for him on the way. They knew he would try to visit even though he said he wouldn't.

Awat looks closely into Macati's eyes as he explains to her.

"As I struggled with them, Obya blew white vodun powder into my face. I blacked out immediately. Later I awoke to find myself tied up in a room. Obya was wiping things out of my nose while my father and Uzaza stood behind him. They said that they knew I would try to visit you despite the hazards. They kept me in that room until last night when I escaped. I am certain they will send warriors here as soon as they find out I am gone. Let's elope and start our lives together somewhere else."

Macati wraps his arms around Awat's waist, desperate to escape with her and start a secret life, far from their families. He so badly wanted to be with her.

Awat is unimpressed and turns down his crazy idea.

She cups his face with her tender hands, and shakes her head, looking directly into his eyes. As he towers her, his eyes plead for her cooperation, knowing it is the only way they could be together during these challenging times.

Awat tells him that he need not to lose his throne on her account, especially now that the disease is gone. She believes she can take him to Bishop Mathew, who will give him the mark of God, thereby preventing him from ever getting smallpox in case Satan returns with his dreadful disease.

She is convinced that as soon as he gets the mark, he can return to Kapora and tell them about the Bishop, his God, the cure for the strange disease and the abundant blessings and gifts from God that the Bishop can bring to the Kapora people.

Deep in infatuation after being apart from her for so long, Macati agrees to get the mark even though he is not completely convinced. However, if that is what it takes to reunite him with Awat, it's worth the try.

He is desperate to be with her and he is willing to do anything for her.

They both rush to Bishop Mathew's house and on the way there, Awat asks him a question.

"So, what is vodun powder?"

Macati explains that every time the Kapora army goes into battle, some warriors will get so badly injured, and adequate treatment may not be available on the battlefield, so Obya or any of his apprentices will blow the powder into the warrior's face.

Once inhaled, it goes straight to the brain and shuts you down instantly, slowing your heart rate and breathing down to the point that you could pass for dead. The warrior feels no more pain and can stay in suspended animation until the battle is over, and he is taken to a safe place where he is revived and treated for his battlefield wounds.

The warrior must be revived the same day lest he suffers brain damage due to oxygen deprivation to the brain. Otherwise, he will be revived with minimal capabilities. He becomes like a walking corpse if revived too late.

The Kapora have spun this known side effect to their advantage.

Sometimes, the Kapora will capture an enemy warrior of great reputation, and Obya will blow the powder into his face. The enemy goes into suspended animation. Obya will keep him under for so long that part of his brain dies from lack of oxygen and nutrients. When he is revived, he will only have the basic functional capability. The Kapora will then parade the enemy in his diminished functional state, reduce him to a beast of burden before the world, thereby reinforcing the belief that anyone who dares rise up against the Kapora cannot escape their wrath.

Even if they died, the Kapora would resurrect you to humiliate you again. You become a Kapora Zombie.

Awat informs him that the Wagombe has a similar powder made of frog secretions. They use them to kill lions and other large predators that kill their cattle.

"How do you get the wild animal to inhale the powder?" Macati asks.

"When calves and cows start disappearing, we know that there is a pride of lion or a pack of wild predators operating in the area. So, we make a paste of the powder and spread it on the back of a calf, then set it out to pasture alone. Lions being opportunistic animals, will see the young calf and attack it. Once dead, the entire pride feed on the calf ingesting the poisoned paste smeared on the calf's back. Soon they fall into suspended animation. You can walk up to them and kill them all with your spear. Some Parapouls take the cubs and raise them."

Ehn? Wont he eat you when he grows up?

He might if you don't know what you are doing. My father raised one but he died shortly before we migrated.

Why would Parapouls do that?

Would you pick a fight with a man with a Lion?

No!

Hence the saying "Speak softly but carry a big stick. He need not shout to get your respect. You will pay attention when he speaks even with a soft voice. Try not to aggravate him lest he lose his grip on the reigns of the Lion.

Macati is intrigued and listens carefully as Awat continues.

"I was on my way to prepare some for Jabu because a leopard recently attacked his cattle. Nandi says if he paid tithes to the Bishop, the leopard wouldn't have attacked his cattle," Awat tells Macati of the big argument they just had.

"What is your take on this, Bishop Mathew?" Macati asks.

He slips his hands away from her body and releases her from his firm hold.

"I'm not too sure, some of the things he says make sense, but others sound suspicious. I know that no one with the mark got the disease, so I'm taking you to meet him."

She believes its Bishop Matthew's mark that gave people immunity, and those without the mark like Jabu were either lucky or beneficiaries of protection prayers from Nandi and other Christians.

"What are you skeptical about then?" He asks.

"His constant demand for bull-sized offerings. Several beautiful young ladies in the church come to his house for special anointing at *night*. Some people who make outlandish testimonies during service and act very holy in the church are the most wicked people I know outside the church. Yet Bishop Mathew raises them to prominent positions due to their contributions and service to the church. It's all eye service to me. They only act holy when there is an audience."

"So why are you taking me to meet such a scoundrel?"

Macati chuckles.

"To get the mark of God, so your parents don't bar you from visiting after they hear that no one with the mark ever got the disease."

Macati tells her that he will return home with the good news as soon as he gets the mark. He tells her that he wants to marry her as quickly as possible, to never separate again.

Awat says he has to follow the proper marriage protocol.

"I am not a piece of fruit you pluck off a tree and walk away with."

She protests, wanting to follow culture and tradition.

"If I am to be a princess or queen one day, you must begin to treat me like one." She bats her eyelashes.

"Of course, my love. Forgive me Princess Awat." He bows his head, fooling around with her.

Awat giggles, and twirls into his arms, embracing the moment as he plants a kiss on her head to mark his promise and his deep love for her.

"*Nakupenda Mkuu wangu.*" She expresses her love for him in Wagombe.

Macati eventually agrees saying that he needs to go through the Kapora rites of passage to be eligible for marriage.

Macati explains the Kapora rite of passage into manhood through solo survival and Awat says she can make the powder for him to paste on a calf so he can catch and kill the biggest lion in the region.

She warns him not to sniff it as it will go straight to his brain through his nose and knock him out. He must not have a cut on his hand either, when smearing the vodun paste on the calf. If that happens while out on solo survival, no one will administer the antidote and revive him.

He just might become food for hyenas and vultures.

"Regular Kapora don't know how to make the powder. It's a secret known only to Obya and his apprentices," says Macati.

"Most Wagombe know how to make it considering wild animals often attack our cattle. I can show you how. We have to catch a few frogs," says Awat.

"Frogs?" Macati raises a brow.

"Some fish have similar compounds, but frogs are easier to catch. They secrete a white substance that covers their skin when threatened, which immobilizes and sometimes kills a predator that swallows it. You get more secretion per frog than from fish glands and it's not every fish that has that gland," Awat responds.

Macati is eager to return home with the mark of God on his arm, the stories of the bishop in his mouth, and the formula for the vodun powder in his head and love of Awat in his heart. He feels like he is walking on air. Life perfect. He has a secret weapon to kill the biggest lion for his manhood initiation.

If he returns from solo survival with a huge lion's skin, nothing can stop him from ascending the throne and marrying his sweetheart Awat.

Chapter Five

Solo Survival

It is dawn. Halima is preparing Zaki's breakfast in the cooking shed. She hears movement on the other side of the wall surrounding the royal compound. She is not sure if it's one of the palace guards or a domestic animal.

"Who is there?"

"Your favorite son," Macati replies as he scales the wall.

Halima is overjoyed to see he returned safely.

"How did you escape? Did you run to the Wagombe settlement? Does your father know you are back? Come here," She rushes to hug him, then stops and pushes him back.

"No, go back!" She peers at him from a distance.

"Did you contract the disease?"

Macati beams at her then speaks gibberish with a thousand words stumbling out of his mouth.

"Have you gone mad?" Halima asks with concern in her voice.

"No, Mama, I am trying to answer all your questions at the same time."

Halima laughs with her son.

"Can't you be serious about anything? I thought several months of detention would change you into a bitter person."

She unfolds her arms and dishes out boiled yam into Zaki's favorite bowl.

"I am bitter," Macati responds, putting on a twisted face, like someone who just bit into a lemon.

"You allowed Papa, Uzaza, and Obya to lock me away. Not once did you try to save me!" He speaks up.

"I was made aware of your incarceration only after they caught you trying to sneak out to the Wagombe settlement."

Halima cups his baby face with her soft and motherly hands.

"I agreed to keep you in custody because I would rather have you in custody than dead or permanently disabled. They won't let me see you because they thought you would convince me to pressure your father to release you. However, I was allowed to prepare and send your meals. I was heartbroken when the food returned uneaten for the first few days, but all that changed when you started eating regularly. Now answer all my questions," she demands.

Macati tells her that the plague has been completely eradicated from the Wagombe settlement because of Bishop Matthew's spiritual intervention. He shows her the "mark of God" he received as added protection in case the evil spirit returns with the disease.

"Oh, so there is no more plague?" Halima moves closer to her son.

A voice from behind them answers her question.

"The warriors we sent to catch him confirm that it is gone."

Halima and Macati swing around and find Uzaza, Zaki, Obya, and the chief palace guard standing behind them.

Halima takes a protective stance between them and Macati.

"Don't take him away!"

"But we have to be cautious that he hasn't brought back the disease. He might spread it to the Royal household," Obya responds.

"He is fine!" Halima shoots back.

"Can't you see he looks healthy?"

"It takes a few days for the sickness to manifest. We know he was with Awat, and it killed her mother and brother. Maybe Awat is resistant, but Macati isn't. So, we need to keep him away until we are certain he is clean."

Obya explains.

Macati shows the mark on his arm, explaining that he has immunity to the disease.

But sensing Obya and Zaki's skepticism, he suggests that he can voluntarily stay away from everyone by going on solo survival — the final rite of passage for the Kapora boy to become a full-grown man. It takes a while to track and kill a large wild animal and return with its skin. If the disease manifests, it would do so while alone in the wild. If he returns from solo survival in good health, he should be permitted back into society and marry Awat.

Halima gasps in pleasant surprise, and as Macati anticipated, she backs him up. Macati's months in custody were painful for her. The sooner the ordeal is over for him, the better for her.

It also gladdens her heart to know that Macati will be eligible for marriage upon completing the final stage of his manhood initiation. Having Awat as a daughter-in-law will fill the void of not having a daughter of her own. Something Nyoka often uses to taunt her through passive aggressive verbal jabs.

Great King Zaki, the one great men tremble at this voice, will do almost anything to please Halima even after twenty-seven years of marriage.

Macati, like all children, knows how to play one parent against the other to his advantage. He turns to Halima and looks at her with puppy-like eyes. Halima's maternal instinct kicks in, and she persuades Zaki to let him go.

Zaki yields, agreeing to let Macati go on solo survival. Zaki observes the smile spread across Halima's face and turns to Uzaza.

Just in case he has overlooked something important, Uzaza will point it out.

Zaki is glad to have Uzaza as his Kasuku.

Uzaza however figures that the sooner Macati becomes a full-grown man, the lesser the chances of Ika becoming king. Ika has already demonstrated that he will violate the old-age tradition of not harming the Kasuku, his family, and property if he becomes king.

With Macati as king, my head is safe.

He agrees to the proposal.

They turn to Obya.

"It sounds fair," says Obya.

"Stop by me as soon as you return from solo survival, so I can ascertain the sickness isn't manifesting."

"Agreed then!" Halima jumps in, almost hyperventilating.

"I will prepare something for your journey," she makes eye contact with Zaki as she makes the next statement.

"And as soon as he returns, we shall visit Awat's family for the knocking of the door."

The phrase 'knocking of the door' varies from tribe to tribe, but the basic concept is the same throughout Africa. A young man seeking a maiden's hand in marriage brings his family's elders to knock on her father's door and formerly ask for her hand in marriage. You don't visit him empty-handed, and you don't speak to the girl's father directly, but rather have an older person talk on your behalf.

"Let's discuss this later, first things first," Zaki studies Macati for a moment, nods, and leaves.

Obya instructs Halima not to hug Macati.

"Come back with a dangerous animal's skin, like me," says the Chief Palace guard, pointing at his leopard-skin armband.

"If I could get past you and your men and get into the compound, I can catch a lion," Macati boasts.

He puffs out his built chest with pride and clenches his jaw. His long and stretched out hair in dreadlocks sways from side to side as he circles the chief palace guard, chanting and boasting.

"We let you think you were getting past us. Didn't you spend the night watching us from the top of a tall Iroko tree on the hill half a mile away? How do you think the King, Uzaza, and Obya got here fully dressed as soon as you started speaking to your mother? I told the guard on the wall facing the hill to pretend to fall asleep the moment he hears your mother in the cooking hearth at dawn."

The chief palace guard points at the smiling young guard beside him.

The young guard gestures to Macati.

"We got you," he smiles in triumph.

"We immediately sent word to the King and everyone here that you are surrounded," the young guard chimes in.

"That you stayed up all night without falling asleep or losing your grip, in spite of the night insects tells me you are ready to stalk a worthy prey. Its good lions don't know you the way we do; otherwise, they will predict your hunting moves before you make them," Uzaza says as he leaves Macati and Halima.

Macati smiles politely.

But you don't know my secret weapon, He turns to Halima after the last man leaves.

"Mama, I'm not comfortable with what Papa said." Halima smiles then responds slowly.

"We dropped the marriage plans on him too soon. He is cautious. You know he must consult the ancestors before making any major decisions. Later, he will consult the ancestors to determine if Awat is good for you or not. Don't worry about that; they will say yes, and I will have my tall, beautiful daughter-in-law, and twin grandchildren, a boy and a girl and you must name the girl after me."

Halima gives him the *mother's look* as if to say *I am serious about this.* It's an unspoken language that all children understand.

"Ah ah? How do you know all that?" He asks.

"I already checked," Halima says as a matter of fact.

"What?" Macati's voice raises an octave in surprise.

"Don't hassle me. What's a mother to do but worry about her children, especially one that is so love-stricken that he risks getting a dreadful disease to visit a girl in a far-off land despite his parent's warnings? Mama's got to do what a mama's got to do. Now you go and bring back the biggest lion out there, and I will start making plans for the knocking of the door. It will be the best knocking of the door this kingdom has ever seen!"

Macati is visibly excited. He moves forward to hug her, but Halima steps back.

"Hey! You smell of sweat and forest. Go wash, and your food will be ready by the time you return. You don't want all the animals to smell you and run away while you are still far off. The only animal you will be able to catch smelling like that is an old tortoise with arthritis."

Macati walks away, mimicking an old tortoise with arthritic joints.

Halima laughs and says after him, "Your daughter's name will be Halima."

She returns to her cooking and mutters, "Don't get all starry-eyed in love and forget your mama; better not give her a Wagombe name."

"Halima! Your daughter's name will be Halima!"

Chapter Six

To Catch A Lion

The dry season has ended, and the rainy season begins. The early rains turn the formerly dry savannah into a lush green land, teeming with gazelle, wildebeest, zebras, giraffes, and millions of herbivores. Where herds of herbivores graze, carnivores stalk, seeking easy prey. It is a natural cycle.

The rains fall to water the earth, grass feeds on rain, grows abundantly, and multiplies. Herbivores feed on grass; they grow fat and multiply. Carnivores feed on herbivores, they grow strong and multiply, and when they die, scavengers feed on their carcasses. What is left fertilizes the soil that feeds the plants, and the cycle of life begins all over again in the African grasslands.

Today, the lion will hunt wildebeest, and Macati will hunt the lion.

Macati traps a young wildebeest. He smears it with vodun paste, and he leads it to a watering hole where he observed a pride of lions drinking from the previous day.

Lions are creatures of habit. They go to the same watering hole every day.

Macati ties the wildebeest to a tree then climbs another tree, north to the nearby bush, so the lions don't smell his scent in the wind.

This time of the year, the wind blows from south to north, moving moisture-laden clouds from the Atlantic to the African Hinterlands ushering in the rainy season. Climbing a tree north of the watering hole ensures the wind will carry his scent away from the lions approaching from the south.

Several hours pass, and a pride of lions troop to the watering hole. They spot the wildebeest, kill and eat it. The Alpha male bites off chunks of the vodun paste as he eats the largest share of the wildebeest. In a short while, the vodun past travels through his digestive system and knocks him out. It could have been faster if the lion inhaled it as it goes straight through the nose to the brain.

By the time the cubs have a chance to eat the wildebeest, most of the skin smeared with vodun paste is gone; they will not be affected by the vodun paste. Their sleep would follow the natural pattern of a lion after it has eaten a heavy meal. They can wake up on their own, unlike the Alpha male and the other lions that swallowed the paste. They will go into suspended animation and eventually die.

Vultures start circling above the wildebeest's carcass. The sight of hovering vultures is a sign to the hyenas that there is food nearby. They will follow the vultures overhead until they smell the carcass in the air.

Macati knows he must move fast. It won't be long before the hyenas arrive to devour the carcass. They will chase away the cubs and vultures and eat what is left of the wildebeest. They might see the comatose lions and think they are dead and start eating them also.

Macati must skin the biggest lion before the hyenas arrive. They move in packs of twenty to eighty and will attack a lone man with a spear. Death by hyena is worse than death by lion.

The lion will kill you first, then eat you. Dead people feel no pain.

On the other hand, Hyenas don't wait for you to die before they start biting off chunks of your flesh. First, they will surround you, all eighty of them, then they sneak up from behind each one, trying to take a bite. Eventually, one of the eighty takes the first bite. When you turn to strike it, four or five of them bite off your calf muscles; you fall, and the others will pounce on you to get a piece before the rest.

And hyenas don't like to share.

What starts like a coordinated attack quickly turns to competition by all pack members. They will bite and eat a chunk of your body as you thrash about in pain. Their bite goes through flesh and bone while you are still alive and run off, so another hungry member doesn't take your body parts away from them.

Macati hurries down the tree and rushes to the sleeping pride of lions, with a spear. He thrusts his spear through a comatose lion just below the rib cage in an upward motion, making sure the spear strikes the comatose lion's lungs and heart. As he thrusts the Alpha male, he accidentally steps on a cub's tail. It wakes up and starts yelping. Macati chases the yelping cub.

The cub, no bigger than a domestic cat, is easy to catch. He ties it to a tree then he skins the Alpha. Unknown to him, two females from the pride did not follow the pride to the hole that morning — they had gone hunting in another part of the savannah, following the herd of wildebeest from which Macati had taken the calf.

Now they are returning home by way of the waterhole, and they hear the cub yelping.

While the male lion is stronger, the female is more dangerous. She runs long distances, is faster than the male, and can take sharper turns. She is better adapted for hunting. To make matters worse, you tied her cub to a tree, and you just killed their entire family. *There are two of them against you.*

Chapter Seven

The New Year Festival

Every year in the lunar month before the new planting season — spring solstice in the Northern Hemisphere, or late March, going by the Gregorian calendar — Vassal chiefs and their entourage come to the Kapora capital to pay tribute to King Zaki and make offerings to the Orishas for a bountiful year's harvest. It's a weeklong festival marked with revelry, pomp, and pageantry akin to a modern-day carnival in Brazil, the Caribbean, and Mardi-Gras in Louisiana, USA.

Masked dancers in colorful costumes fill the streets of the capital, and the streets are filled with the flowing rhythm and sounds from African instruments like the *kudu horn, ngoma drums, wooden mbiras, zithers, shakers, stringed koras, Fula flutes, and the nyatiti.*

Among them are male youths and young women, displaying ritual, war and tribal dances with spears and cultural treasures belonging to the ancestors of Kapora. The dancing is captivating, with the spiritual power and strength that it discharges. The crowd cheers and chants, dancing along and freeing their spirits.

The riverside tribes bring tributes of fish and all sorts of marine creatures. Their entourage dance in costumes that resemble colorful riverside birds and marine creatures. They also bring a giant statue of the water spirit, *Yemoja,* to whom they give credit for their prosperity and safety while on the water. The agricultural tribes bring with them yams, rice, millet, sugarcane, and assorted fruits, while hunters bring elephant tusks, rhino horns, and animal skins.

Each brings a massive statue representing the deity or ancestor to whom they believe intercedes on their behalf to the supreme god to bring success to their various ventures.

Unlike the Wagombe, most African tribes believe you continue living in the spirit realm after you die. The Kapora believe that you join the Creator and other deities in the spirit world as an *Egun* and can influence the lives of living relatives here on earth. The spiritual realm is organized as follows: The Godhead is the sovereign king of both the spirit and physical worlds. Different tribes call the Godhead different names. However, his character and laws are similar to Jehovah in the Old Testament Bible. Beneath him are different deities, each in charge of one aspect of life. So, you have a deity in charge of fertility, another war, and another for the seas and water bodies. Much like a government with several departments, each responsible for administering an aspect of life. You also have regional administrators responsible for specific geographical and celestial regions much like a provinceial governor.

You don't send your petitions to the Godhead directly, but to the Deity in charge of the issue you are petitioning about. Just like in the case of government, you don't go directly to the head of government if you want to send your child to school; you go to the Education department. If you were a shrewd businessperson while alive, your *Egun* would work in the department of wealth creation and luck in business when you pass on to the spirit realm. The wealthier you were on earth, the higher in rank you will get in the spirit world's wealth creation department.

Your proximity to the executive committee of that department enables you to push through the petitions of your living relatives on earth for protection, good health, good luck, and prosperity in all their endeavors.

If you were a great hunter while alive, you will have direct access to the deity in charge of hunting and can assist living hunters in their hunting expeditions. If you were a wise and prudent person while on earth, you will directly access the deity in charge of knowledge, wisdom, and creativity when you move on to the spirit realm as an *Egun*.

Whichever department you find yourself in the spiritual realm, you will expedite the petitions of your living relatives, so they excel in life. Hence, success in one aspect of life runs in families due to their departed relatives' activities in the spirit realm. It is like having a family member in government, however, in this case, it's a government that rules our material world from the spirit realm.

Families with *Eguns* in the right places in the spirit realm fare better than families with no one to promote their interests.

At some point in the future, you can reincarnate into the family from which you came to reap the benefits, the good fortune, and blessings you bestowed unto that family while in the spirit realm as an *Egun*.

The birth of such a child brings with it good fortune to the family. Some parents would call that child their "*good luck child*." Those who knew you in your previous incarnation might recognize your personality and give you the name you had in your last incarnation.

Your character, which is an integral part of your soul, stays with you and never changes, whether you are in the land of the living or the spirit world. Therefore, it is not unusual for people to see a baby with a fully developed personality and refer to him or her as an "old soul." *One who has been here before.*

It is believed that a child in its first incarnation comes as a tabula rasa and will develop its personality as it grows. However, if the person has been here before, that child will not be born tabula rasa but come with his or her pre-existing personality.

The *Egun* of the wicked, insane, and those who commit suicide or die violently before their assigned expiry date takes a different path. Such *Eguns* are not permitted into the realm of the ancestors and deities but remain earthbound. They are not allowed to reincarnate into the land of the living. As one's character never changes, the wicked *Egun* will continue to cause trouble for the living. The *Egun* of the wrongfully terminated, for example a murder victim will seek revenge on its assailants and their living descendants. Their activities are usually around the location of their final departure from the land of the living or to *Ewa-Ufot*, the evil forest where the Kapora throw the bodies of convicted murderers, witches, sorcerers, the insane, and those who commit suicide.

Some wicked *Eguns* may leave their local domicile and wander into public gathering places like marketplaces and festivals to mingle with the living to cause trouble.

The Kapora avoid *Ewa-Ufot,* the evil forest, and places where suicide and violent deaths occurred. If perchance you must go to a place where the evil *Eguns* congregate, take with you, images of your protective deity, something that represents it, and or the favorite colors of your protective *Egun.* If you had a great fighter in the family that has passed on, take his image or favorite item. Your protective *Egun* and deities will keep the wicked ones at bay.

Never wear black in such places, especially for pregnant women, for it's an open portal for one or several of the evil *Eguns* to gang up and chase away the soul of the unborn child and possess its body while still in the womb. This is a loophole through which some of the wicked *Eguns* break the spiritual law barring their reincarnation into the land of the living. They possess the body of the unborn child and reenter the land of the living. Being wicked by nature, they bring their wicked character and bad luck with them. *Many in secret speculate that this is the case for her royal highness, Nyoka, and her offspring.*

The Kapora call such children *Omo-Iya* — a child of suffering also known as a *bad* seed. Such children are evil from birth. Their wickedness reveals itself even before they learn to talk. Unlike their good counterparts, these children bring with them fortune reversal and fruitless toil. Sleep leaves the eyes of the mother, and peace resides in that home no more.

Prominent in this weeklong festival is the fertility goddess in various forms, lewd dancing, and lots of alcohol. It is believed that she will grant a larger harvest this New Year and an increased population.

Lost to most young people is the religious significance of the skimpy-dressed dancing girls and their sexually provocative moves. To the youth, the annual festival is an opportunity to meet other beautiful young people from all over the empire and neighboring kingdoms. Even ugly people look gorgeous after a few drinks. Blame it on the alcohol, skimpy clothed dancing girls, or the fertility goddess; the facts are that everyone has fun this week, and many babies are born nine months later. Mid November to early December going by the Gregorian Calendar. Fondly referred to as festival babies. Which coincidentally is harvest season for most crops.

This is the first day of the festival.

King Zaki and his chiefs of the grand council and representatives of sovereign kingdoms are dressed in colorful regalia, sitting on an elevated podium to watch the procession of dancers and statues of the different deities led by the Vassal chiefs.

Noticeably absent is Chief Obijinaal of the Jinaali people.

King Zaki turns to Uzaza and asks.

"Have you seen Obijinaal or any of his people?"

"No," Uzaza responds.

"He is usually the first in the procession; his gifts and costumes are usually the most elaborate of all the vassal chiefs, praising you in a loud voice until he gets hoarse."

"True," says Zaki.

"It does not look sincere though. It is as if he is overacting to impress the crowd. I do not think it is from his heart."

Uzaza smiles.

"But his eye service compels others to keep up with him in praise and gifts. I am curious as to why he did not show up this time. Maybe we should send Ika and a detachment of warriors to find out what is wrong."

Zaki interrupts Uzaza mid-sentence by pointing at the Wayo contingent dancing in the procession.

"Look, over there, isn't that Buta, Nyoka's cousin leading the Wayo in dance? The Wayo are not our Vassals. I married Nyoka, their princess, to cement diplomatic and trade ties with them. Why are they dancing with the Vassals? They should be sitting up here with the other sovereign representatives."

Zaki points at the fat man in a black woolen tailcoat, white shirt, white silk gloves, a black top hat, black walking stick, and gaudy gold jewelry.

No one in the crowd has seen European clothes before. They think Buta's costume designer has terrible taste to make him a black costume when the occasion requires bright and colorful apparel. More so, it is believed that wearing a black outfit in public gatherings makes you an open portal for the wicked Eguns to work their evil schemes through you.

The blubber around Buta's belly shakes as he lurches on skinny short legs. Dancing in a black woolen coat under the African sun makes him sweat profusely. It pours down his face, making him look like a greasy black ball in a top hat with tiny eyes and white teeth surrounded by thick red lips as he smiles at the aghast crowd.

Buta misinterprets the shocked look on their faces as admiration of his new clothes and gaudy jewelry. Using his walking stick to steady his bulk from losing balance, Buta kicks his short skinny legs high so the crowd can admire his polished black leather boots, another item of western clothing the gathered crowd has never seen before.

Uzaza squints to ascertain if it is, in fact, Buta leading the group.

The last time he saw Buta, he was much thinner. It appears his belly and face rapidly grew fat, and his legs did not keep up. Now he looks like an overweight black potbellied pig dancing unsteadily on skinny legs.

"Maybe Buta doesn't know any better. He is such a low-ranking member of the Wayo royal family; he probably doesn't know the right protocol," he says.

Zaki orders one of the guards to inform Buta and the Wayo entourage that they should sit with the other sovereign delegates, not dance with the Vassals.

It is amusing to watch an idiot make a public spectacle of himself. However, it is not so funny if the laughing crowd knows that the shameless idiot is your relative.

Nyoka asks the guard to stay; she will handle this herself. She apologizes on Buta's behalf, stating he is the family clot. That is why no one trusts him with anything important. Buta had not succeeded in anything in his life until recently when a relative introduced him to long-distance trading with people on the Atlantic coast, so he no longer hangs heavy on the family's more productive members.

Long-distance trading has been quite lucrative hence the rapid weight gain. Nyoka thinks that Buta is using this occasion to show off his newfound wealth. As though to tell the world who once viewed him as a failure, *how do you see me now?*

He is delusional enough to think that the people laughing are impressed with his gaudy jewelry, ridiculous outfit, and idiotic dance moves.

Zaki nods in approval, as Uzaza chimes in.

"Buta must have passed through Obijinaal's chiefdom to get here. Find out from him if he stopped by Obijinaal's palace or has heard anything about why Obijinaal and his people have not shown up yet."

Uzaza pauses as though thinking of an answer to his own question. He stares at Buta for a moment, then blurts out the same question on everyone's mind but are too polite to ask.

"What is that stupid-looking costume he is wearing?"

Halima bursts out laughing.

Nyoka gives her a dirty look and leaves in a huff.

As Nyoka leaves, the chief palace guard informs King Zaki that there is a commotion at the parade starting point.

"Trouble?" Asks Zaki.

"No, joy. It is Obya and several our people jubilating about something. I see the Wagombe doing their jumping dance too."

The chief palace guard replies, referring to the Wagombe style of dancing in which they stand erect and jump high in one spot with very little or no hand movement. The Kapora find it rather odd as the Kapora notion of dance is like most Bantu tribes. It involves bending down and moving all parts of your body, except when you jump to execute an acrobatic move do you jump — not jumping up and down continuously in one spot like the Wagombe, Maasai, and many other Nilotic tribes.

Abero, Halima's maidservant, runs up to Halima and whispers something in her ear. Halima jumps to her feet excited.

"Macati! Macati! Macati has returned. He has the skin of several lions and is holding a live cub. It's like he killed a whole pride of lions; not just one for his solo survival!"

Macati had achieved something that had not been done in by any of his ancestors. Not even the great Ikwunga. He has marked his legacy before it was established.

Halima bounces in excitement, pointing in the direction of the parade starting grounds.

Obya, Awat, and the Wagombe entourage are with him.

"Look, they are coming this way!"

The crowd lining the sides of the parade grounds erupts in cheers as tall Wagombe Parapouls carry Macati on their shoulders.

Macati loves a dramatic entry.

It's been two weeks since he killed the pride of lions, captured a cub, and narrowly escaped death from the angry lionesses. However, he stayed in the wilderness, awaiting the annual festival to make his grand entry.

He had grown his facial hair into a goatee beard and shaved his nape in the wilderness. His new look also came with the new necklace of Lion teeth around his neck to mark his victory.

Looking down at the cheering crowd from the shoulders of the seven-foot-tall Wagombe Parapouls, he remembers how he ran up the nearest tree when the angry lionesses chased him as he skinned the Alpha male lion, and how he looked down from the branches at the growling lionesses. He thanked his ancestors that he got away just in time, and the creator of all life made it impossible for lionesses to climb trees with tall, straight trunks.

If it were leopards after him, they would have followed him up the tree and devoured him.

After catching his breath, he pulled the poisoned arrows from the quiver on his back and shot the lionesses. Waiting for the poison to kill them felt like an eternity. He could hear the distinct calls of the laughing hyenas in the distance. It won't be long before they hear the yelping cub tied to the bottom of the tree. They will come over and feast on the dead lions and the cub, thereby bringing to naught all his efforts.

He recalls hurrying down as soon as the last lioness died. He thrusted through them with his spear and quickly finished skinning the Alpha male, then moved on to the other members of the pride. He took off with the cub and lion skins and stayed on another tree far away from big cats' usual hunting grounds. He selects one with a deep gully around it because hyenas can't jump like most other predators

He stayed there overnight and a few days later, he reappeared at Awat's with the cub and skins. The joy on her face said it all, he is destined to have a great legacy as the Great Macati, and she is destined for greatness as his future wife.

She told him to go to the spot in the forest where she gave him the formula for the vodun paste. She will bring him home-cooked meals, milk, and a small goat for the cub. He stayed in the forest for two weeks and returned in time for the annual festival. Only Jabu and her younger brother Barack knew of this arrangement because she needed their protection when she went into the jungle to meet Macati. They kept his secret.

Now everyone believes he just returned from solo survival with the skins of a pride of lions and a live cub. *Only a great warrior worthy of the throne could accomplish such a feat.* It is a sign of great bravery to kill a dangerous animal, wear its teeth like a necklace, and its skin as a dashiki then walk its cub on a leash as you walk a dog.

Uzaza smiles; he knows the kingmakers will consider Macati's candidacy for the throne with favor, if there was no foul play.

Nyoka watches in disgust; the crowd jubilates as tall Wagombe carry Macati on their shoulders. All attention is on Macati, the lion skins, and the live cub he brought back from solo survival.

Nyoka gets upset when she is not the center of attention. She gets furious when the attention is on her rival Halima, or anyone associated with her.

Even worse is that Buta, her relative, has brought the wrong type of attention to her.

The crowd cheers as Macati jumps off the shoulders of the Parapouls carrying him. He lands and goes into a series of windmill spins. Kapora musicians swing into action beating their drums and playing their stringed instruments that look like bows. The crowd cheers even louder.

Waggy and several young Kapora men join him in dance. The Wagombe young men form a half circle as a backdrop and do their jumping dance to the music.

After impressing the king, the grand council chiefs, and the gathered crowd with his acrobatic dance, Macati announces his intention to marry Awat.

Awat is dressed to impress, in special Wagombe attire for such occasions, consisting of a white beaded dress with a colorful belt attached to her waist, and a matching collar tribal necklace, head chain, earrings and bangles.

The crowd erupts in cheers again.

Nyoka catches sight of her son Ika in the crowd smiling. She forgets her errand to speak to Buta and walks straight up to her son Ika. She can't contain her anger anymore.

First, her idiot cousin embarrasses her before the whole world, now Macati's dramatic return from solo survival endears him to everyone present at the annual festival, and Ika stands in the crowd smiling like a burnt he-goat.

When a goat is burnt in fire, the facial muscles contract, making it look like it is smiling. He-goats have beards like Ika.

In West Africa, the goat is considered one of the most stupid animals on earth because it never learns from its mistake. For example, you can beat a goat for trying to eat a pile of yams you just harvested. It will cry and run away only to return the moment the pain subsides. Then you beat it again and it will cry and run away again. However, as soon as the pain of the beating subsides, it will come back to do the exact same thing.

Nyoka shoves Ika.

"Idiot! Smiling like a burnt he-goat! Look, Macati killed a pride of lions and brought home their cub to domesticate. You big for nothing fool, what did you kill for your solo survival? *Ehn? Ehn?* A Hyena! Look, he has proposed to a tall, and beautiful princess. Everyone will compare her with that fat lazy hippopotamus you married. Now I have a bunch of hippos looking grandchildren while Halima will have tall and beautiful grandchildren. Moron, what is wrong with you? Do you have a Kwagoso spirit? Is that why you can't do anything right?"

Nyoka insults her son with no filter.

Ika hates how his mother turns everything into the "Nyoka show," with him as the villain who causes everything wrong in her life, real or imagined. Nothing he does is good enough for her. If he does anything noteworthy, she will not acknowledge it. Usually, she would point out that someone else did the same thing even better than him. But for the unthinkable horrors that would be meted unto him for striking his mother, Ika would have broken her jaw the moment she started demeaning him publicly.

It is a sacrilege punishable by stiff fines to insult your parent, much less strike them. Ika is relieved to see his mother's cousin Buta walking up to them.

Perfect distraction, I will get away from this irritating gnat.

"Nyoka, come feed your starving cousin. I have not eaten a decent meal since I left Wayo kingdom several days ago."

White teeth flash across Buta's pudgy face.

"You don't look like a hungry man to me."

Nyoka points at Buta's round belly hanging over his belt. A few buttons are pried open from vigorous movement while others stretch to keep the rest of his belly within the white shirt, wet with sweat. The woolen tailcoat, drenched in sweat, stinks like a dirty ram.

"Is that the way you treat your visiting cousin?"

Buta beams a broad smile revealing a gap between his top teeth held by red gums and surrounded by thick red lips. One tooth has a gold cap.

"Idiot! Why do you insist on embarrassing us? Go put on some regular clothes and remove that thing from your mouth before people start asking questions. Why would you tie a leash on your neck like a goat?"

Nyoka tugs Buta's pleated stocks, a predecessor to the modern-day necktie, bringing him close to sniff his sweaty woolen coat.

"You even smell like one!" She pushes him back.

From her peripheral vision, Nyoka notices Ika trying to sneak away from her now that she is focused on Buta. She turns and yells after him.

"Keep on running, *Omo Iya!* Child of suffering, I don't know who is worse between the two of you. I think you should return with Buta to Wayo land and visit Aro, the curer of sick heads. Let him inquire into the spiritual realm whether or not a Kwagoso spirit has been assigned to you the way it was assigned to this fool."

She prods Buta's hanging belly.

"That is why he was a failure in life until recently!"

Nyoka swings around and waves her finger in Buta's face.

"As for you, you too should visit Aro again to make sure the Kwagoso spirit hasn't returned with seven spirits more wicked than the first one. You recently turned your life around for the better. Judging from the way you are acting today; you could lose all your newfound wealth. Humph! Prancing around like a she-goat in heat, with that stupid thing around your neck," she sneers.

Buta starts to protest when he notices Nyoka is distracted, looking at someone approaching them.

Nyoka changes the topic abruptly by asking in a loud voice — one of those voices not meant for the person it is addressed to, but for the other people around you to hear.

"You must have passed through Obijinaal's Chiefdom on your way here from Wayo land. Did you see Chief Obijinaal?"

"No," Buta replies out loud, like an amateur actor reciting memorized lines. "We stopped at his palace and saw the wooden statue on the royal stool, so we assumed he had left already to come here."

He looks around to see who is walking up to them.

It is Uzaza.

It is the custom that when a Vassal Chief leaves his palace to visit a King or pay tribute at the capital, he leaves a statue on his stool to represent him while he is gone. It is believed that the Chief will hear and see anything you say to the statue while on his trip and answer back through his priest or in person when he returns from the trip. Like all monarchies around the world, the nobility and religious elites are intertwined. Chiefs and kings supposedly have strong spiritual connections; in some cultures, they are the direct descendant of the god or goddess worshiped in the kingdom or a representative of the god or goddess or the founding ancestor. That is why no one challenges their authority once enthroned.

Buta turns around and sees Uzaza walking up to them. He repeats himself to Uzaza. But the explanation does not make sense to him.

"If Obijinaal left for Kapora before you, and you didn't pass each other on the way, where could he be?" Uzaza asks.

"Maybe he took a different route," Nyoka cuts in.

Uzaza and Nyoka return to Zaki.

Uzaza tells Zaki what he just gathered from Buta.

Zaki thinks for a moment, then says,

"That is highly unusual for Obijinaal. He is usually the first to arrive and make much ado about his allegiance to me. His praises are usually the loudest of all chiefs. We should send Ika and a group of warriors to Obijinaal's town."

Nyoka tells him not to be too hasty.

"Give him a day or two; there are more pressing matters to attend to at the moment," she refers to the weeklong celebration and the "findings" prior to officially asking for Awat's hand in marriage.

Halima is surprised that Nyoka would bring up the matter of "findings" positively when she is obviously against the marriage.

Does Nyoka know something that would cause a problem?

The term "findings" refers to a background check into the families of the individuals to be married. It is believed that certain diseases and character traits run in families and can be passed down from generation to generation. Certain mental illnesses, suicide, and kleptomania, for example, are grounds for breaking off an engagement if discovered in your family because marriage is seen as the joining of two families, and if there is something bad in one side of the families, it could manifest in the offspring from that union.

When a young man indicates his interest in a girl, both families initiate the "findings" process even before the "knocking on the door." It is embarrassing if you knock on her father's door only to discover later that there is a blemish in the family that can be passed to the next generation. It's therefore prudent to first do the findings, followed by the knocking of the door.

Halima knows that a quarrel spawned by envy never ends. The envious will use anything to bring pain or embarrassment to the person they envy. She fears that Nyoka knows something about Awat's past that could embarrass the love-struck couple; that is why she tells Zaki to focus on the "findings" rather than investigate Obijinaal's non-payment of the annual tributes.

The first day's official opening ceremony ends as the sun stands straight in the sky at noon and everyone returns home to rest in advance for a long night of festivities when it is much cooler.

As soon as the royal family returns to the palace, Halima motions Abero, her maidservant, to come over.

"Run, find Mama Waggy, Waggy's mother. I need to see her immediately."

Waggy's mother is Maasai and is married to a Kapora cattle trader and butcher. She speaks both Maasai and Kapora. Maasai and Wagombe are two languages that evolved from a common root; quite identical that if you speak one, you can communicate with someone from the other tribe. This is similar to a Portuguese conversing with a Spaniard.

Halima wants Mama Waggy to mingle with the visiting Wagombe and find out if there is anything in Awat's background that might cause a problem.

Later that day, Zaki and Halima eat out of the same bowl.

It's a habit they developed many years ago while courting.

Ika comes in and requests that he ride with the Wayo delegation to visit his mother's people. He will return in a few weeks.

"If I let you go, you will miss your brother's knocking on the door," says Zaki.

"You know that it is important for all able-bodied males of the groom's family to be present for the knocking of the door. Your brother has publicly announced his intention to marry Awat now; he is a full-grown man. Tradition requires that we carry wine and go knock on her father's door to formally ask for her hand in marriage after the findings."

"There are enough men in the family to make an impressive showing; my absence won't make a difference," Ika replies.

Zaki stands up from his meal and moves close to smell if Ika is drunk again.

"Stop talking nonsense; it is Kapora custom for the groom's kinsmen to approach the father of the bride with drinks and formally ask for his daughter's hand in marriage. A wife is not an orange you pluck off a tree on the side of the road, and you keep on walking. No matter her social standing, she came from a family that gave her life and loved her for many years. Therefore, a man must meet with the family in their compound and demonstrate to her father that he can take care of her equal to or better than she was treated in her father's compound.

You have a duty to perform as a man in this family. It is important that they see the type of men this family produces -strong men, responsible men of noble character. Let it be known that their daughter is not marrying into a family of irresponsible, stupid men. Also, by merging both families, the union will produce great men of noble character to walk the earth long after they have passed on to the land of our ancestors'. Yes, a lion can only give birth to lions, and roaches, baby cockroaches. We must present ourselves in full force and show them that the house of Ikwunga is a house of lions, and therefore, they should expect great men from this union!" Zaki bellows.

Halima feels sorry for Ika. She knows that Zaki has long waited for the day of Macati's knocking of the door. Zaki will take this occasion over the top.

This ceremony will be bigger than anything anyone has ever witnessed in the kingdom. She knows this will cause Nyoka to rain insults on Ika.

She believes this is the real reason Ika wants to miss Macati's knocking of the door. He is deliberately trying to miss Macati's wine carrying to avoid Nyoka's insults.

He's not drunk; he is scared. Poor boy.

Halima strokes Zaki as she speaks and looks deep into his eyes. He locks his eyes with her and gently places his hand by her hip.

"You know he hasn't seen his mother's people since he was a little boy. Besides, it's been a long time since we sent a royal entourage to the Wayo kingdom. Who better than the son of both royal families to head such a delegation? One man missing from the entourage visiting our future in-laws can be easily excused for attending important state matters. It's an opportunity to express to them how we respect our in-laws by sending the sons of both unions to head the delegation to their mother's homeland. Now they know what to expect when their daughter, Awat bears us a son. Their grandson will one day head the royal delegation to Wagombeland."

Zaki smiles, his wife's wisdom and counsel is always timely.

This can have a positive spin and make a good impression on the Wagombe.

Ika breathes a sigh of relief when Halima intervenes. If only his mother was as tender-hearted as Halima, his life would be so different.

Nyoka's abrasiveness has made him an outsider all his life. Nyoka conflicts with so many people that he can't reciprocate their gestures of love towards him lest she calls him a traitor for fraternizing with the enemy.

Despite the conflict between Halima and his mother, Halima has always been kind to him. No wonder people gladly grant her every request with a smile. Even the great King Zaki, the lion killer, purrs like a kitten when she strokes him.

"Good idea, go and get ready with your entourage. I will arrange with Uzaza what gifts to send to your mother's people," says Zaki.

Ika hurries out of the palace to gather his things for the trip before Zaki changes his mind. In his haste, he brushes past Mama Waggy, Kwabena, Waggy's younger brother, and Abero, Halima's maidservant.

"What is the hurry, young man?" Mama Waggy asks.

Ika grunts and keeps on walking. Mama Waggy stares in shock at Ika's blatant disregard for an elder. Regardless of your social standing, you don't disrespectfully brush past an elder in Africa. This type of disregard for customs and other people's feelings causes concern on the type of a king Ika would be should he be coroneted.

Mama Waggy, still in shock, doesn't notice Halima motioning her to come over.

"Come quick," says Halima, motioning impatiently.

"What's going on? Everybody is in such a hurry today. Ika almost knocks me over and keeps on walking with impunity. Does his behavior have anything to do with your calling me over?"

"No, that is manner less Ika acting like a gorilla. He gets it from his mother's side of the family," Halima replies.

"Oh, that one, she hardly ever talks to me. I was surprised when she walked up to me today and started talking to me as if we have been best friends for eons. I am surprised she even knows my name," Mama Waggy says in a dismissive tone.

"Nyoka spoke to you? What did she want?"

Halima's chest heaves rapidly as she speaks.

Mama Waggy replies in a slow and easy tone.

"She was inquiring about Awat, and she wanted me to go with her to the Wagombe women so she can introduce herself to them and speak with members of the royal family. You know, being the wife of the king and a possible future kin's woman."

"Did you go?" Halima is visibly nervous.

"Me, go, why? I can't go with her. I made an excuse about attending to long-distance visitors staying with us for the festival. She was disappointed. I don't know what she was thinking. Maybe she thinks I should be ecstatic she is talking to me, and I would overextend myself to be in her good graces. I'm certain she is up to no good, and I will not be manipulated into facilitating her evil schemes."

Mama Waggy smiles.

Her young son Kwabena chimes into the conversation, saying,

"You were just telling Papa that you would tell Her Royal highness that Nyoka was up to something when Abero arrived to tell mommy that you needed to see her urgently."

Mama Waggy and Halima stop short and glare at him. Kwabena realizes he has broken a cardinal rule. In Africa, children don't get into adult conversations uninvited. Such an intrusion invites a dirty slap across the impudent face. Kwabena starts apologizing immediately."I am going to play with young Ikwunga.

"Yes, do that," says Halima.

Kwabena runs off immediately, happy that all he got was angry looks from his mother and Halima and not the well-deserved dirty slap. A dirty slap is the type of slap that lands you on the ground, confused and dazed for half a minute before the cry comes out your mouth.

Mama Waggy apologizes for Kwabena's behavior, explaining that Kwabena always follows Waggy anywhere he goes and copies him. However, Waggy gave him the slip and snuck out of the house. Now he is bored and minding everyone's business.

Halima laughs,

"Yes, I often see him following Waggy and imitating him. Macati calls him Waggy's tail. Where did Waggy go without his tail?"

Mama Waggy chuckles.

"Waggy is in hot demand today. With the festival and Macati's dramatic proposal to Awat, love is in the air, and Waggy is out there playing matchmaker to all the love-struck teens from the Wagombe and Kapora tribes. Hence the need to lose his tail. Now, little Kwabena is lost without his big brother and has attached himself to me."

"Young Ikwunga will keep him occupied. I'm glad you are here. I need you to check into Awat's background and find out if Nyoka might use anything against Macati and Awat. I know that they will get married regardless of what the fact-finders say. I am just concerned about a royal scandal before the wedding."

Halima's eyes dart around, checking if someone is listening to them.

"But there are fact-finders who do that," says Mama Waggy.

"The fact-finders take weeks, and they tell their findings to the whole family at the same time. I need to know if there is anything long before they do. You have a language advantage over them. None of them speak Wagombe or any of the closely related languages. Will you help me?" asks Halima.

Mama Waggy smiles as she responds.

"Why ask like you think I might say no? You know Macati and my son have been friends since they were toddlers. Macati is as much my son as he is yours. Besides, it was in my place that they conceived the plan on how to get Awat when the Wagombe first visited us. My brother was their interpreter when they came to negotiate with the grand council. He too likes to play matchmaker, diplomat, and conciliator. He is the one who introduced Waggy to the Wagombe royal family and suggested that he explains the Kapora culture and the symbolism of the dance moves. Waggy has been teaching him Maasai to effectively communicate with Awat without a third party tagging along. We are all in this together," Mama Waggy laughs.

"I'm glad to hear that," says Halima, somewhat embarrassed that she doubted Mama Waggy's faithfulness.

"How do you know all this?"

"Waggy has a tail," Mama Waggy laughs, pointing in the direction Kwabena ran.

"An intelligent and nosey tail... being the last born, he is also my little pet, and he tells Mama everything. Nice little spy he is. Just be careful what you say around him; he will repeat it — like he just did moments ago."

"Enjoy it while you can; he will soon outgrow this phase," says Halima.

Mama Waggy's face turns serious.

"The bigger question is, how do I get the information you need from the Wagombe without raising suspicion?"

Halima already figured that part out. She knows that Mama Waggy is not very outgoing and takes a while before she warms up to new acquaintances. An observer in social gatherings, barely speaking unless asked a direct question.

"Go to where the Wagombe women are gathered and ask which one of them is a good hairdresser. Identify yourself as a Maasai married to a Kapora man and make it clear that you would like them to give you a hairstyle close to your Nilotic roots."

"Hairdresser?" Mama Waggy asks.

"*Ehen*, now, wherever women gather to do their hair, gossip flows unabated. That is where you hear everything. From relationship advice to the hottest gossip in the community," Halima responds.

"Ah, I see, "says Mama Waggy.

"With Macati publicly declaring his intention to marry Awat, that will be the hot topic of the day. Naturally, they would be curious about what an inter-tribal marriage is like between a Nilotic woman and a Kapora man. Naturally, I will paint a rosy picture for them," Mama Waggy chuckles.

"You got the idea. Identify the most flippant of them all and befriend that one — preferably someone with a negative outlook on life. One who is quick to find fault in everything and everyone."

"I find it difficult to be around such people; why can't I befriend a regular person?" Mama Waggy asks.

Halima explains:"Because faults are like hills, you stand on top of your hill and can easily identify other people's faults from your vantage point. The person whose faults pile up high like a mountain is quick to see every other person's fault and pass down judgment from their high mountain. They are usually the most judgmental people. Besides, if you want to discover a woman's faults, praise her to another woman with low self esteem and she will tell you all her faults."

"You only have to deal with the judgmental gossip briefly, and you are free. However, if my baby marries the wrong woman, he will be miserable for life".

"I thought you liked Awat, and you always wanted a daughter. I assumed you would be happy to have her as a daughter-in-law."

"True," Halima cocks her head to one side then to the other — a gesture contemplating both sides of an issue.

"True, I do. However, you can desire something so much that you overlook other things that later come to bite you. It is better to want what you don't have than to have what you don't want. A terrible punishment it is to discover after the wedding that you are now bound to one who makes you miserable."

"True word," says Mama Waggy.

"Didn't you ask the oracle of Ifa?"

"How do you know I did?"

Halima is shocked to hear Mama Waggy knows of her visit to the oracle.

Who else knows and how much do they know?

Mama Waggy notices Halima's apprehension and offers a comforting explanation.

"You told Macati just before he went on solo survival, and Macati told Waggy. Waggy's tail was present, and the tattletale told me," she smiles.

Halima breathes a sigh of relief.

"I did, and the oracle said they would have twins — a boy and a girl. Excited, I insisted he names her after me. The Oracle also told me something I did not share with Macati."

"Was it something terrible?"

Mama Waggy crosses her arms over her chest with her fists clenched — a common African gesture meaning to protect your heart from bad news.

"Yes," Halima looks to the ground.

"It said they would go through several years of tribulation, but they will pull through in the end. I was wondering maybe Nyoka knows something that Macati and I have not yet discovered. That is why she starts talking about findings."

"Did the Oracle say that his marriage to Awat will invite the retrogressive spirit with two left legs into his life?" Mama Waggy asks.

The Kapora believe that some people come into your life and good fortune follows them while other people come in and bad things start happening — missed appointments, opportunities, the list is endless.

Their spirit and your spirit don't work well together, so your walk through life becomes quirky like a person walking with two left legs. That person may not be evil, and their spirit may work well with someone else but not you. Therefore, a permanent union is not advised unless you want to spend the rest of your living years in perpetual struggle and retrogression.

"No," replies Halima.

"It is a rough part of the journey he must take to accomplish the mission he was sent to fulfil on earth."

The Kapora believe that people are spirits on assignment from the Orishas. You are given the necessary tools, physical attributes, and talents to fulfill that assignment and then sent to your duty station to perform that assignment. For example, suppose your assignment is to entertain. In that case, you will be given the talent of song and dance, then issued a body to perform those moves and placed in an environment that will provide the necessary coaches and opportunities to develop and utilize those talents to execute the mission.

Sometimes those coaches and opportunities come disguised as pain. Just as iron ore must be burnt in fire and beaten with a strong hammer into a useful implement.

The hardships of life about to befall Macati will shape him into a useful implement for the Orishas and the benefit of mankind; this assignment is made before birth. However, not everyone fulfills their mission, and another is sent to complete it. Think of the natural-born entertainer who thinks it more pragmatic to become a doctor rather than sing and dance for a living. He will be a mediocre and miserable doctor instead of a renowned entertainer. When the allotted time to fulfill his mission is up, he and his talents are buried on that day.

Mama Waggy understands the Kapora belief system and agrees to execute Halima's plan.

"Okay, so I will ask the gossip questions about Awat..."

"And the character of her late mother." Halima quickly cuts in.

The judgmental gossip will give you all the negative information without much coaxing on your part. Halima hands Mama Waggy a pouch of cowries, a currency used by many inland African kingdoms in the 1800s.

"Buy her nuts and *Ikpakere* - plantain chips. Flippant people tend to talk more when chewing on something. A keg of sweet palm wine would facilitate the talkfest even more. If there is any negative thing in the girl's past, you will get it from the gossip with a negative outlook on life. Pay attention to what she says about her mother," Halima gives her an emphatic look.

"Ah ah?"

Halima explains further,

"*Ehen* now... Monkey see monkey do. If her mother alienated her father from his family, so will Awat alienate me from my son and grandchildren. I need to know if I'm gaining a daughter or losing my son. I went through a lot to have him; I can't lose him to another Nyoka type personality. Nice guys like Macati tend to attract mean-spirited women that bare their fangs after marriage."

"As a mother, I know your concerns," Mama Waggy replies.

Chapter Eight

The Visit

Three weeks later.

It is sunrise. Jabu and Barack are among the first group of teenage boys to be initiated into Parapouls at the Wagombe settlement. King Zaki and delegations from neighboring tribes are present for the festivities. Usually, King Zaki sends representatives for occasions like these; however, this is an important day for him, Halima, Uzaza, and Macati. The entire clan, except Ika, has come for Macati's wine carrying ceremony, also known as "the knocking of the door." This will be done right after the Parapoul initiation ceremony.

This day was chosen to keep in spirit with the initial proposal done during festivities. It saves the royal family from making a separate trip for the knocking of the door.

The fact finders returned with a favorable report.

Mama Waggy's private investigation for Halima yielded favorable news also. Just as the wound on the tiny finger inflames the whole hand, a single negative thought inflames the whole mind. Fortunately, most of the things we worry about never happen, and Halima's first impression about Awat was correct.

Now Halima is at ease again.

As they busied themselves preparing for this day, Halima and Mama Waggy joke about Halima's anxiety when Nyoka started snooping around.

Today the house of Zaki is present to formally ask Makuak for Awat's hand in marriage to their son Macati. They have brought with them kegs of palm wine and gifts to be presented to Awat's family.

As soon as the rooster crowed at dawn, Barack and Jabu ran to *Beny Bith*, the Fishing Spear Chief's hut to receive his blessings, then ran to the village square to take their place amongst the other teenage boys to be initiated into manhood.

They all sit in a row cross-legged, with the rising sun behind their backs. The Parapoul initiator comes to each boy, and in turn, each boy stands up and calls out his ancestors' names.

Like every tribe on the continent, knowing one's ancestry, family tree, and bloodlines are essential to the Wagombe. Stories of the great ones who came before you spur you to do great things yourself.

There are, however, practical reasons why Wagombe boys must learn their ancestry. They are a nomadic group. Not knowing your ancestry and family history in a nomadic society like the Wagombe increases the likelihood of accidentally marrying a blood relative.

That is a taboo punishable by Engai and the spirits that work under him. They will send you deformed, insane, or sick children to make you miserable for life.

Today, modern medicine tells us that the risk of genetic disorders and several mental disorders increases when blood relatives have children together. In the 1800s, the Wagombe believed these sicknesses were the punishment from the gods for marrying a close relative. Your descendants are your legacy.

Considering the Wagombe have no headstones with inscribed epitaphs, your children are the only ones left on earth to carry your memory or any proof of your existence. How they turn out says a lot about you as a person. Sickly, weak, criminal, stupid, or insane children should not be your final testament to the world.

Makuak's heart pumps hard as the initiator approaches his son Barack. Makuak is the *Beny-wut*, the Cattle Camp Leader of the Wagombe. He does not want his son to embarrass him in front of his tribe and the visiting dignitaries.

He pays close attention to signs of weakness, like trembling. He notices Barack's voice strengthen as he calls out the names of all his ancestors and the great things they did when they walked the earth.

Makuak's eyes shift to King Zaki and his entourage to see their reaction when Barack yells out his ancestors' names, starting with Kenteke Shanakdakhete, also known as Candace of Meroe in Greek historical texts, the Nubian queen in 332 BC, and her infamous stand against Alexander the Great. He had previously marched from rather, easily conquering Egypt, and then set his eyes on rich Nubia. He came to the border of Ethiopia only to meet Kenteke Shanakdakhete in personal command of her armies sitting on a huge war elephant and thousands of Parapouls in battle formation on top of a ridge.

In a battle between horse and war elephant, the horse loses or runs away.

In addition to war elephants, Kenteke also had mounted horsemen on Sudanese Barbs, the indigenous African swift light horse faster than most other horse breeds except its cousin the Arabian knight. Several on foot with lions on leashes and others on war elephants like Kenteke. To avoid the risk of having his record ended by a woman, Alexander the Great turned around and ended his expansion into the African continent.

For a minute, Makuak is lost in thought.

The day the children of the porcupine went their different ways was the day they all became food for the cat.

If only the Nilotic people could stay united and act as one, as they did back then, they would be far more advanced than they are today. Now the Wagombe, like other Nilotes, are easy picking for Arab slave raiders and cattle thieves.

He sighs.

It pains him that a descendant from such great leaders to lead his people to become a vassal state of another kingdom. However, he is consoled by the fact that his that his daughter's marriage to the Kapora prince elevates him above other Vassal Chiefs, and one day, his descendant might become emperor of Kapora — to rule over many nations beyond just his tribe.

Makuak's focus quickly shifts back to the initiation as the initiator clasps the crown of Barack's head firmly and spins it past the blade of an extremely sharp knife. Barack does not flinch, and Makuak exhales.

To flinch or scream during the initiation ritual will be to deny his courage, and therefore, disgrace his family and ancestors.

The initiator holds Barack's head firmly again and raises the knife to his forehead for the second scar, and Makuak notices his son's leg tremble. Shaking and jerking will cause a kink in the scar. A kink in the initiation scars on his forehead would brand Barack a coward, visible for all to see. Makuak feels pressure on his upper arm, turns to see Awat squeezing his arm as she sees the blood run down her baby brother's head. Her face twisted like she is the one being cut.

He unclenches her hand from his arm.

"I don't know who is worse; you or your mother. You worry too much about him," he says, trying to hide his fears and appear strong in front of his only daughter.

She always looked up to him for answers and strength since she was a little girl. He is "Super Dad" in her eyes, and he does not want to disappoint her. To show concern would only frighten her further.

"Don't worry about Barack; he's got his father's strength. He will be just fine," Makuak reassures her.

"It's my job to worry about him since mama isn't alive to do so. He is still the baby in the family," Awat replies.

"Not after today," Makuak responds.

"He is a full-grown man now."

She falls silent for a minute, lost in thought, then asks,

"Do you think Mom is with Engai and our ancestors? Macati says that when people die, they join with the almighty creator and intercede on behalf of the living, especially in times like this. They will give Barack the strength to make it through. They love him, and his failure is their failure also, and his success makes them proud — they too have a stake in his success."

Makuak hesitates before answering.

"The Kapora people, like other West African tribes, believe in the dead interceding on behalf of their living relatives. We don't. I think when you are gone, you are gone. The chicken you ate for dinner last night will not reach out from the great beyond to stop you from eating her eggs for breakfast," says Makuak.

"Those who die in battle can't continue the battle from the spirit realm, and neither can they protect their orphaned children and widows from wicked opportunists who exploit and mistreat them after their father's death."

He continues.

Awat is uncomfortable with his response.

"But Bishop Mathew said that those who did good while on earth would go to heaven, and those who were bad will go to hell."

"How does he know? Has anyone come back from the dead to confirm that there is a heaven or hell?"

Makuak thinks this new doctrine of an after-life is bringing confusion into their simple society. After the death of his people, his first son and wife in such a short space of time, Makuak started doubting the existence of any benevolent spirits at all.

Which priest did he not consult when his people died?

What sacrifice did he not offer the gods when his wife got sick?

What prayers did he not make when his first son and heir agonized with smallpox? Each priest gave a different explanation.

"The gods are angry," they would say.

Listening to them was like listening to the local drunkard using anger to justify his dereliction of duty as a protector and provider for his wife and children. *Which sane parent does nothing when their children suffer if it is within their power to stop it?*

It is either the parent is not present, too weak, or like the village drunkard, too dysfunctional to save their child from suffering, so he says.

"They offended me; I am angry with them, so I let them suffer."

Makuak keeps his thoughts to himself because, as Benny Wut, he is required to preserve the cultural beliefs of the Wagombe.

Instead, he asks Awat the question again, half hoping that in her interactions with the people of other tribes and the bishop, she might have some new evidence of a benevolent spirit or another place where people go after death that he is not aware of; maybe his wife and first-born son still live in that place.

"Has anyone returned with evidence proving that there is a heaven or hell?"

"Yes, Angel Gabriel brings messages and gifts from the other side,"

Awat responds.

Makuak is disappointed with that answer. He has heard that before and the rumors that this so-called Angel is Mathew's albino co-conspirator being passed off by the Bishop as an Angel. Makuak does not want to be drawn into another lengthy debate that has divided most Wagombe households since Bishop Mathew arrived with his new doctrine. There are more pressing matters at hand.

Makuak decides to humor her.

"Look, your brother passed the initiation; I think your mother has interceded on his behalf to God. You of all people should know how she gets when it comes to helping someone she loves to attain their dreams."

"Me? How should I know?" Awat asks.

"You are just like her," Makuak smiles.

"No, I'm not like her; I am like you." Awat protests.

While she loved her mom, she adores dad.

"I know what you did to assist Macati in gaining the royal stool even before he proposed to you. That is the type of thing your mother would do if she were in your position," he smiles.

"Who told you I did something to bring Macati closer to the stool?"

Awat demands.

"I am your father; I know what you are capable of doing. I am Benny Wut of our tribe; the good spirits tell me everything. But since it's your little secret, I will pretend not to know anything. Now, go get your brother's song oxen."

Makuak walks towards Barack, leaving Awat on the sidelines wondering who else knows her secret and what harm it might bring Macati if it's exposed.

Makuak wipes the blood from his son's face and wraps a broadleaf around his forehead. He is glad that the lines are straight. Straight lines on the forehead identify the bearer as a full-grown man. They also identify the tribe he belongs to, especially during the war, where one needs to quickly identify friends from foes when fighting in close quarters. The three straight lines on his forehead identifies Barack as a Wagombe. Makuak presents Barack with a spear and a club.

At initiation into manhood, tradition requires that a father present his son with offensive weapons of war and tools of the trade to launch his career to perform his manly duties as a provider and protector.

His mother presents him with protection items - a shield to protect him from the enemy's arrows, a broad hat to protect him from the sun above, a blanket to cover his body from the elements, and sandals to protect his feet from sharp objects on the ground beneath. It is believed that the deities listen to the prayers of the father for the children's victories in career and life's battles.

In contrast, the mother's prayers of protection and wellbeing over her children are quite powerful in the spirit realm. Just as a hen can chase a mangy dog that attacks her chicks, so can a mother's prayer of protection chase any evil spirit that attacks her child in the spirit realm.

Actions in the spirit realm manifest in the physical world, hence the significance of the items given at initiation.

Today, Barack's maternal aunt will present the shield, hat, blanket, and sandals on behalf of his late mother.

Makuak takes the bull from Awat and presents it to Barack; this will be his "Song Oxen."

It is his most precious possession, and he will lavishly care, sing to it and delicately train its horns into unusual, symmetrical shapes. Barack would start his herd of cattle with it.

Barack calls it *MaKuei*, which means a bull with a black and white head. Kuei is also the word for fish-eating eagle, a striking bird of similar black and white markings. Barack announces in a loud voice that he is dropping his boyhood name of Barack, and he should be addressed as MaKuei henceforth. It is the custom that when a son is born, his parents name him eight days after birth. The name his parents give him is based on the circumstances of his birth or the way they pray his life turns out.

Barack means blessed. The day the boy becomes a man, he chooses a name for himself and his song bull.

Makuak heaves his chest.

"My little boy is a warrior, just like his daddy. He gives himself and his bull a name that's identical to mine. Makuak the spotted bull, much like the spots of a leopard."

Jabu's paternal uncle performs the initiation rites on behalf of his late father, and Nandi presents the shield, blanket, hat, and sandals. Jabu chooses to keep the name his father gave him in memory of his father.

Nandi Christianizes the traditional prayer of protection by replacing the war deity's name with Arch Angel Michael and Engai with Jesus.

In the afternoon after the initiation, King Zaki and his entourage leave the village square and troop to Makuak's family compound for "the knocking of the door." Here, Macati will explain to Awat's family how he will provide for their daughter. He should also demonstrate that he can treat Awat equal to or greater than she was treated in her father's compound. If Macati is a farmer, he will bring some of his farm produce and offer it to the father and her family. The Wagombe being cattle herders require he brings cattle and whatever he uses to demonstrate his ability to cater for Awat.

Macati presents double the number of livestock requested and wild game because he is a hunter.

The Wagombe are impressed with the gifts; they bring food and drinks to their guest. It is a sign that they approve of the marriage. Joy fills the air. Amid the excitement, Halima offers to do Awat's "fattening room."

"What is that?" Asks Makuak.

Halima explains that the Kapora prepares a woman for marriage when she comes of age, this includes fattening her up, so she drops her girlish figure for the full-figured body of a healthy woman.

The Kapora custom requires that before the wedding day, the bride will be put in a room for a month, fed, and trained to cook the type of meals her husband likes and how to be a mother and a good wife. It is shameful to the girl's mother if her husband returns her because she is a terrible cook or an unfit mother. They will say her mother did not train her properly.

Success in marriage requires more than good looks and infatuation, and the fattening room is part of the marriage preparation.

Whatever she learns in the "fattening room" is what will prepare her for life's turbulence that comes long after most people forget about the wedding ceremony. Lessons learned make the marriage wax strong long after the festive crowds have gone and the frustrations of life, like ugly buzzards, come from all directions to perch on your marital rooftop, to watch it die and gouge it apart like vultures would a decomposing corpse.

Besides, most Kapora men prefer to cuddle a curvy and full-bodied woman at night than a boney woman that feels like a bundle of dry firewood.

After putting on weight in the fattening room, her husband must provide for her, so she never reverts to her girlish boney figure, lest society views him as a bad provider. The protruding bones of a skinny married woman announce to those who see them that her husband is a derelict.

Nyoka interrupts Halima mid-sentence.

"Isn't it the mother and aunties of the bride who are supposed to do her fattening room?" She demands in a loud voice.

Halima says, "Yes, but as Awat's mother is no more, and I know what my son likes and his peculiarities, I am offering to teach Awat how to cook for a Kapora man. Besides, it will be a good time for us to bond as mother and daughter."

Uzaza joins the conversation.

"I think you want to do this because you only had sons and always wanted a daughter to do girly things with, like plan her wedding ceremony. So, you are using Awat as a surrogate."

It is typical of Uzaza to say what everyone else is thinking but too polite to say.

"Nyoka is right; tradition is tradition, the mother of the bride or female members of her family seasoned in the matters of life and marriage should do it for her, not the mother of the groom. You can do her *omugo* when the first child is born."

"What is *omugo*?" Nandi asks.

"*omugo* is when grandma assists the inexperienced daughter or daughter-in-law to take care of her newborn baby," Mama Waggy explains.

Nandi, not knowing the family politics between Halima and Nyoka, says she will do Awat's fattening room.

Nyoka smiles. She has gotten one over Halima. She knew Halima always yearned for a daughter. Nyoka makes it a point to pet her daughters, do their hair, and other girly things in Halima's presence just to rub it in.

A few days earlier, Nyoka was snooping around the palace and overheard Halima telling Zaki that she planned to make a request. Zaki had informed her that it is not in the tradition for the groom's family to do it, but after hearing her argument, he said maybe they would get away with it considering the Wagombe don't put their girls through the fattening room preparations. Their women do not gain weight like Kapora women.

Nyoka came for this knocking of the door expressly to foul Halima's joy.

Awat notices sadness on Halima's face and nudges Nandi.

"Say something!" She whispers in a desperate voice.

Nandi interjects.

"Considering I don't know how to prepare Kapora meals nor the proper way to handle a Kapora man's idiosyncrasies, I will need a coach. Who's better than Macati's mother to coach me? Since you cannot leave your husband and come here for a month, we might have to take up residence in the capital."

Nyoka cuts off Nandi.

"It is wrong for the woman to move into her husband's family compound before the young man has built his own house. It's as if he depends on his parents to support his wife; that makes him a weakling or a boy. Or you, Awat, a maidservant of the family. You must stay in your father's or a relative's compound before the wedding ceremony!"

There is an edge in Nyoka's voice.

Nandi replies, "We could have a hut in the capital. It need not be in the king's family compound. The Wagombe, as a Vassal state of Kapora, are required to maintain a building in your capital for Wagombe nobles and emissaries to stay when they visit the capital on official business. We are yet to build ours. We can build it quickly, and that is where Awat, the daughter of the Wagombe Chief and therefore a Wagombe emissary can do her fattening room before the wedding."

To Nyoka's disappointment, the Kapora elders in the entourage see sense in Nandi's argument and agree with her.

Most of them caught on to the political undercurrent between the two wives, are partial to Halima, the nicer of the two; reinforcing the saying, people with bad attitudes die twice. First, they die socially, and later, physical death comes to rid society from their antics. Many despise Nyoka and are happy to stick it to her whenever an opportunity presents itself, even if it means modifying an age-old tradition to favor her adversary.

Makuak and the Wagombe elders agree to the plan. Every decision-maker from both tribes agree that the Wagombe will build a hut in the capital for visiting emissaries, and Awat will do her fattening room there.

Chapter Nine

Going Away

A week after the hut is built, Uzaza catches Macati around Awat's new hut. The lust in Macati's eyes for Awat's more curvaceous and thicker body is more than enough for him to see that Macati is a blink away from breaking traditional rules and committing fornication.

"You know better than to visit her during her fattening. You should be building a house where both of you will raise a family. It is shameful for a man to move his bride into his father's house, or even worse, for the man to move into the wife's family house," Uzaza says.

"I was completing my house when my cub ran away. I came looking for him," Macati responds.

"I know that trick," Uzaza points at the rose bush where Awat is hiding behind.

"Better not get pregnant before the wedding! You know he must present evidence of your virginity to the elders on the night of the wedding ceremony."

Uzaza speaks in Awat's direction, then turns to Macati.

Macati avoids eye contact to avoid revealing his inner thoughts and some of the plans he had set out to do before getting caught.

"We have been looking all over for you. Come with me; your father summoned you. We have serious state matters to handle. Chief Obijinaal has not sent his tribute or sent a message explaining why. It has been months since the festival. We need you to take a contingent of men and collect the tribute plus a fine for lateness."

Uzaza speaks as he walks in the direction of the palace.

Macati hurries after him.

"But Ika usually handles things like this."

A trip to Obijinaal's chiefdom will keep him away from Awat for many days.

Uzaza continues walking as he speaks.

"That was before your father decided to make you King instead. It's time you start practicing. Besides, Ika is still with his mother's people in Wayo land, and we cannot delay any further. Failure to do something soon will be viewed as weakness by other Vassal Chiefs, especially when it's Obijinaal, a runt amongst his peers challenging Zaki's authority."

At this point he has Macati's full attention.

"Even though King Zaki is strong and hearty, he will not live forever; the sooner you learn to handle things like this, the better. It's an opportunity to demonstrate to the kingmakers that you are capable of handling matters of state. King Zaki plans to present you to them immediately after your wedding ceremony, as we have never had a bachelor king in Kapora history. It's difficult enough to convince the kingmakers to coronate you while Zaki is still alive and in sound mind. Let's do everything to bolster his efforts to change tradition. I already started lobbying some of them in advance," Uzaza responds.

"From what I know about Obijinaal, he will probably overpay and grovel the moment he sees me and claim it was only a joke," Macati replies.

"That is a big possibility, but I recommend you go with a very large contingent. The sheer size alone should intimidate him into quick compliance. And, if perchance, he defies you, you have enough men to burn down his town. You can take your future in-laws as a sign of solidarity between our people and the tall Wagombe," Uzaza responds, knowing Macati is quite popular amongst the Wagombe Parapouls.

Several of them, like MaKuei and Jabu, will join the contingent without much persuasion.

The next day, Macati informs Awat that he has finished building his house so they can get married as soon as he returns from Obijinaal's chiefdom to collect tributes. She can beautify their home while he's gone.

He hands her his cub to take care of while away.

Several days pass, and Macati does not return.

Days turn to weeks, and still no word — melancholy sets in over time.

Nandi tells Awat that when she feels this way, she goes to church. She suggests returning to their homeland for a few days and attending Matthew's church to get her mind off Macati.

"Time will pass faster when you spend it in the presence of God," she says.

Word gets out that Awat and Nandi plan to visit Wagombe land for a while, and several young Kapora warriors and scouts come for the trip, offering protective services on the journey back. Amongst them is Waggy; he did not follow Macati and the other warriors to Obijinaal's town because he is yet to do his solo survival. Only full warriors can go for such trips.

But there is another reason Waggy is going on this trip with Awat.

Chapter Ten

The "End Times" Are At Hand

At the Wagombe settlement, Nandi and Awat attend one of Bishop Mathew's open-air crusades. Today he speaks about the *end times.*

"The heart of man is desperately wicked, and God has decided to destroy the world and cleanse it of wicked people. He is sending a series of cataclysmic events that will bring untold suffering across the earth."

Bishop Mathew preaches about the four apocalyptic horsemen — Pestilence, War, Famine, and Death. He states that the smallpox epidemic that ravaged the Wagombe is nothing compared to the type of epidemics that will scourge the earth when the pestilence horseman rides through — He will cause multiple wars, mass starvation, and food shortages. God will haul massive flaming rocks from heaven onto the earth, and they will destroy the food supply and poison all drinking water. There will be seven years of tribulation. Those who die during the seven years of tribulation will face even greater torment in hell for all eternity. Mathew would misquote the bible to instill fear, then offer a self-serving solution.

He raises his voice for dramatic effect. "However, in his infinite mercy, God has decided to rapture a hundred and forty-four thousand righteous people to heaven and save them from the years of tribulation. They will be returned to earth to repopulate the world and establish his kingdom here on earth after cleansing it of wickedness. God has done it before, and He is willing to do it again. First, by flood, and He saved Noah and his family by placing them in an ark — a giant boat. He then used them to repopulate the earth after destroying all the wicked people. This time, He will use fire and pestilence, but first, He will send giant boats with big red crosses on their wings to take the righteous to heaven. First, they must go to the baptismal castle, a month's journey away, to be cleaned before shipment to Heaven. God does not want anyone unholy in Heaven.

Several Kapora scouts and young warriors are at the event.

Ever since Macati proposed to Awat, it has become common amongst the teenage Kapora boys to chase after tall beauties with smooth and dark skin. The Kapora teenage girls grew up with these boys and treated them like brothers, whereas the Wagombe girls treat them like celebrities, an ego boost to the Kapora boys. This makes the Wagombe girls even more attractive.

Under the guise of providing Nandi and Awat safe passage back to their homeland, several Kapora scouts and young warriors came to Wagombe land, they conveniently found religion at Bishop Matthew's church.

The Kapora boys heard that there were more females attending Bishop Matthew's church than males. That translates to less competition and good "girl hunting grounds" for the Kapora boys. They view Bishop Matthew's church as how a lion views the Serengeti in the rainy season — teeming with thousands and thousands of gazelles.

In this case, the Wagombe gazelles are willing to be caught by the Kapora lions. The young Wagombe girls love the attention from the Kapora boys. Maybe, they too will be swept off by a strong, responsible Kapora man who will pay double dowry just to prove his love for her, as Macati did for Awat.

There is a local gossip, Amebo, that Mama Waggy befriended to get information about Awat's family and hear what married life between a Nilotic woman and a Kapora man is like. At Halima's behest, Mama Waggy fed Amebo rosy stories. The intention was to make Macati more acceptable to Awat's people. Amebo took the stories back to Awat's family and spread the rosy rumors to the other Wagombe women, thereby whetting their appetites for Kapora men.

Waggy has become quite popular these days. Every love-struck teen from both tribes wants him to interpret for them.

Today he sits half-listening to Bishop Mathew's sermon about the impending cataclysm on earth, heavenly bliss, and terrible hell – something is not quite right as his mind goes on a journey of its own, stopping abruptly when it hit something the preacher said.

He jumps up and interrupts the preacher.

"What happens to the souls of those who never heard of Christ before they died? Do they go to Heaven based on their good behavior or to hell regardless of good behavior because they were not born again and worshiped other gods?"

Waggy directs the question to the white man in long white robes that Bishop Mathew refers to as Angel Gabriel. He reasons that Angel Gabriel is from Heaven and should know whether all the people in Heaven were born again or not. The white man turns to Bishop Mathew and asks in Portuguese to interpret what Waggy is saying.

Bishop Mathew and Angel Gabriel argue back and forth in Portuguese while the congregation sits perplexed. For a while, it looks like they are quarreling. Finally, the banter subsides, and Bishop Mathew explains to the congregation that the strange language they are speaking is called "tongues" — a heavenly language that enables you to communicate effectively with God himself and other heavenly beings. When you speak in tongues, only God and His angels understands your prayer request, and therefore, no one or devil agent can sabotage it. Even the devil himself and his minion evil spirits can't block your prayer or send a counterfeit that will cause you more pain than good because they don't understand the heavenly language called tongues.

As per Waggy's question, everyone who died before hearing the gospel will be judged according to his merit. However, if he was tricked into worshiping another god — which is basically a demon or a familiar spirit — then that demon and its minion evil spirits will stand around the person at the point of death and will capture the person's soul as it leaves the dying body and takes him straight to their kingdom called purgatory.

There, he will be tortured and used as a spiritual slave of the devil, causing trouble here on earth, especially to the family members he loves most. That is why many families disintegrate shortly after the death of a member. The dead person's soul remembers past offenses within the family, and the demons use it to sow seeds of discord amongst the living family members. The devil likes to see people suffer physically and emotionally; he particularly loves strife and division in families. Dead relatives are forced to helplessly watch their loved one's reel from one crisis to another.

The tortured soul will remain in this condition until judgment day, when all wicked people, the devil, and his minion spirits will be brought out of purgatory for judgment. If your crime is equal to or less than your time served in purgatory, you will be washed clean and assumed into heaven. If your sin is much, then you will go to hell with the devil and his demons for all eternity.

Bishop Mathew pauses for effect as the horrible impression he just created registers in the minds of his congregation. Bishop Mathew's formula is simple; creates fear in his victims' minds, then offer a solution that invariably involves paying him in gold, cattle, land, or services.

His congregants can't read the bible, so they don't know whether he is lying. Satisfied with their reaction, he continues.

"God, in His infinite mercy, has created an escape route for the people in purgatory. A captive can get an early release from purgatory if one of their living relatives intercedes on their behalf. Certain sacrifices must be made. Something must be given in exchange for the person or people being released from purgatory."

"Are you saying we should kill someone to release our people from purgatory?" Waggy asks.

"No," Bishop Mathew replies.

"The currency for purgatory is pain, physical and emotional pain. You must do penance, that is, do something that hurts you physically and separate yourself from something you hold dear in your heart. Like a piece of ancestral land that has been in your family for centuries. Surrender it unto the Lord."

Awat gets up, annoyed.

"Honestly, we Wagombe people are having trouble with this life after death thing."

She repeats her father's argument about the inability of the soul of a dead chicken to save their eggs from being eaten and warriors who die in battle unable to protect their widows and orphans from the great beyond.

Bishop Mathew has a ready answer for her. He studied the Wagombe culture long and hard, so he tailored his sermons to focus on prosperity, abundance, good health, and eternal life here on earth after the seven-year tribulation. It was out of desperation from dwindling numbers and the influx of people from other tribes who traditionally believe in an afterlife that he started talking about punishment after death.

"God spoke everything into existence but molded man in his own image. Humans were molded into existence and not spoken like everything else. We are spirits like Him, and we were originally designed to live forever like God until Satan tempted Eve and messed everything up. Chicken, cattle, and everything else were spoken into existence for our benefit and sustenance. Let there be light, and there was light. Let the land be teeming with four-legged beasts, and so it was. Because God didn't breathe life into their nostrils in the same way He created man, they have no soul. That is why we can kill and eat them, and they have no spirit that can harm us later or try to prevent us from killing their offspring later."

Bishop Mathew scans the crowd to see if they believe him.

Nandi cuts in.

"Are you saying, therefore, that my husband, children, and all who died of smallpox are in Purgatory?"

Bishop Mathew puts on a sad face and paces as one in deep thought on how to deliver very bad news.

"Unfortunately, yes for most except your husband," Matthew replies.

Satan knew God loves you and sent me to preach the gospel and save you all from impending doom and eternal damnation. So, Satan sent a wicked spirit with the terrible disease to wipe you all out before I got here. He also sent legions of Kwagoso demons to cause obstacles, detours, and distractions to delay my arrival so the wicked spirit killed you all before I got here with the message. Fortunately, your Bishop discerned the spiritual attacks and distractions. I prayed and fasted for seven days and seven nights, and the Lord sent Angel Gabriel to help me fight them. That is why we had the fire stick that speaks with the voice of thunder the day we met you crying over your husband's body."

He continues, cunningly convincing Nandi.

"His soul was leaving his body, and the familiar spirits were hovering above him to capture him and take him to purgatory. They fled at the sight of Angel Gabriel and me with our holy books and fire sticks. Unfortunately, your children and everyone else who died days before we arrived were captured by familiar spirits and taken to purgatory."

"I don't believe you!" Awat shouts because this means her mother and brother are suffering in purgatory, if the bishop is correct.

"Chiki chiki wawa," Bishop Mathew responds in a high-pitched playful voice, as one would speak to an infant, then he starts a funny dance, shaking his legs and flapping his arms like a chicken.

"*Chiki chiki wa-wa, chiki chiki wa-wa* mommy look! *Chiki chiki wa-wa chiki chiki wa-wa."*

Awat starts crying uncontrollably.

"What is going on?" Waggy asks.

Nandi explains Chiki chiki wa-wa was a pet name Awat's mom called her when she was alive — a name born out of the silly song and dance Awat used to entertain her parents with when she was a toddler.

Bishop Mathew puts on a serious face.

"In a vision, your Bishop saw your dead mother in purgatory. She was sad and tormented, so I tried to lighten her countenance by telling her that you were getting married to the prince. In a flash, her countenance brightened, and she said, "Oh, my baby is getting married. Soon she too will have little children and they will entertain her with silly dances and made-up songs just like my *Chiki chiki wa-wa* did when she was a toddler."

Mathew proceeds to tell her how her mother demonstrated the *Chiki chiki wa-wa* dance in purgatory, shaking his legs and flapping his arms like a chicken.

"Chiki chiki wa-wa chiki chiki wa-wa."

"How is she?"

There is desperation in Awat's voice.

The congregation falls silent in anticipation of his answer for her people loved her very much.

Bishop Mathew raises his voice to ensure the congregation hears what he is about to say.

"She is suffering in purgatory, but for a fleeting moment, she was very happy. You can shorten her misery and that of all your relatives by harkening to my voice."

He scans the audience, making a mental note of the horror on their faces.

Awat and Nandi believe Bishop Mathew because there is no way he could have known Awat's pet name as a toddler or the silly *"Chiki chiki wa-wa"* dance.

Unknown to them, Bishop Mathew uses the local gossip's weakness to his advantage. Amebo's character as a gossiper remains unchanged despite her conversion to Christianity.

He learned about *"Chiki chiki wa-wa"* from Amebo and weaponized it. Amebo's contributions to the church earned her the lofty title of deaconess, giving her a platform to hand down judgment and criticism of other people's faults, thinly veiled in religious piety — a trait Bishop Matthew identified early and capitalized on.

Mathew knows that most adults are aware of Amebo's loose lips and will be guarded when they speak to her, so he made her head of the children's Sunday school and every activity that involves children.

Children see and hear everything going on at home and will repeat it to anyone who listens. Mathew knows Amebo will do what comes to her naturally, extracting juicy gossip from the innocently flippant. And she is just too eager to share with Bishop Mathew.

She usually starts with, "Bishop, we need to pray for the so and so family." Then she launches into the story, and Bishop Mathew listens attentively to her stories feigning religious indignation, shock, and horror. The bishop's response encourages her to talk even more, adding her personal editorial and criticisms, under the guise of religion. Bishop Mathew pays special attention to the stories of people in the upper class. He would repackage these stories and weave them into sermons without giving the names but claim they were revealed to him by the Holy Spirit, thereby gaining credibility as a prophet of God who knows everything.

He often adds a warning of fast approaching calamity to the person that can only be averted after they "sow a seed" to the bishop. "Sowing a seed" translate to "Give me something" gold, silver, cattle etc. depending on what he thinks you can afford.

Bishop would say things like, "If you knew all things, saw all things, past present and future, there are many things you would have done differently."

He would briefly make eye contact with a miserably married congregant, turn away and say, "Married differently," chuckle and turn his gaze on someone else dealing with a crisis in their enterprise.

"Different choices that could have changed the direction of your enterprise significantly," he would say.

"Well, now you have a prophet from God that can help and give you Godly advice to turn you away from your current rocky path filled with thorns, snakes, and scorpions under each rock poised to strike at your feet."

Trouble in life is not exclusively reserved for the poor; trouble like rain falls on everyone beneath, rich, poor, old, young, it does not matter. What matters to Matthew is that the troubled rich pay a lot more than the troubled poor to solve their problems. Matthew uses this scam to gain a Svengali hold on the "troubled rich." Many rich folks with personal issues will not make a move without consulting him first — at a price.

Bishop now plays the role once held by local diviners, fortune tellers, and seers. And Bishop Mathew has long waited for an opportunity to worm his way into the lives of the royal family. He plans to work on Awat's mind now he's gotten her attention with "Chiki chiki wa-wa."

Earlier, he told the white catholic priest his plans to lie to his congregation about purgatory, and they argued in Portuguese. The Catholic priest didn't like the distortion of the purgatory concept. However, Bishop Mathew convinced him that he could gain a lot of gold if he plays to the plan.

If the plan works, all the natives will hand over their gold to him in exchange for their dead relatives' emancipation in purgatory.

What happens in Africa remains in Africa.

The Vatican need not sanction or even know what they do here. The Catholic priest can retire a wealthy man.

"You were sent to Africa as punishment after your failed attempt at becoming a Cardinal. See this is Joseph's pit or Moses' Nile. Though your adversaries in the home church meant it for evil — as in poverty, disease, and possible death in a strange land, thereby preventing you from ever becoming cardinal, much less a pope — it's through Africa that you will come into great riches. Play along with me, and you will be eternally grateful. You can ask God for forgiveness later, Christ died for ALL sins, didn't he? ALL SINS covers scaming Africans out of Gold and Diamonds. Something they have a lot of anyway, one need not dig for it."

That was the argument they had in Portuguese — a language strange to the African congregants, they now call tongues.

The Portuguese Catholic priest agreed to the plan. Bishop Mathew declares to the congregation that they will engage in spiritual warfare with the devil and his legion of demons. They will descend into purgatory and emancipate the suffering dead. Payment for this dangerous battle must be paid in gold ornaments to Angel Gabriel, land and cattle to Bishop Mathew, and penance for those who can't afford to pay. He directs them to a dry riverbed with shiny stones – alluvial diamonds.

You will wear a leather pouch on your neck, crawl on all fours, and put the shiny stones into the pouch — a full bag of stones will liberate your relatives from purgatory. Another pouch of shiny stones earns you a place on the ship to heaven where you will have eternal youth, joy, health, and abundant blessings for yourself and your loved ones forever.

After the seven years of tribulation are over, you and your loved ones will return to a cleansed earth. Much like the Garden of Eden — as God originally planned it before wickedness came into the world through Adam's disobedience.

Alluvial diamonds were so plentiful in African dry riverbeds that you need not dig for them. They were not considered precious stones like gold, silver, or emeralds in the early 1800s by the local population. Mathew knew their value and sold them to Europeans at the trading posts on the Atlantic. That was decades before European miners and explorers started landing in droves to cart them off.

By mid to late 1800s, Cecil Rhodes, would establish De Beers and acquire the largest diamond fields and build an empire out of African Diamonds. Then carve out large territory rich in Gold, Diamond, gemstones, and names it after himself -Rhodesia. Name changed to Zimbabwe after independence. He would later establish the "Phodes Scholarship" to cleanse his legacy from its bloody past and repbrand himself as a philanthropist. Nobody stops to ask, where did the money come from?

Bishop Mathew proceeds to teach tongues to the overzealous deacons he fondly called the holiest of the holies because they were most prone to over-dramatized public displays of religious fervor.

You earned this title through church contributions and shouting out, praising the bishop's eloquence as he preaches. He thought to speak in "tongues" — a mixture of Portuguese insults and gibberish — to this exclusive group of eye-service zealots.

The prayer in tongues must start with the Portuguese phrase, "*Eu sou uma Cabra estúpida*," which translates to "I am a stupid goat," in English. A phrase Amebo said with such religious fervor that she would convulse and go into spastic fits, like an epileptic in the throes of a seizure.

Several nights later, the congregation gathered at the foot of a rocky hill. Bishop Mathew and Angel Gabriel set off mesmerizing fireworks from behind a large boulder at the top of the hill. They told the congregants that as souls get released from purgatory, all blessings and good luck that the devil hitherto bound will shoot up then shower down like shooting stars in the night. The night sky will light up like day as thousands of souls escape from purgatory on this night of ascension to Heaven.

The congregation must sing praises to God throughout the emancipation process so that God will strengthen the Bishop and the archangel in their battle against the Devil and his legions of demons. No one should climb the mountain that night lest they replace those being freed from purgatory.

The Wagombe and Kapora have never seen fireworks before; they are mesmerized by the spectacular fireworks on the night of ascension.

Several unbelievers join Bishop Mathew's congregation that night.

Chapter Eleven

Bad News

A month after Macati left for Obijinaal's town, Buta shows up at the palace with an injured Burley warrior from Macati's contingent. The Burley youth, Bemoi, close to Macati's age explains that Macati and his entourage were massacred. He escaped by pretending to be dead. The Jinaali, Obijinaal's subjects seeking to break away from the Kapora Empire, took Macati's body and those of noble birth as well as the dead Wagombe to display in the town's square.

Bemoi, and several others were left in the bushes to be eaten by vultures. As soon as the Jinaalis left, he ran south towards his mother's village for fear that if he went north, there could be other Jinaalis laying ambushes on the route to Kapora. He blacked out at some point.

He was fortunate enough to be found by Buta who treated him. The injured warrior stated that Chief Obijinaal is in rebellion against the throne and promised to crush the Kapora like a bug if they set foot on Jinaali territory.

Zaki flies into a rage; he summons a war council immediately.

"Every able-bodied man in the kingdom must report to the town square at dawn. We are going to war!"

Horse riders gallop at full speed, executing Zaki's order that all warriors and scouts across the kingdom return home immediately. All able-bodied men are conscripted with immediate effect. Waggy and all scouts at the Wagombe settlement will return to play the role of armor bearers and porters for the warriors when they go into battle.

If perchance, a scout kills an enemy warrior in battle, he is instantly elevated to full warrior status. He will not go through solo survival or kill a dangerous animal, for he has just killed the most dangerous creature on earth — a full-grown man. His armband and warrior garbs will be made of treated leather tanned red.

Word of Macati's death spreads across the land like a wild bush fire driven by the Harmattan winds. There is wailing in every home for the young men that death snatched too soon, and a period of mourning is declared.

Mothers weep, young brides, inconsolable and angry men gather at the town square eager for orders to destroy the Jinaali. Those who pelt the Kapora with pebbles must expect rocks in return. They want vengeance, Kapora style — a head for an eye.

Uzaza looks around the gathering crowd and notices that Bemoi who came back with the news is absent. Something in his story does not add up, and he needs clarification. He sets off in the direction of the young man's house when he crosses the front of Obya's compound.

Oluwo, son of Obya rushes out, calling him.

"My father sent me to find you; he says it's important."

"To your father, everything is important," Uzaza quips.

"What is it about?"

"I don't know," Oluwo replies.

"But I think it has something to do with the survivor from Macati's detachment."

"Is he here?" Uzaza asks.

Oluwo nods yes.

"He was passing by here on his way to the square when my dad insisted that he come in and be checked out, so his injuries don't fester."

"Ah," Uzaza smiles.

That is typical Obya. He leaves nothing to chance. Every detail is important to him.

The lad continues his narrative.

"He saw the warrior briefly and hurried out of his shrine as though looking for herbs then whispered to me that I should find you and ask you to leave whatever you are doing and come over immediately."

"Has the young warrior come back with a contagious disease?" Uzaza asks.

Oluwo shrugs as he responds.

"I don't know, but whatever it is must be important enough to bring my father close to shock — nothing ever shocks him.

Uzaza rushes over to Obya's shrine. There, he sees Buta, and the injured warrior being treated. Buta explains the condition he met the warrior in the forest and the type of first aid he administered. Obya needs this information to determine what herbs to use to effectively kill the infection but not interact negatively with whatever Buta administered earlier.

Much to Uzaza's surprise, Nyoka is in the shrine as well. Uzaza struggles to hide his surprise as the seemingly random dots begin to connect in his mind.

The injured warrior is a mixed marriage child — his father, a long-distance Kapora trader, and mother, a Wayo Buka woman, one who sells food to traders in the market. The Kapora believe that one drop of Kapora blood in you makes you a whole Kapora, and therefore, this warrior is considered full Kapora despite his mother's ethnicity.

Now Uzaza feels the warrior's Wayo allegiance might be quite strong.

Obya greets Uzaza with a smile. The look in Obya's eyes tells Uzaza that he, too, is suspicious of the young warrior's story and his role in Macati's death in battle. The injuries are superficial and could be self-inflicted with hesitative knife marks before the half-inch slash to the chest, that he claims a Jinaali spear inflicted him.

It was this cut to the chest that he claimed led the Jinaalis to think that he was dead and leave him alone.

Uzaza turns to Nyoka.

"What brings you here? Shouldn't you be with the other wives preparing your husband's food supplies, so he has something to eat while he is at the war camp? You know Halima is too distraught to do anything."

"I will go right away. First, I had to find out the well-being of my son. He left for Wayo kingdom with Buta. He is bound to pass through Obijinaal's territory on his way back here. Who knows, Obijinaal might lay an ambush for him also. His demise will kill Zaki with heartbreak, and we will be left without a leader."

Uzaza turns to Buta and asks, "Didn't Ika and his entourage return to Wayo kingdom with you? Where is he now? He should have returned long ago."

Buta turns to Uzaza and replies like one who has rehearsed a speech.

"Ika is taking a long way back home to circumvent Jinaali territory. He should be here in a few days. I was hunting antelopes on the border of Jinaali territory and Wayo-land when I heard movements in the bushes. I investigated and found this warrior dehydrated, delirious, and barely alive. From his dreadlocks, I could tell he was Kapora. I revived him, and he told me that he was part of Macati's entourage, and they were on their way to Obijinaal's town to collect tributes when they were ambushed. He was able to escape by pretending to be dead from a spear thrust to the chest but didn't think it was prudent to run north in the direction of Kapora, as there might be more Jinaali hiding in the bushes enroot to Kapora. Instead, he went south, trying to get to his mother's village, a Wayo trading post. I quickly sent word back to Ika in our capital that he should not cut through Jinaali territory but go through the Kongo kingdom on the way back home lest Obijinaal attacks him also."

Nyoka prods Uzaza.

"What do you think is going on?"

Her eyes dart back and forth like a cornered rat.

"I am confused. I never imagined Obijinaal would raise his heel against the King. We have to crush his insurrection immediately lest other vassal states feel encouraged to rebel against us," Uzaza replies earnestly.

"Yes! Swift and decisive action is required!" Nyoka rises.

"With overwhelming force! Send thousands upon thousands of warriors against Obijinaal," Buta chimes in.

Uzaza observes the blubber around Buta's belly bounce as he speaks.

This fat lazy slob can't catch a crippled grasshopper, much less a baby antelope. He probably never hunted a day in his life, and he wants me to believe he was hunting when he found this teen warrior.

Uzaza usually says what he thinks, but this time, he keeps his thoughts to himself.

"Today! Right now! Show those bastards not to attack our emissaries ever!"

Nyoka's eyes search Uzaza's face for anything that will give her some insight into his thoughts.

Uzaza maintains a deadpan look, revealing nothing. He lowers his voice as one speaking with caution.

"I can only suggest; the war council must decide, then we have to prepare the army for war, then move members of the royal families into separate strongholds in case the unthinkable happens, and the king and army are defeated in battle. The enemy can't wipe out the entire royal family in one swipe."

Uzaza gets up to return to the war gathering. He knows that Zaki would send thousands of warriors to crush Obijinaal. He must get to the war council and urge caution. A rat like Obijinaal does not challenge a cat to a fight unless there is a hole nearby. He must find the source of Obijinaal's newfound bravery.

Obya says to him as he gets up to leave, "I will see you there."

He says, locking his eyes with Uzaza's as he speaks.

"After I have treated this brave and lucky warrior."

Uzaza nods in acknowledgment.

Obya does not want Bemoi the injured warrior, Nyoka or Buta know that he suspects foul play. He plans to discuss his suspicions with Uzaza and Zaki privately.

Afterward, Buta walks back to the palace with Nyoka to prepare to move to one of the strongholds on a mountain outside the capital. After which, he will head back to Wayo kingdom.

At the war council, Zaki wants to head out to war immediately; exactly as Uzaza expected. Uzaza says he should send everyone close to the throne to the strongholds and be guarded by trusted warriors. No one is allowed to go in or out of the strongholds until the war is over.

Uzaza and Obya speak to Zaki privately, stating that they believe someone close to the throne is complicit in Obijinaal's insurrection, which might be a trap. Obijinaal is a rat that wants the world to think of him as a lion. He is too much of a coward to make a bold move like this. There must be some powerful people edging him on. Rather than plunge headlong into battle, Zaki should send spies to determine the source of his newfound bravery before they attack.

Between now and when the spies return, they must fortify their defenses if Obijinaal and his allies attack the capital.

Chapter Twelve

Hidden Traps Uncovered

Spies return with stories of a strange weapon in the hands of Obijinaal and his Jinaali warriors. Fire sticks with the voice of thunder that can strike a man dead from a distance are unknown to the people of Kapora.

They also inform Zaki and the inner circle of the true nature of Buta's "long-distance trading." He has come in contact with some strange-looking people on the Atlantic coast. They look like albinos with straight hair, long noses, and some have colored eyes — blue, green, brown, and hazel - *Europeans.* He sells human beings to them, and they sell him clothes, rum, western manufactured goods, and strange weapons. The awkward-looking clothes Buta wore at the annual festival were not the product of a bad costume designer, but the type of clothes white men wear in their country.

Buta brokered a deal with them — trading weapons for slaves.

A Portuguese dealer sold Obijinaal the fire sticks with thunder's voice in exchange for Macati and his entourage. They are the first installment payment on the deal. The injured warrior, Bemoi is the son of a Wayo mother, and Kapora father is part of the conspiracy. He was supposed to bring back a false report that would tempt Zaki into making an impulsive and hasty decision to attack Obijinaal with a large force armed with spears, swords, and horsemen.

When both armies meet on the battlefield, Obijinaal's warriors will stand in battle formation with swords and spears in their hands, and the secret weapons lying in the tall grass by their feet. Their traditional weapons and small numbers will give the Kapora a false sense of superiority — encouraging a careless charge —and when the large Kapora army charges, Obijinaal's men will pick up the new weapon and fire into the charging crowd, killing many before they make it past the halfway point of the battlefield.

Survivors and injured warriors will surrender, expecting the traditional treatment of Prisoners of War (POW) that has existed in this region of Africa for centuries — ransom paid by the defeated kingdom for their safe return. Ransom is based on the warrior's standing in his community.

A poor warrior fetches a low ransom, and one of noble birth fetches a large ransom. Unknown to the Kapora, the old rules governing POWs are about to change forever. POWs from all battles henceforth will end up on slave ships bound for the Americas. The Kapora have had no contact with Europeans on the Atlantic Coast or any knowledge of their weapons.

Obijinaal, through Buta, has made such contact and intends to use it to his advantage.

What is unknown is the endgame of this plot.

Is Obijinaal trying to capture the capital and therefore make himself the new emperor? Is it the Wiley Wayos' plan to use Obijinaal in a war by proxy to conquer the Kapora? Or does Ika think the throne will be handed over to Macati, so she arranged his sale into slavery and Zaki's death in battle, thereby clearing the path for Ika's ascension to the throne?

Buta's behavior since the annual festival right through to his convenient discovery of Bemoi caused Uzaza to suspect Buta's complicity in Obijinaal's uprising. Buta is much too clumsy to orchestrate an intricate plan so grand, while Ika is too impatient to develop such a complicated scheme — one that requires calm calculations and patience to implement.

Ika is more of an executor of simple direct orders that require brute force and immediate results. Such a diabolical plan can only come from Nyoka's mind.

Uzaza knew that Buta would be long gone by the time the spies return, so he waited until Buta bade Nyoka goodbye then set an ambush for him on his way back to the Wayo Kingdom.

With Nyoka now in a stronghold far away from the capital and other royal family members, she will be none the wiser to Buta's capture. Buta's disappearance went unnoticed as it happened on a lonely path. They were holding him in a secret location unknown to all Royal family members except King Zaki himself, lest word got back to Obijinaal and any other unknown partners in the conspiracy.

Bemoi was asked to stay home to recuperate fully and therefore kept out of the loop of all military affairs. They intend to try him at a later date when they get more information out of Buta.

Armed with the information from the spies, they torture Buta for more information. Zaki personally ties Buta to an anthill, then breaks the hill's top and throws a flaming palm kernel cake into the anthill. The smoke and fire irritate the ants in the hill. They pour out of the hill by the thousands and start biting Buta; he screams for mercy, but the ants engulf him within seconds.

He starts confessing immediately.

He tells them everything; he even answers questions his interrogators have not thought of asking.

Buta tells them that as Macati and his entourage approached Jinaali town, the capital of Obijinaal's province, Obijinaal appeared before them and demanded to know why they were visiting his kingdom. It was obvious at that point that rebellion was afoot. Immediately, the Kapora warriors formed a defensive circle and raised their shields, forming a wall to block any flying arrows the enemy might shoot at them. Macati said they have come to collect tributes for the king.

"The only tribute that old gorilla deserves is rotten bananas," replies Obijinaal.

That was the signal for Obijinaal's men hiding in the trees to start firing their weapons. The Kapora warriors did not stand a fighting chance. Many of them were cut down where they stood in their defensive circle. Bullets passed through the shields and hit the warriors.

After the first volley of shots, Obijinaal offered the survivors terms of surrender.

"Drop your weapons and come with us. We will ransom you for our independence from the Kapora Empire. You live to fight another day, or you can die now, and we will march to your capital and wipe out the rest of the Kapora army with our new weapons, then degrade your lineage for all eternity."

Degrading one's lineage for eternity is the worst type of humiliation a conqueror can inflict on a vanquished kingdom. The last thing the surrendered men see before their eyes are gouged out is their daughters, sisters and wives raped by pygmies, dwarfs, hunchbacks, and midgets brought along by the conquering army, thereby ensuring the future generations of the vanquished kingdom are comprised of short and deformed people — little men that will never rise to challenge the authority of their new overlords.

The surviving males will spend the rest of their living years in shame and darkness, despised by their wives and daughters for failing to protect them, resented by their children for their weakness, and dependent on others for the simplest things in life.

Self-sufficient men turned to blind beggars because they can neither farm, fish, or hunt for themselves or their families; a falling from grace to grass and from grass into the gutter. Their dignity trampled in dung as they grope around the valley of despair, no longer able to perform their natural role of provider and protector. The death they hoped to avert through surrender, often comes to them by their own hands. It is customary that those who commit suicide do not deserve an honorable burial but are thrown into *Ewa-Ufot*, the evil forest, un-mourned by those who love them and eaten by vultures who know them not. Their spirits forever roam the earth in limbo as *Eguns* not worthy to enter the land of the ancestors or given a legitimate chance of reincarnation.

Buta continues his narrative.

"Macati surrendered on a promise that Obijinaal had no intention to keep. He and the survivors were soon chained and led by me and my cohorts for sale to Portuguese slave traders on the Atlantic coast. Macati and his men are in a slave castle by the Atlantic awaiting a Brazilian ship bound for the Alagoas in Brazil. Nyoka put me up to it when she learned Zaki intended to pass up her son and install Macati as the king."

Buta screams as ants crawl into his ear, biting their way towards his eardrum. The words fly out of his mouth in a rapid clip.

"Obijinaal, with his new weapons, will inflict heavy casualties on the Kapora army and fight them to a standstill, then declare independence, which Zaki, if still alive, will have to honor."

"I sold rifles to Ika as well. He and his contingent are waiting at the trading post village on the border of Wayo, the town from which Bemoi's mother hails; he is also part of the conspiracy. Ika has promised Obijinaal a royal pardon if he keeps his end of the plan. However, Ika suspects that Obijinaal might try to take the capital for himself and declare himself emperor. After all, he did the fighting and has the fire stick with the voice of thunder. Obijinaal doesn't know that Ika and his men are also armed with fire sticks with the voice of thunder and a mounted calvary that will invade and destroy Obijinaal as the battle with the Kapora army wanes. He also has Wayo horsemen from the royal house within his ranks. With numbers, rifles, and swift horses on his side, Ika will emerge victorious."

He is confessing the entire plot, he pleads for mercy and relief from the ants traveling deeper into his eardrum.

Tell us more! Zaki bellows.

"Every warrior chief that might pose obstacles to Ika's ascension to the throne will conveniently die in battle, thanks to snipers within his ranks. With no way of telling who fired the fatal shot in the heat of battle, the Obijinaal will be blamed for their deaths. Obijinaal and his nobles will not survive the battle either. Obijinaal's friends and family that survived the battle will be massacred after the victory. Let dead men keep their secrets. Their death will be justified as an act of revenge by grieving Ika for the death of his father and the enslavement of his precious brother Macati."

Uzaza pulls Buta off the anthill before the ants kill him. Some ants had started to crawl up his nose. Buta is worth more alive than dead. Obya throws him into a nearby brook, forcing the ants to get off him. The splash of cold water revives Buta; they pull him out of the brook.

Zaki's head is full of anger; he wants to thrust Buta through with a spear, but Uzaza intervenes, saying he wants to get from Buta, crucial information on where to get the strange weapons, so the Kapora army fights Obijinaal fire for fire.

"It's important they wipe out Obijinaal in a decisive swoop, lest other kings get this weapon themselves and overrun us," he says.

Buta starts talking like a parrot that has eaten too much pepper. He tells them of the Portuguese traders in Luanda that can sell them weapons. Further south are the Dutch and German traders, the Belgians in Congo, and the English along the Zambezi River and the Niger Delta also sell such weapons.

Zaki says he will trade with the English to reduce any chance of word getting to the Portuguese and eventually to Obijinaal, their ally. Zaki and his war chiefs discuss what to exchange with the English. Buta informs them that the English traders are no longer interested in slaves, but gold, ivory, palm oil, and precious metals — something the Kapora have in plenty.

The Belgians and Dutch want slaves, and the Kapora don't have any at this time. When they overrun Obijinaal, Zaki intends to sell Obijinaal, his family, Buta, and everyone involved in the conspiracy to the Belgians or the Dutch. Let them suffer the same fate they have brought unto others.

They force Buta to take them to the English.

After a two-day journey, the Kapora meet white people for the first time.

More impressive are the weapons they have; not just fire sticks with the voice of thunder, but artillery pieces too. One shell can kill a hundred warriors gathered in battle formation.

Waggy's mouth hangs ajar as he observes the Englishman demonstrating new pyrotechnics that will perplex an enemy. Flares that will turn a dark night into daylight; great for night fighting, fireworks that look like falling stars. Waggy realizes that Bishop Matthew and his archangel used this type of equipment to mesmerize the congregants on the night of ascension.

The white man in long white robes, who Bishop Matthew told them was an archangel, was actually an ordinary white man.

Every lie has an expiry date.

Unfortunately, there isn't much he can do to reverse the past events in light of this discovery. The Wagombe and other Christian converts are well on their way to the Baptismal castle on the coast to be baptized then put on big boats with big red crosses on their sails. Waggy wonders if these boats were really sent by God to rapture people to heaven, or are the Christian converts about to go on a voyage to hell as slaves in a strange land?

When news of Macati's death in battle got to the Wagombe settlement, Awat decided to join Bishop Mathew and the penitents leaving for the Baptismal castle on the coast. The Wagombe are not aware of the spy's discovery or Buta's recent confession. As far as they know, Macati and his entourage were killed in battle by Obijinaal and his Jinaali warriors.

Bishop Mathew says the wars and rumors of war have begun — a sign of the end times he preached about earlier.

An aching heart will accept anything that can relieve its pain, including lies. Awat believes life on earth without Macati is not worth living; she might as well join him in heaven. Bishop Mathew told her that Macati received the "mark of God" while alive, so he went straight to heaven when he died in battle.

Nandi decided to join the group going to the Baptismal castle, considering her husband and all except one child, Jabu died of smallpox. Now, Jabu too, is no more. She believes he died alongside Macati in battle.

Bishop Mathew told her that Jabu and her entire family are now in heaven because of the payment she made to Bishop Mathew and the archangel on the night of ascension. Their souls were released from purgatory on that night. Besides, Nandi feels old age and its related ailments creeping up on her. She will be better off in heaven where she will have eternal youth and joy, far away from the crisis of daily life here on earth. The end times are at hand, and life is expected to become unbearable for those left behind after the rapture. Nandi figures her age will be a great disadvantage to her survival during the seven years of tribulation.

Several Kapora converts would have joined the group, but because of Zaki's direct order, every able-bodied man of fighting age returned home and prepared for war. Some wonder if this is one of the apocalyptic horsemen Bishop Mathew spoke about.

"In the end times, there will be wars and rumors of wars spread across the world."

The Kapora purchased rifles and artillery pieces from the English.

"Those who pelt the Kapora with pebbles must expect rocks in return. We will obliterate Obijinaal with heavy artillery bombardment!" Zaki bellows.

"But first, we must save Macati from the slave castle on the coast before the Brazilian slave ship sets sail, after which, we will march Northeast to Obijinaal's chiefdom. Obijinaal expects them to come from the northwest because the Kapora capital is located northwest of his town. He has posted scouts on all pathways from the northwest to inform him when the Kapora are on the move."

Zaki laughs as he imagines the shock on Obijinaal's face when he realizes he has been routed.

The Kapora will position the artillery guns on the southern hills overlooking Obijinaal's town while Kapora warriors will wait in the forest around the town. As the bombs rain down on the town at night, panic-stricken town people and Jinaali warriors will run into the nearby forests seeking refuge, only to be shot by Kapora warriors armed with fire sticks that speak with the voice of thunder.

Zaki and the grand council will deal with Nyoka, Buta, and Ika after Macati's rescue from the slave castle after they have captured Obijinaal.

Judging from his character, Obijinaal will quickly sue for peace when he realizes he is outgunned. He will give up the names of all co conspirators at the trial. That's the way Zaki and his inner circle hope things will play out soon.

However, man's well-made plans are inconsequential when the gods script their own decisions on a matter.

Chapter Thirteen

Pombeiros

Nandi limps under the bundle's weight on her head as she goes up the ramp to the castle's gate. The Baptismal castle looks exactly as Bishop Matthew had described it, massive white buildings with towers and a big church in the middle of the yard. She gazes in awe at the massive structure. A gentle breeze blows from the harbor on the western side of the castle. It cools her from the long and arduous journey in the hot African sun, making her long and arduous travels, through forests, and turbulent rivers worthwhile. She has risked life and limb to get here, and in this absolutely divine place, she will stow away on a big boat which will take her to heaven. Soon, she will be reunited with her late husband and children.

At the castle gate, a light brown-skinned guard with a pointed nose and soft wooly hair is wearing unusual-looking clothes. In his hand is a fire stick with the voice of thunder.

There are several guards with similar weapons on the walls around the castle and in the small building by the gate. Some have white skin and long noses, like the archangel who visits her village with Bishop Matthew. Some are black, and some are light brown like the one slouching by the gate.

Nandi makes a quick, silent prayer as she approaches the guard.

"Father, You said You will neither leave me nor forsake me. You have kept me safe as I made this long and dangerous journey to this castle. Grant me with favor, with these guards to let me into the castle and let them not discover the true reason I have come."

She straightens up and tries to look as confident as possible. At this point, she imagines her late husband talking to her.

"Put on a brave face and keep on walking, don't over-analyze things. Rejection flees in the face of confidence. Walk and act like it's already yours and watch, your request will be granted by the person you are about to meet."

The guard jumps to his feet, opens the gate wide for Nandi to walk through with the load on her head. He points at the church and motions her to join the other Wagombe being baptized.

He says something in Portuguese, but Nandi does not understand a word he says. However, she recognizes it as the strange language Bishop told her was called speaking in tongues. She thanks him with a broad smile. He stares at her with piercing green eyes. Nandi has never seen a human being with such eyes.

She feels as if those green eyes can see all the way through to the back of her head. Nandi quickly turns her head down to the ground as a sign of respect, but more importantly, in her mind, to prevent him from looking deep into her head. He might discover the true reason for her coming to the castle.

The guard covers his pointed nose with a handkerchief and with the other hand, impatiently waves her in the direction of the massive church.

Walking past the guard, Nandi acts as if she is adjusting the load on her head. She turns her head and sniffs her armpit as she hurries past the guardhouse.

"Do I smell that repulsive?" Nandi wonders.

"Do the white-skinned guards with long noses smell me from inside the guardhouse? What of the black ones with short, broad noses? Can they smell me too? Maybe my sweaty odor worked in my favor. The green-eyed guard wanted to get away from me so fast that he didn't ask the obvious question; why did you not walk in with the other Wagombe converts? If he were suspicious of my motives, he would have alerted the other guards in the guardhouse, and they would have arrested me easily."

Nandi smiles as she imagines the voice of her late husband in her head, saying, "Stop over analyzing and focus, Nandi. Focus on the mission! You made it past the guards. Keep stepping, one foot in front of the other, you are almost there."

She follows the sound of Wagombe choral music coming from the church. Christian songs with African musical instruments bring a smile to her face and rhythm to her steps. For a moment, she forgets the pain in her feet and walks past the church. Out of sight from the guards at the gate, she turns a bend and runs behind the building. She can see the harbor from here. In her countless wonderings as a herdswoman, Nandi has never seen a body of water so large. It looks as if it stretches far out to the sky in the distance.

The Wagombe are a pastoral tribe that roams the African savannah where there is plenty of grass for their livestock. They do not venture to the coast because Tsetse flies in the tropical rainforests near the coast kill cattle and horses.

Bishop Matthew was right; there are many giant boats with wings. Many of them have big red crosses on their wings –(galleons with red crosses on their sails). *I have to get on the right one before the baptismal service ends.*

She runs to the harbor, careful not to be seen by the guards or any of the people in the castle.

As she approaches the first galleon, a terrible stench assaults her nose. The suffocating odor of stale urine, vomit, feces, and dried blood hangs heavy in the air.

"This is definitely not the right boat to Heaven." She moves on to the next and the next, then finally stops at the fifth galleon. It is much cleaner than the others and smells of fresh paint.

As she runs up the gangway towards the lone black man mopping the deck of the ship, she greets him and excitedly asks a burning question.

"Is this the boat that takes you to Heaven?"

"What did you say?" He asks in an unusual accent.

The young man steps backward, placing the mop bucket between him and the seven-foot-tall elderly woman in dirty clothes and disheveled hair. She looks like she had not washed in a month.

The stranger, with a funny accent, is muscular and about a head shorter than her. Nandi figures he might be from the Ibo tribe, although his accent sounds like one from another world. She and her late husband have traded with Ibo people in the past. She knows enough Ibo to buy, sell and haggle prices.

She repeats the question slowly in Ibo, so the stranger with the funny accent fully understands her.

The stranger introduces himself in Ibo but with a name and accent that does not match the language.

"Hello, my name is Greg."

Ibos are businesspeople by nature; maybe he traded in a far-off tribe for so long that he acquired a name and its people and their accent. Nandi reasons.

Greg points at the galleons in the harbor with a wave of the hand. There are hundreds of them, some tied to the docks and many more moored in the open sea.

"All these ships will take you as close to *hell* as you can possibly get here on earth. *They are all slave ships*."

Greg informs Nandi that Bishop Matthew is a Pombeiros — a Portuguese name for African agents who bring other Africans called Peças from the hinterland and sell them for Manilas, alcohol, guns, clothes, jewelry, and European luxury goods.

"Peças, Manilas?" What are those Nandi asks?

"Peças means pieces in Portuguese. We, black people, are not considered human beings but pieces to be bought, sold, and utilized like any other commodity you purchase in the market. Manilas are a curved metal currency used in most kingdoms along the African Atlantic coast. They are made of copper or brass. It is the currency of the slave trade."

Greg observes the look of disbelief spreading across Nandi's face. He explains further.

"Europeans, unlike the Arab slave raiders, cannot go into the Hinterlands to catch slaves for themselves. Many of them die of malaria and other tropical diseases, so they stay on the coast in fortresses like this and purchase their Peças from Pombeiros. Pombeiros use different methods to obtain Peças; kidnaps, slave raids, instigate wars and supply weapons to both sides, then sell the prisoners of war. The list goes on."

Nandi's eyes redden with anger.

"Bishop Matthew is not a Pombeiros! He does not kidnap anyone or start wars. In fact, he is a man of God. He preaches hope, prosperity and he brings us gifts from heaven. The devil is a liar! You are a devil agent trying to stop me from getting my blessings. I bind you in the name of Jesus!" She makes a giant sign of the cross in the air as she 'binds' devil Greg.

Greg tries not to laugh at Nandi as he explains to her that self-ordained Bishop Matthew, a silver-tongued orator uses "feel good" religious doctrine to get his Peças.

"The gifts from heaven as you call them are western manufactured goods like umbrellas, iron pots, mirrors, and salt. He told you that God has a lot more in store for you when you get to heaven, didn't he? Is that the blessings you think I am trying to stop you from getting?"

"Yes, and Bishop Matthew said that God in His infinite mercy had sent giant boats with big red crosses on their wings to rapture a hundred and forty-four thousand righteous people. They will take us to heaven where there is no more sickness or death. I will have eternal youth and will be reunited with my late husband and my son, who died in battle last month alongside my future nephew-in-law, the Kapora prince. I went through great pains to make it here; you will not stop me from being raptured! Hallelujah *aaaamen! Eu sou uma Cabra estúpida!*"

Nandi starts to hop around the deck, shaking her fist at Greg and speaking gibberish, believing she is speaking in tongues.

"What is that?" Greg asks.

"Tongues! Tongues! I am speaking in tongues. Get thee behind me, Satan. I bind and cast you into the pit of hell from which you came."

Speaking more gibberish, she reaches inside her bundle and pulls out a gourd of holy water.

"*Hebra! Hebra* Holy Ghost fire! Fire! You and all my enemies that don't want me to go to heaven fall down and die!" Nandi starts chanting in rhythm, "Die! Die! Die! Fall and die. Die die die! Fall and die!"

She splashes the water on Greg then observes his reaction, expecting him to convulse and die.

Greg starts laughing.

"This woman acts like crazy Daisy on the Virginia plantation; she sees the devil in everything. I didn't think I would ever meet her African counterpart."

He points to a chain gang of men in dreadlocks being led to a ship at the furthest dock to the left. It's the first stinky ship Nandi passed earlier. They shuffle along, wet and tired, with chains on their feet, giving just enough room to walk but not kick or run. Hands tied to their backs and braces on their necks with connecting chains to the man in front and the one behind.

Their mouths are gagged so they cannot shout or bite. Their bodies are drenched in water because the Portuguese slavers baptize their Peças and give them Christian names before shipment to the Americas in compliance with Iberian legislation. Hence, many Catholic priests in slave fortresses across the African continent and a preponderance of Roman Catholic names amongst the enslaved and their descendants in Iberian America - Maria, Jesus (Pronounced Hay-Soos) José (Pronounced Ho-Say meaning Joseph. Juan (Pronounced H-won meaning John).

There is a very tall one amongst them with Wagombe style braids matted close to his head instead of the lion mane-looking dreadlocks of the Kapora.

"Those over there are the Kapora crown prince and his warriors, not unrighteous men being condemned to hell. They have been starved for a week, so they are too weak to fight. Notice their mouths are gagged so they cannot shout and alert the happy Wagombe in the church who think they are going to heaven. As soon as the old ships with the forcibly obtained Peças pull out, the happy Wagombe in the church will be loaded onto this clean ship, and all the other new ships moored in the harbor. Upon boarding the ship, they will be overpowered and forced into shackles and leg irons."

Nandi puts both hands on her head, her jaw hangs ajar; she slowly sinks to the deck.

Greg proceeds, realizing that Nandi no longer views him as a "devil agent" trying to stop her from getting her blessings. He informs Nandi that the place she calls "The Baptismal castle" is a Portuguese slave-trading fortress.

It is one of the forty-three slave castles spread across the African Atlantic coast. There are two types of Pombeiros on the premises; the black-skinned ones and the half-castes, as the Portuguese call them. The half-castes are the biracial offspring of the white priests, sailors, Portuguese soldiers, traders, and the local African prostitutes in the brothels near the fort. The pecking order at the fort is as follows: the white priests, traders, and white military officers make the top caste, the free blacks the low cast, and the "half-castes" in the middle.

The light brown-skinned guard with green eyes is a "half-caste," not a guardian angel that can see through your head with piercing green eyes.

It is the practice for Portuguese slave traders to baptize slaves before shipment.

"The white men in white long gowns are catholic priests, not angels preparing righteous people for heaven. Some have blue eyes, some green, some hazel, and some brown, but they see just like the rest of us, and it has nothing to do with the color of heaven from which they came. The grass is green in America as it is in Africa, and we all bleed red. As per the "Mark of God" Bishop Mathew gave you, the biggest threat to a ship full of over 200 slaves is smallpox. One captive with the disease can infect the entire crew and cargo on the voyage. Hence the vaccination of everyone sold into slavery. Smallpox vaccination leaves a mark on your arm. Tall strong vaccinated Peças fetch a higher price than an unvaccinated one. This makes them less likely to catch or spread smallpox to other Peças and crew before they get to the Americas.

Greg pulls off a tarp revealing a pile of leg irons and chains.

"You and your people will be locked down, side by side in layered rows, one above the other in the cargo hold of these ships. Many of you will get sick or die on the journey across the Atlantic. That is why old slave ships have a permanent and distinct smell of stale urine, vomit, blood, and feces."

"After several years of slaving operation, the stench becomes so bad that slavers burn the ship and file insurance claims for fire accident at sea," he smiles.

"It's amazing how the captain and crew always survive the fire accident at sea and live to collect the insurance money only to sail again another day."

"Sharks know the smell and throng behind older slave ships because every so often, a dead Peças is thrown overboard," Greg says as he walks to the rails of the ship, pointing at shark dorsal fins, which circle an old ship in the distance. "When the ship starts running out of food supplies because Peças mortality was lower than projected, several Peças are thrown overboard lest the crew starve. Occasionally, one might escape from the hold below and jump overboard, trying to swim to freedom. None makes it to land. No one returns alive once they pass through "*the door of no return*." He points at the thick wooden door on the side of the slave fortress through which captives pass when herded onto waiting ships…

Nandi remembers Bishop Mathew talking about the "door of no return" in a different context. She turns to take a better look at the chain gang that just came through the door of no return. Her eyes widen as she recognizes some of the captives in the chain gang.

"All these months, we thought Macati and his entourage died in battle!" She wails, interrupting Greg in the middle of his sentence.

"You know the Crown Prince?"

"Yes! My niece Awat is his fiancée. My only surviving son was part of his entourage when he was ambushed. That is him over there! The tall one! The tall one!"

She points at the chain gang and starts to wave. Greg jumps on her and covers her mouth. They both fall on the deck.

"Quiet! Do you want to attract the slave traders?"

"No, but we must save them. We thought they all died in battle. Awat and I decided to join Bishop Matthew's congregations to reunite with her prince in heaven, and my son and late husband. I did not want to grow sick, old alone, and childless. I went over and beyond the duties of a Christian to be taken to Heaven on a giant boat. However, when everyone gathered for the trip to the Baptismal castle, Bishop Matthew said that my time is quarter to dead, so I should stay behind and let a young person go on the boat. Imagine the insult! Calling me a quarter to dead after all I did to grow his church. So, I gathered a few supplies and stayed a non-visible distance behind the congregation. That is why I am not in the church with the others. I intended to hide on the boat then run to Jesus at His mercy seat the moment the boat arrives in heaven. I hoped to state my case and tell him of all the good works I did to advance His kingdom here on earth. He would pardon me for stowing away into heaven and say, *come into my rest, you good and faithful servant.*"

"There is no way Matthew would have let you come," says Greg.

"Why?" Nandi demands.

"Bishop Matthew's contract with my master Mr. Jackson was for young and fertile people of Nilotic stock because Nilotes are naturally tall, strong — and the average Wagombe woman can bear eight or more children. You are obviously past childbearing age. He hit the jackpot when he came upon your tribe of seven-footers. Mr. Jackson wants to breed and sell slaves on his Virginia plantation as his brother breeds and sells cattle. Your age disqualifies you."

"Why would your master do such a thing?" Nandi wonders.

"The Abolition of The Slave Trade Act three years ago empowers the British and American Navy to seize slave-trading vessels on the Atlantic. The Act, however, does not ban slave ownership or the trade of slaves and their children already within the United States. With the increased demand for slave labor and short supply due to the Abolition Act of 1807, the price per slave has risen significantly. To make a windfall profit from this price surge, Mr. Jackson and his investors chattered over a hundred ships and hoisted flags of non-signatory nations to the Abolition Act like Spain and Portugal. They want to import as many Wagombe as possible to breed homegrown, obedient, big, and strong English-speaking slaves."

Greg continues.

"The greater part of the British Navy is busy fighting Napoleon, so they cannot spare many ships for abolition enforcement. The single small ship available for abolition enforcement is reluctant to intercept a Portuguese ship due to Portugal's alliance with Britain against France. Besides, the Portuguese monarch was forced to flee to Brazil due to advancing French troops on their capital. They need the money generated from the slave trade, gold mines, and plantations worked by African slaves to finance the expulsion of French occupiers'."

Nandi looks horrified at this point.

"The U.S. has such a tiny Navy that they rely on privateers to perform Naval tasks. The privateer owners in the southeastern quadrant have a financial stake in this venture. No ship in this fleet will be intercepted if they enter U.S. territorial waters through that quadrant."

Greg stops to catch his breath.

He wants to tell her how he knows all this and why he is here. Nandi cuts him off before he starts another litany.

"I am a cattle herders' widow, most of the things you just said, I don't understand. I see my son and my future son in-law in chains. They are putting them on a smelling ship. My niece is in the church singing and dancing, thinking that she is going to heaven. We have to save them! Or are you too going to benefit from the sale of your people, and why do you call Macati, a Crown Prince instead of Prince?"

Nandi is not aware of the plans to make Macati King instead of Ika.

Greg was present when the head Caçadore told Mr. Jackson about Macati, the Crown Prince, to be shipped to Brazil before they load the Wagombe so they should go into town and return at about noon. By that time, the happy Wagombe would be baptized and ready for shipment.

Nandi glares at Greg expecting an answer to her earlier question. "Will you help me save my people?"

"I can't leave this ship," Greg looks down at his right foot.

Nandi follows his eyes and notices for the first time; Greg's foot is shackled with a long chain to the ship's mast. It is long enough to let him work on the deck but not long enough to get off the ship.

"I will run to the seaside and get big rocks to break these chains. Then you will help me save my son, my son in-law, my niece, and my tribes men and women." Nandi holds her stare at Greg until he nods his head in agreement.

"Be careful that none of the guards or Pombeiros sees you because they want to keep the Wagombe in the church, happy and ignorant. If they see you, they will realize that you have caught onto the scam and throw you on a stinky ship," Greg warns as she rushes off the ship unto the Jetty.

Nandi's mind races through the past two years. It all makes sense now that she is able to put things in their proper perspective.

Over two years, Bishop Matthew visited the Wagombe tribe in the African hinterland with messages from God and western manufactured goods he called "gifts from heaven." Occasionally he visited with a blue-eyed white man in long white robes. This generation of Wagombe has not seen a white man before. Bishop Matthew told them that the white man was an archangel with blue eyes matching the heavens from which he came. They performed pseudo-miracles, preached prosperity, hope and spoke of a wonderful place called Heaven, a glorious kingdom of joy, good health, and abundance.

"These gifts I brought are sent by God in Heaven. God has much more in store for you." Bishop Mathew would say to his large congregation.

And the gathered crowd would shout, "Amen!"

Last month he had declared a promise.

"God in his infinite mercy has sent giant boats with big red crosses on their wings to rapture a hundred and forty-four thousand righteous Wagombe. I will take you to the Baptismal castle ten thousand at a time, and there, Angels will baptize you in the name of Father, Son and Holy Ghost. Then you will go through the door of no return and board the heavenly boats with big red crosses on their wings."

"Hallelujah!" The crowd erupted.

Some burst into songs, some into dances, and others into spastic fits like one in the throes of an epileptic seizure shouting, "*Eu sou uma Cabra estúpida*," and any other derogatory Portuguese word they have learned as the heavenly language called tongues.

"The more you do for the man of God; the more God will do for you. Give me a bull-sized offering, and God will give you ten bull-sized blessings. A poor and hungry shepherd cannot take good care of the sheep. The sheep get their blessings only after the shepherds have been blessed. It is the will of God that your shepherd be bountifully blessed so I can lead you to greener pastures via the still waters by the Baptismal castle."

A popular statement that generates loud resounding "Amens" from thousands of gyrating penitents at his open-air crusades.

Bishop Matthew owns over a million head of cattle given to him by zealous converts in exchange for prayers, miraculous healing, God's blessings on their lives, and an opportunity to be part of the hundred and forty-four thousand granted passage to Heaven in their lifetime. Those who cannot afford to pay their way to heaven can earn their way through "good works for the man of God."

"Good works for the man of God" means the person will serve Bishop Matthew free of charge. Cook, clean, and do anything he tells them to do.

Many young pretty women perform special favors indoors to receive anointing oil of the Lord at night. The not-so-pretty ones and postmenopausal women wear leather pouches around their necks and crawl on all fours alongside the poor men in a dry riverbed to pick shiny stones – alluvial diamonds.

The Wagombe value gold, copper, and iron but do not know the value of diamonds so plentiful in the dry riverbeds; one need not to dig for them. A full pouch of diamonds earns a poor Wagombe penitent passage to heaven on a giant boat with a red cross on its wings. Bishop Matthew sells the diamonds to European merchants on the Atlantic coast.

Bishop Matthew also spoke about a terrible place called Purgatory — a hot place of pain and suffering for unrighteous people when they die. As for those who died in their sin before hearing the word of the Lord, living family members can make offerings to the "Man of God" — Matthew, so their family members will be released from Purgatory into Heaven.

Recently, he acquired gold-rich land in the mighty river basin as payment for the "emancipation of the dead in hell."

Matthew proclaimed a "night of ascension."

That night he forbade anyone to go up a local hill because the departed souls will be released from hell below and ascend to heaven above at midnight. Anyone who climbs the hill will take the place of one being released from hell. As the souls ascend into heaven, blessings and answered prayers, will come down to all believers assembled at the bottom of the hill. That night, Bishop Matthew, and the archangel — the white priest with blue eyes – set off mesmerizing fireworks from behind a massive boulder on top of the hill as the gathered crowd sang, "God of Elijah send fire down."

Ten thousand unbelievers convert to Matthew's brand of Christianity that night. Thousands more offer their gold jewelry to the archangel and their gold-rich lands to the man of God. Bishop Matthew is on his way to becoming one of the richest men in the world. His imported clothes from Europe and the elaborate gold jewelry adorning his fingers, arms, neck, and the gilded Bishop's Miter will make most 19th century European noblemen look like beggars beside him.

Nandi's anger rises as she remembers how she went over and beyond the duties of a devout Christian to secure her place as part of the one hundred and forty-four thousand to be raptured.

Nandi's memory flashback is interrupted by her niece's alto voice in the church leading the Wagombe choir in song.

"Heaven is full of joy."

Anger fills her head with each heartbeat. Adrenalin pumping, she lifts two rocks and rushes back to Greg on the ship.

Watching from the deck as Nandi hurries back to the ship, Greg can't help but marvel at how his fortune has changed. A second-generation African American slave of Ibo ancestry, Greg cajoled Mr. Jackson to come on the voyage as a manual laborer on the ship and attend to Mr. Jackson's needs throughout the journey. Greg intended to run away the moment the slave ship arrives in Africa. He will find his way back to his ancestral home in Ibo land by the seven-round pyramids of Nsude.

Growing up on Mr. Jackson's Virginia plantation, Greg's parents told him wonderful stories of what life was like prior to their capture in West Africa and subsequent enslavement a few years before his birth. Greg often fantasized about a life of freedom, respect, and personal worth amongst people who love him. The moment he heard Mr. Jackson was organizing a fleet of ships to purchase many slaves from Africa, he saw an escape opportunity and seized it. He grilled his parents and many first-generation Africans on the plantation to teach him Ibo and other African languages since he was not certain what part of the continent they would land and what language they spoke on those shores.

He learned enough to navigate his way through the continent back to his ancestral village near the round pyramids of Nsude — an unmistakable landmark. He was not sure if the village still existed after the raid in which his parents were captured.

Was it burnt to the ground?

Were there any survivors?

Will my parent's surviving relatives accept me?

He consoles himself that he bears a strong resemblance to his father and is about the same age his father was when he was captured.

Some of dad's relatives from back then might still be alive and recognize me, he hopes.

As the ship approached the African coast, Mr. Jackson shackled Greg with a long chain to the ship's central mast. He ordered him to clean the ship in preparation for the Wagombe penitents, soon to become field slaves and breeders on his Virginia plantation.

Upon docking at the Fort Harbor, Mr. Jackson and the ship crew left Greg on the ship to repaint it while they went to drink and frolic with local prostitutes in the bars and brothels in the town just outside the Fort gates. Greg just finished painting the ship and was mopping up when Nandi ran up the gangway, asking if that was the boat going to heaven.

He had given up all hope of escape until Nandi came along.

If she helps me break free from these chains, I will help free her people from their happy ignorance. With knowledge and the truth comes mental freedom. The guards and priests in the Fort cannot stop ten thousand strong Wagombe from breaking free. My chances of getting out of this fort just increased ten thousand-fold. Considering Nandi spoke to me in Ibo, chances are she knows how to get to Ibo land. She might lead me back to my ancestral village.

God works in mysterious ways, performs wonders. Meeting Nandi also allayed one of his greatest concerns; recapture by marauding Pombeiros as he navigates his way back to his ancestral village. He knows Krio's fetch a high price at slave auctions because they understand English and need not be broken to become compliant slaves.

"Krio" comes from the African mispronunciation of the American word Creole. It was a name given to the small community of black loyalists who fought for the British during the American war of independence. They were given the choice to settle in Canada or return to Africa. A number of them chose to return and established the town of Grantsville, named after Grant, an abolitionist. They are now recognized as the Krio tribe with a distinct language — Creole English. A mixture of American slave English, French, and anything else their former slave master spoke mixed with a few local African words that enable them to trade and communicate with their new African neighbors.

In 1809 Africa, Greg would be considered Krio by other Africans until he is assimilated into a tribe or joins the Krio community.

Greg breaks his chains with the rocks Nandi brought from the Seaside. Nandi wants to run into the church to warn the other Wagombe, but Greg tells her that she will be overpowered and put on a stinky Brazilian ship like her son. They decide to run off the ship and get help from the bustling community just outside the fort before Greg's master and the ship crew return.

The half-caste guard with green eyes sits half asleep on a chair by the gate. He notices Nandi and Greg walk out of the open gate and yells.

Greg and Nandi burst into full speed.

The guard raises his musket to shoot them; his commanding officer turns up the barrel of the gun.

"Hold your fire, soldier! The sound of gunfire will arouse suspicion in the church."

He orders several Caçadores – 19th Century Portuguese Infantry men – to join the green-eyed half-caste.

"Chase, catch and bring them back. If they resist, kill them with your swords if you catch them anywhere close to the fort. If they get far from the fort, where no one in the church can hear the shot, fire at will. The woman is old, and the American Negro does not know his way around here. None of the natives in this town will give them refuge. They have a financial relationship with the Fort. You are a young and trained Caçadores, and you know the territory; you should catch them easily."

Greg and Nandi make a quick right and run behind a saloon. One guard sees them make the sharp turn, and he blows his whistle. There is a thumping of boots behind Nandi. Greg runs through the local market hoping that the Caçadores won't shoot in a public place and someone might help them.

Nandi runs closely behind him and the Caçadores, in hot pursuit. Merchants and shoppers clear out of their way as Nandi lengthens her strides to increase the distance between herself and their pursuers. The impact of her feet on rough stony ground shoots tremors up her aging knees; her legs begin to wobble.

Earlier in the day, Mr. Jackson and the crew from the clean ships went to town to have fun with the locals while waiting for the forcibly obtained Peças to be taken out of their dungeons and placed on the older ships.

They will leave the bars and brothels by noon in time for the baptismal service to end, and the Wagombe to board the clean ships.

Mr. Jackson stands on the veranda of a brothel, observing the raucous in the market a hundred meters away. He sees a young man and an elderly woman running through the crowd and several uniformed Caçadores in hot pursuit. He recognizes Greg and shoots in the air.

"Greg has escaped from the ship! Catch him!"

Several sailors pour out of the bar below into the street. Greg sees the sailors and makes a sharp right turn into a nearby forest. The ship mate sees him and orders the sailors.

"Follow me!"

Nandi makes the sharp right to the best her aging body can maneuver. Her sixty-five year-old body has taken more punishment today than at any other point in its lifetime.

Her throat feels like it is sucking in fire as she breaths in the hot, and dry air at a rapid clip. Her malnourished heart struggles to pump blood devoid of nutrients to every muscle. The tendons in her legs ache with each stride.

Forest undergrowth whips at her legs, her face, all over her body as she struggles to keep up with Greg. There is a fallen tree in front of them — Greg leaps over it. Nandi's mind tells her to jump, but her aching leg muscles fail to obey. She hits her sheen on the trunk.

A sharp pain shoots throughout her body, and she tumbles over the trunk. Nandi struggles to get back on her feet, with blood gushing down her leg. She stabilizes herself and takes a long stride.

But someone hits the back of her head, knocking her out cold.

Chapter Fourteen

Saving Macati

In the slave castle, penitents queue up to be baptized by white catholic priests they believe are angels. The senior Caçadore officer walks in and informs the leading priest about Nandi discovering their scam. They should speed up the process because his men are taking too long to return, and he is not certain if Nandi and Greg have gotten help from another tribe opposed to slavery.

"I will send one of my men to go into town and get Mr. Jackson and his crew so they can start loading the ships with converts immediately". He says in frustration.

The senior officer is unaware that the ship captain and his crew had already joined the green eyed Caçadore in pursuing Greg and Nandi, and the first mate had hit Nandi on the head with a branch, knocking her out cold in the forest.

Nandi lays face down on the forest ground, oblivious to the fierce battle going on around her. Greg swings a broken tree limb upwards. It impacts the first mate on the jaw, and he falls backward.

Greg is relieved to see strange men in African war garbs join him in battling the ship crew and the Caçadores. He does not know where they came from or why they are helping him, but he is glad they showed up.

As the sound of loud thumps, the snapping of tree branches and grunts arise between the fighting men, Greg bends to lift Nandi, so they can escape while the African warriors fight the Caçadores. Greg is not aware that the half-caste Caçadore with green eyes is charging at him with a sword. The Caçadore is so focused on killing Greg that he doesn't notice Waggy swinging a massive battle-ax at his neck. It's a swift swing and Waggy does not miss. The Caçadore with green eyes will be dead before his body hits the ground, minus his head.

The evidence of Waggy's sharp aim at his neck is evident, as blood gushes out from his exposed neck, and soils the dry ground in a dark and bloody pool.

The African warriors fight their way through, joining Waggy with their crafted weapons. Some of them throw their tribal Kpinga knives towards the enemy from thirty feet away. The twenty-two inches long knives crafted with three blades, each of different shape, protrude out from targeted angles of the shaft, and pierce through flesh and bones. The Caçadores stand no chance with their manufactured weapons, as the blades on the Kpinga strikes them down.

Within minutes, several of the ship crew and Caçadores are either captured or dead. The survivors scurry back to the fortress.

King Zaki, Uzaza, and Obya enter the clearing. Zaki is dressed in a Dashiki made of Lion skin and brown ankle length baggy trousers, with the head of a Lion for his headdress. Obia, in a red leather dashiki, red ankle length trousers and a metal helmet with horns, and Uzaza in a crocodile skinned Dashiki, black baggy trousers and the hollowed-out head of a large crocodile for his head dress.

Obya revives Nandi by smearing a stinking green substance under her nose that looks like fresh cow dung.

Nandi awakens to see King Zaki smiling at her.

"Nandi, what brings you here, and why were those men trying to kill you and this young man?" Zaki points at Greg.

Nandi explains how she got there and what she discovered. She informs Zaki that Macati, Jabu, MaKuei, and the survivors of Macati's contingent are being loaded onto a stinking ship. Awat and the Wagombe will be loaded onto a white ship with red crosses as soon as Macati's ship sets sail for Brazil.

Greg draws a map of the castle in the sand with his finger.

With Nandi as an interpreter, he tells them that the fort is under-guarded. Many of the experienced Caçadores that would have guarded the fort were shipped to Europe to fight Napoleon. Just a handful are left behind, half of whom the Kapora warriors have killed or captured already. Those left at the castle are mostly new recruits — half-castes and native Africans — who enlisted for the money, not out of love for Portugal. They will run away at the first sign of real trouble.

The local Wayo's have a lopsided but beneficial economic relationship with the fort, so Zaki should not expect any cooperation from them. Macati and his warriors on the ship are so weak from starvation that they can't offer any resistance even if they tried.

The converts in the church are delighted to be here. They out-sang, out-danced, and out-prayed even the most religious priest in the slave castle.

Greg suggests they attack from the east because the fort's artillery pieces and cannons are positioned on the western wall facing the Atlantic Ocean. Seldom would you find the cannons of a slave castle facing inland — towards the African continent. Most of them point to the Atlantic Ocean. The greatest threats to this and most other slave forts come from other European powers, not the indigenous population, as trade in Western manufactured goods and the export of slaves, gold, ivory, and cash crops make them wealthy.

Europeans fight each other for control of these fortresses. They attack from the sea. Slave fortresses or coastal trading posts have changed hands from one defeated European power to the other, for example, Elmina on the Gold Coast (present-day Ghana) has changed hands three times. First the Portuguese, then the Dutch, and now the English.

There is a town called Escravos, which means *slave* when translated from Portuguese, on the Escravos river dedicated to the slave trade. This was snatched from the Portuguese by the British for its profitability.

Note:

The town still retains its "Slave Name" in 2022 – sixty-two years after independence from the British. As at the writing of this book, the indigenous people of Escravos work for pennies while Europeans, Americans and modern Pombeiros make billions of dollars from African labor and the crude oil beneath and around Escravos.

Up until now, the only possible threat to this slave castle is the French Navy and the English West Africa squadron dedicated to abolition enforcement. However, the French Navy is overstretched trying to protect whatever territories they have left in the Americas. They recently lost Haiti to a slave revolt. The bulk of their navy is busy fighting England.

The English West Africa squadron had only two ships dedicated to intercepting slave ships. One of which sank earlier this year (1809

), and its replacement is yet to arrive in Sierra Leone.

The Germans and Dutch are further south. They have no interest in the fortress because they are profiting heavily from the gold and alluvial diamond trade in the rands of South Africa. There are no other European ships within a thousand miles except for the American ships in the harbor flying Portuguese and Spanish flags to circumvent the abolition act.

Zaki jumps to his feet.

"We must move in fast before the other guards in the fort realize that something's happened to their counterparts, and they mount a defense. We need to get to the Brazilian ship and rescue Macati before it sails off!"

Greg picks up a rifle and bullets from one of the dead Caçadores, while Nandi picks up his sword.

"And where do you think you are going with that?"

Zaki points at the sword in Nandi's hand.

"This is a job for warriors." He protests.

"Who will show you the right ship to board? There are hundreds of them in the harbor. Besides, you need me to translate what he says," Nandi points at Greg.

"She has a point," Says Uzaza.

Waggy chimes in.

"If the Wagombe in the church see her with us, they will believe and join us, not resist thinking we are devil agents sent to prevent their rapture to heaven. Or worse, they might even fight us because they think we are trying to get on the giant boats and invade heaven."

He further adds, mimicking the Bishop.

"I've heard the Bishop say things like, *the Kingdom of God suffers violence, and the violent take it by force.* He will claim that we are the violent he preached about who have come to capture the Kingdom of God by force. When they see Nandi with us, they will join us. We need them to gain a quick victory so we can save Macati and quickly move on to Obijinaal before he finds out we have left our capital under fortified and capture it."

Waggy takes the ammo belt off the headless body of the Caçadore with green eyes as he speaks.

Zaki nods in approval as Waggy stands proud.

Now he is a Kapora warrior of the highest order, for he has killed the most dangerous animal on earth — a full-grown man, an enemy warrior in battle. Greg shows him how to load the gun.

Chapter Fifteen

Fight For Freedom, Who Wins?

The castle gate takes a direct hit from Kapora artillery, turning the huge wooden door into a smoking hole in the wall and shattered wood strewn across the ground. Hordes of Kapora warriors armed with battle-axes, spears, swords, long bows, English rifles, Kpinga knives and light artillery storm through the smoking hole where the gate once stood. The castle guards barely mount a defense against the hordes of warriors, fast covering every inch of the fort.

Light artillery shells blow up guard towers. The newly recruited African and half-caste Caçadores in the slave castle scatter in different directions. Some run unto the Brazilian ship seeking refuge.

Kapora warriors crash into the church, and Nandi shouts to the shocked congregants that Bishop Mathew sold them all into slavery. The Wagombe join the Kapora; they break pieces of furniture and use them as clubs. Bishop Mathew and the Catholic priest run out through the back door, heading to the docks.

Nandi, King Zaki, Awat, and a dozen warriors chase them to the docks, wanting blood.

Bishop Mathew, the priest, and Mr. Jackson run onto the first ship to escape the rampaging warriors. The old king ignores all age-related pain and outruns his strong men. Sweat trickles from his face as he bolts towards the ship. Throwing caution to the wind, he leaps off the gangway unto the Brazilian slave ship only to be stopped by a bullet from the priest's pistol.

The warriors catch up and overpower the priest before he can reload his pistol, and they throw him overboard. The gold in his pockets weighs him down as he tries to swim and keep his head above the waves. The sharks that follow slave ships hear the splash and rush in for a feast.

Uzaza and Greg pull the bleeding King off the ship. Awat, Nandi, and a few warriors run below deck to free Macati and the others. Waves of warriors surge towards the galleon. Bishop Mathew cuts the ropes tethering the ship to the docks so no more warriors can board it. The ship eases away from the piers leaving behind angry warriors and the burning fort.

The warriors on the ship are too few to overpower the Caçadores and the crew of the Brazilian slave ship; Nandi and Awat are soon captured, and Mr. Jackson tells the Caçadores on the ship to shoot at the warriors at the dock.

"Aim for the man in western clothes. He should be easy to distinguish from the other black folk in African war clothes," he says, referring to Greg.

The Brazilian captain says he is short a few slaves to make a profit on this trip. He takes the captured warriors as slaves. The ship crew and Mr. Jackson strip Bishop Mathew of his elegant clothes as payment for their troubles.

Mr. Jackson takes all of Mathew's jewelry as compensation for funds lost in this venture, and Bishop Mathew will replace Greg, who just escaped. Stripped to his undergarments, Bishop Mathew breaks away and runs to the back of the ship. He is about to jump off and swim away when he sees sharks feasting on the Catholic priest. The sea is red from his blood, and the blood curdling shrieks from the priest sends tremors down Bishop Mathew's spine as the sharks bite chunks of the priest's body. The silence ensues as he slowly sinks below the waves.

Mathew turns and tries to talk his way out of trouble. He starts negotiating for his freedom in perfect English, then in Portuguese, and back to English. Mr. Jackson is shocked to hear Bishop Mathew speak fluent English.

"All this time you sat in negotiations with the Catholic priest as an interpreter, I had no idea you spoke perfect English."

Mr. Jackson says as he motions to the Brazilian captain to order his men to stand down.

Mathew explains he is a Wayo prince.

When the Portuguese explorers and missionaries first arrived in the Wayo Kingdom seeking converts and trading partners, his father, the king, made him go with them as a child. His father wanted him to be educated in the white man's ways and to act as an interpreter and ambassador to Portugal, as was practiced between the Portuguese crown and African royalty for most of the past two hundred years in the 1600s and 1800s.

Historical backdrop:

Between the 1600's and 1800s, the Portuguese recognized African kings as legitimate monarchs. They neither had a military large enough to conquer nor the population to colonize the continent, so they traded with African leaders instead of subjugating them. Conquest and subjugation came later with the Berlin conference of 1884 – 85 when the ground rules for the partition and colonization of Africa by European powers were enacted. Prior to the Berlin conference, it was common practice to take African royal family members back to Portugal to be educated. These young men would act as ambassadors and trading partners with the Portuguese traders and African nobility; this arrangement was more profitable than conquest and occupation. The latter would require large armies and administrators. The Portuguese barely had enough to occupy and administer their colonies in America and Asia. Trade and diplomacy with African leaders proved lucrative. Several kings like the Oba of Benin had Portuguese wives in their harem.

Intermarriage between the Portuguese royal family and Africans produced the "Black De Souza" bloodline of the Portuguese Royal family.

The practice of diplomatic marriages between royal families is not limited to Africa alone but has been common practice worldwide dating back thousands of years.

For example, all of Europe's monarchies were related to each other by the 1800s. For example, The Black De Souza of Portugal was intermarried with the nobility of the German principality of Mecklenburg-Strelitz and produced princess Charlotte.

King George III of England marries Princess Charlotte of the black De Souza royal bloodline.

Coincidentally, England would abolish the African slave trade in 1807, during Charlotte's reign and her sick husband King George III. The repatriation of blacks from Jamaica, Canada, and the USA will occur under the reign of her son King George IV. Under her sponsorship, the eight-year-old German Composer Wolfgang Amadeus Mozart rose to prominence amongst the British elites.

Charlotte North Carolina USA, Charlottetown Canada, and Fort Charlotte in Saint Vincent are named after her. Charlotte's famous descendants include her son King George IV, Granddaughter Queen Victoria, the current British royal family, and David Cameron, former British Prime minister.

Mathew's father noticed young Mathew was not physically strong like his brothers, but he had a sharp mind. He is so far down in line for the throne but close enough to have aligned interest with the ruling class. Mathew would be useless on the farm and as a warrior but was excellent in learning the white man's ways.

Mathew was trained in the classics, English, Latin, French, and divinity at Coimbra University in Lisbon. He returned to Africa seventeen years later and was instrumental in enriching the Wayo nobility through trade with Europe.

Mathew is Nyoka's youngest brother and the one who introduced Buta to "long-distance trading."

Mathew informs Mr. Jackson that there are several rich investors in this venture expecting a handsome profit. Mr. Jackson cannot return to the United States empty-handed.

The jewelry they took from him in no way comes close to recouping their investment. Mr. Jackson's reputation and creditworthiness in the business circles of the emerging wealthy class in the United States will be ruined.

"I have a plan that will turn this into a temporary setback, and you will return to the United States as a very rich man," he says, knowing full well the power of greed.

Promise a man the thing he desires most, and he will do your bidding, even the most ridiculous.

Mathew muses as he observes Mr. Jackson pull a crate to sit on so they can discuss this proposal even further.

Bishop Mathew says he can help them get more slaves.

Fortunately, none of the American slave ships were destroyed during the attack. He can fill them up with tall and strong slaves.

Mr. Jackson says the gig is up in this part of the continent.

That word of Mathew's religious scam will spread quickly. He cannot get any more Wagombe. He promised his investors tall and strong slaves that will breed generations of tall, strong, and obedient slaves to be sold within the United States when the price of slaves rises from the scarcity of new slaves caused by the abolition of the slave trade.

Bishop Mathew informs him of the Anago, the pre-19th-century name for the Yoruba speaking people. Other names include Nago in present-day Togo and Aku in present-day Sierra Leone, and the thick of war with the Dahomey kingdom. Strong young POWs are sold by the thousands out of three slave ports: Goree Island, Eko, and Porto Novo.

The Brazilian ship captain says he knows the slave port at Eko well; and the Portuguese call it *Lagos* — the Portuguese word for Lagoon because Eko sits on a lagoon.

He is concerned about the British presence there. The British have been encroaching on Eko and the nearby trading posts at Porto Novo, also known as New Port in English, and Escravos town on the Escravos River. Escravos is the Portuguese word for slave.

Mathew says there is nothing to worry about the British in Eko, for the English merchants there do not favor the abolition of slavery but rather sell guns to the Yoruba war Chiefs to defend themselves from Dahomey incursions, while Francisco Felix De Souza sells weapons to the expansionist king of Dahomey.

"Good, I can select the tall, strong ones to fill my ships."

Mr. Jackson says in an authoritative tone,

"That might meet your quota, but it will cause trouble for you later." Bishop Mathew says.

"Why?" Mr. Jackson asks.

"A warrior is always a warrior. A warrior will do what comes to them naturally the first chance they get —*fight!*'

Bishop Mathew points out that most of the slave insurrections in the Americas were led by former warriors and captured nobility forced into slavery without implementing the tenets of the Willie Lynch letter. This includes Nene, leader of the maroons in Jamaica — a captured Ashanti Princess sold into slavery. France lost its most profitable possession Saint Dominique (now called *Haiti*), to a slave revolt fought by POWs sold to the French by the expanding the Kingdom of Dahomey. This was part of the Haitian slave revolt's success; thus, making it easy for them to organize and overthrow their French overlords.

Historical backdrop:

Francisco Felix De Souza, descendant of a Portuguese Nobleman/first colonial governor-general of Brazil, was the biggest slave trader in West Africa. He would build a massive palace for himself and fathered eighty children with many women.

His success came by propping up expansionist kings like Adandozan and Ghezo by supplying them with weapons in exchange for POWs which he sold as slaves. These leaders were so power-hungry that they expanded their armies by conscripting legions of women into the ranks. With the gun, one need not the male strength required to wield the sword, spear, or hand-to-hand combat to fight your opponent's warrior.

A good eye and the willingness to squeeze the trigger took out the enemy before he gets close to you with his sword or spear. The Dahomey called them 'Minos' European explorers called these female warriors "Amazon Warriors."

Unsuspecting slave owners who failed to read or implement the tenets of the Willie Lynch letter of 1712 (the making of a slave) often discovered too late when the warrior code within their captives got triggered.

For example, Gaou Guinou, a warrior prince of Alada in the Kingdom of Dahomey, was betrayed by his brother and sold into slavery. His grandson Toussaint Louverture would lead the first successful slave rebellion that resulted in Haiti's independence. This rebellion's success is rooted in the fact that enslaved POWs of the Dahomey and Anago kingdoms united to fight their overlords using their military experience and religion. Hence the need to Christianize all slaves, erase their language, histories, and traditions after that.

For better or worse, family histories tend to reoccur in one's bloodline even several generations later. Louverture would be betrayed by one of his own at the edge of victory, and his position usurped.

A similar fate to his African grandfather, prince Gaou Guinou of Alada, Louverture dies in a French jail far from home while another ascends the leadership role that should have been his.

Another famous son of a Dahomey POW/slave turned soldier is Thomas- Alexandre Dumas, the first black general in a European Continental army who led several successful campaigns for France. He is the inspiration of several of his son's (Alexandre Dumas) characters in, "The Three Musketeers" and "The Count of Monte Cristo" amongst other famous novels, and the reason Napoleon ordered the Sphinx's nose to be shot off because he was jealous that such a great monument would have identical facial features as the black general (Alexandre Thomas Dumas) – who was more popular than himself. Erasing Dumas, his accomplishments, and anything that would cast a shadow on his (Napoleons) personal glory would satisfy the little man with a mighty ego.

The Brazilian captain chimes in.

"We have the same problem in parts of Brazil. We have lost control of vast territories in Brazil's Alagoas and Bahia regions from slave rebellions and runaways. Several of them have joined with native Indians to fight us, hence the need to import more slaves to backfill the escapees on the plantations. He has a point."

Bishop Mathew smiles.

"Enslaving me will not profit you at all. I can make you a very rich man, Mr. Jackson.. If you give me back all my jewelry and a cut in the profit, I can help you obtain a mix match of Peças from different tribes so they can't communicate with each other; preferably from kingdoms currently at war with each other. After purchasing Dahomey POWs from Lagos, we can stop at Porto Novo — a former Yoruba province annexed by the Dahomey Kingdom and purchase Yoruba POWs from there as well. Put them on the same ship. They (Yoruba POWs and Dahomey POWs) hate each other more than they hate you and are more likely to fight each other for past offenses than unite and fight you, their common captor. Neither group will submit to the other's leadership in a rebellion against you. Imagine what would happen if you put British and French combatants from the ongoing war in Europe on the same ship?"

Mathew says, knowing that Britain and France are currently embroiled in the Napoleonic wars.

Mathew notices this new insight enthralls Mr. Jackson into the slave trade from the African standpoint. He continues to make his case.

"Some unscrupulous Pombeiros obtain criminals and lunatics cheap from communities seeking to rid themselves of troublemakers and *efuleefus* as well as the village idiot. They sell them to unsuspecting and inexperienced slavers like you."

He explains.

"When the Peças start acting crazy, you think it's just angry Peças resisting slavery. It's no different from an unscrupulous businessman selling you a defective product knowing full well that by the time you discover you have been scammed, it's too late to do anything about it. There are scammers in every line of business; slaving is no different. For a price, I can help you identify the least troublesome ones."

Mr. Jackson agrees.

Bishop Mathew directs them to Calabar and Bonny's kingdom in the Gulf of Guinea before heading to Lagos, Porto Novo, the Gold Coast and on to the mighty Jollof Kingdom currently in decline due to internal strife. They will skip Sierra Leone and the Gambia to avoid the English West African Squadron.

"You wouldn't have any investors from South Carolina or Georgia?"

"No," Mr. Jackson replies.

"Why do you ask?"

"Rice plantation owners in South Carolina and Georgia's low country regions prefer Peças from the Jollof Kingdom, Wolof, Temme, Serbro, Galo and Mende tribes. Those tribes are known for rice cultivation. They call that part of the Africa continent the rice coast. I got Mr. Tucker shiploads of Mende, Sherbo, Gola, Peças for his rice plantation before the Abolition Act. Hence, my relocation to these parts when I learned the British were planning to base their anti-slavery operations off Sierra Leone's coast."

Chapter Sixteen

Put me under

"He is bleeding out. The bullet cut an artery, and I cannot get it out. I do not know how much longer he will live," Obya says with fear written all over his face.

Zaki grabs Obya's arm with a tight grip.

"Keep me alive long enough to see Obijinaal's destruction. We ride to Jinaali tonight."

"You are not in a condition to ride to Jinaali. As your heart pumps, you will continue to lose even more blood through the lacerated artery. Riding a swift horse will make it worse. You could die from blood loss by the time we get there," Obya replies.

"You will put me under with your vodun powder and revive me when Obijinaal is captured. We will try him, Nyoka, and Ika and execute them on the spot with everyone associated with this conspiracy. After that, if I die, I die."

"Ok, I will put you under and mount you on your horse propped up with sticks under your Dashiki, so the people think you are alive. We will cover your eyes in war paint. It is dangerous, but I will do it," says Obya.

The battle for the fortress is over. The Kapora and Wagombe celebrate victory and the fact that they narrowly escaped slavery with very few casualties.

Warriors bring the captain of the Caçadores along with several white men and a few African Caçadores. One of the black Caçadores speaks is of the Wayo tribe and able to communicate with the Kapora.

Uzaza yanks him before the war chiefs to act as an interpreter between the white men and the Kapora war chiefs. They negotiate a hostage swap – bring back Macati, Awat, and the Kapora people on the Brazilian ship in exchange for all priests' Caçadores and European traders' lives.

Warrior's salvage one of the burning slave ships. They load the captain of the Caçadores and the ship crew and tell them to sail after the Brazilian ship. The War chiefs find that more expedient than loading the ship with Kapora warriors with no naval experience and forcing the crew to chase and engage the Brazilian ship in battle.

All the while, King Zaki is propped up in a chair flanked by two trusted warriors. Only his inner circle knows he is dying. He turns to his chief bodyguard as soon as the Caçadores' captain and his interpreter are ushered out of the room.

"Ride back to the capital and inform the elders and kingmakers of the latest developments except my current health condition. Have them declare young Ikwunga King with immediate effect, so Kapora isn't left headless if I die tonight. We are fighting a new type of war with strange weapons. Victory is certain, but casualties will be high."

"My Lord!"

One of the warrior chiefs, Ayilara, tries hard to control his voice's rising anger as he speaks.

"Ikwunga is a child, why bypass your eldest son full of years and experience in handling matters of state, and hand over the leadership of our great kingdom to a boy who was weaned off his mother's milk just yesterday? Why would you do it in the middle of a war with the Jinaalis…"

He stops mid-sentence when another war chief motions him to shut up.

Uzaza is not surprised that Ayilara would protest bypassing Ika. Whatever is in his head gushes out of his mouth un-filtered. It is bad when he is nervous and worse when he is drunk.

He is not the type of person you tell a secret.

What surprises Uzaza is the one who motioned him to shut up — they are both Ika's drinking buddies and are sure to gain lands and titles if Ika becomes king. One would expect him to also protest, not motion his drinking buddy to be quiet.

"Could the chief who motioned Ayilara to shut up be one of the conspirators? The conspirators probably did not bring Ayilara into the loop because of his loose lips, lest he exposes the plot in a drunken stupor." He wonders.

Obya notices Zaki's facial muscles tighten as he struggles to suppress his pain. A trickle of blood slides out the side of Zaki's mouth. Obya rushes everyone out before they notice. He lays Zaki down and blows vodun powder into his nose. Zaki's facial muscles slacken as one who's fallen asleep.

Chapter Seventeen

Death by Bunta

From the crow's nest of the Brazilian ship, a sailor yells that there is a ship fast approaching. The captain pulls out his telescope.

"It's one of your fleets." The captain says to Mr. Jackson. "It's the captain of the Caçadores and some white sailors."

Mr. Jackson grabs the telescope to look at the oncoming ship. One of its cannons goes off, and a sailor starts waving flags.

"Are they shooting at us? What is he doing with the flags?"

Mr. Jackson demands.

"No, the cannon shot was to get our attention; they want us to stop." The Brazilian captain signals a sign.

"Don't stop! It's a trap. We have the Kapora prince and Wagombe princess in our cargo hold. They will rescue them and kill us all!"

Bishop Mathew yells out of fear.

"I don't see any warriors on the ship. Maybe they want to negotiate an exchange for the prince and princess for the Europeans they have captured in the fortress," says the captain.

"Kapora are good at concealment. You don't see them approaching until they are on top of you. I tell you, there are hundreds of them hiding below the deck on that ship. They will storm this ship the moment their ship pulls alongside us," Mathew turns to the captain.

"They will keep you alive long enough to take them back to shore then kill you slowly. Prince Macati will see to that personally. His capture and sale was your arrangement."

He then turns to Mr. Jackson.

"Death by a shark is better compared to what they will do to us. I'll take my chances with the sharks following these old ships than death by *bunta*. You have a choice, Mr. Jackson; we can get away from them and sail into a great fortune or stop and die by bunta. Your children will grow up as orphans and be forced into indentured servitude when your creditors come to auction off everything you own, to settle the debt you incurred to finance this venture."

Mathew pauses for effect.

Images of his pampered children being forced into a life of indentured servitude flash through Mr. Jackson's mind. The life of the indentured servant in 1809 America is just a little better than the life of a slave.

Let not the sins of the father be visited unto my children.

"What is death by bunta?" Mr. Jackson demands.

"They tie you down and bite off pieces of your flesh and eat it while you are still alive," Mathew responds.

Death by bunta doesn't sound like a pleasurable experience to the Brazilian captain. He tells his signalman to reply to the ship to come along, then tells the crew to slow the ship down and keep it stable.

Next, he runs to the back and tells the cannoneer to load the cannons with hot balls and fire on the oncoming ship. A hot ball is a cannonball that's heated before loading into the cannon muzzle so that it sets anything it hits on fire.

The hot ball rips through the lower bow of the ship and hits a powder keg causing a massive explosion. The front of the ship erupts, and sailors drop onto a lifeboat into the sea. The front of the ship dips into the sea — dead sailors from the blast slide into the water. Blood from the dead and injured sailors in the water attract the sharks following the ship. The scent of blood in the water attracts the sharks trailing the Brazilian ship. They turn around and rush to the sinking ship for a hearty meal.

Kapora warriors and Wagombe watching events unfold from the fort, wail in lament as they watch the ship sink. They know that all the hope of getting their prince and princess back just went down with the ship.

Bishop Mathew marvels at his ingenuity as he observes the captain congratulating the cannoneer for such an excellent shot. Mathew had used an old trick coastal African chief's play on European traders to prevent them from venturing into the African hinterlands and retain their profitable position as middlemen in the transatlantic trade with Europe.

Coastal chiefs would discourage European traders from going into the hinterlands with their western manufactured goods to exchange for precious metals, ivory, cotton, and palm oil. Coastal chiefs would purchase items the Europeans needed from the hinterland and bring them to the coast for sale at prices ten times more than they purchased them from the interior. Then they would purchase western manufactured goods like umbrellas, mirrors, iron pots and sell them to people in the hinterlands at marked-up prices, but do not say where they got it from.

The coastal chiefs told the European traders about the horrible stories of human sacrifice and cannibalism to scare them from venturing into the continent and trading with hinterland kingdoms directly, Thereby keeping their position as middlemen and enjoying the profit that came from it. Stories of adventurers that were eaten alive or used for ritual sacrifice kept most European traders from venturing past the trading posts' fortresses and safe confines at the coast.

The fact is the Kapora will not eat any animal that eats human flesh, much less a human being. Their god of creation forbids them from mistreating anyone with any form of imperfection like blind,criple, albino except in self defense. Such an act would incure his wrath directly and personally. Europeans are covered under the "albino" statute. None of their gods would accept such a sacrifice.

The Kapora would not eat anything with the life blood still in it, neither would they eat any raw meat. Even their westernized descendants will not eat any raw meat with blood oozing out, much less something that is still alive. However, the tales of cannibalism feeds European xenophobia and make good business sense to the African middlemen on the coast.

Death by bunta was a product of Mathew's imagination, and it achieved its purpose effectively. Bunta is in fact his cousin's name – Buta with an 'n' before the 't'.

Mr. Jackson acts on Bishop Mathew's advice.

They pick up slaves from several ports along the West African coast. They place Awat, Jabu, and Barack on the U.S. bound ship.

All tall POWs from warring tribes are placed on the US-bound ship. Upon getting to the U.S., they will be put to forced labor and sold as breeders.

Macati, Waggy, and several Kapora are mixed with Yoruba POWs, and captives from other tribes known for their artisan skills and kept on the ship bound for Brazil. Many artisans would be sold to Brazil's Bahia region, where the demand for artisans runs high. Others will be sold to sugarcane plantation owners in the Alagoas to backfill those that ran away.

After the ships are loaded, Mr. Jackson reneges on his agreement with Bishop Mathew and chains him down below with the people he helped capture. Mr. Jackson plans to use Mathew to understand and manage his slaves on the plantation in America.

Chapter Eighteen

If I survive this one

If I survive THIS one. If indeed I survive THIS one, I will lavish thanks upon my maker for many a suffering have I known, but THIS one is the father of them all!

Ola Rotimi, Ovonramwen Nogbaisi

The lower deck of the slave ship has less than five feet of standing room. Three hundred to four hundred Africans from different tribes are crammed into this space. Chained to each other on sleeping shelves, they lie side by side in a head-to-foot fashion called "spooning" with barely enough room to turn. Spooning is when your head is next to the feet of the two people on either side of you — so instead of shoulder to shoulder, they cram more people into a tiny space. The holding space is dark with very little ventilation and barely enough room to place buckets for human waste. The tightness of the cargo hold, the poor ventilation, and the oppressive heat bearing down on the galleon as it travels along the equator westbound to the Americas is stifling.

The heat produces a suffocating stench, bringing sickness and death to many in the ship's hold. Only the strong survive.

Macati wonders what offense he has committed that the Orishas would bring this type of punishment unto him and Awat.

Are they offended that he cheated on his solo survival? If it's because he cheated, and Awat, her brother, and cousin aided and abetted the crime, what of Nandi and all the other innocent people on slave ships who had nothing to do with the offense?

He starts to pray again for forgiveness and deliverance and then stops confused. Who should he pray to this time? The deities? His ancestors? The almighty God of creation? Which spirit has he not prayed to? Which one should he promise to make restitution for his sins and offer multiple sacrifices if he survives this ordeal?

He lays quiet and listens to all the people around him cry and pray to their respective gods. Beside him, an Ibo captive prays to Chukwu. The Yoruba prisoners of war across from him pray to Ogun, the god of war. The Mandingo, Fulas, and Hausa captives pray to the Muslim God, Allah. Lying next to him is a Krio praying to the Christian God Jehovah. The highways to the spirit realm must be congested with prayers of the afflicted.

The Orishas do nothing and the ancestors do nothing.

The Eguns are silent. The spirits are deaf to the cries of their children. Not even one rescues or tries to comfort the faithful adherents crying out for help on the middle passage. The old galleon creaks as it rocks from side to side — it is as if the ship is groaning in agony.

On this journey of despair, suicide begins to look like an appealing solution.

Macati's thoughts are interrupted when the Krio's prayer to the Christian God turns to loud songs of thanks and praise.

Macati nudges the Krio and says, "Why would you praise the God of the very people who put us in these chains? Their Jesus looks like them and his enemy satan, black is like us. If it is His will that we become captives and He empowered His people to lock us down here, what makes you think He would help you?"

"Because He helped me escape slavery before," the Krio replies.

The Krio explains that Krios are former American slaves who joined the British in the American independence war of 1775 – 1783. Many fled their plantations and joined the British on promises of freedom from slavery by Sir George Clinton. But George

Washington, himself a slaveholder, was fighting for American liberty, but not blacks' freedom. Over three thousand slaves escaped and joined the British in hopes of gaining true liberty — they were called black loyalists. When the US got independence, it did not include black folks.

This Krio was one of the 411 black loyalists brought over by the British to establish the West African colony called the "Province of Freedom" in May 1787 and the settlement was called "Granville Town" named after the English abolitionist Granville Sharp on land provided by a Temme King Tom. Their name "Krio," is an African mispronunciation of the word Creole, which is the language of the American returnees.

Creole is a mix of English, French and African languages. Krio or Creole language would later evolve into what is now known as *Pidgin English* after the massive infusion of Jamaican Patois introduced by the Trelawney town maroons that would arrive later.

Upon his death, King Tom's successor turned on the settlement. By 1792, there were only sixty-four settlers left in Granville Town. Many had died or moved to form new settlements in other parts of the West African coast. This Krio tried to navigate his way through the West African tropical rainforest to another settlement of returnees when he was captured by Pombeiros and resold into slavery.

Krios' fetch higher prices on the slave auction block, for they are former slaves or children of former slaves and need not be broken or thought to obey orders of their English-speaking masters.

"If that god helped you escape, what did you do that he let Pombeiros catch and resell you into slavery?" Macati asks.

The Krio replies, "I will answer your question with another question. What offense did all these people commit against their gods and ancestors that they let this happen to them? Some questions I can't answer. What I know is that he helped me escape the first time as a child, and he will help me escape again."

Macati listens intently to the Krio's story of escape from slavery. How he pretended not to understand English, so he doesn't get sold to the US but to Brazil instead. He heard that it is easier to escape in Brazil and disappear in the dense jungles of the Amazon than in the US where they have bounty hunters and native American Indians who would turn you in for a bounty. Whereas the Indians in Brazil would not turn you in because they too were forced into slavery prior to the enslavement of blacks. This news opens Macati's mind to the possibility of returning to Africa. Then he prays to any god that's listening that they let him survive this ordeal and more importantly, return him and Awat to Kapora as King and queen.

On the other side of the Galleon, an elderly Krio woman lay motionless — she has not eaten in days. There is no point living anymore. She is not the first captive who decided to take her life by starving rather than remain in this hot, dark, and stinking ship, only to get out in the Americas to spend the rest of her living years toiling in the sun as a slave. She was a slave before and escaped as a young woman.

She can't go back into slavery again.

She doubts if she has the strength to escape a second time in her old age. Young captives on the ship who try to starve themselves to death are tortured, and when that doesn't work, they are force-fed with a contraption called a speculum orum which holds the mouth open, thus taking away the choice of suicide; the captain would rather keep his human cargo alive.

An elderly woman will not fetch much in the market due to her age and the fact that she is a woman. Unlike the Arab slave trade, which preferred African female slaves to work as domestics and sex slaves, young male slaves were preferred in the Americas to work the plantations and mines. The captain orders the crew not to force-feed the elderly Krio woman. He would instead save the food rations for those that will fetch a high price in the slave market. The elderly Krio succumbs to death and is thrown overboard to be eaten by sharks.

Chapter Nineteen

Sweet land of liberty for some people, not all.

Nandi is glad to breathe fresh air for the first time in weeks. She looks around for anyone she recognizes as the other captives are brought up from the ship hold. A month earlier in the slave port of Fernando Po off the West African coast, the Wagombe Peças and tall POWs from other West African kingdoms were carted unto a ship bound for the United States, while Macati, Waggy and a number of the Kapora were left on the Brazilian bound ship.

In the US-bound ship's hold, the captives were separated from other members of their tribe as per Bishop Mathew's instructions. Two enemy POWs have a non-aligned prisoner in the middle, so they don't kill each other. Nandi was sandwiched between a Yoruba warrior and a Dahomey Mino for the entire trip. The expansionist Dahomey kingdom sent legions of brutal female warriors called "Minos" (Amazon Warriors in French historical texts) against the Yoruba kingdoms.

Minos would torture, kill, or sell their vanquished to French and Portuguese slave traders while the Yoruba killed or sold the Dahomey Minos to English and Portuguese slave traders. These enemies were put on the same ship with captives from non-aligned kingdoms between them, thereby ensuring the captive would not unite to overpower the ship crew, whom they outnumbered ten to one. If they all pulled the long chain that bound them all to the shelves in unison, they could rip it out and break free.

Where disunity resides, suffering takes residence also.

And so, Nandi lay on the bench, surrounded by hatred, darkness, and stench for weeks on end. Today, she stands chained at the docks not knowing the fate of her loved ones; she watches the captives brought out of the hold. Her face is covered in dirt and sweat, and she feels her strength going.

She pauses hearing the shuffle of several feet and the grunts of familiar voices. Finally, she sees familiar faces — Jabu is on the ship. Next to come up is Awat; she looks ill and thin. Nandi tries to go over to them, but the sailors force her back in line then herds them all into a huge building with rusty iron doors. Normally, captives will be examined, washed then transported to an auction house. However, this set will not be auctioned but taken straight to Mr. Jackson's plantation to be prepared for their new role as farmhands, breeders, and — in Nandi's case — infant caretaker while the young men and women work the fields. It is the Jackson plantation practice to separate children from their mothers shortly after they are weaned. The children are cared for by elderly slaves that are too old to work in the field, thus freeing young mothers to work alongside their male counterparts and get pregnant again.

It also has the added effect of breaking up family bonds and atomizing the slave community.

Each person sees himself or herself as an individual separate from the rest of the community. With the communal spirit effectively destroyed, each one seeks their interest without regard for other members. Those who don't fare well are not looked upon with sympathy but shunned as weak, inferior, and deserving of their unfortunate condition. The overlord, however, sees no difference between the less fortunate and the self-perceived superior black person — in his eyes, they are all chattel and beasts of burdens, no different from how he views his workhorse.

The practice of grandmothers playing the role of both father and mother to children in the black communities of the British colonized Caribbean and the United States has its genesis in this practice.

Seldom do the men grow to see old age. You can kill a man at fifteen years old and bury him at fifty by breaking his spirit before his fifteenth birthday. The years in between will be spent in endless toil as a mindless zombie to the benefit of his master. Those who refuse to be broken mentally will be physically broken in the presence of others as a warning to others not to think outside their assigned boxes.

The women who live to old age will bury their brothers, husbands, sons, and several grand or foster children before they too finally pass on.

At the building with rusty iron doors , men and women are separated into two large dungeons to await the taskmasters that will march them to the Jackson plantation. In the female dungeon, Nandi finally gets to speak with Awat for the first time since their capture two months earlier. They rush into each other's arms and hug for a long time. Awat's temperature is quite high, probably from the trauma they are going through, Nandi thinks. They barely start a conversation when loud screams from the men's dungeon fill the building. They recognize the voice but not the language.

It is Bishop Mathew screaming in English.

Nandi asks, "Is that animal screaming in tongues? Who is he trying to impress here?"

Nandi and Awat don't know English, and they think any European language is "tongues."

"*Aargh! Aaaargh save me before these savages kill me!*"

Bishop Mathew screams in perfect English from the men's dungeon. The guards are shocked to hear a captive speaking English. Most captives speak only African languages when they first arrive. The guards start running down the stairs to the men's dungeon.

Jabu, MaKuei, several Wagombe and tall Kapora captives got hold of Bishop Mathew in the men's dungeon and beat him. A massive Wolof joins the fray. He remembers Bishop Mathew from when he operated amongst the peace-loving Wolof and Mende people from the West African region called the "rice coast" because these tribes are known for rice cultivation. Mathew used his false religion to catch Temme, Mende, and Wolof people. He sold them to slave traders on the Atlantic coast that resold them to rice plantation owners in South Carolina who were willing to pay higher prices for slaves from this region.

Krios who returned to Africa just after the American Revolution settled on Temme land in the "rice coast" of West Africa and informed these tribes of the hellish lives Mathew's victims underwent upon getting to America. Life on a rice plantation is worse than on a cotton plantation. Life expectancy was a lot shorter on a rice plantation than any other because the slave spent unending hours in the scorching sun with his feet sloshing through mud, breathing steamy humid air.

Slaves from the rice coast cleared over 40,000 acres of land and dug 780 miles of canals across the United States' Carolinas. They carved rice fields out of tidal swamps filled with huge cypress trees, alligators, snakes, and disease-carrying mosquitoes. If heat stroke didn't get you, one of the others listed above would.

The massive Wolof takes out the agony meted out on his people on Mathew's mouth.

His fist slams into Mathew's mouth, breaking a front tooth upon impact and sending it down his throat.

Mathew coughs to stop the tooth from going down his windpipe.

"Lying rat! Son of swine! Die!"

The Wolof yells in his language as he strangles Mathew.

MaKuei pulls off the Wolof, allowing Mathew to catch breath.

"You don't deserve quick death but a slow and agonizing one."

MaKuei tells Mathew.

The Wolof protests that this might be their only chance to exact revenge on Mathew. Mathew scrambles on all fours to get away from his assailants. MaKuei runs behind Mathew, who is still crawling and kicks him so hard in the groin that the force raises Mathew off the ground causing such excruciating pain — anguish that takes you beyond screaming. Mathew's red eyes and mouth open wide but bring forth no sound. By the time the guards get to the gate of the cell, they see Bishop Mathew curled up in a corner with his hands between his legs.

Jabu lifts him by the shoulder, and MaKuei grabs him by the torso. They position him like a battering ram and smash his head against the iron bars of the dungeon. His scalp splits open, and blood gushes out.

"You sold us into slavery; now you will pay with as much pain as possible." They tell him.

The guards open the gate and use a horsewhip to disperse the men from around Mathew. They drag Mathew out, barely conscious.

Jabu shouts after him.

"If you survive this one, we will beat you again every day and twice on Sundays for the rest of your wretched life!"

"You should have let me kill him,"the angry Wolof protests. "Now they have taken him away." The guards drag Mathew past the female dungeon as they head to the medical officer's office upstairs.

The women hurl insults at him.

"I hope you die. The gods punish you."

Nandi calls out to Jabu, "I hope you broke his bones!"

"I told you the bastard was a charlatan," Jabu yells back.

Guilt and sorrow bear down on Nandi.

"It's all my fault," she sobs.

"I championed his religion to our people, and many joined because of me." She looks down in regret.

The medical officer revives Mathew.

"You are quite hated amongst your people," he says, stitching the gash on Mathew's head.

"Those are not my people; I am a free-born prince educated in Coimbra University Lisbon," Mathew replies.

"And I am the Czar of Russia," the officer snickers.

"I sold them all to Mr. Jackson, and he double-crossed me and threw me in with the rest of the cargo. Give me justice, and I will reward you handsomely," Mathew continues.

"King, prince, bishop, or whatever you call yourself in Africa, you are just a nigger here. No courts will listen to your case. You got your reward and justice — becoming a slave like those you sold," Mr. Jackson says as he enters the office.

"Double-crossing sidewinder," Mathew retorts.

Mr. Jackson strikes him with his walking stick. Mathew falls to his knees.

"From now on, you call me Master Jackson," Mr. Jackson smiles.

"Everything is different from now henceforth. You are in God's own country, the United States of America. Here, you do as I say with a smile. You start work in the cotton fields tomorrow morning," Mr. Jackson turns to leave.

"You might as well shoot me now."

There is a quiver in Mathew's voice as he tries to feign bravery.

Mr. Jackson turns around.

"Why would I mess this office up with your blood? There are many niggers eager to kill you." He moves closer to Mathew.

"I'll have some friends come over this weekend and toss you in with a few of the men you enslaved. Then we will place bets on how long it takes them to beat your brains out. You want to die? I'll make money watching you die."

"I won't give you any trouble," Mathew mutters.

A smug smile spreads across Mr. Jackson's face. He places his hand by his ear as though he misheard something.

"Master Jackson." Mathew bows.

Mr. Jackson taps his walking stick on the ground. Mathew kneels.

"That's better. Now we understand ourselves; I will do you a favor. Tonight, you will sleep in a separate cell from those you enslaved. Tomorrow after you all have washed, fed and recovered from your voyage, I will return with my taskmasters and a few of my trusted slaves. You will be chained in a line and you all will march behind my coach to my plantation. Save your strength and rest well. You will need it for the long march tomorrow. You will be at the back of the line, so no one beats you up."

Mathew bows repeatedly from his kneeling position.

"Thank you, master; you are so kind."

Chapter Twenty

Have you seen my son?

The next day, Ellen Jackson sits on the furthest side of her husband in the coach. Barely speaking, with her arms folded and her legs crossed, she looks outside the window, and Mr. Jackson pretends to read the newspaper he already finished reading on the two-hour ride into town. Last night was a long night for them, and they are both exhausted, but not from what you would expect from a married couple who have been apart from each other for several months. It was a long night of arguments. And to think of it, Ellen can't even remember the last time her husband initiated a simple hug, let alone a night of romance. The love in their marriage is long gone, not that there was any before, at least there was some semblance of a kindling that might glow.

Happiness in the Jackson home is an act for public consumption, especially when they are among their high-class friends, at balls, galas, and church on Sundays. But resentment and distrust are permanent residents of the Jackson mansion, and they have mastered the art of masking it when they are around their friends.

Ellen normally does not go to the slave auction house with her husband. It is way too barbaric for her civilized Christian sensibilities. However, she knows her husband has an animalistic barbaric side. She believes he has had a few flings with the slaves on the plantation, even though he vehemently denies it. He has been in Africa for several months. It's hard to believe he was celibate all that time.

So many scenarios run through her mind, and after last night's argument, she just couldn't contain her curiosity any longer. So, she insisted on coming with him to the auction house to see which one of them he could have messed with. She knows his taste in women; he likes them caramel, heavy chested with big butts — areas Ellen is highly deficient. She doubts he married her for love but the love of her father's money and access to the Virginia banking community. That's how a cattle rustler's son rises into the Virginia elite class. Raw guts, animalistic brutishness, a sharp mind, and the tenacity of an angry pit-bull. The Virginia elite tolerates him if he does their dirty work.

She has tried to clean him up, make him more presentable to the Virginia elites. As an eager student, he quickly learned the social graces and etiquette of the elite. Her invested effort, time and her father's connections have been profitable for Mr. Jackson. However, there has been no personal return on investment for Ellen except that she is saved from the social stigma of being a pale old maid.

He wasn't Ellen's first choice either, for her first choice faked his death to get out of the wedding she manipulated him into. A year after playing the grieving spinster mourning her beloved's death, the young doctor resurfaced in Boston. He is now married with three children.

Ellen's fast approaching expiry date made her agree to marry this upstart, the only bachelor in her horizon that cared to spend more than a passing glance at her sickly pale and boyish figure.

The newly arrived slaves are chained to each other in a long line. One of Mr. Jackson's elder slaves approaches the taskmaster. The taskmaster is sitting on a horse and chewing tobacco. He spits brown tobacco slime on the ground, barely missing the elderly slave's worn-out shoes.

"Wat daya want?"

The elderly man removes his shabby hat as a sign of respect, revealing a sweaty bald head.

He forces a smile and says, "It looks like the iron neck brace on some of them are too tight."

He points at Jabu struggling to breathe.

"He might faint from poor circulation to the brain before we walk a mile. There isn't enough room in the cart at the end of the line to carry many people if they all start fainting," he beams a broad smile at the taskmaster sitting on his high horse.

"If they faint and don't get up, I'll whip them! If that doesn't work, I'll just shoot em," the taskmaster replies.

"That works good for those pretending to faint but if you shoot em, Massa Jackson loses money, and he might take it out of your pay suh," the elderly slave replies.

"Alright, alright. Check the neck braces. Leave enough room for two fingers to pass through. That's circulating noff. If you help any escape, I'll shoot you first, old man," the taskmaster brandishes his rifle.

The elderly slave shakes his head vigorously as he speaks.

"No suh no suh. Nobody gonna scape suh."

The elderly man hurries off to the front of the line and gradually works his way to the back of the line.

As he checks each one's neck brace, he says to the newly arrived slave in a low voice, "Onye huru Opara'm," which translates to *have you seen my son* in Ibo.

But the newly arrived slave does not respond. He is a POW from Dahomey. They have no connection with Ibo people linguistically or by trade.

When Mr. Jackson returned to the plantation yesterday, he did not explain to anyone why Greg did not return with him. Mr. Jackson has not yet decided if he should tell them that Greg successfully escaped, thereby encouraging other slaves to escape or telling them that Greg tried to escape and died on the docks of the slave castle from a rifle bullet fired from the ship. Nothing in his behavior towards Greg Sr. gave any hints as to what happened to Greg Jr..

As a matter of fact, he acted as though this is just another regular day, and he asked Greg Sr. to drive the wagon to the rusty warehouse at the docks just to create further anxiety and confusion in the old man's mind. Mr. Jackson loves to keep people on shaky ground. It gives him a sense of power.

Greg Sr. is afraid to ask Mr. Jackson what happened to his son, so he hopes that one of the new arrivals can tell him something. But new arrivals from Africa usually can't speak English except for recaptured Krios, and there aren't any Krios on this ship — they were on the Brazil bound ship. So old man Greg speaks his native tongue, hoping that one of them understands Ibo and can put his fears to rest.

Greg Sr. goes on to the next one.

"Onye huru Opara'm."

Still, he gets no response; the man is Ashanti.

He repeats the process over and over again as he goes down the long line. His breathing gets labored as he drags himself to the next. Silence makes the dread of bad news heavy on the heart.

There is a heavy lump in his throat. The old man staggers on down the line to the last one exhausted.

Fighting back the tears he says in a breathless whisper, "Onye huru Opara'm."

This is it; if she doesn't know, then I will never know what happened to Greg, and his mother will keel over from a broken heart, he thinks to himself. He repeats the question, and Nandi responds.

"Eee ahurum ya," she responds to say *yes, I have seen him.*

"Move on!"

The taskmaster yells from the front of the line, cutting short the old man's joy and unleashing an avalanche of questions into his mind. Old man Greg struggles to contain his emotions as he hurries to the cart.

And so, the long march to the Jackson plantation begins.

Mr. Jackson's stately coach in front and the long line of slaves in chains trailing behind flanked on both sides by white taskmasters on horseback. At the back of the line is a water cart driven by Greg Sr. with barrels of water and a few trusted slaves to serve the water. His mind is not at ease. Nandi telling him that she saw his son now opens new unanswered questions like, did he find his way back to my hamlet by the round pyramids of Nsude? How is he adapting to Africa? How does he support himself?

Greg Sr. strategizes how he can spend time with Nandi to get as much information as possible. News of Greg's sighting in Africa by one of the new arrivals will gladden Greg's mother's heart. She has been worried sick since he left the plantation.

The march goes into the fourth hour. The sumer heat bears down, and Awat is throwing up again — she is unstable in her gait. Up the hill, a Mulato woman in a torn white ball gown holding a pink umbrella with frills around the edge's waves at the carriage.

She smiles as she does the dainty princess wave at the occupants of the gilded coach.

Mr. Jackson focuses intently on the newspaper, pretending not to notice with his wife next to him watching his every move.

"I see you looking at her."

Ellen says from the other side of the coach.

"You would like to bury your head into her bosom like you're burying it in the newspaper."

Mr. Jackson raises his head above the paper.

"There you go talking crazy again."

"Everyone calls her crazy Daisy not me. Look at her in rags, thinking she is a princess," Ellen chuckles.

"She was normal until you pushed her over the edge; cruelly mistreated her and sold her children because of your insecurities. And to think she is your cousin..."

"Hypocrite! Being my cousin did not stop you from sleeping and having children with her," Ellen shoots back.

"So, you finally admit she is your cousin. You are so paranoid that her children bear such a striking resemblance to ours and it makes you conclude that they are mine, and so you instigated our children to mistreat them regularly. You accused her daughter of stealing your pearls and had the taskmasters' strip and flog her publicly, then you wear fancy clothes with the magically recovered pearls and go to church acting all pious. You have the audacity to call me a hypocrite?

Daisy's children look like our children because they share your crazy genes, not mine! I try to talk sense to you to stop your cruelty towards them, and you accuse me of trying to protect my bastard children."

"Yes, you were trying to protect your bastard children! Don't think I don't know of your arrangements to send them off to your brother so he would free them and send them to school. That's why I sold them all while you were over in Africa frolicking with savages," Ellen replies.

"You did it to hide your ineptitude as a mother! Your uncle Will stated that you'll free Daisy when she turns eighteen or marries a free-born negro — whichever comes first —you kept her under your thumb instead. She has children and is a better mother to them than you ever would be to ours..."

Ellen rises and serves her husband with a dirty look.

"How dare you call me a bad mother!"

"Because you are!"

Mr. Jackson throws the rolled newspaper in her face.

"You love the accolades of being a married woman but don't act like one unless you have an audience. You love the title of a mother, but you never show love for the children nor spend time with them but would rather prance around from one high class function to another. Daisy was a better mother to our children than you ever were. You turned her into a field slave and tried to raise our children yourself. However, your ineptitude as a mother became increasingly apparent over time. So, you shipped them off to boarding school."

"I sent Daisy to the field, so you don't have easy access to her in the house," Ellen points her bony finger at her husband.

"And our children? What's your excuse other than you wanted them out of the way? Now our son has turned into a homosexual in that boarding school thanks to you."

Mr. Jackson points his finger at her.

There is a raucous behind the coach, and Mr. Jackson turns to look. He sees crazy Daisy trying to lift a fallen slave.

Awat lies on the floor unconscious, and the taskmaster whips her.

"Get up, lazy nigger!"

"What the devil has gotten into you?"

Crazy Daisy points her umbrella at him.

"Can't you see she's pregnant? You will kill her if you make her walk in this heat any further."

The taskmaster raises his whip to flog Daisy when Mr. Jackson yells from the coach.

"Enough! Put her in the water cart and keep moving; one more mile, and we'll be home."

Greg Sr. disconnects Awat from the rest of the chain gang. He and crazy Daisy help Awat to the water cart. As they approach the end of the line, Nandi says something in Ibo.

"Father of Greg, I can make her well."

Greg Sr. seizes the opportunity and requests Nandi be released to help.

"Why should I?" The taskmaster growls.

"She is her mother", old man Greg lies.

"She can't run away and leave her pregnant daughter behind; besides, she is old."

The taskmaster unlocks Nandi then points his gun at Greg; then Nandi to warn them if they try any mess, he will shoot.

Greg Sr. hands the reigns over to another loyal slave and goes to the back with Nandi, Awat and crazy Daisy. Old man Greg plans to use this opportunity to find out all she knows about young Greg.

Awat confirms to Nandi that she is, in fact, pregnant and Macati is the father. Awat and Macati figured that they would be married in a few weeks, so if the pregnancy started showing a month or two after the wedding, everything would have been all right; that is what they were discussing behind a rose bush when Uzaza came looking for Macati and told him that he had to collect tributes from Obijinaal.

Nandi is shocked to hear that Awat and Macati had broken traditional rules, but a part of her wasn't surprised, seeing how close the two had been since Macati announced his plans to marry her.

"But he was supposed to display a bloody cloth to the elders after your first night together as proof that you were still a virgin on your wedding night. How did you plan to get around that?"

Nandi asks Awat, with her arms folded.

Awat explains that they planned to dip a cloth in a cow's blood before going in together on their wedding night, then display it in the morning. She explains further that when she was told Macati died and went to heaven, she had to get on the boat and join him because with him dead, how would she explain the pregnancy? Especially with people like Nyoka lurking around seeking anything embarrassing to use against them and Halima. She figured that if she joined Macati in heaven, they could get married, have children, and return to earth after the seven-year tribulation, when the world is rid of wicked people.

Nandi tells Greg Sr. how she met young Greg in Africa and how he is now with the Kapora. They might help him return to his homeland, or he just might settle with them. The Kapora are quite generous when you do right by them. His efforts to save the crown prince will be handsomely rewarded. Nandi points out that Greg told her all about crazy Daisy.

Greg Sr. explains that Daisy wasn't always crazy but has sought refuge in madness to escape the wicked blows life has dealt her over the years. Daisy used to belong to Ellen's uncle.

It is rumored that she was his daughter — the product of an affair with a beautiful Creole slave he brought from Louisiana. The Creole slave was the plantation midwife and nurse, for she was great with herbal remedies and healing potions. Ellen's uncle was married, and the wife died after a brief illness. Ellen's uncle never formally married Daisy's mother because the law in Virginia forbade mixed marriages; but he treated her well, practically moving her and her children into the house and treated Daisy like a princess.

Ellen believes Daisy's mother poisoned the legitimate wife with Creole hudu to get her out of the way and did roots on her uncle, so he never remarried. However, he could not legally marry Daisy's mother; he promised to free Daisy and let her marry a freeborn when she comes of age. He would give them land to start their lives.

Historical backdrop:

In 1809, the number of free blacks in the United States reached 186,446 -about 13.5 percent of the total black population. Most of them were in the upper south and northern states. A good number of free blacks had fought in the war of independence on the American side. Many were owned by crown loyalists and joined the Union Army on the promise of freedom after independence. If their masters were crown loyalists, they were set free. Some slaves belonging to patriots were also released. However, most were returned to their pre-revolution patriot masters, like old man Greg.

Some like Cuffee (the American mispronunciation of the Ashanti name Kofi — meaning born on Friday) were owned by Quakers and were given their freedom due to religious conviction.

The fortunate free blacks in America were artisans or were skilled laborers. Others were sailors and dockworkers. The unskilled were worse off, as freedom in the 1800s came with no land or job guarantees. The less fortunate were forced to indenture themselves.

Some of the free blacks in the United States became quite successful and were able to build schools to educate their children when it was illegal for most blacks to read.

It was this class of successful blacks that Daisy's white father was grooming her for. Unfortunately, he died while Daisy was young, and Ellen's father inherited her. That ended the plans for emancipation and marked the beginning of Daisy's life as a domestic and personal caretaker of her cousin Ellen.

Time passed, and Daisy grew into a beautiful woman. That was not the only thing growing. Ellen's insecurities grew after her fiancée faked his death. No one else was on the horizon until Mr. Jackson came to the house seeking a financier for his business startup. Daisy and all her father's slaves went to the Jackson plantation shortly after their wedding. Shortly afterward, Ellen had Jamie, and the birth of their son tampered Ellen's insecurities for a season.

Mr. Jackson once injured his shoulder after falling off his horse. Daisy helped him recover. Her nursing skills became apparent, and she soon became the plantation nurse and midwife, just like her mother. Ellen started suspecting an affair between Mr. Jackson and Daisy and often accused her of witchcraft, concocting evil brews she learned from her Creole mother. It was barely three years later, and Ellen found out Daisy was pregnant. Daisy's baby Jason could pass for white and bore a very strong resemblance to Jamie, her son.

Daisy claimed the child belonged to one of the white taskmasters. But he denied it lest he loses his standing in the community. Consequently, Daisy lost her position in the house and became a field slave. Mr. Jackson did nothing to save her lest Ellen use it as evidence that they are having an affair.

Mr. Jackson is venturing into the maritime business and needs Ellen's father's financial support. Given a choice between his ambitions and Daisy, he chooses the former and tries to help her secretly not to create waves.

None of this helps Daisy's case but instead heaps frustration on top of disappointments. First, Daisy sought refuge in religion.

The religious leaders would tell her, "Cast your troubles unto the Lord, and he shall sustain thee," yet her troubles continued.

Like all house slaves, Daisy perfected the art of smiling at her oppressor while her heart ached. She had mastered pretending to have no thoughts of her own but to present her ideas to the boss as though it was the master's. She often defended the master and Ellen's indefensible actions more vehemently than those who committed them because her life depended on remaining in their good graces.

But a person divided against oneself will eventually go mad.

Her condition worsened when Ellen turned her into a field hand, and no one did a thing to stop it, but rather everyone turned on her. Some of the house slaves openly cheered in the presence of the master lest they too lose their privileged position in the house if they objected. Having lived in the big house all her life, Daisy was terrible at fieldwork — she never worked a day in the field. Amongst the field slaves, she was an outcast, for they viewed her as an uppity aristocrat whom God was punishing by bringing her down from her privileged position "down to the rest of us field niggers." Those she considered friends because she had provided medical treatment or helped as a mid-wife distanced themselves from her at her lowest point.

It is not prudent to be associated with anyone Ellen hates. Daisy started imagining that the devil himself and a legion of demons were working against her. Everywhere she turned, there was a demon seeking to harm her; she spiritualized everything. That's when people started calling her crazy Daisy.

It is rumored that Mr. Jackson had arranged with his brother to marry her off to a free black furniture maker upon his return from Africa, but Ellen sold off her children to strangers when he was out of the country. Daisy finally embraced madness — she slipped into a different reality in which she is a dainty princess. In this world, no one can harm her. It was at this point that Ellen asked the taskmasters to let her out to pasture.

Letting a slave out to pasture is a term used for old milk cows that have stopped producing milk. It is also used for elderly and handicapped slaves that can no longer generate revenue for their masters. Daisy now lives in a shack in the woods beside Mammy Watson — the old plantation childcare provider. It was Mammy Watson's duty to take care of the children while their parents work in the fields.

Now that she is too old to take care of anyone, including herself, she was moved out to the woods to make it on her own or die out of sight and far away from the master's conscience.

If it had not been for the occasional late-night visitors bearing food they had gathered from the other slaves, she would have died long ago. Visitors have noticed a marked improvement in Mammy Watson's health since Daisy's arrival.

"It's her duties as child minder of the slave children that you will take over when you get to the plantation," Greg says, referring to Nandi.

Chapter Twenty-One

A slave in Brazil

When most people think of slavery, the United States comes to mind. However, the largest number of slaves in the Americas was further south — in Brazil with over ten times the number of slaves than the U.S. Brazil needed slaves to work the massive sugarcane plantiontions to produce sugar, an essential commodity in Europe, and a source of wealth for the Portuguese aristocracy. Over four million Africans were imported to replace the fast-dwindling Native-American population hitherto enslaved to work the sugar plantations. Native American Indians were not accustomed to large-scale agriculture. European diseases like measles, smallpox, and the common cold killed those who didn't die from exhaustion. The lucky ones ran away into the forests and quickly mingled with other Indian communities.

A plantation of hundreds could be reduced to a handful of Indians in a week. Those who run away quickly disappear into the dense jungles of Brazil. This is a territory that most European planters are not familiar with, hence the need to import slaves from Africa. Africans were resistant to European diseases, with a history of agriculture, physically strong, easy to identify and unfamiliar with the Brazilian terrain.

The Portuguese perfected mass sugarcane plantation farming on two African islands Sao Tome and Principe for 117 years, beginning in 1502, before any slaves were shipped to the Americas and Caribbean's in 1620. The wealth generated from these two islands led to its replication in the Caribbean's and the Americas.

Though rich in gold and sugar, Portugal's ambitions of colonizing the non-European world was restricted by its small population. Small compared to other European powers at the time.

With a total population of barely one million, they could not establish large settler colonies like other European nations. So, they encouraged their adventurers and traders to have children with locals and recognized them as Portuguese offspring wherever they established a foothold. Most of the adventurers, soldiers, colonial administrators, and fortune seekers were male. Therefore, it was not unusual for these men to seek the company of black and Indian women — by consent, force, or prostitution. Unlike the British, the Portuguese recognized their children born of African and Indian women.

Some were fully trained in Portuguese culture and made heirs. Black and white made brown children, while white and Indian made light brown children. So, the browning of Brazil's population begins.

Macati stepped off the slave ship into a country full of mixed races. He notices that different shades of brown segregate society.

The Caboclo are European and Indigenous Indian mixed heritage, and they were fully assimilated into Portuguese society.

The Mulato were both European and Black heritage. The name is derived from the word Mule: a beast of burden bred by crossing a horse with a donkey for the sole purpose of spawning an animal with characteristics of both parents. In most cases, the Mulato remained a slave. However, there are exceptions, especially when the European father was rich or an aristocrat; the Mulato child was recognized as a Portuguese free born.

A Pardo, a person of all three races mixed was treated based on which gene or features are most dominant, as well as their family's pedigree.

Zambo pronounced Sambo was of a Black and Indian mix — this often occurred when a black slave ran away and sought refuge amongst the indigenous Indian population or settled in a Macombo or Quilombo. If recaptured, the Zambo was put to work with the blacks. The Zambo is resistant to western diseases and can work as hard as the Africans.

Portugal's small population and its desire to colonize the world make them open to co-mingling the races, reproduction, and assimilation of these offspring into Portuguese culture through baptism into Roman Catholicism, adopting Portuguese culture and language. White, Arab, and Jewish indentured servants from across Europe and the Ottoman Empire were encouraged to immigrate to Brazil on the promise of freedom after their tenure as indentured servants. The possibility of wealth through sugar, tobacco, and gold mines lured young non-Portuguese fortune seekers to Brazil.

There was no promise of freedom for slaves like Macati, Waggy, and the others who survived the forty-day journey across the Atlantic from Africa. The end of the horrible trip gave no occasion to jubilate but rather the introduction to a new reality they never before imagined.

Macati, Waggy, and several Kapora warriors, along with the POWs sold by warring West African kingdoms, now work on sugarcane plantations across the Bahia and Alagoas in Brazil.

Rumors abound across the region about thriving communities of escaped slaves deep in the Brazilian jungles called Macombos, an African Ambundu word for hideout or small settlements, and larger communities called Quilombos – the African Kimbundu word Kilombo meaning "Encampment of Warriors".

The warrior spirit in the slaves on the plantations once suppressed by the master's whip gets reignited by these rumors, and they start making plans to escape.

Stories of a successful slave revolt in the French colony of Saint Dominique, now called Haiti, strengthens Macati's hope of leading his people to freedom. Saint Dominique, originally called Ayiti by the indigenous Taino Indians, meaning *land of mountains*, was France's most profitable colony. Chief export was sugar from its sugarcane plantations to Europe and the United States.

Historical backdrop:

Toussaint Louverture, a former slave, and leader in the slave revolt successfully overthrew the French overlords and established an independent state on the Island. Napoleon Bonaparte sent an expedition to retake the island under his brother-in-law General Charles Leclerc. Initially, Leclerc had some victories.

Louverture is betrayed and captured. He dies in prison.

Jean-Jacques Dessalines finally defeated French troops at the Battle of Vertières. Over 50,000 French troops, including 18 generals, died trying to recapture the island, and Napoleon was forced to remove his remaining 7000 troops from the island. That ended Napoleon's dream of a North American Empire. Over 10,000 white French, Creole refugees, and blacks loyal to the French status quo left the island during the war. They poured into the North American French colony of New Orleans, thereby doubling the city's population, and helped preserve its French language and culture for several generations. Funding a protracted war on multiple fronts proved expensive for France. The loss of Saint Dominique and its associated revenue stream left Napoleon no option but to sell New Orleans to the United States as part of the "Louisiana Purchase" in order to replenish his fast-dwindling funds. War costs money.

Chapter Twenty-Two

I Can't Live Like This Anymore

A few months later, Macati and Waggy are part of a crew of slaves taking tons of sugarcane to the sugar mill at the village of Maceió on the Atlantic coast one morning. Waggy nudges Macati and reveals a shank he has made from a piece of iron.

"If we overpower these overseers, we can escape into the bushes and join a Kilombo," he says.

"Any attempt to escape now will end in death," Macati points at the rifle in the overseer's hand.

"You will be shot before you get anywhere close with that knife."

"I can't live like this anymore!" Waggy protests.

"You won't live like this much longer," says Macati.

"I am working on a plan that will enable a lot of us to escape this plantation and eventually return home."

"To Kapora?" Waggy's eyes widen.

"Yes," Macati replies.

"But this is not the time or the place. Besides, I have to bring in a few more trustworthy men into the plan."

"Good!" Waggy exclaims.

"Now you sound like a Kapora prince. If we succeed, great! And if we die, we die like men!"

"I won't die here," Macati shakes his head, refusing to accept that fate.

"Oh? Have you joined the Anago and their Ogun rituals?"

Waggy asks.

Historical backdrop:

Many slaves turned to their traditional religions because they were dissatisfied with Christian doctrines promoted by the Portuguese masters that encourage slaves to turn the other cheek when slapped, forgive their oppressors and work for their masters as they worked for God. Prayers and rituals to the "Orishas" were disguised as prayers to Catholic saints. The Orishas are Yoruba Deities, and Ogun is the Yoruba god of war, iron, and male children. Anago is the term for Yoruba people prior to the 1900s.

"What do Ogun rituals have to do with escaping slavery?" Macati asks.

"Oh, I thought you have been listening to the Ogun priest who claims that if he performs those rituals for you, nothing made of iron can kill you. Ogun being the god of war and iron, iron is subject to him, and therefore his followers who perform the ritual can't die from anything made of iron." Waggy explains.

"I don't want to find out whether or not it works after a bullet hits me in the head. I am referring to the words of the oracle who foresaw my appointment as king and warned of physical forces that would bar me from ascending the throne for a time but eventually, my descendants and I will sit on the royal stool of Kapora."

"I am all ears," says Waggy, eager to hear Macati's thought-out escape plan.

"How do we get off this plantation and even more, how do we sail back to Africa with no boat or navigation skills?" He asks.

Chapter Twenty-Three

Escape From The Plantation

"One does not try the monkey's tricks on the bush-pigeon, my people. It will fly away… fly, I tell you… and that is what I'm going to do… vanish! They will search for Ovonramwen, but the gods of the earth and sky shall blur their vision and confound their minds. I said so!"

Ola Rotimi, Ovonramwen Nogbaisi

The dry season is when most expansionist African kingdoms like the Oyo Empire, Dahomey, and the Kapora embark on expansion wars. It is a season when men need not tend their farms, and the weather is favorable to traveling long distances with little or no undergrowth to slow the Cavalry's advance. It is also the time when you shoot blazing arrows from long bows into the air, and they land on your enemy's dry thatched roof, setting it on fire with no rains to quench it. This strategy is effective in destroying walled cities as blazing arrows fly above the walls and land on the roofs of the buildings within the walled city turning the walled city into an incendiary trap to its inhabitants.

Now your opponent is torn between saving his household, his possessions from the fire and fighting you. A divided and confused opponent is easy to defeat. Victory is usually swift, and the warriors return home in time for the rainy season, which is the planting season when warriors become farmers once again.

In Brazil, the dry season is when the sugarcane fields are set on fire before harvest. This eliminates the trash, kills snakes, and enriches the soil for the next crop. The sugarcane plant's dry leaves burn up, leaving the sugarcane stem standing and ready for harvest. However, this dry season, the fire at the plantation rages out of control. It threatens the big house and other parts of the farm that don't grow sugarcane. Everyone on the plantation is called out to put out the fire that mysteriously leaped from the plantation and onto the mansion's roof. Free men, rich, poor, indentured servants, and slaves all struggle to fight the fire. The thick smoke rises, and the fire, blown by strong winds, continues to spread.

Macati ties a brush of dry leaves mixed with oil to a large rodent's tail at a far corner of the plantation. He sets the brush on fire, and the rodent darts off into the plantation dragging the flaming torch along, setting dry leaves on fire as it runs. Macati runs to a bush near the barn and shoots a blazing arrow into the barn. Soon the hay in the barn is engulfed in flames.

Horsemen with buckets rush to put out this second set of fires. Macati runs to the stream with a wooden bucket in his hand to join the others fetching water to douse the flames. A lone gunman is guarding the slaves fetching water; he turns in Macati's direction.

"Hurry! Hurry! Flying ambers have started another fire in the barn!" Macati shouts to the men at the stream.

He quickens his pace.

The guard turns away from Macati and yells at the men at the stream.

"You heard the man. *Move!*"

The last words barely leave his lips when Macati's wooden bucket slams the side of his head. The man stumbles forward. Macati's foot catches him square in the nose with a swift kick. His rifle falls to the ground as he drops to his knees in a daze. Macati grabs the barrel and swings the weapon at full length. The butt of the rifle smashes the guard's skull on contact, and the guard drops to the ground dead.

The men at the stream rush in and remove his ammunition pouch, machete, and bullets. A Zambo takes his boots and tries them on. Waggy and the men in the stream toss the guard into the stream and let his lifeless body drift downstream with the current, towards the east of the river where the Yacare caiman reptiles reside. Waggy smiles. *"They will eat him like the sharks ate those who died on the slave ship coming here".*

Macati exhales in relief.

"I killed an enemy; I am now a real Kapora warrior. This now cancels out how I cheated my way through solo survival," he thinks to himself, then yells, "Follow me!"

Waggy makes a loud sound like a bird. A woman in the field repeats the sound. Thirty slaves abandon their post and come running to the stream to join the dozen already there. They cross the stream and run into the forest. About half a mile beyond the stream, they stop and catch their breath. Macati climbs up a Brazilwood tree, which has dense, orange-red heartwood that takes a high shine. It is the premier wood used for making bows for stringed instruments. The wood also yields a red dye called brazilin, which oxidizes to brasilein. The country (Brazil) is named after this plant, for it grows here in abundance.

Macati reaches for a sack with bows arrows blow darts, shanks, and spears at the top of the Brazilwood tree. Macati and the escapees had fashioned these weapons with their shanks and farm implements over the past three months. The arrows and blow darts are made of sharpened dry bamboo dipped in a concoction made predominantly of curare plant extract created by a Zambo and Oluwo, son of Obya. Oluwo was one of those who boarded the Brazilian ship to save Macati at the slave port and was captured alongside Awat. The warrior spirit rises in the men and Minos, the Dahomey female warriors, as they pull their weapons out of the sack.

Back at the plantation, the overseer notices that the buckets of water from the stream have suddenly stopped. He rides to the stream and notices everyone is gone. He shoots in the air, and seventeen men gallop in the direction of the shot.

Two men wade into the stream and pull out the clothes of the dead guard stained in blood.

"Several slaves have escaped! You! You and you!"

He points to six men.

"Round up the rest and lock them up. You!"

He points at a fat Caboclo.

"Bring the hound dogs and the militia. The rest follow me. They couldn't have gone far."

The overseer, himself a Caboclo of mixed European and indigenous Indian ancestry, is versed in the art of tracking runaways in the Brazilian forests. He leads his party across the stream and follows the broken twigs in the bushes that give evidence of people recently passing through. Usually, it's one or two that escape at a time — but this time it's over forty of them. The trail of bent brushes and footprints in soft soil is easy to follow.

"Cock your guns," he warns the ten men with him.

There are many, and they probably have the guard's gun with them. The men lock and load their weapons and ride further into the bushes following the tracks. They get to the Brazilwood tree and notice that the tracks go in different directions.

"It appears they have scattered in different directions," says one man.

"Let's split up and go in different directions," says another.

"Let's wait for the bloodhounds or follow the direction of the largest group," says another.

A fourth man starts to ride in the direction of the largest set of bent undergrowth saying, "If we wait, they shall have gotten further away."

Soon after he utters those words, a blow dart strikes him in the neck. Curare poisoned blow dart kills its target quickly when it hits any part of the body. It need not strike a vital organ or cause the target to bleed to death, as is the case with western arrows. With the poisoned dart, death comes by suffocation when curare laced poison in the blood reaches the lungs. It causes the respiratory muscles to fail, and the victim's lungs collapse. The man falls off his horse without a scream. The overseer notices several of his men suddenly start dropping. Confusion sets in, then panic.

The survivors look around to see where the arrows and blow dart are coming from. A shot rings out from the bushes fifty paces west of the gathered men striking another man in the chest. Waggy never misses.

The overseer knows it will take at least ten seconds before Waggy can reload the rifle and fire again. He charges in Waggy's direction at full gallop. His men follow him into a trap. They ride into a torrent of poisoned arrows, and poisoned blow darts hit them from all sides. The panic-stricken men start shooting at random at their unseen assailants. The escapees had climbed the trees and laid in wait for their arrival.

These former African warriors understand jungle warfare better than their European and foreign enemies do. Waggy's shot was to attract them into the trap and signal them to shoot their arrows in unison. Each one is shooting at a preselected target from his fighting position on the top of trees near the Brazilwood tree; they are careful not to shout during the attack as that would give away their position. The battle lasts a few minutes, and all the pursuers are dead.

No horse was shot during the melee. The warriors come down from the trees and strip the pursuers of their weapons, ammunition, and anything useable. Warriors load the dead bodies unto the back of the horses. The Minos cut off one of the dead bodies' arm and dangle it off one of the branches of the Brazilwood trees. It hangs dripping with blood and is visible for any pursuer to see. Then they drag the body behind them into the jungle, leaving a trail of blood for their pursuers to follow. Two miles later the Mino cuts off the other arm and lets it dangle on a branch visible for pursuers.

On the bank of a brook, another mile later, the genitals are impaled on a reed. On the other side of the brook, the headless body and twenty feet away, the head impaled on a long stake.

It is a form of psychological warfare that the Mino warriors use to strike fear in the enemy's hearts. Any man seeing this will think of his mortality and walk-in trepidation of meeting agonizing death at the hands of the Mino. When you fight a man, he fights you blow for blow, fist for fist. When you fight with a woman, she fights you with everything — physically, spiritually, and psychologically. With the introduction of guns to West Africa, the Dahomey kingdom had legions of female warriors called Minos, which means *our mothers* in English. Initially they defended the kingdom while the men went out to war.

Think of what happens to anyone who tries to attack a child in the presence of their mother who has a loaded gun and knows how to use it. She may not have the physical strength to overpower the assailant with a knife or a spear. However, with a gun, all she needs is a trigger finger, an angry eye, and a willingness to kill the person attacking her child; this is why their neighboring kingdoms lived in fear of the Mino. The POW Minos sold into slavery in Macati's group reverted to their traditional tactics and now use them on the slave masters that have oppressed them for so long. The French would later call these legions of female warriors the "Amazon warriors".

The fat Caboclo and the militia arrive an hour later at the Brazilwood tree with bloodhounds. They stop to examine the bloody arm hanging off the branch. It is evident that a battle has taken place, but the blood localized to the spot where the arm was cut gives them hope that the overseer and most of his men might be captured alive. The militia now knows that these runaways are armed and willing to use the weapons seized from the overseer and his men. They proceed with caution, thereby allowing Macati and his group to run at full speed deep into the jungle.

The bloodhounds follow the trail of blood. Soon the blood is gone, but they can follow the scent of the warriors and horses. About a mile and a half into the trail, the pursuers have quickened their pace to a jog behind the bloodhounds. The lead hound steps on a twig, and the broken twig triggers a dangerous trap similar to the type tribesmen use in killing wild boars in Africa. A spear-like stake springs out of a pile of fallen branches and thrusts through its abdomen. The dog yelps and keels over, with blood rushing out of its abdomen and its mouth. Its muscles twitch, and limbs stretch then relax as life ebbs out of it. The hound owner pulls back his other dogs lest another trap kills them also. The pursuers proceed even more cautiously from there. They strike the bushes ahead of them with sticks to ensure there are no hidden traps under the brushes — none want to die like the dog.

Half an hour later, they find the second arm swinging on a tree branch. One of the militiamen proceeds to cut the rope tethering the arm, as he mutters under his breath.

"Savages."

He cuts the rope, and suddenly a big bloody mass pours all over him. Another contraption designed by the Minos in the group to induce dread in their enemies. The militiaman shrieks in fright. Everyone behind him leaps backward. Human entrails dangle all over him.

Fear grips the militiamen.

"I have a wife and children to take care of; let's turn back while it's still daylight," says the fat Caboclo.

"Oh? Turn back? Does the man they killed not have a family too? What if you were one of the men they've captured? Wouldn't you wish we rescued you?" The captain replied.

The lieutenant chimes in.

"You were supposed to be with them, but the overseer asked you to come for us. That could have been you! Selfish bastard."

The group moves forward cautiously. It takes them an hour to cover distances that would have taken fifteen minutes. As they encounter each body part, dread fills each man. The setting of the sun and the rising noise of nocturnal wildlife increases their anxiety. They are used to chasing the solitary runaway or a group of no more than five, but this is the first time they have dealt with a large number of armed runaways willing and able to fight.

By the time they get to the staked head, it's become apparent that they need a large number of troops to deal with this band of runaways. Night falls, and the pursuers turn back.

Horse meat is lean and has a slightly sweet taste like a combination of beef with venison. The hungry warriors roast one of the horses' meat over an open fire until it is well done. Most West Africans and their westernized descendants will not eat flesh still fresh with blood no matter how hungry they are. The Wagombe don't mind bloody meat; however, they are totally different from the typical West African.

Besides, there are no Wagombe in this group of escapees. The Wagombe captives are far away on the Jackson Plantation in the United States. Macati looks up to the clear sky, sees the North Star and wonders how he can get up north to the United States where the love of his life, Awat is. He thinks about what is happening to her, and sighs in regret.

But the thought of her raising their child alone brings him back to reality and reminds him to keep fighting and persevering.

"I have to get to her, I have to." He whispers to himself.

While the others feast on horsemeat jubilating about their successful escape from slavery and the hope of a future devoid of the master's whip, Macati's mind is not at ease.

Waggy's voice disrupts Macati's thoughts.

"The entire region is booby-trapped. The enemy can't come close without incurring heavy casualties. I have posted sentries on the perimeter."

"Do you think they will find the bodies?" Macati asks.

"I doubt there will be any pieces left. This dry season has decreased the river size and number of marine animals that alligators have to feed on — they are quite hungry. You should see the way they rushed at the bodies of the Overseers and guards as we threw them into a brood of alligators on the muddy banks of the river."

The group had split into two earlier. One group led by Macati created a false trail of highly visible tracks leading west while Waggy led the main body south, leaving a trail of ground dry pepper in their wake starting at the point where the groups separated.

When the bloodhounds get to the point where the two groups separated, the ground pepper sprinkled on the ground is mixed with dirt and therefore not visible to the human eye. However, they will irritate the dog's noses, and they will take the path of least resistance by following Macati's group scent than Waggy's. Fortunately, dogs don't speak, and the militia will be none the wiser to the fact that the runaways have divided themselves into two groups.

Waggy got to the riverbank and threw the bodies off the horses unto the muddy banks where alligators breed, then got on the horses and rode off, leaving a trail of ground pepper behind them to prevent the dogs from following their scent. A mile northward, they turned and galloped to catch up with Macati and the rest of the group. The militia might never get to that part of the riverbank and even if they do, the alligators would have eaten all the bodies, leaving no evidence of their existence. Nothing will be known about their whereabouts, thereby adding further fear of the warriors and their capabilities, while at the same time giving the militia the false hope that the overseer and his men may still be alive as hostages for future negotiations.

The Zambo joins Macati and Waggy.

"We are a day's journey from my mother's village. They have been friendly to runaways, and they are bound to know where the nearest Quilombo or Macombo is."

The Zambo and his parents once lived in a Macombo, but it was overrun by the military. He and his father were captured and returned to slavery. The Zambo promises to ask his mother's people to take them to the nearest Quilombo.

"That will bring great joy to your mother's heart," Macati says.

His mind goes over to his own mother and imagines her joy to see him and Awat return home. Then anxiety gradually covers him like a cold blanket.

"Is she alive? Is my father alive? Has Nyoka killed my baby brother? Did Awat survive the journey? Did she give birth to a boy or a girl?"

Chapter Twenty-Four

Searching For A Safe Place

The next morning, the men head deep into the jungle in quest of a Quilombo. As they traverse a wide plain, Macati notices a group of birds suddenly fly from a cluster of trees a thousand feet ahead. They fly swiftly in his direction, making a quick turn in the air as they approach him. He orders the men to stop. For the sudden flight of birds hitherto perched means that there are people in the area.

Macati breaks the group into three — a small group of eight armed with captured guns, arrows, and machetes will serve as the advance party. The Zambo, Mino, Ijaw, and Ashanti, first-generation warriors versed in jungle warfare, two-second generation slaves, and one Mulato make the advance party. They would go ahead of everyone else to make sure there is no ambush up ahead.

Another group of four will form the rear guard. They are also responsible for cleaning all the tracks left behind by the main body and look out for enemies approaching from the rear.

The main body will be in the middle. Macati orders the main body to hide in the bushes while the rear guard moves further back to scan for enemies behind. In doing this, they will map out an exit route in case they have to make a hasty retreat. The fastest sprinter, a Kanuri warrior of Nilotic descent heads that group. The Kanuri warrior is the fastest runner in the group. Everyone will move forward only after the advance party gives the all-clear signal of waving a red cloth tied to a spear shaft like a flag.

Strict silence is required so as not to give their position away.

The advance party approaches the cluster of trees from which the birds took flight. As they get close, an anaconda rushes out in their direction. The group freezes. The snake gets a few feet from them then turns right and quickly disappears into the thicket.

The Ijaw man in the group says, "Quickly turn left and take cover in the crevasses over there. There is a large force fast approaching."

The advance party rushes and takes cover in the crevasses and waits. Soon they can see movement in the bushes. Human forms dart from tree to tree, steadily making their way in the direction of the advance party. The Ijaw people on the Atlantic coast of West Africa view boa constrictors as messengers of the gods. A snake heading in their direction while on the warpath, is believed to be messenger from the gods warning them that a large number of the enemy is approaching. If the snake runs left, you run right. If it turns north, you turn south, and if it turns east, you turn west. Simply put, whatever direction it goes, go the opposite way. Anacondas are in the Boa Constrictor family and therefore get the same reverence from the Ijaw man in the group. Several other African tribes have a different interpretation of snakes showing up around their dwelling and in time of war.

Snakes are sensitive to vibrations — they can detect large herds like buffalos stampeding in their direction from a long-distance away, thus giving them enough time to move away, lest they get trampled under their hooves. A hundred men running in the same direction have a similar effect of stampeding animals on snakes. Regardless of the reason, scientific or spiritual, the advance party run to the cravens as the Ijaw man instructed.

Macati sees movement in the tree from a distance. He signals his warriors to fan out to the flanks of the trees but stay low to the ground. It is obvious that these people have spotted the advance party and intend to attack them. By the time the group gets to the cravens, he and his men have formed a half-circle around them.

"Each one take one," Macati sends the message to the men.

Each man aims at an individual from the other group.

"I will stand up and give them an ultimatum; surrender or die. If they fight, fire at will."

It is better to capture them whole than engage them in battle. From his vantage point, he notices that they are not white men but native Americans. From his new yet strange experience, he has learnt that plantation owners have been known to use some unscrupulous chiefs to recapture runaway slaves in exchange for iron pots, metal tools, guns, and salt. Macati's men inch forward to get within an effective shooting range of the Indians. They want to ensure that every arrow, bullet, and blow-dart shot in the first volley takes down an enemy because this group is much larger than the runaways.

The first volley should take down half the group and the second volley a lot more before the survivors can engage in close combat. He knows that the Mino in the advance party is a good shot and will take out a few Indians before they get to the cavern. The enemy has only one way out if they are to survive this battle, the way they came.

The Indians get closer to the cavern and suddenly the Zambo starts shouting in a strange language. The leader of the group shouts something back in the same language. Next, the Zambo jumps out of the carven and runs towards the leader of the group. The leader of the group drops his weapons and rushes towards the Zambo. The sound of joy fills the air — it is the Zambo's mother's tribe.

Macati is glad he never gave his 'surrender or die' ultimatum for they wouldn't have understood a word he said and would have been compelled to fight to save their tribe. Several people would have died needlessly.

The Zambo calls his friends out of hiding and introduces them to his mother's people and their allies.

The night before, foraging Indians noticed the escapees in the area. They ran back to their village and informed the community that a large band of people were in the area. It was dark and the foragers could not determine the race or the total number of the intruders. This tribe sent emissaries to other nearby villages and by morning, they had assembled a large force to fight the intruders.

The Zambo's Indian relatives are glad to see him alive and well. They inform him that a Kilombo is built at the top of a rugged mountain with natural fortifications. They will take this group of runaways there.

"But first we will take you to our village to celebrate your life," says the leader.

"My sister will be glad to see you."

He barely finishes his sentence, and a middle-aged woman comes running. Good news travels fast. It is the Zambo's mother. She is one of the few survivors of the attack on the Macombo by the Brazilian military, in which this Zambo and his black father were captured.

Macati observes the Zambo rush into his mother's arms and imagines the same scenario reoccurring in Africa the day he and Awat return home to their family.

Chapter Twenty-Five

Victory Belongs To Those Who Profit From It.

"Come here, boy!" Mr. Jackson calls out to an elderly black man working on a drafting table at the shipyard as he climbs down his gilded coach. Beside the black coach driver sits Mathew. The elderly man leaves the drafting table and goes to Mr. Jackson, hat in hand with a sway in his stride. "Yes, Suh!" The elderly man responds.

"This is Mathew, he will be working with you from now on," says Mr. Jackson. Mathew rushes down from the front of the coach.

"You are welcome," says the elder, extending his hand to Mathew. "My name is Charles Huggins," he says as he studies Mathew's face. Charles Huggins has perfected the art of disconnecting his thoughts from his face — a good survival skill of the powerless while in the presence of their oppressor. "Concealment and cover," he would say to himself; something he learned as an infantryman in the American war for independence. Huggins' face displays a polite welcome of a revered stranger, but his mind says, "So this is the black slaver I've heard so much about. Slithering snake, how did he get out of fieldwork to get this job?" Mathew responds to Huggins welcome with a wide smile revealing a perfect set of teeth minus one. "Charles Hug what?" He says, trying to hug Charles Huggins.

Mr. Jackson laughs. "Just call him old man Huggins. Everybody calls him that."

"Come with me, I'll show you around," Charles Huggins beckons Mathew, ignoring the stupid joke at his expense.

Bishop Mathew is relieved to be removed from the cotton fields and made to work in Mr. Jackson's new shipbuilding yard alongside white indentured servants and black freedmen like Charles Huggins. Prior to slavery, Mathew had never done fieldwork. Foremen at the plantation have saved Mathew several times from a well-deserved beating from MaKuei, Jabu, and other slaves on the plantation. Even second-generation slaves not sold by Mathew beat him on general principle after word got around that he was a "black slaver" (an American term for Pombeiros). Today is the second-best day of his life in America — the first was the day the big Wolof (renamed Frank). The one who broke Mathew's tooth was sold to Mr. Tucker, A rice planter from South Carolina. This was after Frank's third attempt to run away. Frank would ferociously attack Mathew any time he saw him. While other slaves would not attack in the presence of a taskmaster, Frank would pummel Mathew no matter who was present. He has a stubborn side to him; when he sets his mind on something, nothing stops him. He was bent on letting out the frustrations of his life as a slave on Mathew's face and nothing would stop him. The more the taskmaster flogged Frank, the worse a beating Mathew got. Killing or disabling Frank for Mathew's sake was not an option as his hard labor earned Mr. Jackson great profit. However, upon his third escape attempt, Mr. Jackson decided to sell him off. It was better to make a profit from his sale than lose him altogether to the next escape attempt or accidental death when the taskmasters try to pry him off Mathew. Judging from Frank's size strength and determination, Mr. Jackson was concerned about what Frank would do to him or any of the white folk on the plantation if he ever caught them alone. Frank was a commander of Wolof warriors on the "rice coast" of Africa. Hailing from the "rice coast" made him an easy sell to a rice planter. The demand for Wolof and Temme people is high amongst rice planters in the Carolinas, but the supply is low due to the stationing of the British West African Squadron in the "rice coast" of West Africa. Mr. Jackson touted Frank's stubbornness as the tenacity to Mr. Tucker and he paid more than the asking price.

A few weeks on the job and Mathew with a college education from Coimbra can read, write, and produce better technical drawings than many of his white counterparts with limited formal education — a source of hatred towards Mathew. However, they console themselves in the fact that they get wages for their work or are working off their debts. They will one day be able to set up their businesses. However, they don't see Mathew ever tasting freedom no matter how well he works. Mathew works alone most of the time. He is an outcast amongst his peers including the free black artisans' carpenters and draftsmen at the shipyard except for old man Huggins who deals with him with curious civility. Quite humbling for someone who was once worshiped by throngs of people. Mathew misses the lifestyle he once had, and it pains him to part with the gold-rich land he's left behind.

Charles Huggins once asked if he felt any remorse for the lives he ruined to acquire those riches. To Huggins question, he replied yes, feigning remorse. However, to himself, not at all. To Mathew, it's the way of nature. You pass through life once, so make the best of it with what you've got: good looks, physical strength, or intelligence. In nature, the strong devour the weak and grow even stronger. Life is neither fair nor charitable. It's not fair to worms that birds eat them. Neither is it fair to birds that men eat their eggs before their newborns hatch to see the sun. But such is life. Mathew sees his victims as stupid goats to be eaten. The weak and stupid deserve what they get. Mathew's feeling towards them is reflected in the translation of the Portuguese words he thought them as tongues: Eu sou uma Cabra estúpida (I am a stupid goat). Mathew chuckles as he remembers how his ardent congregants memorized these words and prayed them fervently. The zealous ones he thought even more degrading insults in Portuguese. If anyone's to blame, it is God. The same God who made the Gazelle a herbivore and made the Lion a carnivore who must eat gazelle to survive. When the hungry Lion and the Gazelle meet in the wild, they both pray to the same God who made them both. The lion, - "Give me this day my daily bread lest I starve to death" the Gazelle, - "Deliver me from the evil one oh God". At the end of the day, it's the one who maximizes their God given ability to run faster than the other that will thank God for answering his prayers that day. If the Gazelle outruns the Lion, she will thank God for answering her prayers for deliverance from the evil one. If Lion out runs Gazelle, He too will give thanks for answered prayer in giving him food this day. So it is in the lives of man. The days of free food (Mannah) falling from heaven are long gone. You must utilize what you have to get what you want. In Mathew's case, it's intellect and manipulation.

One day, Mathew notices Charles Huggins stuffing some discarded newspapers into his bag. "I know you are up to something," says Mathew. "If you don't let me in, I will tell Master that you are stealing from him."

"I didn't steal anything, just picked up some discarded newspapers at the site; see," Charles Huggins thrust them at Mathew.

Mathew catches a glimpse of the headlines, "America declares war on Britain!" Mathew exclaims. He tries to turn the page.

Charles Huggins yanks it away from Mathew. "Sniveling weasel, I'll tell master, I'll tell master. Get away from me! I know your type."

"I'm sorry," Mathew responds

"I'm the only one nice to you and you would step on me given half a chance. Black slaver. I see why the others beat you up on the plantation."

"How did you know?" Mathew is shocked that the elderly man knows so much.

"Just take these and get out of my sight. I want them back tomorrow." Old man Huggins ends the conversation abruptly. He realizes that he let out too much by the last statement and any further information about himself and his family could be used against him. It's a cardinal rule: You don't give the likes of Mathew any information about yourself. They will weaponize it.

Just before the war of independence, he was separated from his family on the Morris tobacco plantation and sold to architect Huggins to settle a debt. His last name changed from Morris to Huggins; Young Charles Huggins worked in his master's construction company learning woodwork and draftsmanship. Architect Huggins, his new owner was a crown sympathizer. At the break of War, Charles Huggins ran off to join the black patriots fighting for American Independence. He was one of the few lucky ones who gained their freedom after independence. The architect's family immigrated to Canada when Britain lost the war. However, Charles' family on the Morris plantation was not released, for the Morris tobacco plantation owner was with the patriots. They were sold to Ellen's father who in turn gave them to Mr. Jackson as a dowry. Charles Huggins traced their whereabouts to Mr. Jackson's plantation and offered to work for Mr. Jackson with the understanding that part of his wages will go towards buying the freedom of his children and grandchildren. He visits every weekend and will not let a small issue like old newspapers bring negative attention to himself. "Concealment and cover," he muses with a smile, looking at Mathew.

Mathew thinks he has gotten over and feigns gratitude thanking Huggins over and over again. He takes them home to read at night by candlelight. From the papers, Mathew learns that Britain is embroiled in the Napoleonic wars and needs men to fill the ranks of its military. Young men are seized off the streets and pressed into military service. Life in the British Army is bad and life in the Navy is worse. The living quarters are squalid, food is deplorable, and the officers mete out harsh punishment to dissenters. Several British Navy men escape to the whaling city of Boston Massachusetts. Life as a whaler or American merchant marine is significantly better, the pay is great, and the living conditions are a lot better. Out of desperation, the British Navy intercepts American commercial and whaling ships and captures American sailors. Many British Navy deserters are recaptured, punished, and forced back into military service. They call it impressment into service. A few American-born sailors got caught in the mix.

Gold and glory are the real motives of all wars regardless of what banners they wave; religion, Ideology, altruism, or any other "ism" he contrives to justify it. Man, by nature is greedy covetous and wicked in his methods of feeding that greed. Victory belongs to those who profit. Those who invest their life and blood profit least in that victory. In fact, the greatest victors seldom smell death or the cries of the wounded on the battlefield. The US has been profiting from the Napoleonic wars without committing troops. The first victory was a triple territorial expansion without firing a single shot. The discounted purchase of 828,000 square miles (2,140,000 km2) of French North American territory is the cheapest real estate deal recorded in history at less than 3 cents per acre. France desperately needed money to fund its wars in Europe but revenue from its overseas territories was either cut off —in the case of Haiti — or disrupted by naval, pirate, and privateer interception on the high seas. Internally generated revenue was decimated as most men of working age were engaged in the war effort, and so Napoleon sold their North American territories to the US that was already profiting from supplying both sides of the war. The French North American territory called Louisiana (named after the French King Louis XIV), covered all of the present-day states west of the Mississippi River; including the city of New Orleans, Arkansas, Missouri, Iowa, Oklahoma, Kansas, and Nebraska; parts of Minnesota that were west of the Mississippi River; most of North Dakota; most of South Dakota; northeastern New Mexico; northern Texas; the portions of Montana, Wyoming, and Colorado east of the Continental Divide; and portions of land that would later become part of the Canadian provinces of Alberta and Saskatchewan.

European powers at this time are overstretched militarily and financially. They barely have enough forces to maintain their existing empires in the Americas much less protect them. The US economy, on the other hand, was booming from the sale of desperately needed goods to both sides of the war. The US has expansionist plans of its own — go beyond the current boundaries of the thirteen colonies along the east coast, to territory west of the Mississippi even though the total population at the time was barely above seven million. The new government knows that this is the best time to wrest under-guarded North American territory from the world superpowers at the time: France, Spain, and Britain.

The British on the other hand would rather have a small United States than a large and powerful one that could later challenge the global balance of power. Britain supplies modern weapons to indigenous chiefs like Tecumseh through agents in Canada to forestall further American westward expansion. Tecumseh on his part wanted to stop further incursions on Indian land by frontiersmen rendering the original inhabitants destitute on their ancestral land and to establish an Independent Indian confederate nation in the Midwest. Everybody coverts something that belongs to another or will fight to stop the courteous from robbing them. Therein lies the root of most wars.

President Madison threatens to declare war on what he perceives to be a vulnerable Britain on several grounds that include stop supporting Indian resistance, the disruption of American maritime activities, and the impressment of American sailors.

Congress sends an ultimatum to Britain and a list of grievances. The British know that they can't fight multiple wars at the same time. On the European front, they and Prussia are the only formidable force standing in the way of Napoleon's march to European domination. The defeated Portuguese monarchy has fled to Brazil and set up its new capital in Rio De Janeiro. Napoleon's attack on Lisbon Portugal was described as an armed parade — barely any resistance. The few surviving Portuguese Caçadores legions have regrouped under the British command. Spain has switched sides in the war and joined France with Napoleon's brother Joseph Bonaparte as its King. Britain has no resources or the will to fight another war with the Americans — they already lost the independence war at a time when they were unencumbered with a raging war in Europe. A second war with the US at this time was not so enticing. The British sign the treaty agreeing to All of America's terms. Madison does not wait for the emissaries sent to negotiate with the British to return with the signed treaty. He declares war on Britain two days after the treaty is signed and sends a detachment of troops to Annex Canada from Britain. This will also end the prospect of an independent Indian Confederate state in the Midwest under British sponsorship as they would no longer be able to send Tecumseh weapons through Canada. The British has a little over 6000 troops to defend Canada. The U.S marches on Canada and attacks its capital, York (present-day Toronto). An easy victory is expected after defeating British troops at York, where American soldiers plundered the town and burned its parliament. The war of 1812 between the US and Britain begins.

The British, unable to muster enough troops in Europe rely on local Canadian militia and Indians to defend their North American territory. They send out letters of the marquee to governors of their Caribbean islands authorizing privateers to blockade the United States and disrupt its maritime economy — the main source of US wealth at the time.

A privateer is a private maritime investor, shipowner, or ship captain authorized by letters of marquee from their government to attack enemy commercial and navy ships during wartime, capture and keep for themselves enemy ships and cargo. A small portion of which is given to the authorizing government. It is legalized piracy. The letter of marquee and the flag you fly during the attack is the thin line separating the pirate from the privateer. Privateers and pirates prefer to capture an enemy ship and cargo intact than to blow it up as would a typical Navy frigate; something that English sailors in the Caribbean have done to French and Spanish gold-laden ships for years. Privateers are in the war for profit, not nationalism and it was a very profitable venture for the ship owners, financiers, and sailors alike. While it did generate some income for the authorizing government, more importantly, it freed up the Navy to focus on military targets rather than disperse their forces chasing commercial ships to cripple the enemy's economy. War costs money. Crippling the enemy's economy deprives them funding to fight you while creating social and internal unrest at the same time. Many privateers turn pirate when the war ends, and the letter of Marquee is terminated.

To capture an enemy ship intact requires you to pull alongside the vessel, tether your ship to it and a large number of men storm the vessel, overpower its crew then take over control of the ship, and then steer both ships back to port. Where a government official was waiting to take custody of the captured crew and a portion of the loot from the privateer, it was common to have a lot of black able-bodied men on an English privateer ship. The captain and ship officers were white and a large number of men who storm the target vessel were blacks from the British West Indies, particularly the Bahamas, Bermuda, and Jamaica. The blacks on privateer ships did get a share in the plunder. Life as a black privateer was a lot better than on the plantation. The crossover from privateer to pirate was also common out in the open sea. Why share your hard-earned loot with the government or turn in your prisoners? What the government doesn't know won't hurt you. The captives were sometimes dumped on a desert island, put in a small lifeboat to fend for themselves, or killed. If dead men tell no tales, who will report to the government?

Privateers set out from British colonies like Bermuda, Jamaica, and the Bahamas, amongst other English-speaking Caribbean islands in search of quick profits and to expand their fleet with captured American vessels; over 516 registered privateers on the British side supported by 85 Royal Navy ships. The entire United States Navy of only 8 Frigates and 14 sloops to guard the eastern seaboard of the United States was about the size of only one British squadron based in Halifax. The deck is stacked overwhelmingly in favor of the British dominating the war at sea, resulting in the loss of 1600 US merchant ships and a massive drop in revenue for the United States from $130 million before the war to $7 million. Prices of imported items like coffee, tea, and sugar rose in the US. The US issued letters of marquee to citizens, investors, and ship captains to stop the onslaught of American merchant ships and stem the economic hemorrhaging.

American privateers capture British ships carrying valuable cargo like sugar from the British-West Indies and bring their cargo to US ports for sale at exorbitant prices. The captured ships are used to expand his privateer fleet. Insurer Lloyds of London reported 1,175 British ships captured of which 373 were recaptured for a total loss of 802 during the war of 1812.

By 1813, the US was losing the war at sea. The nimble Bermuda sloops were faster and more agile than American frigates and converted merchant galleons fitted with cannons. They conducted swift raids on American ports and harbors in the Chesapeake Bay area and soon the British have full control of the Chesapeake Bay. Several slaves in the Chesapeake Bay abandon the plantations and join the British occupiers on the promise of freedom to any slave who fights on the British side against their American oppressors. The pot is further sweetened by the promise to return the former slaves to Africa if they so desired or given fertile land in the British colony of Trinidad where they could farm their lands as free men. The US could not make a counteroffer to those already in bondage without offending its landed gentry who owned these slaves. So, they offered land to the already free blacks that earned their freedom in the war of independence but got no land or jobs after the American Revolution. To increase enlistment from the white population, the war was touted as the second independence war from the British. In essence, the British were trying to recolonize the US and force them to pay taxes to the British crown, conveniently omitting the fact that the US first attacked the British Empire when they were most vulnerable by trying to annex Canada two days after the British had agreed to all of America's terms. Victory belongs to those who profit from it and four sides fight one war for profit. To Napoleon, victory or profit is world domination, to the US, victory is an occupation of the North American continent, to Tecumseh, victory is halting the seizure of ancestral land and forced incarceration of native Indians unto reservations, while to the black slave, victory is liberty and a chance to return home or live as free men in Trinidad.

British attacks on American ships give Mr. Jackson's creditors serious cause for concern. Building ships that could be destroyed by the British Navy or captured by privateers do not guarantee a quick return on investment that Mr. Jackson promised them. Today, Ellen's father will be leading a group of creditors to the shipyard to call in their loan. Mr. Jackson dreads this visit. It will take a major miracle for them not to cut off the financial supply and demand full payment of loans already disbursed. Mr. Jackson even made up with Ellen and convinced her to plead with her father to no avail. Mr. Jackson is in dire straits, and Mathew knows it and plans to use this information to his advantage.

Chapter Twenty-Six

The Quilombo

In the Alagoas of Brazil, Macati, Waggy and the men who escaped from the sugar plantation have settled into their new lives at the Quilombo. The fledgling community is made up of escaped Africans, Native Americans, Jews, Arabs, and runaway white indentured servants. Macati and Waggy and the other runaways assimilate quickly. Waggy has given up hope of returning to Africa, and with no navigation experience, he figures there is no way they can cross the Atlantic Ocean. He decides he might as well make the best of his newfound freedom in the Quilombo.

Huge walls made of clay and rocks surround the Quilombo nestled on the top of a rugged mountain. A long road runs down the middle with African style huts and western styled houses on either side. Each building reflects the origins of the inhabitants. Some with strong Ottoman features, African and Portuguese styles. At the center of the Quilombo is a marketplace where the wives of hunters, farmers, fishermen, blacksmiths and artisans gather to sell products brought in by their husbands. Next to the market is Skies place, a shed, simply a roof supported by bare poles. Here free men of all races seat on logs made shiny and smooth from use to drink local brew, debate affairs of the Quilombo, tell jokes after a long day in their farms, hunting fishing or working their crafts.

Further down the road is a large garden with every tropical fruit tree you can find in it. Here children play between the trees. Pluck and eat whatever fruit is in season.

All men are required to do a tour of sentry duty on the walls and the outer perimeter look out points. The threat of an attack is not lost on them.

Soon, Waggy meets and marries a Native American girl — the Zambo's Indian cousin, and they have three Zambo children - Ferdinand, Orlando, and his little princess Marcelina. One evening, Macati and Waggy teach the next generation the traditional Kapora war dance and fighting techniques. The Quilombo's very existence is a threat to plantation owners and the Alagoas government. Slaves in nearby sugarcane plantations run away to escape the hellish life of slavery.

To the young men in the Quilombos, the Kapora war dance now pronounced Capoeira by the Portuguese speaking Quilombolas is a dance of survival, and a dance that reminds them of their glorious past.

Word of the total annihilation of Macombos nearby demonstrates the Bahia and Alagoas state government's determination to eliminate all Macombos and Quilombos in their states. The young men have three choices: fight, die fighting, or return to slavery. To the warriors, the royals, and their sons, the decision is predetermined in the blood, and so they dance. With rigor and strength, they dance the capoeira — a blend of African war dances, martial arts, and music.

Members of the Quilombo gather round to watch the young children spar. The children of mixed heritage, with curly, afro, soft, silky and wavy hair move around in clusters, forming their own defensive circles as they chant words in their native tongues.

"The boy has moves," Macati says referring to little Ferdinand who is three years old.

"Just like his daddy," Waggy responds.

"No, I taught him those moves," Macati counters.

Waggy looks at his little princess Marcelina in his arms and says, "Daddy is right." The baby smiles back at him.

"See," he says to Macati.

"The queen has spoken and that's it."

She can't even talk yet. She can only say "Yaya". Macati responds.

My princess Yaya does not need to speak words her smile says it all. Waggy counters.

She always takes your side even if you are wrong; even her mother has no chance. Macati takes Marcelina from Waggy. Her beautiful light brown eyes twinkle, as she stares at her godfather Macati. She reveals her gums, as a big smile is spread across her lips. Macati fails to hide his smile, as he embraces her and brushes his thumb against her soft and smooth light skin and says to Waggy. See, she's smiling at me now. I am right. He smiles back at her.

Macati mind drifts to Awat, and the family they would raise together, if they were not separated. He is lost in his thoughts and Waggy brings him back, as he taps his shoulders.

"Okay, don't be sad; the gracious princess Yaya lets you carry her sometimes…" Waggy abruptly changes gears.

"Don't make it obvious; look over there, my sister-in-law is staring at you. I think she likes you," says Waggy.

"You haven't left your matchmaking ways," Macati steals a glance at the Native American Indian young woman standing by the musicians but says nothing else.

"Ehen?" Waggy wants an answer.

"She is pretty," Macati replies and says no more.

"Ehen," Waggy gestures him to say more.

"She is short," Macati replies.

"Nice and portable, make a move, or do you need me to talk to her on your behalf?"

Waggy gets up as if to walk over to the Indian girl who is now talking to Waggy's wife.

Macati grabs him back down with speed.

"Your wife put you up to this, didn't she?"

"What difference does it make? You need to start having children. Then you too can have a little princess like my Yaya here."

He looks at Marcelina and she smiles back at him.

"See, the princess Yaya agrees that it's a good idea; she needs a friend. Also, a daughter will give you joy and never leave your side. If we are in-laws, all the better; our children can grow up together. Besides, the girl has a good character; she is pretty and a good cook. What else do you want?" Waggy demands.

"She is short," Macati replies.

"I know what it is. You are missing Awat, and you hope to reunite with her and return home. Sorry, it won't happen. The ocean is too big for you to swim to the United States. The U.S. is too big for you to locate the exact plantation she lives on. They will catch you and re-enslave you before you get anywhere close to her as you try to navigate your way around that strange country. Besides, she has probably delivered children for another man by now…"

Waggy stops abruptly realizing he has gone too far.

He braces himself for a blow. Macati bows his head down; images of Awat lying with another man reels through his mind. Frustrated, he stands up and walks away.

"I… I am sorry. I didn't mean it like that," Waggy hurries after him.

"Only a true friend tells you the truth," Macati stops walking, with his head still down.

"The slave master got them to breed tall children on his plantation. He will force her to give birth to many children so he can sell them. I just am not ready to give up yet." Macati refuses.

"Give up on what? Your marriage to Awat? She doesn't have a choice," Waggy explains.

"Everything," Macati continues.

"Awat, our children, returning home and restoring greatness to our people. Not just the Kapora; all black people, as was promised the great Ikwunga."

Waggy looks into Macati's eyes, searching for the glare of madness but finds determination instead.

"And how do you propose to do that?"

He asks anticipating an elaborate scheme.

This is something that he has spent countless nights trying to come up with since the middle passage but couldn't find one, thus giving up and deciding to settle and have a family here in Brazil.

"I have been praying to Jehovah and he spoke to me in a dream that he would restore all, and I will see Awat and our children with my own eyes," says Macati.

"Your disappointments in life have driven you to madness brother," Waggy thinks to himself but asks a question instead of saying what is really on his mind.

"Which Jehovah are you referring to? The God of Bishop Mathew and the blue-eyed Catholic priest who baptized slaves before shipment? The one they say looks like our white oppressors with a black enemy who looks like us? Is that the God you think will save and elevate us black people to the same level of the white, blue eyed Jesus? Every Sunday the plantation owner brought a priest to tell us that the bible says we are descendants of Ham and therefore should be enslaved, exploited, and oppressed by every other race?" Waggy questions him.

"The one that helped the Krios escape slavery in the United States and return to Africa is the one I am referring to. That priest twists the bible to justify the wickedness of the master to keep us compliant while at the same time ease their conscience from the wickedness and violations against God" Macati replies.

"You can't read the bible, so how do you know that its message is misquoted?"

"True, I can't, and neither can most slaves read. In fact, that is one of the major reasons why they don't want us to learn to read. If we read, we would discover the lies. However, Bro Doks has been reading it to me." Macati confesses.

He stops and looks at someone approaching behind Waggy. Waggy turns around and greets Russ, a Jewish member of the Quilombo. Russ speaks excitedly to them.

"I was down at the docks with a few of our people pretending to be my slaves. We went looking for stores we could raid at night. While in town, we learned of a warehouse full of guns, cannons, and powder. I think we should raid the place. I asked Oluwo, and he said we should gather men and plan, but not execute the plan until a night of heavy downpour. He will summon heavy rains in a few days after we have organized a team to raid the place. The storm will force everyone in the town to stay indoors. We are organizing a large group of men from this Quilombo and several neighboring Macombos to break into the warehouse and steal the weapons under the cover of darkness and heavy downpour."

"I will join you," Macati says instantly, expecting Waggy to do the same, but notices a look of disapproval on Waggy's face.

"This Quilombo is running low on ammunition. We can't repel a sustained attack by a large force. The government forces have intensified their attacks on our settlements. Their victories in the small Macombos will embolden them to come for us next. We need to arm ourselves. Here is our chance to arm ourselves and mount a formidable opposition or even attack them causing such heavy casualties that would deter any future attempt to recapture us," Macati tries to convince Waggy.

Macati is confident of going to battle with Waggy at his side knowing Waggy will always cover his blind spot.

Russ likes the idea of taking the war to the enemy instead of being reactionary.

"I was thinking of a formidable defense. I didn't think of us attacking them first," he says.

"It will take them totally by surprise because they have always been the attackers while we defend then run away when we run out of ammunition. It's not like we can go to a shop and buy guns and ammunition. It's whatever we scavenge from their dead soldiers that we use. They won't expect us," says Russ as he turns to Waggy expecting him to join.

"I will think about it," says Waggy.

"If you decide, let me know. I'm heading to Skai's place, where men gather to drink and catch up with the news of the day. I'll find more interested fellas and bend the elbow with them," he bends his elbow making the motion of a drinking man moving a cup to the mouth then walks off in the direction of Skai's place — a makeshift bar that serves locally brewed alcohol.

Macati turns to Waggy after Russ is out of earshot.

"I have never known you to shy away from a good fight to protect your home."

"What if it's a trap?" Waggy turns to Macati squarely.

"Oh, because he is white? Do you think he will rather sell us out for profit than join us to fight white people? Russ is Jewish. He left Europe to escape persecution. Having nothing; he became an indentured servant in return for passage to Brazil. His master mistreated him and soon Russ realized that other indentured servants found themselves further indebted to the master over time and could never leave. So, he ran. He is one of the founders of this Quilombo. There is a bounty on his head."

"Do you remember how we caught fish as children?"

Waggy asks and Macati nods.

Waggy continues, "We throw a palm kernel into the brook, and about a hundred fish rush to eat the palm kernel. We cast a wide net over the fish feasting on the palm kernel and catch them all."

Waggy motions as though he is casting a net over Macati.

"You and all the men from the neighboring Macombos are the fish and the warehouse of weapons is the palm kernel. Russ might not be part of the conspiracy and when they catch him, they will hang him before they hang the rest of us. I think it's too convenient that there is a stockpile of weapons at the docks waiting to be stolen."

"In the recent past, I've been fasting and praying for guidance and an opportunity to return home. The last two days, I keep getting the same dream. Bro Doks says it's a message from God," replies Macati.

Waggy pauses before he responds. He knows that Macati's gotten deep into the Christian religion in recent months. He has spent a lot of time with Bro Doks, a first-generation Kalabari slave who learned how to read while in captivity and stole the master's bible when he was escaping. Most people in the Macombo are skeptical of anything Christian and mock him when he preaches.

Now everyone calls him Bro Doks instead of his full name, Dokubo. Bro Doks has been telling people that the messages from the pulpit are false doctrines meant to perpetuate oppression and enrichment of the religious elites. He has read the bible himself cover to cover and the messages are of freedom, not bondage.

However, the establishment knows that the congregants can't read or won't read the bible for themselves and therefore accept whatever comes from the pulpit. To many, the bible is used as a talisman to ward off bad luck or used as a display piece in their homes.

It was Doks message of freedom that caught Macati's ear that he started spending a lot of time with Bro Doks.

In the recent past, Macati has spoken a lot about reuniting with Awat and returning home. Waggy is unsure if Macati's newfound religion under Bro Doks' guidance is sending Macati down the road of delusion and false hopes.

"What is the message and how did you get it?"

Waggy asks cautiously.

Macati notices the caution in his friend's voice but proceeds anyway.

If I can't run this by Waggy, who else can give me an honest second opinion?

"I saw myself standing in front of a ship — my own ship. The wind was blowing us toward land. The vegetation of the land ahead was green with palm trees and white beaches. There was my guide standing just behind my right shoulder. He said look ahead, Awat your mother and children are waiting for you over there. I looked but the landscape didn't look like home although I knew it was Africa."

"What was different about it?" Waggy asks.

"The landscape by the sea had mountains shaped like a lioness. I said to the guide, that does not look like the mountains near Kapora and the symbol of Kapora is a male Lion with a full mane, not a lioness. The guide said you must first reunite with your family under a large cotton tree near the hills of the Lioness before regaining the throne at the home of the lion. I asked him, do you think that I will reunite with my family and regain the throne? He said, definitely! I am aligning events and ordering your footsteps to fulfill this very purpose."

Macati continues.

"I stood in awe of the mountain shaped like a lioness and muttered, thank you. My guide thanked me for listening and allowing myself to be used in fulfilling the plan he had for me and my people from the beginning of time."

Waggy is perplexed, "What did he mean by that?"

"I don't know. The dream stops at the same point every time. With the same message, *I am aligning events and ordering your footsteps for this very purpose.* That is why I think this raid is part of God's plan."

"What does he look like?" Waggy asks.

"Who?" Macati asks.

"God, the guide in the dream. What does he look like?" Waggy responds.

Chapter Twenty-Seven

Let's Make A Deal

Mathew greets Ellen's father and a group of creditors as they disembark their coach at Mr. Jackson's shipyard.

"What if I told you how to make a fortune in thirty days?" He asks.

"Are you talking to us?" The eldest member of the group says to Mathew with disgust in his voice that a slave dares to address him directly.

"Oh, Mathew, are you up to your tall tales again?" Ellen's father asks, and then he turns to his friends.

"Never mind him; he claims he is a prince in Africa and will make you rich if you set him free."

The group burst out laughing, one of them motions like a gorilla. "Uh uh uh, unga unga; will you pay us in bananas?"

"Dollars from sugar, guns, and ammunition sales," Mathew replies.

The men stop to listen.

Mathew smiles, revealing a perfect set of white teeth minus one.

"Oh, the power of greed," he muses, then speaks.

"Because of the war with Britain, there is a shortage of sugar in this country. If we brought in shiploads of sugar, you could sell it at any price you want. It's a seller's market. The military needs guns and ammunition, and there isn't enough produced in this country."

"And where do we get the sugar and guns? We can't buy from the British sugar Caribbean colonies," Ellen's father cuts him off.

"Brazil is desperate to sell their sugar as their European trading partners either have their own sugar-producing colonies or are going through financial crises from the war with Napoleon. We can buy sugar and weapons from them and bring them here for sale," Mathew replies.

"Sounds like a good idea," says the elderly man.

Mr. Jackson had walked up to the group and was listening to the conversation. He is relieved that Mathew is creating a distraction from the issue at hand — the debt he owes them.

"How do our ships get past the blockade?" Mr. Jackson asks.

"You have a large fleet of ships sitting around, not making money, but just waiting for a British frigate to blow them up or Bermuda privateers to take them away thereby ruining your business and any chance of repaying your debts to these gentlemen."

Mathew pauses for his message to sink in, then continues his point.

"The British Navy is in the North targeting Europe-bound ships. If your ships are fitted with cannons and travel south in a large convoy, no privateer would dare attack. They prefer to attack lone ships. Remember, they are in the war for profit and won't take on an armed convoy."

The men take the conversation into Mr. Jackson's office at the shipyard. Mathew explains that he speaks fluent Portuguese. He will go with Mr. Jackson to Brazil to purchase the sugar and weapons. The profits will be shared amongst the investors, and Mr. Jackson's share will cover his debts and have some to spare.

Mathew doesn't share in the profits but will be given his freedom and returned to Africa at the end of the war. That is Mathew's proposition to the people in the room.

"That sounds like a reasonable proposition," says Ellen's father. "Now we know how we will make our money; how do you intend to return to Africa?"

Mathew had a ready answer to that question.

Old man Huggins told him about Paul Cuffee and his efforts to return free blacks to Africa.

Historical backdrop:

Paul Cuffee was of Aquinnah Wampanoag Indian (aborigines of present-day Mathers Vineyard in Massachusetts) and of African Ashanti descent. Kofi, meaning born on Friday in Ashanti, is mispronounced and misspelled Cuffee in American history books. Son of a former slave, Cuffee, built a lucrative shipping empire and established the first racially integrated school in Westport, Massachusetts.

Before the war of 1812, he got involved in the British effort to resettle freed slaves, many of whom had moved from the US to Nova Scotia after the American revolution to the colony of Sierra Leone — originally called Serra Leoa, which translates to Lioness Mountains in English from Portuguese, by a Portuguese explorer Pedro de Sintra. Pedro de Sintra had named it Serra Leoa to describe the mountain formations surrounding the natural harbor of the present-day "Free Town" where freed slaves from the Americas would later settle after the British kicked out the Portuguese and acquired it for themselves, as was the practice before the Berlin conference of 1884. Cuffee helped establish The Friendly Society of Sierra Leone, which provided financial support for the colony. He believed that African Americans were more likely to rise to be a people in Africa than in the U.S. where slavery and legislated limits on black freedoms were still in place despite one's education, achievements, or standing in the community.

Cuffee also had the support of several white elites who were pushing for an African American colony. Not for altruistic reasons but out of concern that the gradually increasing number of free blacks in the U.S. could cause slave rebellions and other types of trouble for the country. The American Colonial Society (ACS) co-founders, particularly Henry Clay, advocated exporting freed Negroes as a way of ridding the South of potentially "troublesome agitators" who might threaten the plantation system of slavery. Their fears were rooted in the successful slave rebellion in Haiti led by free blacks like Toussaint Louverture and Alexandre Sabès

> *Pétion, which the French referred to as Affranchis (Freedmen). The four thousand slaves that joined the British in the Chesapeake Bay in the war of 1812 give further credence to the possibility of blacks joining a foreign power against the U.S. and their general distrust of the free black population. America's enemies will have a large army within the U.S. borders eager to fight their current overlords if given weapons.*
>
> *By 1812, Paul Cuffee had successfully returned 89 African Americans to Free Town Sierra Leone. He returned from Africa with a shipload of goods for sale in April 1812 only to have his ship the Traveler and its cargo seized on the grounds of "trading with the enemy" — Britain. This would prompt him to seek an audience with President Madison to secure his ship's release and persuade the President to establish a colony for freed blacks. Though Cuffee got his ship back, Madison, a holder of hundreds of slaves, would not grant his request for an American colony for free blacks. Cuffee's dream of an American colony in Africa for free blacks would come four years after his death through Madison's successor President Monroe. Liberia (Liberty Area) 's capital would be named after Monroe (Monrovia). Its flag closely resembling the U.S. flag — red and white stripes and a single white five-point star with a blue background instead of fifty.*

Cuffee had just got his ship back at the point of this meeting, and several free blacks like old Man Huggins were hoping Madison would grant his request for an African colony of free blacks.

Mathew, on his part, planned to go on Cuffee's ship back to the continent. It matters not if it was to free town or the territory to its west, the Liberty Area where Cuffee and the American Colonial Society were hoping to establish a colony. He would find his way back to the Wayo kingdom and reclaim the vast wealth he left behind, especially the gold and rich land and diamond fields.

Chapter Twenty-Eight

Voyage To The U.S

Brazil is known for its nice weather. Seldom do you have hurricanes, typhoons, or cyclones. However, this night, fierce tropical stormy winds approach hurricane levels. The moon and stars hide behind the stormy clouds. The streets are desolate as everyone stays indoors from the thunderstorm, just as Oluwo predicted.

Macati uses a crowbar to break the lock of a warehouse by the docks. Russ and twenty men run into the warehouse. Waggy's brother-in-law pulls up with a stolen wagon. The men in the warehouse start loading the wagon with crates of guns and ammunition.

"Where is Waggy?"

Macati asks the Native American with the wagon.

"He and fifty others have positioned themselves a mile away to cut a path for your escape in case you get surrounded," the man replies.

Macati remembers how hard it was to convince Waggy to come along for the raid. Waggy finally agreed, stating that he would get several men to provide perimeter defense. If perchance Macati, Russ, and the twenty men on the raid get surrounded, he would attack those surrounding the warehouse and cut a path for Macati's escape.

The cart is loaded, and Russ instructs the cart to pull out. He gives a high-pitched whistle and the second one pulls into the warehouse. Everything is going according to plan — a white-skinned member of the Quilombo would ride in the cart of weapons in case the police or the army stops them and would claim to be part of the militia and the Indian, Zambo, or black person riding with him is a loyal slave. As one cart leaves the warehouse, another pulls in. Russ stays in the warehouse coordinating the loading of arms and directing traffic.

Macati and the twenty men in the warehouse fill them up. Each one has a weapon hidden at an arm's length away in case they have to fight their way out.

As the fourth cart comes in, Macati hears a familiar voice shout at the cart driver.

"You are going the wrong way!"

It is Bishop Mathew's voice.

"This is not your shipment," Russ replies. "Yours is in the warehouse." Sounds of boots are heard running towards the warehouse.

Macati and his men in the warehouse hide behind crates. They cock their weapons, ready to shoot their way out of the warehouse. Mathew rushes into the warehouse, behind him is Mr. Jackson. Macati recognizes Mathew and signals the men to hold their fire and keep out of sight.

"I thought they were closed for the day," says Mr. Jackson through Mathew.

"We are closed," a Caboclo on the fourth horse-drawn cart says as he dismounts the cart.

"However, we expect trouble, so we have come to replenish our supplies."

The Caboclo is one of the runaway indentured servants seeking refuge at the Macombo. He recites the script of the plan in case they are confronted. Russ and the white members of the Quilombo pretend to be militia officers getting supplies, while Macati and the other blacks pretend to be slaves working for the militia officers.

So far, everything was going according to plan until Bishop Mathew and Mr. Jackson showed up.

Three weeks ago, Mr. Jackson's creditors liked Mathew's plan to purchase sugar and weapons from Brazil and sell them in the U.S. at exorbitant prices. Mathew came to Brazil as Mr. Jackson's interpreter. They arrived from the U.S. that evening as the rains began to fall. It was too late in the day for them to load their ships with weapons and sugar. First thing in the morning would be much better, as advised by informants.

"What type of trouble?" Mathew asks.

The Russ turns to Mr. Jackson as though to ask who gave Mathew, a black man, the impetus to engage him in conversation like they are equals.

Mr. Jackson knows the look; he gets it a lot from friends whenever Mathew steps outside his assigned position as a slave and dares contribute to a conversation amongst white men.

"He is my interpreter," Mr. Jackson replies in broken Portuguese.

"Oh, okay," replies the Caboclo.

"The army attacked a Macombo and recaptured several Quilombolas. However, several escaped to nearby Quilombos, and we expect a retaliatory attack, so we need to prepare. That's why the warehouse was opened for us," he lies.

"We have a shipment in there," says Mathew.

"Come on in and identify them. I wouldn't like to take your weapons and sugar by mistake," Russ says.

He doesn't know how many people are at Mr. Jackson's party. It's better to bring them into the warehouse and kill them quietly than out in the street lest someone witness it and alerts the authorities.

Chapter Twenty-Nine

The Blue Coats

Old man Huggins has been reading discarded papers and learned that the British need local recruits to defend their interests in the Americas until the end of the Naploeonic wars. Then they can send in troops from Europe. It is 1814, and the war has turned against Napoleon Bonaparte. Spain has dethroned his brother Joseph Bonaparte as their king and joined Portugal to march on France from across the Pyrenees. Russia, Austria, and their allies have invaded France from across the Rhine. Tsar Alexander of Russia is leading an army to personally avenge the mayhem Napoleon caused in Russia two years earlier. The coalition occupies Paris, and the French Senate sign the treaty of Fontainebleau — deposing Napoleon as its leader and sending him in exile to the isle ofElba's. The British needed local American conscripts to contain the U.S. incursion on its North American territory, Canada, until they can unleash their war-hardened military on the fledgling United States.

The U.S. counters with similar offers, much to the annoyance of several slave owners who paid for their slaves, plus their entire fortunes depended on slave labor.

Old man, Huggins, visits his grandchildren on the Jackson plantation on Sunday to give them the news. The British are offering freedom to any slave who joins them against the U.S. With the boss away in Brazil, everyone's at ease this Sunday morning at the Jackson plantation. Huggins delights in watching his grandchildren play when an old comrade in arms greets him. During the American independence war, Greg Sr., a black patriot infantryman, fought in the same regiment as Huggins. Greg Sr. was promised freedom but was returned to his master right after the war of independence.

Huggins informs him of the British stationed in the Chesapeake and his plans to join them.

"We are too old to fight," says Greg Sr.

"True," says old man Huggins.

"However, if the British know that you were instrumental in their recruitment efforts, they will reward you handsomely."

"Okay, I would like the British to take my descendants and me back to Africa. I could reintegrate my children into the Ibo community there. What about you, what's in it for you? You don't know what tribe your ancestors came from?"

"The British have a town called Freetown on the west coast of Africa where they would return the freed slaves. Those who can't return to their tribe can stay in Freetown or be given fertile land on the southern part of Trinidad, a British Caribbean colony. I think I'll take my children and grands to Trinidad." Says Huggins.

Old man Huggins and Greg Sr. spread the word around the Jackson plantation and several other plantations in the DC and Virginia area.

To Awat and her relatives on Mr. Jackson's plantation, the choice was simple. First, there was no guarantee the U.S. would keep its promise. Black Patriots like Greg Sr. were returned to his Patriot master after the war. Even if the U.S. government kept its promise, the condition of many of the Negros freed after the independence war twenty-nine years earlier was deplorable.

Yes, the United States did free some of the blacks that fought on the American side in the war of independence, like old man Huggins. Though they were legally free, they were unemployed, landless, viewed with suspicion, and as a menace to society. Some of them, like old man Huggins hire themselves out for peanuts while others indenture themselves to avoid starvation. Education does not guarantee gainful employment either, as Edward Jones, the first black man to graduate from Amherst College, learned the hard way. He was biracial but not light skinned enough to pass for white and therefore had difficulty getting gainful employment in the U.S.

Daniel Coker, also mixed-race, Irish/Black learned to read by accompanying his white siblings to primary school as their "valet" and later on relocated to Africa to improve his lot in life. Coker founded the West African Methodist church while Jones became the founding principal of Africa's first western University, the Fourah Bay College in Free Town Sierra Leone — this is all in the future. As of today, these free men and their enslaved counterparts had life-changing decisions to make if they wanted to improve their lot in life.

The British had a foothold in the Chesapeake area of the United States. Over two thousand slaves had joined them, and hundreds more were abandoning the plantations to join them every day.

"How do I enlist?" MaKuei asks old man Huggins.

"Tonight, follow the drinking gourd until you get by the river. I will be waiting for you at the riverside tonight. I'll take you to the British."

The drinking gourd refers to the big dipper asterism used by fugitive slaves as a point of reference, so they don't get lost as they escape to freedom in the north.

"Ellen and the taskmaster will find out that we have escaped and send a posse after us," says Jabu.

"Comatose people can't call no posse," Daisy says as she produces a bottle of concoction from under her petticoat.

"I've arranged with some of the house slaves to knock them out with this. The house slaves will mix it in with their food tonight and join the field slaves to escape."

Old man Huggins is glad to see his people finally unite for a common cause that benefits them all. Some of his light-skinned grandchildren worked in the house and hitherto felt superior to their darker cousins in the field. The darker cousins in the field resented and distrusted their lighter-skinned cousins in the main house, viewing them as suck-ups and traitors who benefit from their suffering.

In the Jackson plantation, every tiny difference was used to keep the slaves divided. The foundation was laid on the ship when they placed warring factions on the same ship. Upon getting to the plantation, tiny differences were exploited to keep the slaves divided. First, the eradication of common bonds starting with the family unit, physical features like skin color, hair, clothing, diction, and destroying the man's innate propensity to provide for and protect his family.

You can only teach what you know. If all you know is brokenness, how to run, hide and suck up to the master, then that is all you can teach the next generation: brokenness, run, hide, and suck up to the master.

Every Sunday, old man Huggins has taught his children, grandchildren, and anyone who would listen that there is an alternative lifestyle to what they are used to. This turn of events reassures him that his preaching has not been in vain.

Historical backdrop:

Vise Admiral Cochran, commander of the British forces on the North Atlantic station, ordered black soldiers' recruitment to form the Colonial Marines as he had done earlier on Marie Galante. Marie Galante was a French colony that the British seized from France with the help of local slaves promised freedom. Unlike their British counterparts, these slaves were resistant to tropical diseases. They were able to resist the French governor's forces from Guadeloupe, who sought to take advantage of the tropical deceased weakened British soldiers garrisoned on the Island. Cochrane's order was implemented in the United States by Rear Admiral Cockburn, Cochrane's second-in Command. The Colonial Marines corps served as part of the British forces on the Atlantic and Gulf coasts of the United States during the 1812 war.

Cochrane's proclamation stated that all persons wishing to emigrate would be received at a British Military outpost or aboard a British ship. One could enter his Majesty's service (King George III, husband of Queen Charlotte, a descendant of the Black De Sousa bloodline), or go "as free settlers to the British Possessions in North America (Canada, Nova Scotia or British possessions in the West Indies. Trinidad would get the largest number), similar to Dunmore's proclamation of November 7, 1775. Although it only offered freedom to those who bore arms with the British forces in the American Revolution. This time, it gave freedom to any enslaved black person. By May 10th, 1814, the British occupied Tangier Island off the Virginia coast and offered an accessible location to Virginia slaves seeking refuge from their slave masters. Able-bodied men were given the option to take up arms or become blue jackets - the "working party" constructing Fort Albion.

Chapter Thirty

Us Bound

In Brazil, the storm is over, and the clouds give way to the morning sun. The warehouse owner approaches the front door of the warehouse at the docks and reaches for the padlock. It falls apart as soon as he touches it and his heart jumps out of fear.

"Have I been robbed, or the stupid foreman broke it last night and replaced it to look like nothing happened?"

He swings the door wide open and realizes most of the contents are gone. He starts shouting, and passers-by gather to see why he is yelling. He runs through the warehouse, taking quick stock of what is left. His voice echoes across his warehouse.

"I am ruined!"

Bishop Mathew and Mr. Jackson walk through the open door as the warehouse owner shouts.

"We saw the men who did this. They said they were from the militia, preparing for an attack from Quilombolas."

The owner grabs Mathew by the coat lapel.

"You did this!"

"Not me! Not me," Mathew replies.

"If I had stolen them, I wouldn't be here," Mathew says desperately.

"You are coming with us," says a big man with a gun as he pulls the warehouse owner off Mathew.

Mathew glances over to Mr. Jackson for help. He knows that he could easily be framed for this theft and flogged then hung.

"He didn't do it," says Mr. Jackson in English.

The huge man turns to him and says, "Inglis?"

"No, American," Mathew replies on Mr. Jackson's behalf.

He goes on to explain that they came to purchase sugar and weapons from the warehouse owner but could not load their ships because it was late and heavy rains were about to fall.

The huge man is the local chief of police, and he leads them to the police station. On the way, he orders one of his men to call the local militia officer. The young man gallops away while the officer, his men, Mathew, and Mr. Jackson walk over to the police station. To his surprise, the militia commander is already there by the time they arrive at the station.

"I hear a lot of weapons and ammunition are missing from the docks," he asks.

"Did you take them?" The police chief asks.

"No, we have our own, but I think I know who did," the colonel replies.

"Who?" The chief asks.

The colonel points at a composite sketch on the wall.

"Him!"

"That's one of the men I saw last night," Mathew says.

"That's not good," says the Colonel.

"What's going on?" The police chief asks.

"They have armed themselves in anticipation of our attack on their Quilombo," says the colonel.

Then he turns to Mr. Jackson.

"They let you live?"

"Yes," Mr. Jackson replies through Mathew.

"They asked me a few questions and set aside my sugar and ammunition crates while they took the rest."

"I think they spared you to warn us that they are armed and ready for us. Nothing to do with your purchase," says the Colonel.

Hot sweat runs down Mr. Jackson's face upon realizing how close to death he came.

What they don't know is this is one of two reasons they let Mr. Jackson live. The second reason is - Macati sent a message to his comrades to spare them so he can ship himself to the United States in a crate. He climbed into one of the crates with a carbine and had some men nail it shut. That crate would be loaded unto one of the US-bound ships, and he would get out when the crate is deposited on Mr. Jackson's property. Macati did not have time to prepare an elaborate plan but seized the opportunity to get to the U.S. when it presented itself.

"If I survived a slave ship, I can survive a cargo ship. I will figure out a better plan for the voyage."

The warehouse owner says the price of those goods has gone up and wants to recoup some of his losses. Mr. Jackson and Mathew haggle prices with the warehouse owner. Mathew points out that they can purchase from any other person on the docks if the warehouse owner insists on the high price.

"It's better to get something than nothing at all," he thinks and quickly agrees to the original price.

"You didn't see anything unusual?" The officer turns to Mathew.

"No," he replies.

"They acted like soldiers, and the blacks acted like loyal servants to the white officers.

Later that day, Macati's crate is moved by the ship crew to create more room for additional sugar. Macati finds himself upside down, with bags of sugar over the crate. He stays motionless for a while, not to attract attention as he watches men move about through cracks between the planks in the wooden crate. Once the ship set sail and the crew left the cargo hold to attend to the masts and other tasks above deck, he straightens out and realizes his crate is weighed by the bags of sugar piled on top of it — he can't get out.

The tropical heat bears down. This condition is worse than the slave ship that brought him to Brazil. He hangs tough, knowing he will soon be reunited with Awat. Soon it dawns on him that he hasn't hashed out a plan to find Awat, but he knows that Mr. Jackson and

Mathew know where she is. He holds tight to the carbine as though to reassure himself that he will fight his way to freedom if necessary.

Night falls, and the heat gives way to a cool breeze. The sea is smooth tonight, but the visibility is low due to fog. Mr. Jackson's convoy travels slowly under a moonless sky, keeping a reasonable distance between themselves to avoid a collision — a privateer frigate leads the way. Merchant galleons are fitted with cannons in the middle, Mr. Jackson and Mathew are on the last galleon so that he can keep an eye on the other galleons laden with sugar and ammunition.

He bet everything on this trip; if things go wrong, he will be financially ruined with no hope of recovery. If it succeeds, he would be a multimillionaire. Only two things can stop him from realizing his dream: bad weather and an attack by British privateers.

All is well; the storm has passed, and the sea is calm, except for the fog. He forces himself to retire for the night before midnight. Exhaustion from Brazil's activities coupled with the long day vigilance watching the fleet takes its toll, he falls into a deep slumber.

It is after midnight, and the man in the crow's nest on Mr. Jackson's galleon struggles to stay awake as the gentle waves rock the ship lulling him to sleep. To stay awake, he focuses on the light of the ship in front of him, half a mile ahead. But sleep sometimes is a sneaky enemy when you sit motionless for a while. You think you are awake, but your eyes have shut themselves from the realities around you, and your visualization goes into the dream world. Here, everything is perfect for the man in the crow's nest.

The fleet is traveling along safely, and by daytime, they should be closer to homeport. However, in the real world, a silhouette of another galleon emerges from the fog and silently pulls up to the port side.

Ropes with hooks fly overboard from the other galleon, and within seconds, both ships are tethered side by side. The sound of loud shouts and gunfire into the air startle the man in the crow's nest awake. Hundreds of men board the vessel with pistols, swashbucklers, and swords. Mr. Jackson scrambles off his bed groping around in the dark for his pistol. He scampers up the ladder to the deck when the ship rocks violently. Another ship hits them on the Starboard, the right side of the ship. Hundreds of more men pour onto the ship.

Within minutes, the crew and its passengers are overpowered by the throngs of privateers from the British colonies of the Bahamas and Barbados — majority of the marauders are black.

Taking over an enemy vessel intact requires a large number of able-bodied men armed to storm and take it intact with little or no damage to the cargo or the ship itself. Such captured ships become the property of the privateer and their financier. With the shortage of white Englishmen in these colonies and blacks' ratio to whites being ten to one, privateers fill their ranks with strong black men. The life of a black privateer is better than that of a slave.

On the open sea, there is a greater semblance of equality amongst pirates and privateers. You treat each other with respect and trust. Mistreating a fellow privateer could earn you a bullet in the middle of an attack in a friendly fire.

After subduing Mr. Jackson and the other crew members, the English privateers go through the cargo hold looking for treasure and assessing the value of their catch.

They take off the sacks of sugar from the top of Macati's crate and pry it open to see what valuables may be inside. To their surprise, they find Macati. Macati had his carbine cocked and ready to shoot as they were prying it open but decides not to shoot when he hears the accent of one of the men opening the crate — the man has an African accent.

"The enemy of my enemy is my friend," he thinks to himself.

He passes his carbine to the man butt first.

"Thank you for saving me," he says in Kapora.

The man replies in a Niger-Congo dialect similar to Kapora.

"Did they capture you for sale to slavery?" The man asks.

"No, they captured my wife and child, and I am going to save them," Macati replies.

The man laughs.

"Come out," he turns to his comrades.

"We have a lovesick fool trying to stowaway into the United States to rescue his wife and child."

The men take him above deck. Macati complies without resistance until he sees Mr. Jackson and Mathew tied up on the deck. He breaks free from his captors, jumps on Mathew, yelling in Kapora.

"Where is Awat? What did you do to her?"

Initially, the privateers enjoy the spectacle; then they separate the fight. Just as things subside, a cannonball rips through the sail. Two American privateer ships protecting Mr. Jackson's convoy had turned around and come to rescue one of their fleet. A battle ensues between the ill-experienced Americans and the battle-hardened British privateers. The British privateers turn the captured ship around and run while their toughest gunship holds off the Americans.

The gunship is a captured French Man "O" War manned by seasoned gunners. The battle between the Man "O" War and the American galleons fitted with cannons rages like two dogs against a grizzly bear. The American galleons take on heavy casualties, but their odds of victory increases, as the American frigate leading the convoy turns around to aid their embattled counterparts. One of the American galleons is in flames. They lower the lifeboats, and the Man O War retreats just as the American Frigate arrives.

Its withdrawal leaves room for the American privateer galleons to rescue their sinking comrades. The American frigate pursues the Man O War into the fog. Soon the Americans realize that while they focused on the Man O War at the back of the convoy, the Bahamian privateers had regrouped and captured another unprotected vessel laden with sugar at the front of the convoy. The American frigate realizes that their cargo ships are getting boarded, stop chasing the Man O War, turn tail, and run to protect the rest of their fleet.

The Bahamian privateers turn their ships and set sail for the Bahamas at full speed. The American privateers give chase then turn around when they hear another of their own firing its cannons. The British privateers had kept a fast Bermuda sloop in the fog, and it moved in to shoot at the unprotected fleet of merchant ships, not knowing how many British privateers might be in this fleet. The Americans think that the fleeing ships are luring them away from the merchant's vessels so their counterparts can attack the merchant ships just as they did with the Man O War; they go back into formation. The lone attacker disappears back into the fog.

As the British privateers return to the Bahamas with their captured vessels, Macati begs the first-generation African privateer to take him to the U.S. The African explains that there is a war between the U.S. and Britain, and they are in the business of capturing American ships — they can't take him to the U.S. Finally, they settle on Macati joining their group. When the war is over, he can find his way to the U.S. He might make enough money as a privateer to purchase Awat's and his child's freedom.

With no other options available, Macati agrees to join them.

"What about them?" He points at Mr. Jackson and Mathew.

"They will be handed over to the British governor-general of the Bahamas colony to be used in negotiating prisoner exchange with the American government in the future." The first generation African explains.

On the way to the port, Macati and the first-generation African, acting as an interpreter interrogate Mathew and Mr. Jackson about Awat and his child. Mr. Jackson tells him that Awat was pregnant when they captured her and gave birth to twins named Mark and Hali.

Macati can't contain himself on hearing that his twins and queen are now slaves. He jumps on Mr. Jackson to strangle him, but an English officer knocks him over the head. Mr. Jackson is worth more to them alive than dead. Macati goes into despair.

Upon arriving at the port, Squire, the Governor General's special assistant, is waiting for them at the docks. Armstrong, captain of the privateers, knows Squire well. He wants a share of the loot found on the ship; he has an arrangement with the privateers within his jurisdiction –

give him a portion of the spoils, and he will under-report the total amount taken to the crown. It is unknown if the Governor-general is part of the scam but is too much of a gentleman to dirty his hands with such bribes, sending Squire to do the dirty work instead.

Mathew and Mr. Jackson are handed over to Squire, who in turn hands them to the local jailer. They will remain until such a time when the British need POWs to exchange for one of their own with the Americans.

Mathew cozies up to Squire, claiming that he is Mr. Jackson's slave, and the US will not offer any exchanges or ransom for a slave. His master is the only person who could pay his ransom, but that is not possible as he is a captive himself, and even if Mr. Jackson were set free, he is financially ruined. His slaves, plantation, shipyard, and mansion will be auctioned off to settle his debts.

Mathew offers to go with a British convoy to the U.S., and he will help recruit blacks for the British war effort.

"Really? do you think I am stupid?" Says Squire.

"You will run away the moment you set foot in America."

"Run away to what?" Mathew replies.

"To become a slave yet, again? It is in my interest that you win this war so I can return to Africa as promised by the crown. That is why I am offering my services. The slaves would rather listen to me, a black man. It is easier for me to sneak on to a plantation as a slave and convince other slaves to run away and join you," he says.

"Okay, the fleet you came in will not be going out for a few days. You can go with the squadron that will be strafing the Carolina coastline."

Mathew marvels at his power of persuasion. He knows that the war in Europe will end soon, and it will not be too long that he will return to a life of luxury if he returns to Wayo kingdom.

Chapter Thirty-One

The Reunion

Captain Armstrong has a black flag and has severally turned pirate when it suits him, only to revert to being privateer when it suits him. Macati becomes a skilled pirate and amasses a small fortune. He and his cohorts focus their activities within the Northern Caribbean, an area poorly guarded by the virtually non-existent U.S. Navy — picking off ships from the U.S. as privateers and turning pirate at the site of gold-rich Spanish ships. Today they pursue a Spanish ship bound for Cuba. They will attack the Spanish ship as pirates, not privateers because Spain is an ally of Britain. Spanish ships often have gold.

The captain plans not to inform the British governor of this attack. As they approach the ship, they notice there are just a few men on the ship with no cannon to defend itself.

This will be easy, they think.

The captain fires a cannon and announces they intend to board, and the Spanish ship gives no resistance. The passivity of the crew discourages the pirates. The cargo must be worthless otherwise; they would have given more resistance. Captain Armstrong orders the man in the crow's nest to scan the perimeter to see if there are any other ships nearby, just in case it's a trap by the Spanish Navy, and they are using this ship as bait.

When they attack it, the Navy will encircle them.

The crow's nest report nothing on the horizon, and the captain orders them to pull up alongside and prepare to board. Macati feels uneasy as they get close to the ship; it smells familiar. He looks about and his black colleagues look uneasy as well. The captain orders them to board — fifty men jump across. The crew stands in surrender with their hands up. Macati and the men run through the ship looking for cargo, hidden holds where the crew might have hidden their gold. Captain Armstrong holds a sword to the throat of the captain of the Spanish ship.

"Where is the gold? He asks.

"There is no gold on this ship," replies the captain.

"What are you carrying?" Armstrong demands to know.

"Slaves from Africa to Cuba, most of them are sick. Bad for business," he replies.

Spaniards, contrary to popular belief, held more African slaves than any other European group. They occupied all of gold rich South America, a large part of present-day USA and several islands in the Caribbean. They needed African labor to farm their plantations and work the gold mines.

Macati tries to hold his breath as he walks through the cargo hold of slaves. The heat and the stench bring memories of his journey.

He says in Kapora, "For long you have prayed for deliverance. Today your prayers have been answered. We are here to release you."

Shouts of joy fill the air as Macati, and his cohorts force the crew to unlock the chains. From amidst the shouts of joy, he hears a familiar voice say, "The Orishas bless the mother who bore you."

Several other voices respond, "Ise."

Macati is both elated and concerned that several the captives speak Kapora. He turns to the nearest of the group and asks.

"Are you Kapora?"

The man says yes.

"I am Macati, son of Zaki,"

The man responds, "I am Akibu, son of Uzaza. They said you were enslaved!"

"I was, and now I'm free, and I am here to free you too! How is my father?"

"Do you not know? He is dead." Akibu replies.

Macati freezes, at a loss for words. He takes a second as he digests the news of his late father. An uncontrollable tear rolls its way down his face as his eye twitches. He wants blood, somebody must pay for this.

"And my mother?" He clenches his fist.

"Enslaved like the rest of us loyal to the house of Zaki. Ikwunga is here with us."

"*Ikwunga!*" Macati yells above the noise.

Ikwunga responds from the other end of the ship.

Macati rushes over, not waiting for the man with the keys to catch up. The man was busy unlocking the shackles on Greg Jr.

Macati starts breaking Ikwunga's chains with an iron rod. He hugs his brother tight and kisses his head, relieved to know he was ok.

A million questions run through his mind.

"How did Zaki die? How did Halima and those loyal to the house of Zaki become enslaved? There are so many captives on this ship; how will they be maintained? Where can they settle? Will Captain Armstrong and other members of the group be accepting of so many new people?"

Akibu, son of Uzaza and Ikwunga, fill him in on the events following the attack on the Baptismal Castle.

Five years ago

The sniper's bullet from the rear of the ship misses Greg on the docks due to distance and wind from the sea. The Kapora are too distraught to see the ship sent to rescue Macati and the other captives on the Brazilian slave ship go down in flames; this strengthens their resolve to march to Obijinaal that day.

Zaki is propped up with sticks on his horse covered by flowing war garments, so no one knew he was in suspended animation, thus dispelling any rumors of his death and the cascading effects on the army's morale. Uzaza and another war chief ride alongside his horse, guiding it on the march to Obijinaal's kingdom. The troops behind feel encouraged to march behind their leader.

That evening, the Kapora warriors joined by the Wagombe from the Baptismal castle camp in the hills surrounding Obijinaal's town.

Darkness falls upon the land, and the artillery bombardment began. The Jinaali people ran into the bushes to hide only to be captured or killed by the Kapora and Wagombe warriors. Obijinaal and a handful of warriors get on horses and start galloping out of town.

Uzaza leaves Zaki on his horse unattended to join the horsemen chasing Obijinaal. In the melee, a bullet hits Zaki in the head. It's unknown if the bullet came from one of Obijinaal's men or one of the Kapora horsemen working for Ika.

Zaki's horse is spooked and starts running.

A second bullet strikes the horse's leg as it gallops at high speed. It topples over, tossing Zaki off. He lays motionless on the ground

Word of Zaki's demise spreads through the ranks. Anger and revenge fuel the others to press on the pursuit. Obijinaal and his men head towards a marshy narrow pass.

Several Jinaali men jump off their horses and take up fighting positions behind trees at the marshy narrow pass while Obijinaal and his officers ride through. The Kapora calvary would be forced to slow down in these marshes and funnel through this narrow pass, thereby making them easy targets for the gunmen behind the trees. The pursuing Kapora realize that they are about to ride into a "turkey shoot" stop beyond effective range of the Jinaali snipers.

While contemplating their next move, they hear shouts of victory from the other side. The Jinaali gunmen behind the trees abandon their position and scatter into the swamps, then Ika and his men ride in from the pass Obijinaal rode through. They had ambushed Obijinaal, and his officers on the other side of the pass and killed many top-ranking officers. Ika rides in gallant strut dragging Obijinaal's body behind his horse, leaving a trail of blood and brain matter in the mud.

Obya turns to Uzaza and says, "He was shot through the mouth and the bullet blasted through the back of his head."

Uzaza scans the cheering warriors as he replies.

"I think he was captured alive and shot through the mouth not to divulge the conspiracy at trial," Uzaza says to Obya.

"The people will think Ika did it in anger for Obijinaal's enslavement of Macati, the murder of Zaki, and the insurrection against the empire. They will crown him king. Forget about making Ikwunga king; none of the kingmakers will listen to us."

Obya and Uzaza return to where Zaki lay and remove the gold wrist cuff with the lion head and hide it. Only legitimate heirs to the throne can wear the cuff of the great Ikwunga.

If Ika becomes king without the cuff, his reign will not have the backing of the Orishas.

Zaki's inner circle starts disappearing within days of Ika becoming king. Ika has an imitation cuff made to legitimize his claim to the throne. Under Ika's reign, the Kapora begin trading with Europeans in palm produce to the English, cocoa to the Belgians, and slaves to the Spaniards and Portuguese.

Nyoka becomes the power behind the throne, taking prominence at all royal functions. The disappearance of its citizens and lopsided trade with the Europeans sends the Kapora economy downward.

Consequently, a tiny elite class emerges during Ika's regime. They are only interested in pomp, pageantry, and elaborate display of wealth. They surround themselves with sycophants and "yes men. All state officials are corrupt, and there is no sense of honor or moral decency. Anyone who speaks against this turn of events disappears or is accused of treason and sold into slavery. The middle class virtually disappears, melding into the poor and downtrodden.

Uzaza and Halima know it's a matter of time before Nyoka manufactures enough false evidence against them. The day Obya and his household disappeared, Halima did not wait to confirm rumors that the newly appointed chief palace guard, Bemoi, the burly youth of mixed Wayo and Kapora parents, had whisked them away at night to be sold as slaves.

She, Ikwunga, Uzaza, and his family flee the following night. They head to the only people they trust, the Wagombe.

She believes that if Nyoka and her cronies can make a prominent member of society like Obya disappear with no reprisal from society; they too would disappear soon.

Now

"Where is Mama?" Macati demands.

"Wayo Pombeiros ambushed us. They separated us. The last time I saw her, she was being loaded onto a ship with Uzaza."

Ikwunga continues.

"We were outside the kingdom. Nyoka visited us at the slave castle to gloat. She thanked us for making this easy for her. They didn't even have a monkey trial with solid enough evidence to convince the few warrior chiefs still loyal to the house of Zaki that their beloved Halima was responsible for the economic demise of the kingdom. Now she can spread a rumor that Halima and Uzaza were having an affair and Ikwunga is Uzaza's son, unbeknown to Zaki. The rumor is that our family was frolicking in the countryside when they were captured by roaming Pombeiros. That is the story Nyoka will tell the people of Kapora."

Chapter Thirty-Two

Revenge

With Napoleon dethroned and forced into exile on the Isle of Elba, the British redirect their battle-hardened troops from the European war front unto the U.S. They are joined by the 2nd corps of colonial marines and Canadians seeking revenge from the destruction of their capital. The second corps of colonial marines is also known as the "Blue Jackets" because of the uniform worn by the former escaped slaves that joined the British Army to fight their oppressors while in base camp but wore red uniform when on the battlefield. They know the lay of the land they once worked as slaves even better than the U.S. army officers who were, in most cases, landed gentry pulled away from the comfort of their mansions to defend Maryland. Mathew is one of the Corps of Colonial Marines attacking a coastal town in Maryland.

He had successfully convinced the British governor General in Nassau to let him join the colonial marines. He knows the area well and can guide the British troops through the region while helping to recruit blacks. But unknown to him, Jabu and MaKuei are part of another regiment attacking from the east. The British are using this attack as a ruse to draw the U.S. army away from Washington DC.

Another battalion of Britons and Canadians wait for the U.S. army to leave the capital to reinforce their comrades in Maryland. The ruse works, and the U.S. army leaves the U.S. capital undefended. When the East and West British regiments join, Jabu spots Mathew and wants to shoot him. But MaKuei stops him.

"I have a plan worse than death for him."

The battle between the British corps of colonial marines intensifies as the fresh American units from DC join their weary embattled comrades in Maryland. Then as planned, the bugle sounds for the British troops to retreat. There is pandemonium in the town — everyone is running in different directions. The British set buildings on fire as they leave town. Jabu and MaKuei corner Mathew and drag him into an empty house. They cut his Achilles tendon in one leg and drag him out as though saving a wounded comrade. He is sandwiched between MaKuei and Jabu.

Jabu presses a knife unto Mathew's side, just enough to inflict pain but not draw blood.

"Scream for help, and I will plunge this knife into your lower abdomen," says Jabu.

"The knife will not kill you immediately, but the acid in your stomach will seep out and burn you from within. You will die a slow and agonizing death if you don't cooperate," MaKuei says.

The hatred in his eyes is glaring.

"Have mercy on me," Mathew begs.

"As you had mercy on others?" MaKuei kicks the cut tendon.

Jabu and MaKuei lag behind the retreating British troops as they cross a wide meadow, they can see the Americans a couple of thousand feet behind them. They turn around and shoot at the Americans knowing they are beyond the effective range of their guns. It's to inform the Americans that they are armed and willing to kill.

The Americans shoot back, and they drop Mathew and run, leaving him in full British uniform and an empty musket for the advancing American troops to capture. The Americans are not merciful to turncoats, especially black ones that have demonstrated a willingness to kill white men.

Historical backdrop:

On May 18th, 1814, the Blue Jackets made their combat debut in Pungoteague Creek's raid and their second mission in Rumley's Gut, where they captured an American artillery battery. Subsequent actions include the Chesapeake campaign, Calverton, Huntingtown, Prince Frederick, Benedict, and lower Marlborough. On July 19, they were joined by a battalion of Royal Marines from Bermuda and, on August 19, accompanied by recent arrivals —seasoned Veteran units of the Peninsular war with Napoleon. They joined in the attacks on Bladensburg and Washington DC, where the president fled, and they burnt down the city in retaliation for U.S. burning of the Canadian capital York, (later renamed Toronto in 1834).

July 19, 1814, a battalion of Royal Marines arrives from Bermuda and enables them to make further incursions into American territory and liberating many slaves until Ghent's peace treaty on December 24th, 1814. Four groups fought in the war – Blacks, Indians, Britain, and the US. Only two were represented at the treaty negotiations. No Indians and no blacks. The Treaty of Ghent restored all original borders. The return of Florida to Spain though not present at the meeting, but made no provision for the creation of a Native American territory between present day Ohio and Wisconsin. Tecumseh and his people fought and died for nothing, and their stories remain untold in history class. In the U.S., the story is told as a second victory over Britain's attempt to recolonize them. Their failed attempt on Fort McHenry immortalized in the verses of the National Anthem – The Star-Spangled Banner.

Greg Jr. and Macati's group separate from their unit and head to the Jackson plantation under Greg's direction, for he knows the terrain. They run into a Wagombe man and his family on their way there. The Wagombe man recognizes Macati and informs him that Awat and the children are already in a British camp in the Chesapeake. His wife was on another plantation; otherwise, he would also have been with Awat and the other Wagombe from Jackson's farm.

Macati and his crew turn around and head to the British on the coast. The Wagombe and his family double up on the soldiers' horses.

Chapter Thirty-Three

Two Sides Three Missions

In war, you don't only strike enemy military installations or forces; you also destroy their ability to produce, cripple their economy and obliterate their food supply. An impoverished enemy lacks the funds to finance his fight against you. Hunger weakens them and exposes the enemy to disease. Soon your enemy's leaders face many perils from within — weapon shortages, sickness and hunger cause desertion within the ranks and possible mutiny, splintering the enemy's forces into factions in their struggle for limited supplies.

Internal strife and suffering worsen as the war drags on, this ushers disaffection to the leadership and its cause.

The British destroy both military and economic targets. September 12, 1814, about nineteen British warships approach the Baltimore harbor. The port of Baltimore Maryland provided much economic value to the U.S. economy and a haven for American privateers that had raided British shipping.

While the battleships take up the formation, landing troops led by Major General Robert Ross and Rear Admiral Cockburn – who implemented Cochran's order to incorporate American slaves into the second corps of Royal Marines – face the off Baltimore City Brigade at the battle of North Point. Amongst the Royal Marines are Macati and a dozen Kapora pirates who enlisted into the British ranks in Bermuda.

In the battle of North Point, there are two sides and three missions. On the British side the mission is to attack the Port City of Baltimore and capture or destroy Fort McHenry. On the American side the mission is to defend the city of Baltimore and buy time for reinforcements to be built into Fort McHenry. On Macati's side, though fighting on the British side he has his own personal mission: to use the attack on Baltimore as a ruse to rescue Awat and his people before the fall of Fort McHenry.

They meet several former slaves from the Jackson plantation along the way who inform them that old man Greg was at a British recruitment camp by the river. Awat and several women and children are there awaiting orders to relocate after the Baltimore Harbor's planned capture.

The results of the plans of men, no matter how well laid, are ultimately determined by God. Although the Americans retreated from battle – a technical win for the British – the British objective of capturing the city and the fort remain unrealized. Major General Ross' death from an American sniper's bullet causes demoralization of the British troops, and they scatter into the nearby swamps and forests.

The scattering was a perfect cover for Macati and his gang to gallop to the recruitment center to save Greg's parents, Awat and the others.

He and his men arrive at the recruitment camp at dusk, amid torrents of rain. The camp looks deserted. Tent doors flap in the wind. The grounds are muddy, and there is not a human in sight, just the sound of thunder and howling winds. He walks cautiously through the camp, looking into buildings and peering into tents — still there is no one.

He gets desperate; throwing caution to the wind, he fires a shot into the air. The gunshot will notify anyone around that there are armed men in the area. In one of the buildings, a man hears the shot and reaches for a musket. He drags himself to a table with great pain in his left leg and lays the table on its side, facing the front door. Behind him is an open door to the kitchen in case he must make a hasty retreat. The man rests the musket's barrel on the table and takes a kneeling position with his weight on the good leg.

Whoever comes through this door will meet hot death.

There is an elderly woman with him. She stands behind thee kitchen wall. Her eyes are open wide in fear, and her face pours down sweat as her lips move in silent and fervent prayer.

Macati's walk from one building to the next turns to a trot and he gradually picks up speed. He is running at full speed, from building to building and tent to tent shouting Awat's name until his voice gets hoarse. Ikwunga catches up with him as he approaches a building at the end of the muddy road and says, "She is gone. If she were here, she would have come running the moment she heard your voice."

Macati's lips begin to quiver. He drops to his knees and belts out a loud cry. His hands gather the dirt on the ground as spreads them across the ground and mourns for the love of his life. He rolls his fists into a ball with sadness and anger written on his face. Wrinkles form around his mouth as he cries. He has not cried like this since he was on the slave ship. He begins to think of the worst with little hope left.

"If God exists, He must be very wicked," he thinks to himself as his knees sink into the mud. Grief engulfs his soul. He calls their names through his tears.

"God, why did you let me live through all this, giving me false hopes only to let me down time and again with multiple disappointments? What does it profit You to cause such pain to those who worship you?" He screams at the top of his lungs.

As though in response to his question, there is a loud clap of thunder.

"Is that all You can do? Make noise and threaten us lowly like subjects with damnation? Kill me now! Isn't that the end of all Your works?" He begins to curse.

The door to the last building opens slowly. The man with the musket slings it over his shoulder and limps towards them with the aid of a stick. He walks towards Macati and Ikwunga in the rain. The elderly woman tries to pull him back, but he shrugs her off. She stays behind, peering through the window.

Chukwu Emeka, referred to by his pirate colleagues as Chuck Mike runs to them and points at the solitary figure walking towards them.

He says with a strong Ibo accent, "Look, dya iz somebody coming."

"*I don't care!*" Yells Macati.

"I have been young, I have been old, and I have never seen the righteous forsaken nor his children begging for bread," the old man with the musket says to Macati.

Chukwu Emeka raises his rifle at the man.

"Who are you?"

"Ndewo, Aha'm wu Greg," old man Greg replies in Ibo, meaning, hello, my name is Greg.

Old man Greg recognized the accent and decided to reply in Ibo, knowing that hearing one's mother tongue in a strange and hostile place changes one's demeanor instantly.

Chuck lowers his gun and steps closer to take a better look at the old man smiling at them. Macati looks up from his kneeling position and sees the strong resemblance between Greg Sr. and Greg Jr.

"Oh my God, you are wonderful," he mutters.

"*Greg! Greg!*" Chuck Mike yells.

"*Your father is here!*"

"Your son is with us," Chuck says in Ibo as he points at young Greg running down the road.

Old Greg hobbles fast towards his son. The elderly woman dashes out from her hiding place and runs to Greg Jr. almost falling a couple times. Greg runs and catches her in a hug to stop her from falling. Old man Greg laughs – I've never seen her run like that. For a moment, joy fills the air, and the heavens cry joyful tears of rain.

Greg Sr. informs Macati and his crew that he was one of the recruiters for the British. He processed MaKuei, Jabu and everyone on the Jackson plantation. He chose to stay behind and process as many people as possible as long as the British needed soldiers, and there are black folk willing to fight for liberty. He figured he would leave when the British close the camp. However, when word of Major General Ross' death reached the camp, the commander ordered a hasty evacuation. He got a leg injury while escaping the plantation, which worsened over the last couple of months due to diabetic complications. He could not keep up with the young men and women abandoning the camp, so he stayed and prayed.

In one swoop, God has answered two prayers; the reunification with his son and an opportunity to get to the British ships bombarding Fort McHenry.

"Have you seen Awat and my children?" Macati asks.

"Yes, they were here two months ago. Your son Mark looks so much like you. The young men willing to fight have been absorbed into the British military. The women and others unable to fight will head for the barges near Fort McHenry. They will board the ships during the artillery bombardment of the fort. Later they will be taken to the Royal Naval Dockyard on Ireland Island in Bermuda. They will be shipped to their various destinations like Nova Scotia, Free Town in Sierra Leone, and Princes Town Trinidad after the war."

"We have to hurry back to the ship, or we will be stuck here when they pull out."

The British had numerous successes in the Chesapeake region, and they were confident Baltimore too would fall just like Bladensburg and Fort Warburton. However, this time things would be different. Baltimore was protected by Fort McHenry — its outer works heavily reinforced. The Americans sunk several of their tall ships at the harbor entrance beyond the range of standard cannons and artillery pieces carried on enemy ships. No British ship could go beyond the sunken ships without destroying their hulls on the sunken tall ships' masts.

The Americans in the fort do not know that the HMS Erebus vessel has the latest and deadliest weapon known to man at the time: Congreve rockets — a precursor to the modern-day missile. Hundreds can be fired at a time. They leave a fiery red trail in their wake as they leave their rocket launchers, similar to modern-day fireworks. They travel greater distances than artillery shells of the day and will explode in the air spreading shrapnel, death, and fire upon the enemy below. They inflicted heavy casualties on Napoleonic forces. The American military fell to their power in the battle of Bladensburg, The US Army ran from them in the battle of Fort Warburton and now the thousand men in Fort McHenry are about to receive a baptism of fire from these rockets.

The Americans in the fort hunker down in reinforced bunkers as bombs explode overhead. The flag flying overhead is tattered from flaming shrapnel from the Congreve rockets. Watching the barrage is an American attorney Francis Scott Key. He had come on board the Tonnant to negotiate the release of American POW Dr. Dean.

After the negotiations, the British wouldn't let him return immediately lest he provides the Americans with information about their fleet positions and troop movement. He was brought onboard the HMS Tonnant as a guest to three British officers until the bombardment is over. From the HMS Tonnant, Francis Scott Key watches in horror as the fiery trails of hundreds of Congreve rockets launched off the British ships explode on, over and around Fort McHenry. He wonders if anyone would survive such a barrage.

His hosts also watch the bombardment, eagerly awaiting word of an American surrender. But none came from the fort. The British intensified the attack through the night to break the American resistance. They pray to God for victory and punishment for those who attacked them at their most vulnerable moment.

Hundreds of Americans hunker down in a desperate effort to hold the fort, believing they are fighting a second war of independence and liberty. They too pray to God for victory over their former overlords who've come to re-colonize them.

Hundreds of slaves run through the night towards the British ships in a desperate race for true liberty. If the British pull out of the area, they will spend the rest of their living years as slaves in America.

Let not the bombardment end until we have gotten on the ship.

They pray.

Old man Greg, Macati and hundreds of slaves run and pray to God for liberty and the destruction of their oppressors. All the three sides offer up fervent prayers to the same God for victory and the other's punishment. However, God had plans of His own.

Several hours later, there is no word of surrender.

At dawn, Major George Armistead orders the lowering of the tattered flag and raising of larger ones to fly over the Fort, as though to taunt the British saying, “I'm still standing despite your best shot.”

Cheers of joy rise from the battered Fort. They suffered only five casualties out of a thousand people in the Fort — a woman, cut in half by a bomb, three white men, and one black soldier – Private William Williams; an escaped slave who chose to fight for the United States instead of joining the British who offered freedom. His story remains untold in American History class.

The sight of the rising flag inspires Keys to write the poem: Defense of McHenry. A line from the poem “Star-Spangled banner” describes the awe-inspiring event and would later be applied to the tune of “To Anacreon in Heaven” — the official song of the Anacreontic Society. This song would become the U.S. National Anthem.

Up until this point, the young nation did not have an official anthem.

The British suffered one casualty, but Macati, Greg, and their company sustained no casualties and board a Bermuda sloop shortly before the British decide to withdraw. The escaped slaves on the British ships and the Americans in the Fort send prayers of thanks up to God for answering their prayers.

Chapter Thirty-Four

Schadenfreude

Joy that comes from witnessing the misfortune of another.

The Spanish leadership was reeling from American expansion into their North American colony of Florida. However, they lacked the manpower to garrison their territory. The war between the U.S. and Britain was as welcoming as watching the neighborhood bully fighting with another bully from the next street. As payback for the things your bully neighbor forcibly seized from you last week, you discreetly assist the other bully. The U.S. had recently annexed the Mobile district of Spanish West Florida and included it into the Mississippi U.S. territory. This territory would become two states Mississippi and Alabama, with Mobile on the Alabama side, thereby reducing the Spanish colony to the current borders of Florida State.

Spain permitted the British free passage of their troops through their territories and built a fort in the Apalachicola River region of Florida where they armed and trained Seminole Indians and runaway slaves from the American plantations from Georgia and South Carolina.

The fort was under the command of a black officer Garson and a Choctaw chief. Members of the 2nd Colonial Marines and Seminole Indians conducted raids into U.S. southern territory in the war of 1812 while the British, Canadians and blue jackets attacked the north; this forced the already overstretched U.S. army to fight on two fronts while crippling its economy that was dependent on slave labor.

Soon, word of the Negro fort spreads rapidly across the southern states of the U.S. Calls for its immediate destruction came from plantation owners across the south.

Benjamin Hawkins, a planter and U.S. political leader, sent two hundred armed men to take the fort and were defeated. This emboldened slaves in the southern states to flee to the Negro Fort in Spanish Florida. This frightened plantation owners in the American south and annoyed the plantation owners in the Spanish colony of Florida, who initially welcomed the Fort as a deterrent to American annexation of their colony but didn't anticipate their own slaves running off to this fort to be armed and trained by the black British Royal Marines. Garcon was all too happy to enroll runaways into his ranks regardless of who they ran from, whether American or Spanish slave holders.

Amongst those who heard of the Hawkins defeat at the Negro fort was Frank, the big Wolof commander who was sold to Mr. Tucker — the Rice plantation owner in South Carolina — after several attempts to escape from the Jackson plantation.

Life on the rice plantation is worse than on a cotton plantation. The death rate in a rice plantation averages sixty-six percent. If the southern heat does not get you, snakes in the rice marshes would. If you escaped the snakes, sickness-bearing insects would get you. In some rice plantations, the death rate is known to go up to ninety percent.

Sunday is the only day of rest on the plantation.

The master goes to his high society church, and a preacher comes to the plantation to preach a variant of the same five messages of; one, turn the other cheek when they slap you; two, pray for those who persecute you; three, love your enemies; four, obey your master as unto the Lord; and five, the more you suffer on earth, the greater your reward in heaven, after you die.

This Sunday, Frank feigns sickness, so no one disturbs his sleep. The foreman would rather have him rested and recovered than too sick or dead to work on Monday. Frank is strong as an ox and works hard to bring the master much profit. Previous failed attempts to escape have taught him to plan and speak nothing of his plans to anyone.

Today, he feigns sickness to conserve energy for tonight.

Darkness falls, and Frank sneaks out of the cottage, runs to the edge of the plantation and pulls out a bag of supplies he has been gathering over the past four weeks. He runs through the night heading south. By the time the master discovers he has run away, he should be several miles gone. With a stolen machete from the plantation, he fashions a bow and arrows made of sharpened sticks and hardened by fire he started with flint rocks.

He travels for several days living on wild berries and game he hunted with his arrows, finally arriving at the Negro Fort in August 1814.

Here, he joins the 800 runaways living around the Fort, where the British had recruited Seminole Indians to curb American expansion into Spanish territory. The British would typically support any group opposed to American expansion — Indians, Spaniards, Blacks — it didn't matter. Three hundred former members of the 3rd battalion colonial marines, thirty Seminole and Choctaw Indians occupied the Fort equipped with three artillery pieces, a thousand muskets, and ammunition.

The land around the Fort is fertile and suitable for planting. Frank sets about building a small house and a farm to sustain himself. It is hard work; something he is not afraid of, but this time he is working hard for himself. Occasionally he goes hunting for food with the Seminole Indians.

The war between the U.S. and Britain comes to a standstill, and they sign a peace treaty (Ghent's). The British leave behind the 3rd battalion colonial marines' members in the Negro Fort to fend for themselves. They figure that they would help curb American expansion beyond its current size for it's always been Britain's goal to keep the U.S. small.

With the war over, the U.S. could now focus its energy on the southern threat. Andrew Jackson informed the Spanish governor of West Florida José Masot, that if the Spanish do not eliminate the Negro Fort, he would. José responds, saying he doesn't have the troops to take the Fort, so Jackson orders Edmund P. Gaines to attack and destroy the Fort.

Frank is out fishing at dawn; he shows his new Seminole Indian friends the Wolof people's fishing methods using a large net he made and two canoes. The Indians are impressed with the number of fish caught by the net compared to the single catch you get with a fishing spear or hook. While in the river, they notice American gunboats sailing in their direction. They paddle to the bank and run into the Fort to inform Garson. They hatch a plan to defeat the Americans.

Frank goes to a sandbar on the river and makes himself visible to the approaching boats. The Americans see a lone black man on a sand bar and decide to capture and force him to can tell them about the inner workings of the Negro Fort. The gunboat lowers its lifeboat full of soldiers, and it heads to the sandbar.

The trap is sprung, and the cannons in the Fort open fire. The Colonial Marines and Seminole Indians open fire from the riverbanks.

Frank dives off the sandbar and swims over to the side. The lifeboat is sunk, and all soldiers in it are killed. The gunboat pulls back, realizing that they cannot take the Negro Fort.

A second attempt on the Fort is made in July.

Being aware of previous failed attempts, Gaines induces Creek Indians from Coweta to join the attack by promising that they can keep whatever they salvage if they help capture the Fort. The Creek Indians were at war with each other, and a cache of weapons would ensure the victory of the Coweta Creek Indians over their Seminole Creek brothers, and so begins the first Seminole war.

In a war where chickens fight themselves, victory belongs to the cobra who joins the fight for he will eat his enemy for breakfast and allies for lunch. The Coweta Creek Indians and the Seminoles Creek

Indians have had skirmishes up until recently. Now the Coweta have a new ally in the Americans — at least for now.

On July 18, a U.S. Navy Gunboat pulls up quietly at the river. The Fort spots them, and fires its cannons at them, and the battle begins. The Navy boats fire five to nine shots to test the range before firing hot balls — a cannonball heated up until it glows orange. The first hot ball is loaded on U.S. Navy Gunboat 154, and they aim high. It's a long shot expected to set whatever it hits ablaze so they can determine from the smoke where it landed and how to adjust fire for the subsequent volley.

The hotshot flies high, missing its mark, then hits a tall cypress tree and bounces off into the fortress, hitting its powder magazine, setting off a massive explosion that is listed as the deadliest single cannon shot in U.S. history.

Almost all the occupants in the Fort were killed or wounded. The blast threw body parts into branches of nearby cypress trees. Soldiers on the boat stormed off the boat, killing off and capturing survivors. Several residents around the Fort escape, running south when the fight began. Survivors within the Fort are captured. Amongst the survivors are Frank, Garcon and the Choctaw Chief. Frank is returned to Tucker, the rice plantation owner. Those who ran at the onset of battle escape head further south into the Florida Peninsula and then to Bahamas where they form a new settlement on the east coast of Andros to get away from the Americans and Spaniards in Florida.

Garcon is killed by firing squad for the earlier defeat. The Choctaw Chief is handed over to the Coweta Creeks Indians. They kill and scalp him.

The Coweta also gain whatever weapons they can salvage from the Fort. Today, the cobra eats his enemy for breakfast. Tomorrow, it will attack its ally the Coweta, swallow up their best land and confine the survivors to reservations. The Spaniards too, will lose the colony of Florida to the United States. History is retold by the victor to vilify the vanquished.

Chapter Thirty-Five

Reunification In Bermuda

Old man Greg is happy to have escaped from the U.S. He and several injured soldiers are taken to the Royal Naval Dockyard in Bermuda for treatment. Young Greg assists him to the sickbay of the naval station when they run into crazy Daisy. She is in a nurse's uniform. She sets elderly Greg up in a bed and starts treating him immediately. A young girl assists Daisy and Greg Sr. recognizes her.

"Hali, where is your mother? Your father is here looking for all of you." He blurts out.

Greg Jr. looks at his father, wondering how they know each other.

"Hali is Macati's twin daughter who was born on the plantation. Hali is Americanized Halima, named after her grandmother, Halima. She has developed an interest in healing and volunteered to assist in the sickbay. Her brother cannot be called Macati — his African name, so they call him Mark. They came over with the British and stayed in Bermuda temporarily before the freed slaves were shipped back to Africa or Trinidad as free landowners."

Greg Sr. explains to his son, as he struggles to get off his bed.

"Where are you going?" Daisy demands.

"To find Macati." He insists.

"You are in no condition to run around the island looking for him. I have to treat your leg." Daisy refuses.

"The leg can wait." He sighs, resisting treatment.

"No, it can't. It's gotten so bad from infection. If the doctor sees it, he will amputate it. I can reverse it, so it's salvageable."

"What of their family reunification? It's important," says old Greg.

"I know how important it is; I just got reunited with my children. Let Hali call her mother, and young Greg will bring Macati here."

She turns to Greg Jr. as she speaks. Greg Jr. looks at his father, and Greg Sr. nods. Young Greg runs off.

"You said you reunited with your children?"

Greg asks with a smile.

"I knew the plantation Ellen sold them to. When news of the British approaching Virginia spread, we went with old man Huggins with a gun stolen from the Jackson big house. See, Ellen had sold some of his granddaughters to the same planter when she sold my children. She noticed that Mr. Jackson had been giving the Huggins girls preferential treatment due to the installment agreement between him and old man Huggins. However, Ellen, in her insecurity, thought the Huggins girls were having an affair with her husband."

"They just let you take the gun?"

"Comatose people can't stop anyone. I had the house slaves knock out the entire family with a potion I made."

Greg Sr. gives her a strange look.

"Don't look at me like that. I could have killed them, but I didn't. For years I turned the other cheek while they slapped. For years I took insults and beatings, forced to smile outside while I cried within. The dual life of suffering and smiling will drive anybody mad. All the while I was praying and hoping that God would deliver me, but nothing changed. I soon realized that there were only two ways out — death or insanity. So, I put on the crazy act convincing everyone that I've slipped into an alternate place where I was far from the harsh realities of life. That was when they put me out to pasture as they do to insane, elderly and handicapped slaves that can no longer produce wealth for the master. And one day it occurred to me as I prayed. For the first time, I actually sat and waited for an answer, not just shouting and crying my problems to God.

"What did he say?" He asks.

"I demanded to know why He let all these wicked things happen to me."

"What did he say?"

"He said it's not just you asking this question; many others asking the same question, and My answer to you is the same I gave to others."

"What is the answer? I've asked the same question myself."

The tone in old man Greg's voice reveals anticipation and impatience. A divergence from the usual calm and stable tone he usually speaks.

"He said that he gave man the earth to have dominion and take care of. We are the custodians. We choose to make a mess of things, and we say it's His responsibility. God said, let us make man in our image, after our likeness: and let them have dominion over the fish of the sea, and over the fowl of the air, and the cattle, and overall, the earth, and over every creeping thing that creepeth upon the earth."

"But didn't that end with the disobedience of Adam?"

Old man Greg asks.

"No," Daisy replies.

"He did not take away Adam's mandate; He cursed the earth stating that man will work hard before it yields its fruit, but He did not take away our mandate — free will, or the ability to do things for ourselves; He gave us the wherewithal. It's up to us to use it, and He will bless the fruit of our labor. So, I decided to stop waiting for Him to do something about my situation and got up to do it for myself, and He will bless my effort. The days of manna falling from heaven are long gone."

"He did deliver you in the end," old man Greg smiles, returning to his usual paternal nature.

"Hmph. I had to take matters into my own hands. Old man Huggins and I got there and noticed that the white folks had abandoned the plantation. Finding his grandkids and my children was easy. We told the other folk on the plantation to run away with us." She adds.

"You must have liberated a hundred people," old man Greg says, excitedly.

"No," only a handful followed us.

"Many stayed right there."

"Why?" Old Greg is shocked.

"I don't know, it makes no sense, yet people call me crazy. Why would enslaved and oppressed people see an open door to escape and not run through it? Some people love their chains, I guess. They don't mind complaining about their oppressed state, but when the opportunity for liberty presents itself, they are scared to seize it. So, we left with our kids and a handful of people to Saint Augustine on the Atlantic coast. That's where I volunteered as a nurse. Then they shipped me here after the war."

Awat comes running into the sickbay.

"Where is he? Macati, Macati, where is he?" She is almost in tears.

"Good morning to you too," says Greg Sr. in his usual self-assured tone.

"Pardon my manners. Hali said Macati is here," says Awat, almost hyperventilating.

"Yes, he is. He and his men rescued me from the deserted recruitment camp and brought me here. I don't think he knows you are here. He's with the Colonial Marines stationed by the Navy Dockyards."

"I'm going over there." She jumps.

"The dockyard is big, and there are thousands of soldiers and sailors over there. It's easy to get lost or even raped by drunken soldiers and sailors that have not seen a woman in a long time…"

Old man Greg's voice trails off as he observes two people approaching — one has a blue jacket on.

Awat turns to see who it is, her heart racing in the hope that it's Macati and Greg Jr.

"I heard you made it," says Huggins, beaming from ear to ear at his old comrade in arms.

"It's even better than that; I reunited with Greg Jr.," Greg smiles.

"We just ran into him outside. The last person I expected to see is a blue jacket. I heard from Forbes that he made it to Africa and back. I need to speak with him before I decide to return to Africa with my family or to settle in Trinidad." Huggins mentions.

"Yes, he escaped but was resold into slavery by other Africans, enemies of his host."

Huggins turns to Forbes. You could hear his thoughts screaming out loud.

Forbes verbalizes the thought.

"So, they still sell people over there?"

"Yes", Greg replies with a tone of disappointment.

"That's it," says, Huggins. My family and I are going to Trinidad!"

"Me too," says Forbes.

"I'm not taking any chances of losing my hard-earned freedom; I suggest you do the same," he glances at old man Greg.

"I know my tribe in Africa. We are old. Mama Greg and I would like to die and be buried at home," he reaches for Mama Greg's hand to reassure her.

She pulls her hand back, speaking for the first time.

"I plan not to die anytime soon. We don't know if our village still exists or the current environment there. Should we spend the rest of our lives in fear of recapture?" She asks.

"Have you changed your mind?" Greg turns to her.

There's shock in his voice.

"I agreed with you before the Prince Town Trinidad and Nova Scotia options became available. Back then, it was a choice between Free Town Sierra Leone and Nova Scotia. I don't like the cold, so Free Town was more appealing. Prince Town Trinidad is warm like Africa without roaming Pombeiros, and we will be under British protection plus, our young men in the Colonial Marines will be allowed to keep their weapons; we will be among friends and people who have a common history with us…" She eyes old man Huggins.

"We should reconsider."

Old man Huggins notices the disappointment spread across old man Greg's face.

"I think we should leave you two to talk this over."

He looks at Mama Greg as he says the next statement.

"I sure do hope to be your neighbor in Prince Town."

Then he tugs Forbes and says, "We need to talk to our families about this.

"Let's leave them to decide." He says, before they disappear.

That night, newly liberated African Americans gathered in small groups to make similar decisions; go to Free town in Sierra Leone, West Africa, or Prince Town in Trinidad.

It is a long night of tough decisions on the Island.

Do you return to Africa and risk hostility from the locals, re-enslavement, or even death from those enemies who sold you in the first place, now in prominent positions with the wealth and power to do with you as they please?

Many Pombeiros used their wealth to buy their way into prominence. From their prominent position in society, they now sell people and resources to Europeans for personal gain. It's a parasitic arrangement where the European in turn, provide weapons to the new Pombeiros to secure his position as chief in a retrogressing society.

Think of the modern drug lord holding unto his blighted section of town with guns he does not produce, flooding it with drugs he did not manufacture or import. He has money, women, and all the outer trappings of success. However, he creates no real jobs or business to develop his community — just minions working for his personal profit, each one of them hoping one day to topple him and become the new neighborhood drug lord. That's the same principle with the Pombeiros. He sells out his people in return for luxury goods and outer trappings of success. His minions justle amongst themselves until they have an opportunity to topple Chief Pombeiros and install themselves as new chief, thus bringing constant warfare and retrogression to the community. Nothing prospers on turbulent land, only misery.

The demise of the first settlement of returnees in West Africa after Chief Toms death also caused concern amongst the newly liberated.

Will they, too, suffer the same fate?

Another option was Nova Scotia — part of the British Empire but cold. The third option was the southern Trinidad.

Huggins, Forbes, and several others would choose Trinidad.

They would establish independent communities headed by their platoon leaders in southern Trinidad. They will be known as the *Merikins* — derived from the mispronunciation of Americans.

Streets to the various settlements are named after the companies they fought under, like the first company, and the third company through the fifth company. Some of the Merikins include William Richardson, Samuel Webb, Amphy & Bashana Jackson, John Milton Hawkshaw, Arthur Sampson, William Hamilton, and George Elliot.

George Elliot was a first generation Yoruba, son of an Orisha priest who chose not to return to Yoruba land because the Yoruba kingdoms were at war with each other and Dahomey. The risk of capture, death, or re-enslavement was high.

Some from the Elliot plantation chose to return to Africa. Today you have Eliots in Trinidad and Yorubaland West Africa.

Augustus Lewis chose Trinidad while some Lewis family members chose to go to Africa instead and reintegrated into the Yoruba community. The Black Americans who returned to Africa and reintegrated with the Yoruba tribe will be called *Saro-Yorubas.*

Chapter Thirty-Six

Where Is Macati?

At the Royal Dockyards Greg Jr. sights Ikwunga at a distance and rushes up to him.

"Ikwunga, where is Macati? His wife and children are here," Ikwunga turns and recognizes Awat speeding up with Greg. His eyes swell up with tears as he runs to her. He hugs her, then sweeps up the children, hugging them tightly as he speaks.

"Uncle!" They smile, looking at him.

He was just like how they had imagined. Awat hadn't missed an opportunity to teach them about her in-laws. Ikwunga couldn't believe how grown they were, and how much they looked like Macati.

"My sister!" He breathes out in relief, glad to see she was well.

"Thank God you're ok." She wipes the tears on his face.

Greg gives them space, as they share words after years of being separated and broken apart. But they don't have much time.

"Young man, where is Macati?" Greg repeats himself.

"He and Captain Armstrong put on their best uniforms and went to the Sinclair mansion. Lord Sinclair is the head of the chamber of commerce, is having a ball for his Majesty's service officers. All the rich folk on the island will be at the ball." He explains.

"So why is Macati going?" Awat asks.

"He is pretending to be Armstrong's aide decamp. They want to meet with a senior British officer and purchase weapons from him with the booty we've saved from our pirate raids. We will go back and regain the throne of Kapora. The officer will claim that the weapons are being shipped to Fort Gadsden, the Negro Fort."

Awat cuts in.

"Which way to the mansion?"

"It's no use. The red coats at the gate won't let you in without an invitation."

Ikwunga notices Awat's countenance fall and quickly adds, "We can wait outside the mansion gate until he comes out."

"It's been years since I saw him; we can wait a few hours," says Awat, desperate to see the love of her life.

"Yes, yes, we have a lot to catch up on while waiting," Ikwunga reaches for the children.

"Oya lets go."

Across town, Macati walks through the imposing brass doors to the grand ballroom of Lord Sinclair's mansion. This hall is built for royalty; he thinks to himself as he takes in every detail of its magnificent splendor. His eyes are drawn up to the gilded ceiling centered above the inlaid marble floor. At the center of the gold leaf honeycombed design, sits a 3000 square foot-stained glass ceiling and regal granite walls.

Corinthian marble columns adorn each end of the hall's oval. Armstrong nudges him. The nudge brings Macati back to the present.

Macati notices their guide, Squire, the Governor General's assistant walking towards a British colonel in a dashing red uniform adorned with medals. Macati rushes to keep up.

It takes one to know one, Macati thinks to himself.

Squire is the corrupt official who took the governors share of the booty each time they do their privateering runs in the Bahamas. He is now the Bermuda Governor General's special assistant.

Macati doubts how much of it the governor gets and how much the man keeps for himself.

Today, Squire's unscrupulousness will work for us.

Armstrong is suddenly self-conscious of his captain's uniform as he walks up to the colonel to be introduced by Squire, who invited them to the ball. Armstrong, a descendant of coal miners, has never been to this type of event in his life. He observes Squire and mimics him, for he knows not how to act in such a grand setting.

In Britain, not every white man is of equal standing. Coal miners and their families were bound to the colliery in which they worked and forever in the service of its owner — usually titled men of a similar pedigree with the officers in this ballroom with whom he is trying to rub shoulders with; this bondage was set into law by an act of parliament in 1606. It stated that no person should free or hire salters, colliers, or coal bearers without written authority from the master they had last served. His former master could reclaim a collier lacking such written authority.

Though abolished in 1775, the Armstrong's, like most colliers, remained in the mines for several generations as they had no skillsets, education, or any place else to go. Captain Armstrong broke out of the familiar to seek his fortune in the high seas and the British colonies at the young age of sixteen. Life out there cannot be any worse than in the coal mines, he figured. Though he had risen through the ranks, made a fortune, and owns a fleet of ships, he is nervous if he can fit in with the British blue-blooded pedigrees in this room.

Armstrong loathes them for their privileged head start in life, yet he longs to become one of them because life as an "English Gentleman" has its privileges. Out in the colonies is the only place he can mix with their kind. In London, they won't look at him twice – despite his newfound wealth. He put on his best clothes to maximize this opportunity and make a good impression and hopefully establish contacts that would introduce him to London's high society when he returns to Britain as a wealthy man with vast enterprises across the British empire, a new man undefined by his humble beginnings.

Captain Armstrong also knows that most pirates' end is death at sea or the gallows when caught. Neither feels appealing to him. The end of the war with America will bring the rescinding of the letters of Marquee that legitimized his activities on the high seas.

To the white pirates, life as a merchant marine does not pay enough, and to the black ones, life as a slave is even worse, so with the option of growing old and grey removed, most pirates live a life of pleasure, rum, and women today, for tomorrow could be your last.

Armstrong and most of his crew are different.

They all plan to reenter civil society as wealthy men.

The black ones are enlisted in the Royal Marines, so they too can reenter society as rich free men or return to Africa with prominent positions in Macati's government when he regains the throne.

At the moment, the British authorities have not labeled Armstrong a pirate. While Squire suspects Captain Armstrong plays on both sides of the law, Squire will keep his peace if Armstrong breaks him off a piece of the loot. Armstrong figures that if he helps Macati regain the throne, he can do legitimate business with the Kapora empire, trading gold, ivory, cotton, cocoa, sugar, and palm oil. That's a lot safer, more respectable, and much more profitable than piracy.

"I'd like to introduce you to Colonel Crowley," says Squire in a squeaky voice.

Armstrong steps forward to shake the Colonel's hand, speaking in his best English accent.

"How do you do?"

Colonel Crowley takes the hand as though to shake it and then turns it to the side, glancing at Armstrong's fingernails.

They are long with dirt under them.

"Jock," Crowley mutters under his breath, loud enough for Armstrong to hear.

Squire notices a flash of anger in Armstrong's eyes on hearing the derogatory term.

"Come now, come now," he says.

"There's no need for that; we are here to discuss a profitable enterprise for all of us."

Crawley waves his hand dismissively at Armstrong and Macati. "What profit could they possibly bring me, Jock and the chimp?"

"Gold! Bags of gold like I told you yesterday" Squire glares at him. If eyes could speak, Squires eyes would scream.

Don't mess it up, arrogant snob!

"Them? Give me gold?" Crawley sneers.

Macati opens the bag in his hand, revealing the shiny metal in a flash, then shuts it from peering eyes.

"Let's talk then," Crowley smiles.

"Not here," says Squire.

"I will ask our host for a room, so we discuss like gentlemen."

Crowley gives him a bum stare. Squire hesitates, expecting a nod of agreement from Crowley.

"Very well then, run along, get on, chop-chop," says Crowley clapping his hands, then abruptly turns to walk away.

Squire turns white in shock.

"Where are you going?"

"They will soon blow the trumpet for the dance to start; there's a young lady I'd like to dance with before we talk. I'm sure you would have gotten a room by then. You wouldn't be joining the dance, would you Jock?" Crawley directs the question to Armstrong.

"I will go with him," Armstrong points in Squire's direction with a smile, trying hard to hide his disdain for Crowley.

"Jock" is a derogatory term the English use for Scotts. Crowley is using it to throw Armstrong off balance — an intimidation technique he uses when negotiating with those he deems lower than himself.

Throw the other negotiator off balance by putting them in a defensive position with an accusation or highlighting their imperfections. No battle is won by defense alone, and it is difficult to plan an effective counteroffensive while harried on the run.

The same principles apply when negotiating with Crowley. His victim is eager to escape the personal attacks and will quickly settle for less just to get away in one piece. While that strategy works well on many, it ignites the street fighter in people like Armstrong.

Squire knows Armstrong is no wimp. Crowley's insolence might blow the whole deal apart; he fears.

It is in the ballroom that British high society put on their best behavior. Everything is regulated according to the strictest code of "good-breeding." Any departure from this code became a grave offense. It was imperative that the ballroom's etiquette and its false pretenses were well mastered by the well-bred. Something Armstrong was not used to. It dawns on him that he has a lot to learn if he's to ever get into the London high society. He does not know how to waltz, hold his cutlery properly or make small talk.

"It will please me to watch you waltz Colonel," he responds with the fakest cheery face he has ever put on, hiding his true feelings.

"I've met better players than you Crowley, I got something special for you, snob." Armstrong thinks to himself.

Squire motions to Armstrong to walk with him to the host's smoke room. As they get out of earshot, Squire says, "Never mind him; it's a hollow show to put you down, so he feels important."

"Will he deliver the weapons?" Macati asks.

Squire knows that Armstrong has the same concerns. He needs to reassure them lest they walk away with their gold, and he loses his commission. Squire had arranged a ten percent cut with Armstrong and another ten percent cut with Crowley unbeknown to both men.

Initially, Crowley refused the terms, and Squire informed him that if he did not sell the weapons to Armstrong, someone else would sell them and claim that the weapons were used or destroyed in battle. Squire wants to squirrel something away for his retirement from his Majesty's civil service in the colonies.

"That's all a show," Squire repeats himself, then goes further to convince them that Crowley needs the gold more than they need the weapons.

"The house of Crowley is impoverished nobility living on past glories," he explains.

"They once owned sugar plantations and rum distilleries in Jamaica. All that got destroyed by Cudjoe Town maroons (Also known as Trelawney town Maroons in some historical texts) during the second maroon war."

They head up the stairs to the second floor, and Squire tells the story of Crowley's fall.

Historical backdrop:

Historical details and translations in brackets are included for the benefit of the non-African and non-Jamaican readers.

Nanny (an Ashanti princess), Acheampong (one that gives birth to kings – mispronounced as Aconpong by Jamaicans), Cudjoe (Jamaican mispronunciation of the Ashanti name Kojo meaning born on Monday) Johnny and Quao were born into an Ashanti royal family in West Africa. During an intertribal war, they were captured and sold into slavery to work plantations in Saint James Parish and Trelawney in Jamaica while it was still a Spanish colony. They escaped the plantations and ran into the Blue Mountains, then found their own maroon communities. Nanny and Quao founded Nanny town, Acheampong founded Acconpong town, and Cudjoe founded Cudjoe's town, also known as Trelawney Town in St James Parish. From their strongholds in the mountains, they freed many slaves in the surrounding plantations.

There were several attempts by the Spaniards to overrun them failed. The Spaniards gave them the name Cimarrónes from which we get the Anglicized name — maroons.

When the British came to snatch the island for themselves because it was so lucrative in sugar production, the Cimarrónes aligned with the British against the Spanish overlords in hopes of establishing a sovereign state for themselves. But soon after the British successfully kicked the Spaniards of the Island and became the dominant power in Jamaica, they replaced Spanish plantation ownership with themselves as the new overlords. Lord Crowley was one of them.

In typical British fashion, they turned on their former allies to dominate them. That is how the tiny island of England conquered the world — an ally with one group to fight another.

Postwar friendships last until they consolidate their hold on the conquered territory, then they turn on the weakened former ally, sometimes with the remnants of the formerly defeated foe eager to feed fat on anyone who brought about their defeat. It wasn't long after Britain consolidated power in Jamaica that they turned on the Cimarrónes. The Cimarrónes, now called maroons, fight the British to a standstill, and peace treaties were made. They agree that maroons will stop attacking and pillaging plantations. Runaway slaves will be returned for a ransom, and in return, the British won't attack their communities; an agreement was honored until there was visible strife between Trelawney Town maroons (Cudjo's people) and their brothers.

When cattle stand together, the lion goes hungry. However, when they scatter, the lion attacks the furthest from the herd, so it is in the lives of a men. The one who isolates himself quickly falls prey.

The British attacked Cudjoes Town, and none of the other maroon communities came to their aid.

The second maroon war was long, fierce, and bloody. The maroons attacked English plantations, factories, and rum distilleries, removing anything they could carry and destroying what they couldn't carry. Chickens, goats, and pigs, they pillaged and would cook them over a low burning fire jerked with spices learned from the Arawak Indians and laden with pepper, for the Ashanti love pepper more than any other West African tribe. The maroons covered their cooking fires to suppress the smoke, so it doesn't attract the British or the hundred bloodhounds and their Spanish handlers imported from Cuba.

Steep-sided hollows mark the cockpit country of St James, some as deep as 390 feet and are separated by conical ridges. They launched their guerilla warfare against the British and the Cuban/Spanish allies from this rugged terrain. Under the command of rugged captains like Montague James, Leonard Parkin, and James Palmer, the maroons destroyed several English rum distilleries and plantations.

Landed gentry like the Crowley were financially ruined and faced the risk of going to debtor prison.

Outnumbered with ten English/Spaniard to one maroon and no support forthcoming from their brothers, the Trelawney Town maroons agreed to a ceasefire. The terms of the truce were the promise of repatriation to Africa. The repatriation of the Cudjoe Town maroons from Jamaica to Africa meant one less maroon community to contend with. To the Cudjoe Town maroons, it meant passage back to the motherland —an agreement the British intended to fulfill partially.

On 21 and 22 July 1796, the Dover, Mary, and Ann landed in Halifax Harbor, carrying between 550 and 600 maroon men, women, and children. This was a Canadian outpost in the North Atlantic Ocean with very long cold winters. There, the British left them, then burnt down Cudjoe Town in retaliation for the destruction meted unto the English plantations and industries.

They sold 1,500 Acres of their land then built a military barracks.

Today, maroon town stands in the same spot where Cudjoe Town once stood. The Fort the maroons built in Nova Scotia (Halifax Citadel) still stands as a tourist attraction.

George Crowley was barely ten years old when his family's fortunes were burnt to ashes in the second maroon war. He was old enough to understand and but too young to do anything about the social humiliation and emotional turmoil attached to the family's downward plunge from grace to the gutter of society. He witnessed his mother's futile attempts to keep up appearances at the occasional social function when an old friend invited her out of sympathy or felt morally compelled to invite them. Their misfortune and her desperate effort to keep appearances became the favorite subject of high society lady conversations over "tea things and crumpets." – behind her back. Somehow, word always got back to her.

George got to find out what high society thought of them the day he tried to tell the "official family lie" about why he could no longer attend elite boarding school.

He barely got out the lie about traveling to their summer villa in the northern countryside when a classmate blurted out the truth to the hearing of all his classmates — bringing forth loud laughter. Even Squire, the class runt, stood above him that day as he sprawled out on the floor red-faced with opprobrium and crying uncontrollably, an image that still runs through his mind to this day.

His father had a heart attack and died struggling to rebuild his fortunes, and his mother had a nervous breakdown from the pressures of life and shame. George was forced to live with relatives until he was old enough to join the army. Being of noble birth, having some formal education, plus the connections of the former family butler, now employed by the governor of the Royal military college got him admission to be trained as a commissioned officer. His salary as an officer is barely enough to pay for his mother's treatment and maintain the crumbling family manor — evidenced by the tattered roof and overgrown weeds in the drawing-room bereft of furniture.

"Now you know why he called you coon," Squire points at Macati. "It is obvious you are the first-generation African undiluted with white or Indian — just like the maroons who brought ruin to the Crowley Empire."

"He deserves it," says Macati with a stern look.

"I cannot tell him that," Squire replies.

"Like I said," Squire reiterates.

"It's all hollow bravado; the need to put you down to feel important. He needs your gold and will do anything to get it. Britain's arch enemies are neutralized, and the end is in sight for his career. He hopes to marry Miss Sinclair and get a huge dowry from her father, Lord Sinclair. However, it's improbable that her father would give his pretty little princess to a man of title, but little means to provide for her."

"Why do you want the weapons anyway?" Squire asks abruptly.

The quick change in topic reflects what has been on Squire's mind for some time. Armstrong fires off the pre-rehearsed script he and Macati had worked on earlier in their preparation for this meeting and possible questions that might come up.

"To resell in the black market,"

"Not piracy?" Squire probes, seeking to confirm his suspicions about Armstrong.

"No, too dangerous, especially now that the Navy is free from war and can deploy resources to combat piracy. I love life and the good things money can buy, just like you." Armstrong turns his gaze on Squire.

Squire deflects.

"Ah, here comes our host," he motions at a distinguished elderly gentleman with two young ladies on either side.

Squire struggles to remember which one is his wife, and which one is the daughter. They are both so young, and he has met the daughter only once before.

"Good evening, ladies," Squire bows down low and places his hand out front.

Armstrong and Macati imitate him. Macati and Armstrong recognize the one in blue. It's been a few years since they last saw her in the Bahamas, and she looks a lot different now.

The young lady in the light blue ball gown brushes past the one in pink and stretches out her hand, placing it in Squire's outstretched hand. On her finger is a large loose-fitting ring. On close inspection, Squire can tell it was sized for someone else.

"Lady Sinclair," she says in a loud voice to assert her position in the house.

"Of course, your ladyship," Squire responds as he kisses her hand. "And you are…" She lets the words hang.

"Mr. Squire, the special assistant to the Governor General."

The maiden in the pink ball gown cuts in quickly to establish that she knows her father's friends and is better connected on the Island than the new wife, who recently took over her mother's room.

Macati recognizes the power play between the young women immediately. It reminds him of the silent war between Nyoka and his mother. Lord Sinclair, however, is oblivious to the ongoing contest in his mansion in which he is the prize.

His daughter resents the upstart that has moved into her mother's bedroom and taken over her titles and jewelry and is now trying to force a wedge between her and her father. All her life, she has been "daddy's little princess." She is concerned that this young woman will get pregnant with a son then divert the family wealth, land, and properties to him, leaving her with nothing.

Lady Sinclair though young in years, is quite experienced in life and light years ahead of the pampered little princess in pink. She is the one who prompted Lord Sinclair to have the ball in hopes that a young British officer will sweep daddy's little girl off her feet, marry her and take her back to England, far away from Bermuda, giving her ample time and space to work on the elderly rich man.

Squire requests a private room to discuss important business. Elderly Sinclair smiles and asks, "What are you up to, Squire?"

The squeal in Squire's voice raises an octave when nervous.

"I want to introduce Captain Armstrong to one of the officers. The army needs private ships to backfill those lost in the war, so they can transport men and material back to England."

"I am certain there's a little profit in it for you," Lord Sinclair quips.

A large drop of sweat rolls down the side of Squire's face as he responds.

"No sir, nothing of the sort, my lord. I'm just doing his majesty's service."

"Good evening, Captain," Lord Sinclair beams a friendly smile at Armstrong.

"I am a shipbuilder myself," Sinclair continues.

"I have sailed some of your Bermuda sloops in the war with the United States," Armstrong responds.

"The best and fastest sloops I've ever captained. I hope to purchase one from you soon, sir."

Flattery gets you far with ego driven men, and Lord Sinclair is no exception.

"You are a man after my heart. Care to dine with me tomorrow? We can discuss your proposal further." Lord Sinclair smiles.

"I am ill-disposed tomorrow, what of the day after?"

Armstrong responds.

"Certainly! Day after tomorrow it is. Seven o'clock, shall we say?"

Sinclair smiles as Armstrong nods in agreement.

"Very well then..." He turns to Squire.

"You can use my smoke room. It has the best tobacco and rum money can buy," he points to the door at the end of the hallway.

"Don't drink it all and keep away from the sweet white rum," Lady Sinclair quips.

"I know your sort," she winks at Armstrong standing behind Squire.

"I don't drink," Squire protests, thinking the quip was directed at him.

It's only a joke Lord Sinclair chimes in, not realizing the coded message from his wife to Armstrong.

"And if you would excuse us, my little darling has to make her grand entrance at the ball.

He holds out his elbows and the two young women slip their hands in. They walk towards the curved grand staircase, where they would be announced before they walk down the stairs. First, the lord and lady of the house, then the naïve little princess in pink, will be announced. The eligible young men in the ballroom will admire her as she walks down the spiral staircase. Several will ask to fill her dance card and make their acquaintance. Every eligible bachelor knows she will bring a large dowry being the only child of Lord Sinclair.

Squire had intimated Crowley of the order of events at the party, and Crowley positioned himself at the foot of the stairway, so he would be the first man she sees.

Squire, Armstrong, and Macati bow down low as the trio leave.

Lady Sinclair lets off an eerie laugh in the distance as she watches daddy's little princess rush to take her place at the top of the curved staircase. With his head bowed down and sense of hearing sharpened by the lack of sight, her evil laugh is magnified in Armstrong's head.

Images from his last encounter with Lady Sinclair rush back to mind when she was a high-class prostitute in the Bahamas, passing herself off as the young widow of a merchant marine who died at sea, leaving her a sizeable inheritance. Hence the fancy clothes she wears to differentiate herself from cheap harlots in the bars and brothels around town. In that encounter, she got him drunk on love and sweet white rum, only to wake up the next day, heartbroken naked and poor — no clothes, gold; nothing but a bad hangover.

She knows he's a pirate and the statement about sweet white rum was a covert warning: *I know your secret, keep mine, or you will hang at the gallows.*

Chapter Thirty-Seven

The Hyena Flirts With The Hen

The Hyena flirts with the hen, the hen is happy, not knowing that her death has come.

- Ola Rotimi, *The Gods are not to blame.*

Outside the mansion gate, Awat waits anxiously with Ikwunga and her two children. Greg had to return to his parents in the sickbay. The children listen eagerly to the pirate tales and exploits of the father they have never met. Ikwunga tells them about Macati's ordeal on the slave ship and how he, Waggy, and the others escaped from the plantation and joined a Quilombo. He talks about the stowaway on Mr. Jackson's ship and how he saved Ikwunga, Greg, and other Kapora on a slave ship. Awat listens attentively to hear anything that would indicate Macati had another woman or children in Brazil or anywhere else, but non forthcoming from Ikwunga's lips.

Inside the mansion, a game of high stakes is underway. Armstrong, Squire, and Macati have secured the room for negotiating with Crowley, now they stand on the sidelines watching the military officers in their uniforms and the gentlemen in their tailcoats take their place on the dance floor. In their beautiful ball gowns, the high society ladies take their place on the opposite side of the hall, facing each other for the slow waltz — a stiff and strange dance to Macati's eyes. Everything looks scripted, choreographed, lacking spontaneity or any genuine facial expression that speaks from the heart.

Macati thinks about the first time he saw Awat, and how he caught her attention with his dance moves.

Once the music starts, both sides take a step and bow. Colonel George Crowley and Miss Sinclair circled each other; their gaze remained locked. Crowley places his hand on her back, and she places one hand on his broad shoulder. Their free hands finally meet. Together they dance to the music, their feet in perfect sync to the beating of her heart.

As the waltz progresses, she feels relaxed, and a small smile forms on her lips. He is perfect, she thinks, *exactly how I dreamed my future husband would look like* — a perfect English gentleman, a senior officer of his Majesty's army. Nothing like the roughnecks she sees in Bermuda; sailors, dockhands, merchants, and drunkards.

His red uniform with shiny medals adorns his broad chest. His eyes, aquamarine like the Bermuda sea, are deep and irresistible. He turns his body in tune with the slow waltz, yet there is a sort of assertive confidence to him. Like he is someone who should not be underestimated, she doesn't care at the moment.

Was it because she was falling in love with a man she hardly knew? The warmth between them grows more powerful by the second, and her heartbeat increases steadily along with it. Their dance was perfect — everything from their breathing to how their feet moved in harmony. Crowley guides her across the ballroom floor as if she were in a dream. She opens her eyes and sees his eyes fixed on her; yet he knew exactly where to take her. Every moment, every angle seemed to be planned in advance — nothing felt forced. She feels as if she is floating.

The young princess is caught up in the flow and decides there and then to let go of sorrows of her mother's passing, the pain of her father bringing in a new woman into the house so soon, and her worries and fears she kept buttoned up inside her.

Right here, right now, she was living; nothing else matters anymore.

She allows him to take her anywhere he pleased in the ballroom. He went right, she went right, he sped up, she sped up. They became one with the music, the dance, and with each other.

"George," she whispers.

"Everyone is looking at us," he squeezes her hand slightly and smiles. "Really?" He chuckles softly.

"I haven't noticed." He keeps his eyes fixed on her.

Lady Sinclair noticed everything, watching from the sideline. The elder Sinclair had gotten tired after the first waltz and took her to the sideline. For the three minutes it lasted, he was tough and harsh, jerking her about the floor, thinking about his desires and showing off his best over-practiced moves, not considering her.

She was glad it was finally over but longed for a younger virile and considerate gentleman like the one little princess has.

Macati also was watching from the sidelines, noticing the spirit of envy grow in lady Sinclair. He also observes the love in Miss Sinclair's eyes and the look in Crowley's eyes, like that of a hungry hyena looking at a chicken.

The Hyena flirts with the hen, the hen is happy, not knowing that her death has come, he thinks to himself.

Chapter Thirty-Eight

Sealed The Deal

The music ends, and Crowley politely excuses himself from Miss Sinclair. He knows he has the naïve little princess on the hook and now wants to create an air of mystery by becoming unavailable for a while.

He walks over to Squire.

"Let's get on with it."

Squire scurries off in the direction of the smoke room. Captain Armstrong and Macati walk in a quick pace close behind Squire. Crowley walks casually behind the trio, occasionally stopping to tip his hat at a young maiden, a high-ranking officer, or a gentleman who looks worthy of his respect and could be of use to him in the future.

He knows that dancing the first three waltz with the host's daughter gave him an instant status elevation and the party guests' esteem. He is pleased to leave a good impression with the guests.

In the smoke room, Squire motions to the drinks at the ivy oak wine cabinet filled with bottles of fine wine, spirits and whiskey.

"Drinks anyone?" He asks.

"No thanks," says Armstrong, remembering his last encounter with Lady Sinclair and sweet white rum.

"Pour me a glass of sherry," Crowley settles into an armchair crossing his legs and expecting to be served by underlings.

He is celebrating early; Squire thinks to himself as he pours him a glass. Crowley brings the glass close to his nose, as he inhales its crisp scent with notes of hazelnut.

Crowley takes a sip and says, "Hmm good, let me see the bottle. Ah, 1796, classic."

This is a good sign; he thinks to himself. Squire selected that bottle on purpose, knowing that was the year the second maroon war ended and the beginning of the Crowley's financial demise. He knows how George thinks. He would interpret this as a sign of changing fortunes.

George raises his glass as one giving a congratulatory toast, smiles and takes a long sip. George Crowley becomes super cooperative in the negotiations, as Squire estimated. He needs the gold desperately.

To Armstrong's surprise, the deal is wrapped up quicker than expected. Macati hands over the leather bag of gold with the first installment. Crowley's men alongside Macati and his Blue Jackets will load Armstrong's ship with fifty Congreve rockets, four crates of rifles, a barrel of gunpowder, and a crate of musket balls at dawn. The official story is that these weapons are being shipped to Fort Gadsden in Florida if anybody asks at the docks.

Historical backdrop:

Fort Gadsden also was known as the Negro Fort (Now a U.S. National Historic Landmark in Florida) was established by the British in the Spanish colony of Florida during the war of 1812 to recruit runaway slaves from the southern states of Georgia, the Carolinas, and Mississippi. The war ended in a stalemate and the war-weary British, having fought to stop American expansionist designs on Canada, needed to put measures in place to curb American expansionism across the continent to become a big and powerful nation that could one day challenge British world dominance. Slaves who find escaping north to Canada in the north too far can run south into Florida and take refuge in the Fort strong enough to fight any posse trying to re-enslave them.

More importantly, a few runaways' success would encourage a mass exodus from the plantations, thereby crippling the U.S. economy that was heavily dependent on free slave labor.

Though reluctant for fear that their own slaves would run, the Spanish crown felt Gadsden was remote enough from their important towns like Miami, Santa Fe, Largo, and Boca Raton. A British Fort with trained members of the Colonial Marines under a black officer — Garcon and a Seminole Indian chief would impede U.S. expansion into their territory. The U.S. had already annexed the Baton Rouge district of its western territory in 1810 and the Mobile district in 1812, thereby reducing the Spanish colony to the current borders of the Florida State.

Arming the Negro Fort was in line with the British practice of supplying arms to Native Americans to prevent Americans from settling in their territories. Native Americans do not manufacture guns, and their bows, arrows, tomahawks, and spears were no match against the rifles Americans used in conquering their ancestral lands. Native American Chiefs like the Seminoles were happy to receive British guns to fend off the American invaders.

For a tidy sum of gold coins, the supply sergeant would look the other way when the weapons are moved out of the warehouse unto Armstrong's ship. If anyone got too curious, they would say that they were being shipped to the Negro Fort. The fact that Macati and his men in blue jackets are seen moving the equipment would make it even more convincing. Crowley will receive the second installment for this shipment after the goods are on board the ship.

Macati and Armstrong excuse themselves and leave the room.

"We need to rest up for tomorrow's busy day," says Armstrong.

Crowley raises his glass in acknowledgment.

"Squire and I will return to the ball shortly; I have unfinished business to attend to," Crowley raises his glass in an imaginary toast to himself for a deal well done and success on his next move on the naïve little princess in pink.

Macati exits the door to the smoke room ahead of Armstrong and is shocked to see Lady Sinclair standing there. He wonders how long she has she been there, and quickly hides the shock on his face.

"Such a beautiful home you have," he says in a loud voice trying to hide his shock and to warn Armstrong about Lady Sinclair's presence. Armstrong quickly shuts the door behind him, blocking off Squire's peering eyes.

"Much better than the Blue crab," he says in a low tone, referring to the brothel she once worked as a prostitute.

"Yes, and much more comfortable than a hangman's noose. I hear that's what they do to pirates these days," she counters.

"They need evidence to convict besides, I have a letter of marquee. However, the young Miss Sinclair doesn't need much evidence to tell her daddy about her ugly past," Armstrong says in a hushed tone.

"You wouldn't dare!" Her face turns red.

"Just pay me back what you took, and I'll go away quietly," he makes a walking gesture with his fingers in the direction of the exit.

"This is all I have right now," she says, pulling out a small bag of jewelry.

"Ah, you came prepared," he says.

She responds with a smile.

"I've always outmaneuvered you, sentimental fool." She thinks to herself.

"I take it you will disappear from my life now." She says out loud.

Armstrong chuckles, "Not so fast; your husband wants to sell me a sloop."

"Take the money and get lost," comes her sharp response.

"All I did was love you," Armstrong's tone goes soft.

"I would have given you anything you want. Especially now that I'm rich."

"I need something I can never get from you even if you tried," her tone is stern.

"What could that be?" Armstrong looks about, confused.

"Respect," she replies, moving away from the smoke room door to lure him away from Squire's inquisitive ears.

"I always loved and respected you, treated you like a goddess even with your ugly past," he protests.

"I treated you better than your father did, and every relationship you ever had; why mistreat the only man who put you on a pedestal?"

"I don't respect you, so it matters not what you do for me, there will always be a void. So rather than lead a miserable life with me, its best we go look for a young maiden who will respect you."

"And the old man can?"

Armstrong points in the direction of the ballroom.

"He looks like he will keel over and die soon."

"Precisely," she smiles.

"Soon, he will be incapacitated from a stroke, unable to run his businesses, and I'll run the empire until he dies eventually. At that point, I inherit it all."

"Is that what you want?" Armstrong's face is beetroot red.

"Partly." She responds like a purring cat.

"So, what is all this talk about respect? You don't respect him." There is a sharp edge in his voice.

Her face is expressionless as she speaks.

"No, I don't, and honestly, I doubt I can respect any man. You know the story of my father and all the other men in between. Who knows, I just might prefer women…"

"Huh?" Macati can't contain his shock.

Armstrong and Lady Sinclair forgot they had company.

She chuckles at Macati's reaction then says, "We have a lot to talk about, but this is not the place or the time; you should get out of here before someone sees you with that and arrests you for petty theft."

She points at the bag of jewelry.

"So, find yourself a naïve little girl who will respect you, and I will work on my rich old fool over here. We could become friends after that," she studies him with catlike eyes.

"You have always been blunt," Armstrong looks to the ground in submission.

"Just to you, Armstrong. Just to you. No point putting up airs and graces; you know the real me. Do you want more money?"

Her voice softens, playing on his sense of chivalry.

"No, it was never about the money. You can take your jewelry back," he hands her the pouch.

"Fair is fair, I robbed you, and now I'm paying it back. Take it and leave," she holds it out.

Armstrong hesitates, and Macati grabs it.

"You have always been practical, Macati," she says to Macati but smiles at Armstrong.

Macati nods and says to Armstrong, "Let's go before people come and start asking questions."

Turning to Lady Sinclair, he says, "Nice seeing you again, ma'am. My regards to Moose."

Moose is Lady Sinclair's son from forced relations with the Hartwell's of England. She doesn't know who's the father — Lord Hartwell himself or his entitled and spoilt sons. She passes Moose off as her son from the previous marriage to Mr. Griffith — a merchant marine who died at sea. That's the story she gave her rich clients at the Blue Crab when she plays the Damsel in distress card on them.

Every man loves to be a hero, especially rich and powerful men, when they meet a pretty woman with a sad story. Lord Sinclair married Catherine and adopted her son, nicknamed Moose. Sinclair will soon marry off his daughter to an English officer who will take her far away from Bermuda. Lady Catherine Sinclair, or rather Catriona, does not need people from her past ruining her nice little plan.

Chapter Thirty-Nine

The Father's Prayer

Macati and Armstrong leave the mansion and walk down its long carriageway with manicured hedges on both sides towards the main gate.

"You need a good night's rest; the Colonel and his men will be on hand to transfer the weapons to our ship at dawn. We set sail to our deserted island at sunrise, so we offload and return by tomorrow evening," Armstrong says to Macati.

"Don't worry about me," Macati responds.

"I am concerned about you after what just happened," he says, still trying to figure out how Catriona rose from the Blue Crab to the mansion and how she can fit in with these aristocrats. She talks like them, dances like them, and even walks like them."

Armstrong smiles, before confessing her past.

"She learned the mannerisms of the rich by working as a chambermaid for an English Lord since she was eight years old. Her real name is Catriona which she Anglicized to Catherine. We come from the same Scottish coal-mining village. Her drunkard father indentured her to pay a debt. She stowed away on my ship to the Bahamas to start a new life when she discovered she was pregnant with Moose."

"Ehn? Discovered? Who is the father?" Macati asks.

"She doesn't know if it's the Lord himself or one of his sons. They all had their way with her. The Lord is married and respectable in society. His wife would kill Catriona if she said it was her husband or her sons who got her pregnant, so she ran away."

"And your role in all this is?"

"Macati! Macati!"

Two voices shout in unison from the other side of the decorated iron gate at the estate's entrance, interrupting the conversation. Macati recognizes the voices. It's Awat and Ikwunga. He could still recognize them both, and Awat was how he had envisioned her to look like.

He runs towards them, shouting.

"*Awat! Awat! Is that you?*"

"Yes, it's your children and me!" She shouts back in excitement.

Macati races out the gate and runs to her. He lifts her into his built arms, swirling her around as if she is as light as a feather. He pulls her close for a long and sentimental kiss. They both laugh in relief, embracing the surreal moment that they had both hoped and prayed for, for years. Macati leans in close and buries his face in her thick afro hair and neck, inhaling her sweet scent in relief.

He barely put her on the ground when the little five year old girl tugs at his coat. Her twin brother stands back, observing them. Macati stops, turns and hugs Hali, then drags Mark into his arms. Mark is a little hesitant in getting close. He is aware that this is his father from the striking resemblance and everything Ikwunga and Awat have said tonight. However, he didn't know how to feel or react now that his father is here.

"Come here! Come here!" He hugs them tight.

"Visions of this day kept my heart beating even through the toughest times. Stand back, let me take a good look at you..."

His eyes well up with tears.

Mark stands stoically while Hali twirls around.

"She looks like my mother," he says to Awat.

"She's named after her too," Awat responds.

"But we had to Americanize it to Hali as the slave masters don't allow African names."

"Not anymore," he says, forcing strength into his voice to push back tears.

Armstrong introduces himself to the family then takes his leave, saying, "See you at the docks at dawn."

"Certainly," Macati responds, beaming from ear to ear.

He turns to his family, "We have a lot to talk about."

He looks at his son.

"What's your name son?" He says tugging the boy towards him. "Mark," he responds shyly.

He turns and looks at Awat, "Huh?"

There is a clear frown on his puzzled face.

"American for Macati," she explains.

"Your name is Macati," he says to the boy in a dominant tone.

"Repeat after me, M-a-c-a-t-i – one who causes people to dance with joy!" He exclaims with pride.

He lifts Mark unto his shoulder and starts the father's prayer, "Anything I say, shout it loud," he says to the boy.

"You will do the father's prayer out here in the street?"

Ikwunga asks.

"The condition's right, besides I ought to have done it years ago when he was a toddler. Besides, the moon is in full bloom today. Tomorrow may be too late, and who knows if we will have a chance to do it in the near future considering tomorrow's trip and the possibility of getting double-crossed." Macati insists.

"We passed the perfect place for you to do the 'father's prayer' on the way here. It's a high mound overlooking the sea. There you can shout to the heavens in a loud, clear voice, and no one will arrest you for disturbing the peace."

Ikwunga points in the direction of the camp of the new black arrivals from the U.S.

"What is that? The father's prayer?" Awat asks.

"The Kapora woman carries her children on her back or her side — a protective and nurturing position. The men carry their children in front or on their shoulder when infants are old enough to sit or stand with their head over Dad's. It has spiritual symbolism beyond the natural feeling the child gets from being bigger than everyone around him or her, including the father on whose shoulder he's sitting or standing on." Ikwunga explains.

Awat is listening carefully.

"When the child is able to speak, his father takes the child out under the brightly lit sky, putting the toddler on his shoulder and prays to the ancestors and family Eguns. It is important that the child agrees with the father's prayer, so whatever they say, that night on earth will be established in the heavens. The central theme of the prayer is that the child rises above the father in life. If the dad gets to a certain level, the child will leverage that achievement and build upon it to a higher level. Standing or sitting on the father's shoulders symbolizes standing on your forebears' achievements and using that advantage to reach even higher than those before you."

Hali tugs on Macati's free finger and says, "Me too, make me big."

She also wants to be carried on daddy's shoulder. Like most twins, whatever you do for one, you must do for the other. Hali is no different, and her gender is no obstacle.

"Can she do that?" Awat asks.

"Yes, she can, and she is also eligible to share in the father's inheritance with her brothers. In situations where the Kapora man has no sons, she can also take on the family name and titles. Imagine if a great man has no sons, or the son grows up spoilt and useless? You can't let the father's toil go to strangers. Give it to the daughter that will continue the father's legacy. "

Satisfied with the response, she changes the topic to Armstrong's parting statement that's been bothering her.

"Oh, ok, now what is that talk about going away?" Awat demands.

Macati notes the edge in her voice. He puts down the child and lets the children walk alongside them towards the mound.

He reaches for her waist and pulls her close. She snuggles in, feeling the warmth of his body and enjoying his physical touch. He grabs her hand and kisses it.

"My love, you know that we are all returning home," he says.

"Yes," she nods in agreement.

"Nyoka and her son Ika are ruling the kingdom." He adds.

"Ikwunga told me." She mentions.

"I doubt they will welcome us with a feast when we return. More than likely, they will try to kill us or sell us back into slavery. Who's to say we will survive or escape the second time?" He raises a good point.

"We can stay in Freetown." Awat suggests.

"That may be a short-term solution, but the English will not feed us indefinitely, and owners of the land may not eagerly give up their ancestral lands for us to farm and sustain ourselves. One or two people okay, but hundreds? No. You know how we Africans feel about giving up ancestral land — more so as the incoming visitors are numerically equal to or greater than the original inhabitants of that town."

He goes on to tell her the plight of those who helped the British in the American war of independence, the destruction of Grantsville, the Krio he met on the slave ship en route to Brazil and the elderly Krio who chose to die rather than be returned into slavery.

"Okay, where are you going with this?"

Wrinkles form around Awat's lips, as she frowns.

"We just purchased weapons from the British, and we plan to reclaim the throne." Macati makes his plans clear.

Awat is quick to pull away from his hold.

"Aren't, you done fighting? What if you get killed? Just come with us, and we will manage together."

Macati's voice is emphatic as he responds.

"As a Kapora man, I was created to have a vision for myself and my family. I have to teach my son to conquer or die fighting anything seeking to destroy that vision or his ability to provide and protect his own. Giving up now is to teach my son to run, hide, acquiesce to the enemy, play the role of slave and or buffoon to the amusement of his oppressor and the supplanter of his inheritance." He refused.

Awat looked at him in disbelief. She was tired of fighting and spending every day as if it was her last. They were finally reunited, and the last thing she wanted was to lose him again.

"Sorry, I cannot do that — to live dependent on the handout of those who once enslaved me and thinks he does me a favor by feeding me crumbs from the table I built. Remember the prophecy when we were teenagers. We will be prevented from ascending to the throne for a season. The kingdom will go through a period of suffering, and our lives will be like a terrible nightmare. After which, we will regain the throne and pull our people out of the darkness back to greatness bringing with us cause to dance for joy again. For this purpose, we must fight. As per death, it will come someday but not while I'm working on the purpose for which I was sent."

Ikwunga sees the confusion on Awat's face, so he explains.

"When a Kapora child is born, their birth circumstances tell their life story and mission from the spirit world from which they came. It's the basis of the name given to the child seven days later — if female — and nine days later if male. We live out the meaning of our names. Everything will work together to ensure that the purpose is fulfilled. People you meet, experiences, skills, natural talents, and knowledge gained over time move to ensure the mission you were sent to accomplish; no one else to do it but you. In Macati's case, he has a mission that goes beyond his lifetime. To which I thank you for naming your son Macati for I know that where Macati stops, his son will continue."

Satisfied with the response, she turns to Macati, "So you bought weapons, and you are going to keep them somewhere safe until we return to Africa?"

Awat knows she can't fight him on this. He had already made up his mind. Though a little worried, her respect for Macati grows.

"Yes. Armstrong is also selling me one of the cargo ships we captured from Mr. Jackson at a discount. He plans to backfill it with a fast Bermuda sloop from the owner of the mansion we just came from."

"Up ahead over there," says Ikwunga pointing at a high mound in a clearing overlooking the sea.

Away from the street's lights and noise, the full moon shines brilliantly here — a beautiful sight over the Bermuda Sea. Macati raises his son over his shoulder as he gets to the top of the mound. Awat watches the sequence of the father's prayer, as Ikwunga explains the symbolism of each action.

"Are you big?" He asks the boy.

He might be a little child but standing on the shoulders of his father and his ancestors before him, he is elevated to greater heights.

"I am big!" He shouts at the top of his voice.

"Bigger than everybody." He smiles.

"Can you see far?"

What a child cannot see standing up, an elder can see while seated. However, if that child leverages the wisdom of his elders, he can see further than anyone, even with his youthful eyes.

"Yes," he responds.

"Further than everybody because I am big." He adds.

"Stand on my shoulders, and I will hold you, so you don't fall."

Macati helps him move from the sitting position to a standing position. There is nothing like a self-made man. Your success is the cumulative effort and success of others who help you rise and those who hold you up lest you tumble down from your new height.

"Shout it loud. I am big. Anything daddy does, I shall do even greater," he repeats.

"Whatever legacy I start, you finish," the boy repeats after him, then Macati and Hali go through the same routine.

Shortly afterward, Ikwunga departs with the children leaving Macati and Awat on the mound overlooking the beach.

Macati and Awat sit on the mound under the moonlight, telling stories of their journeys up to this point and doing what lovers who haven't seen each other in years do.

Time passes fast, and the cock crows at dawn to awaken the sun.

"Morning already?" Macati sits up, squinting his eyes.

"Can't wait to spend all day with you," Awat pulls him back down.

"We have a whole lifetime to do that," Macati gets up slowly.

"Hope you can function without sleep," Awat smiles.

"I'll catch some rest on the way to the island. It looks like it's going to be a calm day."

"Can you tell?" She wonders.

"I've been doing this for years now. Besides, it doesn't matter, storm or no storm out there. The storm within has ended now that I have reunited with you. When I return, I'd like you and the children to come with us. We will go to Brazil and pick up Waggy and the warriors there, then return to Kapora and regain the throne." He is certain.

"You sound confident that you can defeat Ika and the Kapora army." Awat brushes off the sand from her clothes.

"Considering the way Ika and Nyoka have treated the people, I believe the army and the people will defect to our side as soon as they know we have come to reclaim the throne. Akibu, son of Uzaza knows where his father and Obya hid the wrist cuff. With it on my hand, the people will know that I have the backing of the Great Ikwunga. Speaking of which, I need to go to the ship and meet with Armstrong to load the weapons. We will take them to one of our hideouts and be back tomorrow night."

Chapter Forty

Double Crossed

The first pickup was successful. The weapons were stashed in a cave on an uninhabited island. Two days later, Crowley, Armstrong, and Macati meet in a Tavern. Crowley is sober, barely touching his drink. Squire sends his apologies for not making this meeting.

"I am certain we can proceed with the sale of the second batch of weapons without him," Crowley's eyes shift to the left as he speaks.

Armstrong drops his pipe on the floor and gets up to pick it up, taking a quick glance behind him in the direction Crowley looked. He recognizes a man from the governor's office drinking with two other men. He notices a bulge under one of the men's coat — it must be a pistol. He turns around and sits by Macati, reaches over to him under the table and taps his knee while looking straight at Crowley.

"Do you have the gold for the next installment?" Crowley asks.

Armstrong squeezes Macati's knee under the table as he raises his voice with an emphatic "No!"

Macati is shocked at the response. He was already reaching into his side bag for it.

"Too dangerous to transfer that amount of gold in this type of place. Someone might rob us."

Crowley's face turns red.

"Don't you trust me?" He says, rising to his feet.

Armstrong's response is icy calm, "I'm not worried about you..."

His eyes locked onto Crowley's as he moves his overcoat to reveal two pistols in his waistband.

"I never miss, even when agitated. Now sit down, act calm, no sudden moves." Crowley sits back down and forces a smile.

"Come on now, what's this all about?"

"Are they with you?" Armstrong's eyes shift in the direction of the men as he speaks.

"Who?" Crowley turns his head in the opposite direction of the men to feign ignorance.

"Never mind. If you aren't with them, come and meet us at Prince's Bay — with a wagon of guns, and we will give you the gold there." He tosses Crowley a Spanish gold coin.

There's a lot more.

"How am I sure you won't kill me then?"

"Because you have something we want. Besides, we don't need His Majesty's army looking for us, especially since Squire and the governor have our description."

Crowley's face turns snow white. Macati and Armstrong leave the Tavern. The governor's staffer and the two men with him try to get up, but five well-built pirates stand over them revealing their weapons under their coats. The biggest one puts his large and rough hand on the staffer's shoulder.

"Sit and drink some more. What's the hurry? The night is still young!"

They sit, looking at Crowley sweating profusely.

A gigantic black man with a Jamaican accent stands by him with a menacing smile, saying through his teeth, *"Go eeezy mon. Unah want di man dem to panic an start shoot up de rassclaat place? Wi have nuff man an gun dan yu. Go easy. Easy now, easy, yu zimme?"*

He counts words for emphasis.

"Let - them – walk - away."

Crowley knows that the Jamaican maroon is on edge and anything can set him off from the look in his eyes.

"You are right, no panic shooting here. It's a little misunderstanding. I'll meet them at Prince's Bay."

Crowley forces a nervous smile.

"We need to sail out now!" Armstrong says to Macati.

"What of my family?" He frowns.

"You put them in danger if you stay."

"Crowley wants the gold at all costs. He will say we stole the weapons from the warehouse. Squire has double-crossed us. The judge is on the take; there will be no fair trial. We will all hang after they have tortured us into giving them all our treasure and the weapons. Catriona warned me that Crowley and Squire were up to something, but she couldn't expand."

Macati quickens his pace to a trot, "Mrs. Sinclair? I thought… when? How?"

He is baffled.

"I had dinner with Lord Sinclair earlier. She warned me that Squire and Crowley were up to something. She didn't have details. I didn't believe her a hundred percent, but I took precautions anyway. Her words were confirmed when Crowley changed the meeting venue. That's why I had our guys seated in the Tavern before we arrived. I had the Jamaican in our group stand down Crowley because I know he dreads maroons, especially after what they did to his family's distilleries. Run, we don't have much time before the local militia and the Colonel's men come after us."

Armstrong quickens from a trot to run.

Macati catches up, "I thought she hated you?"

"Not enough to see me hang. We have deeper roots than that."

"Getting you killed would remove the threat of you telling her past."

" She doesn't know what I might say if Squire and his cohorts torture me for my hidden treasure."

They get on the sloop and start preparing the sails when the rest of the crew except Greg Jr. run up the plank and join them. They cast off and sail into the night.

Chapter Forty-One

Separated Again

"Where is he?" Awat demands.

"He had to sail away in a hurry," Greg replies.

"Why?" She begins to worry.

"Someone set them up to be arrested, so they ran away."

"What about us?" She is now close to tears.

"I think he will come back for you. However, if he does not, I suggest you and the children join the others heading to Nova Scotia and from there, to Free Town, Sierra Leone."

"And you?"

"I'm coming with you," says Greg.

"My parents have decided to return to Nsude."

Onboard the ship to one of the islands of the Bahamas, Macati and the Kapora discuss their next move with Armstrong.

"Returning to Bermuda is too dangerous. Crowley and Squire have double-crossed us. They will torture us until we tell them where we stashed our loot, then hang us for piracy," says Armstrong.

"We all have spoken frankly about our exit strategy from this life of piracy. The clampdown on pirates will soon begin as the World Navies are no longer at war, and letters of Marquee's have been rescinded. We get out while we still have our health, youth, and gold. I want to return to Scotland as a fleet owner and decorated veteran of His Majesty's service. Who knows? Buy a coat of arms and become a Scottish gentleman."

"Not English?" Macati laughs.

"After that stint at Sinclair's, I now know that they will never accept me in their circles," Armstrong replies.

"You want to return to Africa and regain your throne?" He asks.

"I will be happy to ship palm oil and other goods from your kingdom and Britain."

"Many of the second generation blacks on this ship want to get parcels of land and settle in Trinidad. They will board another vessel and return to Trinidad in their blue coats, so they are recognized as veterans of the war with America and given their due benefits and pay. Those who want to return to Africa with you can board the ship we seized from Mr. Jackson."

He proposes.

"I suggest you first get your friends from Brazil then go to Halifax to pick up your family. By then, Crowley and his cohorts shall have returned to London, and the authorities in Halifax don't know of the issue between Crowley and us. We have talked, dreamed, and fought together. Now is the time to make those dreams materialize."

Chapter Forty-Two

The Old Cotton Tree

By 1815, it began to look like the British would renege on their promise to return freed slaves to Africa. They took Awat, Greg, and thousands of the freed American slaves from Bermuda to Nova Scotia and left them there. Napoleon escaped from the Isle of Elba, overthrew the French King, and is on the march again. The British and their allies are gathering forces to counter him before he gains strength. All resources are geared towards this war effort and nothing for land acquisition, protecting, or supporting a colony of returned slaves in Africa.

The British also knew what happened to black returnees' previous settlement from the American independence war. There was always the possibility of the new settlement getting overrun by the local population or a conflict over scarce resources between Grantsville survivors and the many newcomers. The Freetown population was already rapidly increasing with the influx of liberated captives by the West African squadron intercepting slave ships en-route to the Americas. The new settlement had to be garrisoned, and that would cost money. European soldiers don't do well in tropical West Africa for long periods.

The Merikins, former Colonial Marines, who settled in Trinidad fared much better. Southern Trinidad was sparsely populated due to the decimation of the native population decades earlier by communicable diseases. As such, the British crown was able to allocate large tracts of land to the Merikins without paying anyone.

Soon after Napoleon's final defeat at Waterloo, Europe begins a slow recovery from multiple wars. The Nova Scotia winters are long and brutal. The plight of the blacks in Nova Scotia was quickly becoming a source of embarrassment to His Majesty's Government — as they would recruit these people to fight on the promise to return them to Africa, then abandon them in a temperate region. Eventually, the money to purchase the land surfaced.

Next, they resolved the security issue by relocating the Trelawny Town Maroons from Nova Scotia to Freetown. They became the law enforcers and protectors of the colony — the first organized armed force of British West Africa — something they did with ruthless efficiency, for they had been fighting for centuries. First as African Warriors, then against their Spanish slave owners in Jamaica and then the British.

While in Nova Scotia, the Trelawny Maroons built schools and the Halifax Citadel's bastions — a fortress that saw action from the 1790s to the First World War. It's now one of the most visited historic sites in Atlantic Canada. The Trelawny Maroons were happy to leave the temperate North Atlantic for tropical Freetown; building skills and fighting skills would be used to protect and prosper the new settlement in Africa.

In 1823, the ships started moving the Americans from Nova Scotia into Sierra Leone. Awat and her children walk down the gangway of the ship. Thoughts race through her mind as she sees uniformed men in brown Khaki drill shorts, red fezes, scarlet zouave style jackets edged in yellow, and red cummerbunds holding long wooden clubs. They form two lines at the foot of the gangway. Then use their clubs to form a link chain like guide rails for the returnees to walk through. Awat is happy to set foot on African soil for the first time in 14 years. Something she prayed for but didn't believe would ever happen. Her thoughts are interrupted be a familiar voice. "Who are these people with long sticks?" It is Nandi. An elderly black man in a white single-breasted cassock with thirty-three buttons (for the number of years Jesus Christ walked the earth) answers Nandi's question. They are the paramilitary come to give you safe passage to the old cotton tree. "Cotton Tree!" Nandi grabs Awat's hand to run. A clergyman talking about cotton tree to a former slave sold by a Bishop Pombeiros gives Nandi instant flashbacks. Oldman Greg holds her back. "I don't think he means that type of cotton tree." He turns to the clergyman. "We were told that you will come to lead us to our new settlement. What is this about a cotton tree? By this time the returnees have stopped in silence. Some in fear and others glance about looking for anything they can use as weapons against the paramilitary that have formed a chain link on both sides of the dirt road. Sensing their apprehension, the clergy man explains. "At the center of the new settlement is a large cotton tree where returnees have gathered for a thanksgiving service since the very first settlers of Grantsville arrived in 1789. The paramilitary is here to protect you from being rushed by locals. As soon as word gets back to town that a ship of returnees has gotten into port, throngs of people seeking their family and tribes' people who might have been saved from slave ships by the anti-slave squadron come to the harbor and the old cotton tree.

The returnees follow the clergyman. The maroon paramilitary march alongside them to protect them from the curious crowd as they walk up to the old cotton tree.

Just as the clergyman explained, the local town people come rushing out to greet the returnees. Word had gotten out that this ship had escaped slaves from the United States. As they approach the tree an elderly woman stands on the side of the road shouting out the names of her children. Tears stream down her face. Her voice is hoarse from crying and shouting. Her town was raided by Fulani slavers ten years ago. She and her family were put on separate slave ships. Her ship was intercepted by the Anti-slavery squadron while her children's ship sailed on to the US. She built her hut by the road leading to the tree and comes out every time a ship arrives hoping against hope that one day her children will arrive on a ship. Today she leans on her staff and shouts with the same vigor she has always done since she first came to Free Town. From the back of the line of returnees a tall man in a blue jacket shouts back. Mama!! It is Sergeant Lewis of the 2nd battalion colonial marines. He breaks rank and runs to the old woman. A woman holding a baby and a five-year-old struggles to keep up with him. Sergeant Lewis breaks through the line of Maroons. Ayodele! Is that you? The old woman shouts. Yes, mama it is me he replies. What of Dayo? Is he with you? No mama. She hugs him tight. They both cry out loud. Where is Dayo? She asks again. He chose to go to Trinidad.

Why? The strain in her voice reveals great pain.

Because he wasn't sure what was waiting for us on this side. Sergeant Lewis explains. Is our village still there or was it destroyed? Where would he go, what will he do if he comes to Freetown? Would the local people be accepting of us or would they re-enslave us.

Haaa!!! She cries from the bottom of her soul.

Awat feels her pain watching from the sidelines. She clutches the hands of her children beside her. Tears stream down her face. Mommy, you are squeezing my hand. Mark says. Don't ever leave me she replies. No, we won't he says as he tugs her along to keep moving with the crowd.

As they approach the tree, Jamaican Maroons turned local militia /police, form a perimeter around the tree to give the new arrivals space to have their thanksgiving service uninterrupted. This was necessary because, quite often, the service gets interrupted by anxious residents looking for family and tribesmen and women that might have been saved from slave ships by the anti-slave squadron or just returned from the Americas.

Among the crowd on the outside perimeter is Uzaza, the former Kasuku of Kapora; his vision deemed with age. Word had spread through the burgeoning settlement around the cotton tree that a ship full of American returnees just arrived. Uzaza pushes his way through the crowd closer to the group of arrivals hoping to recognize any of them. A Maroon in uniform and a big stick blocks him.

"Steady man make, una tanda dat side," he says, meaning *relax, stand over there.*

Uzaza steps back then goes looking for an unguarded part of the perimeter that he can breach and mingle with the returnees.

Historical backdrop:

In 1800 when the British offered the Cudjoe town Maroons an opportunity to leave Nova Scotia for jobs in Africa as local law enforcement, or paramilitary force in British West Africa, they jumped on it. Five hundred of them returned to Africa with their fighting skills and their language — Jamaican (Trelawny) Patois. Trelawny Jamaican Patois would become the dominant language of the British West African armed forces across the sub-region and evolve into present-day West African Pidgin English. Nowhere else in British-occupied Africa would this language evolve because the Maroons did not go to those parts of the continent like Kenya, Uganda, and South Africa. Those who did not remember their African names retained their Jamaican English names like Braithwaite, Palmer, Ferguson, Gladstone, Jones, Williams, Higgins, Clarke, and Thomas.

By 1823, when the Americans from the war of 1812 started arriving in Freetown, the Maroons were already established, serving a dual role of law enforcement and protectors of the growing community to prevent a reoccurrence of the Grantsville decimation.

The local pastor who led them to the tree scans the gathered crowd and identifies the oldest man amongst them. His eyes with Old man Greg lock. The wisdom of elders is highly valued in Africa. It is believed that God listens to their blessings, curses, and prophetic declarations — a holdover of traditional beliefs into Christianity and Islam as practiced across the continent. Numerous passages in the Old Testament of the Bible and Quran justify these beliefs.

The pastor motions old man Greg to come forward. Greg nods in acknowledgment.

Now I know I am back in Africa. I have a duty to perform as an elder.

He opens his speech in traditional Ibo style greeting but converts the words into English for the benefit of the non-Ibo speaking audience.

"People of Freetown, I greet you," he waits for their response, then he repeats it, and they respond even louder.

He then shouts it a third time, and they respond not just in words but in shouts and claps. Like what you would see in a predominantly black church in the US.

"I start by overstating the obvious. Put God first in everything you do. Everything that we've done and everything I have is a gift from God. Forty years ago, I was young, strong, and free. Then one day, everything changed. I was a slave, taken from everything and everyone I loved and forced to work in a strange land to enrich those who treated me worse than a goat in my father's house in Nsude. I'm sure many of you can relate to that."

He pauses for effect for a few seconds before continuing.

"In the depths of despair and anguish, physical and emotional, I had this feeling that there was more to my life than this. The problem was I couldn't articulate it, and the physical realities in my life screamed the exact opposite. In everything I've been through, I've been protected; I survived the middle passage in the belly of the slave ship — death from overwork. I've been guided and corrected, and I'll tell you this, I've not always been with God. However, He's always been with me, especially in the down times when I was angry with Him for letting these things happen to me or doubted His existence at all for doing nothing while His children suffered oppression by the wicked. Hunger, disease, and bitterly cold winters, and you know we Africans were designed for hot weather, not the cold."

The crowd laughs.

"When God presented the opportunity to escape, we took it regardless of the fatal consequences if we failed. Many of you put on the uniform and fought. Those who couldn't fight supported those who did, for the price of freedom is paid in blood and courage."

"Hear hear!" The blue jackets in the crowd shout.

"Today is the beginning of a new phase of our lives, and it's frightening. It's a mean world out there with Pombeiros roaming in search of Krios — that's what they call us folks, the Krio people. We have no land to farm, no money, for we were slaves who worked to enrich others while we got no wages in return. At least the children of Israel left Egypt with gold and livestock. We have nothing but our God, the skills, health, and strength He gave us. Like the children of Israel, He will be with us, guiding and protecting us, and we stand strong, free, and victorious in every facet of life. This is the promise He has made to our children — yet unborn — and me."

He stands tall, proclaiming his plans.

"We must plan and set goals, apply discipline, consistency, and hard work to achieve them. A deficiency in any of these areas will lead to mere pipe dreams and frustration. You might as well go back into slavery; at least they feed you enough to keep on working."

Historical footnote:

The Krio used their skills to become modern furniture makers, built American-style houses, schools, churches, and the first modern western university from timber growing wild in the region. The old cotton tree still stands near the Supreme Court and National Museum in Freetown. People still go there for thanksgiving prayers, peace, and prosperity.

The Maroon policeman catches Uzaza trying to cross another part of the perimeter, hoping to get a closer look at the new arrivals. The policeman rushes at him, shouting in Patois. Uzaza sees the Maroon with a raised baton. He yells, attracting the attention of those in worship. He tries to get away but stumbles to the ground. The service stops in hushed silence as they watch the old man sprawled on the ground.

The policeman raises his stick to hit Uzaza when Greg grabs it mid-air.

"That is my uncle; he has come to welcome me back home."

He lies.

The Maroon backs down and a teen girl in western clothes helps Uzaza up. Uzaza peers into her face and starts yelling with tears in his eyes. He can't believe what he was seeing.

"Halima, Halima!" He says in Kapora.

"You look young again. Have you passed on?"

The girl responds in English, "How do you know my name?"

Uzaza sits on the ground with his hands on his head, crying and speaking Kapora. The young girl is confused, and almost frightened.

Awat explains, "This is Uzaza, the Kasuku of your father's kingdom. He thinks you are your grandmother."

Uzaza stops crying instantly, the minute he recognizes Awat. "Awat! I recognize that voice. Awat, wife of Macati; is that you?"

"Yes, wise one, it is me, and these are my children. Macati and Halima." Her face beams with a smile.

"Is Macati here?" He looks around.

"No, I've not seen him." She explains.

"His mother and I come here every time a ship arrives to see if he or anyone we know is among those returning. Was he not with you?"

"Halima is still alive?" Awat raises an eyebrow.

"Yes, but down with malaria. That is why she did not come to the cotton tree today. I thought your daughter was her Egun coming to say her final goodbye. They look so much alike." Uzaza says.

They all rush to the hut where Halima lays sick.

On the way, Uzaza tells them how they were captured and sold into slavery. The antislavery squadron intercepted their ship and brought them to Sierra Leone. He tells them how many people have been saved by the squadron and how Halima is convinced her children will be returned. Halima makes it a point to visit the cotton tree daily until her health finally failed her.

She made Uzaza swear to do the same until all her children return or he returns to the land of the ancestors.

Chapter Forty-Three

The Malee Revolt

Brazil, 1835

Ferdinand rides his horse hard towards the Quilombo. Armed men on a ridge watch the horse jump over a gully, almost throwing Ferdinand off. Orlando raises his blunderbuss in the direction of his older brother and scans right. Orlando is one of the guards on duty. Soldiering is not his thing; making business deals is more his thing. Though he has large eyes, he is nearsighted. For this reason, they give him a blunderbuss when he goes on sentry duty.

All you need to do is point it in the general direction of an intruder, and it will hit the approaching intruder along with everything else around the target. Orlando can see the form of the horse and its rider fast approaching them but cannot identify the rider's facial features.

A hand reaches out and upturns the muzzle of the blunderbuss. It is Waggy.

"Why are you pointing a weapon at your brother?" He asks.

"I am not pointing it at him but aiming behind him for whoever is chasing him. Ferdinand is a gentle rider. For him to ride like that, someone or something is chasing him. So, I'm steadying my aim to shoot who or what is chasing him."

"Your bad eyes are the reason we gave you the blunderbuss," Waggy replies.

"If you fire that thing, you will hit your brother, his horse, and everything around him. Stand down." Waggy commands.

Orlando turns the weapon down.

"Okay, dad, you shoot whoever is chasing him."

Everyone in the Quilombo knows Waggy never misses his target.

"Joy is chasing him. Look at his face; he is happy about something that's why he's in such a hurry. The only danger is he might fall and break his neck — the way he is driving that horse. It bucks and throws off its rider if driven too hard."

He turns to Orlando, then chuckles.

"Oh, I forgot, you don't see too good with those big eyes."

Waggy leaves the hiding position and stands in plain view of his son. Ferdinand rides up to him.

"What is the hurry, young man?"

"The government has granted free passage to any free black, mulato, and sambo who wants to return to Africa."

"Why would they do that after fighting to keep us for all these years?" Waggy frowns in disbelief.

"Because our continued presence encourages other slaves to revolt." Ferdinand continues.

"We provide weapons and refuge to rebellious slaves. The government figures all this will stop if we leave the country."

"Oh, I thought they would come after us after the failed Malê revolt, especially as a number of the fighters have taken refuge with us."

"That is part of the reason. Though the revolt failed, the government is worried that they may not be so lucky the next time. It was well planned and executed. But for one minor issue, it would have succeeded, resulting in the second successful massive slave rebellion in the Americas next to Haiti."

Waggy is referring to the Malê revolt of 1835.

Historical backdrop:

In 1835, Muslims in the Bahia region were called Malê — derived from the Yoruba word for Muslim 'Esin - Imale,' (Religion of the Malians) depicting Malian Gold/Kola nut traders who introduced them to the religion in the 14th century. The Yorubas in Brazil were called 'Nagô,' derived from "Anago" — a term used by the Fon people to describe their Yoruba-speaking neighbors of the Ketu kingdom, from where you get the popular South American religion Candomblé Ketu. Most slaves in Brazil were POW from the wars between the Fon kingdom of Dahomey and the Yoruba kingdoms. It's understandable, therefore, why disunity and distrust ran deep in the black communities of Brazil, going two or more generations after capture. It required a third factor into the equation (Islam) to unite these oppressed groups and fight their common but numerically smaller oppressor.

Though there were several non-Yoruba members from the Hausa and Nupe tribes, many of the leaders were Nagô Muslims educated in Islamic studies and Arabic – the language of the Koran. A language their Portuguese overlords could neither read nor speak. Written communication within the leadership was in Arabic to avert leakage if intercepted.

The Malê rebellion was scheduled for January 25 to coincide with the celebration feast of "Our Lady of Guidance," in the Bonfim's church's religious holiday cycle. Many worshippers would travel to Bonfim for the weekend to pray or celebrate. Authorities would also be present at Bonfim to maintain order at the celebrations. Consequently, few people and government troops in the city would make it easier for the Malê to capture the city.

Sabina da Cruz, an ex-slave of Nago ancestry, fought with her husband, Vittorio Sule, the day before. When the quarrel got hot, he left home with a change of clothes. Like all "right fighters," Sabina had to win the argument with her husband at all costs.

And not satisfied with the outcome of the quarrel, she went looking for him to finish the fight. She found Vittorio in a house with many of the other revolt organizers, where they told her, "Tomorrow we will be masters of the land," she reportedly said.

"Tomorrow, you will be masters of the whiplash, but not of the land."

Vittorio chose to stay with his friends and plan for true liberty than go home to capitulate to his wife. Words were exchanged between man and wife with no clear victory for either side. A stalemate in a lover's quarrel brings out the worst in "right fighters." The right fighter loses all objectivity and will sacrifice anything to win and prove themselves "right in the fight." Including things of greater value than the original issue of contention; this is often forgotten in their blind furry to win.

Dissatisfied with that round, Sabina left the house and complained to her friend Guillermino, a freedwoman, whom Sabina knew had access to whites. Guillermino then proceeded to tell her white neighbor, André Pinto da Silveira. Several of Pinto de Silveira's friends were present, including Antônio de Souza Guimaraes and Francisco Antônio Malheiros.

Within a few hours, the revolt plans got to President Francisco de Souza Martin and the police chief. The palace guards were reinforced, army barracks put on alert, and night patrols doubled. At around 1:00 am, the night patrol knocked on the door of Domingo Marinho de Sá. - the house where Sule and his cohorts were. He informed the patrol that the only Africans in his house were his tenants. However, sensing fear and tension in Domingo's demeanor, they demanded to see for themselves. They went down into his basement and found the ringleaders, discussing last-minute details. A fight ensued, and the Africans were able to turn the officers out into the streets. The fighting saw its first real bloodshed; several people were injured, and two Africans were killed.

One of the dead was Vittorio Sule, Sabina's husband. Something must die when you disagree with a right fighter —trust, ego, relationship, marriage, children, your life, other people, etc. Capitulation can determine where death stops, but the price of being "right" sometimes escalates beyond the control of the right fighter themselves. Not that it matters to them who suffers, so long as they win. Capitulate early, and the casualties are few. Capitulate late, and the casualties increase.

The revolt was forced into motion ahead of schedule, with the Malês reacting to events rather than taking the initiative. They split up to go in different directions throughout the city. Attempts to take the city jail near the palace to free their leader Pacífico Licutan and supplement their short supply of arms with the jailers were met with stiff resistance from the guards who were aware, ready and waiting for them. Soon they found themselves caught between lines of fire from the prison and the palace across the square. Under heavy fire, they retreated to the Largo de Teatro.

Reinforcements arrived on the Malês' side, and they attacked nearby barracks to take their weapons. They pressed toward the officer's barracks; however, the soldiers were ready and pulled the gate shut and fired at them. So, they retreated to the Merce's Convent, a pre-determined spot for regrouping.

A police patrol met them at Merce's Convent but were beaten back by the Malê. The police retreated to Fort São Pedro — a stronghold the Malê did not try to assault. They numbered in the hundreds at this time but were low on ammunition. They now headed towards Cabrioto, outside the city to rendezvous with slaves from plantations outside Salvador. To get to Cabrioto, they would have to pass the Cavalry barrack in Água de Meninos. At about 3:00 am, they sought a way around the barracks, knowing they had not enough weapons to attack it.

The foot soldiers took up fighting positions within the confines of the barracks while the Calvary stayed outside. Soon the Malê started taking fire from the barracks, followed by a Calvary charge. The Malê realized that their only chance of victory is to take the barracks – a futile and desperate attempt that left many dead and wounded. The survivors, faced with certain death, fled, and the Calvary mounted a final charge to finish them off. Those survivors that weren't killed or captured found their way to Kilombos and Macombos.

With the crushing of the Malê revolt, the Brazilian government realizes that the increasing number of free blacks and Sambo would continue to pose a threat to society's existing order and serve as an encouragement to those still in bondage, that they too could be free. Several of the freemen had gained wealth through commerce and as skilled artisans. It has been demonstrated throughout history that all successful revolts were led by members of the middle class and above. This wealthy class of free blacks might pull off a successful revolt the next time. The threat of another

Haiti in Brazil continues to grow as the burgeoning middle, and nouveau rich class of free blacks and Sambos grow.

They adopt a multipronged approach to the problem.

Remove as many of the freemen from the country.

Christianize the slaves and demonize all other religions.

Destroy their history, so they believe life in bondage is an upgrade to where they would have remained in Africa.

Several successful slave revolts were led by the Noble and Warrior classes' first and second generations. This includes Nene in Jamaica — Ashanti Princess. De Saline in Haiti - Grandson of a Dahomey Prince was sold into slavery by a rival to the throne.

The Brazilian government decides to allow any free blacks in Brazil to pay their way back to Africa. Many got on the SS Salisbury and were received by Mantse Nii Ankrah of the Otublohum in the Gold Coast — present-day Ghana. They settle on land issued by Ga King Nii Tackie Tawiah. This group of returnees will be called the Tabom people because they only spoke Portuguese when they arrived in south Ghana. Africans heard them greet each other with "Cómo está?" (How are you?) to which the reply was "Ta bom," so the Akan people and Ga-Adangbe people in southern Ghana and Accra started to call them the Tabom People. Another group would settle on land given to them by the King of Eko (present-day Lagos Nigeria). This group of Brazilian returnees is called the "Agudas," who are named after the land the King granted them.

The news of the government's decision to return free blacks and Sambos to Africa, if they can pay their way, is encouraging but useless to Waggy and others in the Quilombo.

Do we qualify as free blacks in the eyes of the government?

Second, how do we pay for passage back to Africa if we have no money, as the Quilombo is self-sufficient and therefore not integrated into the Brazilian economy? You need to trade to get the currency to purchase passage to travel. Survivors of the revolt are on the run. We should prepare for an influx of runaways and provide food and shelter for them until they get integrated into the Quilombos' economy as farmers. The threat of government forces attacking the Quilombo in pursuit of runaways remains.

They must prepare for war amidst the struggle to accommodate the new Quilombolas.

Chapter Forty-Four

Macati Returns To Brazil

On April 13, 1836, a British ship registered in Barbados arrives in the Brazilian port of Jaraguá. Captain Armstrong walks down the plank and greets the harbormaster in English. He will go by the name Captain Martins and Macati will be his black interpreter on this journey.

Macati greets the harbormaster in broken Portuguese.

"Where did you learn Portuguese?" The man asks Macati.

Macati points at Captain Armstrong as he responds.

"He won me in a card game with my former master in the port of Lisbon. I work for him now, and we have come to purchase sugar and Brazilwood."

"Ah, over there," he points to a warehouse at the far right.

"It belongs to my cousin. He will give you all the sugar you want at a very good price. As for Brazilwood, you will have to go inland for that."

Macati recognizes the warehouse. That is where he entered a crate to stow away on Mr. Jackson's ship to the U.S. twenty years ago. It looks weather-beaten now.

He turns to Captain Armstrong and says in English, "Let's go meet the owner."

The owner and Armstrong haggle the price for sugar and agree to load the ship the next day. He needs to go inland to purchase Brazilwood for his trip to Europe.

The man rents him a horse-drawn cart and driver, overcharging him. Macati, Ikwunga, and several men from the ship pile into the cart's back while Armstrong and the driver stay upfront. They head inland on the same road he told Waggy about his vision of returning to Africa and reinstating the Kapora to their rightful place in the world. Nothing has changed since Macati left.

They get to a fork in the road, and the man tries to make a left turn that would take them in a long loop to the sawmill, and Macati corrects him. *There isn't much time to lose; they must get to the Quilombo before dark.*

The driver turns to Macati with a frown on his face and asks, "How do you know that is a long way?"

"I saw a regional map," Macati lies, saving face.

"Can you read?" His suspicion rises.

"A little," he lies again.

They continue up the road in silence, each to his thoughts. They get close to the sawmill where he, Waggy, and the other slaves used to take the master's timber for sale. Macati is concerned that the owner might recognize him or, worse, his former master and armed taskmasters could be there doing business today.

Not taking chances, he pulls out a pistol and holds it to the driver's head. Wrinkles form around his lips, as he threatens him.

"Now you go to the back, and I drive from here."

Ikwunga and the men in the back cover the driver's head with a sack and make him lie down on the floor of the cart.

"You do as we say, and you will live. If you try to be a hero, you die, and we'll throw your body in the forest by the road."

"Please don't kill me," he begs, pleading for mercy.

"We have no quarrel with you. However, if you jeopardize our mission, you die. Now lay there and be quiet."

Macati takes over the reins, and they speed off to the Quilombo, using the same route he and the Quilombolas used the night they raided the warehouse at the port.

As they approach the Quilombo, a voice yells from a boulder ahead, "Halt! Who goes there!"

Macati stops the cart.

"I am Macati, a friend of Waggy," Macati replies.

"Advance to be recognized," the voice responds.

"No sudden moves; keep your hands where I can see them." Macati moves the cart towards the boulder from where the voice came from.

"Leave your weapons in the cart and get down slowly."

"I have a captive in the back." Macati mentions, coming clean.

"I see him," says a voice behind them.

The men swirl around and are shocked to see five men of different races; Black, White, and Zambo men behind them, with rifles raised.

"No sudden moves I said," the leader of the five says.

"Which of you says he is Macati, the friend of Waggy?"

"Me," Macati responds.

"I've heard of you," the man responds.

"I am Ferdinand, Son of Waggy; I was a baby when you left."

The man becomes more visible in Macati's sight. He is a Sambo of average build and stands approximately 5'7.

"You can't be Ferdinand; he was old enough to dance the Kapora war dance and would recognize me at first sight."

Macati lays the facts straight.

"Marcelina was the baby when I left, not you. We called her Yaya because those were the first words she ever uttered."

"You know the family well. You are right, I am not Ferdinand, but I am Yaya's husband. That was a test. Why are you bringing white men to our Quilombo?" He folds his arms.

"He rescued me from the ship that I tried to stow away into the U.S. to save my family. He is instrumental in fulfilling the dream of returning home. As for this one," Macati points to the man with the sack over his head.

"He's not one of us but the driver of the cart. We covered his head so he can't lead his people back to the Quilombo."

"Why not kill him then? Dead men can't lead anyone back to here."

The Sambo is already thinking of ways to kill him, quickly.

"I promise I won't tell anyone about you!" The driver shrieks.

"See, he's been listening," says Marcelina's husband."

"Bring him here," says a voice from the rock.

Macati turns around. A slim tall Sambo stands upon the rock with a rifle in his hand.

"Now, that is Ferdinand," says Macati, recognizing him. Ferdinand looks like a brown version of Waggy with curly long hair

"Uncle, welcome back. I've sent word to my father. We can go up to him in the Quilombo." Ferdinand smiles revealing big white teeth like his father and a wide forehead like his Maasai ancestors.

Ferdinand studies Macati's face as he walks up to him smiling. Macati smiles back observing the mixed emotion in the young man. Joy but cautious.

Macati and his friends walk towards the boulder.

"No, only you can come, your friends can stay here. You might have been one of us, but we don't know if you have turned coat. Besides, the path is booby-trapped. To undo them all, so your cart can come through will take too long and isn't prudent to keep the path open in view of the government's renewed efforts to destroy Quilombos."

"You will not have to live like fugitives anymore; we have come to take you back to Africa," Macati smiles.

"We've not agreed to return with you," Ferdinand responds.

"Ah, ever so cautious like your father. No problem, we have had this dream for many years. He will return home."

Chapter Forty-Five

The Great Empire Falls

Economic deterioration is the new normal for the Kapora Empire. Its borders have shrunk significantly. Several tributary states backed by one of the European powers through arms sales have broken away to form their independent kingdoms. Soon there are wars on top of wars. Africans kill each other with European weapons. And when these kingdoms became weak from slavery, multiple wars, and related consequences like economic breakdown, food shortages, and diseases, they turn to their weapon suppliers for protection and sustenance, thereby ushering the phased colonization process by those who once sold them weapons. This is contrary to popular belief; Africa was not colonized by hordes of European soldiers fighting their way across the continent. While there was some resistance, you had African kingdoms seeking European protection from their brothers in many cases.

It was more like desert storm in 1990 where foreigners were invited by one Arab state to repel another. The difference is that the foreign power becomes the permanent protector, economic exploiter, and eventually administrator after the war is over. In some cases, it was the foreign power that instigated the conflict in the first place that led to their invitation.

Presently, American, and European military bases dot Africa, Asia, and Latin America's landscape to protect them from their neighbors who look like them.

In the 1800s, however, inviting a European power to protect you from your neighbor or brother was tantamount to offering to become a vassal state of that European imperial power. The protectorate system that became prevalent across Africa, especially in the English territories, is identical to the vassal state system. An African King gives up his sovereignty to become a protectorate of European power. The European power assigns him colonial military officers for protection and the King, in turn, levies taxes on his people and pays it to the protectorate government. Through charters given to corporations like the Royal Niger company, the protectorate government has unlimited access to the natural and human resources of the kingdom.

Rulers like Ovonramwen of Benin, who refused to sign such agreements, were forcefully evicted by the European power led by European officers while the bulk of the fighting forces comprised of African infantrymen from other kingdoms that hitherto were hostile to Benin. It was a system the British perfected in India years before, then applied unto Africa.

In this arrangement, the Pombeiros takes on a new role. The Industrial Revolution in Europe made slavery increasingly irrelevant as machines took over the jobs of humans. However, the Industrial Revolution increased demand for raw materials like palm oil, peanuts, cotton, rubber, copper, silver, gold, and diamonds. Rather than sell Africans to work in Western mines and plantations, the new Pombeiros sells his kingdom, its resources, and its people's labor to work in mines and plantations on the continent to profit the colonial master.

The new Pombeiros gets a kickback and protection from the colonial master. The new Pombeiros, like the old Pombeiros, uses their wealth to buy titles in the new order. Some even got knighted by the Queen of England. The new Pombeiros spent their money on luxury goods. They had multiple women who bear them numerous children, some of whom they acknowledge while others are abandoned to grow as bastards — unacknowledged and unsupported by their daddy Pombeiros when their mother falls out of favor with them. They and their mothers who drop out of favor with the man will stand as outcasts to watch him live in obscene affluence while they wallow in abject poverty.

If crocodiles eat their own eggs, what shall they not do to the flesh of a frog? The larger society's fate from whom the new Pombeiros derives their wealth fare no better than the Pombeiros' neglected children. The Pombeiros, ancient and modern, never build industry or anything that promotes their community's good. The damage is worse when the ruler himself becomes the chief of Pombeiros. Such is the fate of the Kapora kingdom under Ika, son of Nyoka.

The once-great Kapora Empire is now carved up into multiple protectorates. Kapora is now a tiny speck on the map of the British Empire that spans the globe – rich in natural resources supplying vital raw material for the Industrial Revolution to resource-depleted Britain.

Its once-proud citizens are reduced to peasants; many of the able war chiefs have been killed in battle by the enemy fire or assassin bullet from within the Kapora ranks.

Ika has grown increasingly paranoid. He fears that the evil he has done to others will return to smite him. He increasingly isolates himself from the public and appoints a British Colonial Army Captain Ferguson as his chief security officer — a Scotsman.

The colonized see all Europeans and Britons the same, but the British segregate between the English, Scots, and the Irish. The Scots were often sent to Africa, Asia, and the Caribbean to explore, fight, and convert the people to obedient Anglicans – the Episcopal Church – and administer the colony. That's about the quickest way they can rise in wealth and status. While dispensable and easily replaceable by another Scotsman, the colonized hero-worship them as next to God and their names memorized in schools as they would memorize the names of the twelve disciples: Mungo Park, Lugard, MacPherson, Mary Slessor, and so forth.

Captain Ferguson's Sergeant Major is a burly local called Samanja. He oversees the rank and file of African palace guards.

The grand council is full of "yes men" and praise singers. Ika is threatened by anyone capable of independent thought. Anyone who speaks against this administration or is perceived to question their policies gets arrested on trumped-up charges, disgraced, and severely punished.

Money can't talk; however, it can make a lie look true. Paid witnesses show up at kangaroo trials with damning evidence against the innocent. Prisons hitherto nonexistent in African communities start sprouting like mushrooms on a decaying tree.

Strange things happen to popular and highly respected members of the community who refuse to grovel as sycophants. And such people are not given the benefit of a kangaroo trial for fear of public backlash. Sudden disappearance is common before one reappears in a forced labor camp working in a mine.

Nyoka, the queen mother, has elevated herself to the status of a demigod. She is more feared than her son, the King, for it is well known that she controls him. Nyoka has her circle of praise singers who jostle for her favor. In every institution, she has a spy eager to report disloyalty in return for favors.

Nyoka demeans Ika's first wife Jumo, mother of the heir apparent. Depression and binge eating to feel good have taken permanent residence in Jumo. The heir apparent, so stripped of his self-esteem, has grown into a chubby "people-pleasing chameleon" with no personality. Everyone calls him Kinyonga — Chameleon — literal translation to mean harmless little lion. A derogatory name Nyoka called him that has taken root in everyone's mind.

Most people don't remember his real name. Kinyonga is great at using many words to say nothing. When pushed hard for an opinion, Kinyonga will reassemble your words, mix it with anything he thinks you want to hear, and present it to you like an original thought. Lack of protection from dad, mom's depression, and Nyoka's constant badgering has made him an expert in reading people from afar and taking the necessary steps to preserve himself from attack — shape shifting, concealment of real emotions, and disappearance being his top three.

Nyoka takes it a step further by bringing into the palace a new young and docile wife she can dominate. She wants the new wife to bear Ika a son. This son will become King instead of Jumo's son Kinyonga whom she hates, and fears will someday retaliate the pain and humiliation she has brought him and his mother. Kinyonga has an exceptional memory for past offenses, and she has caught flashes of hatred in his eyes a few times. Something he quickly suppresses and denies with a smile. Such a person can offer you a cup of sweet poison to drink with a smile for decade-old offenses.

It takes one to know one, and Nyoka recognizes herself in those quick flashes in his eyes. To her disappointment, the young wife only has daughters. Every year she gets pregnant, but each time, it's a girl. Nyoka kicks her out and brings in another docile wife. Again, the new wife has a female child. Nyoka accuses Jumo of using witchcraft to prevent any male children from being born in the royal family.

Jumo fears that Nyoka might arrange her disappearance or even her sons' death the moment a new wife or any of the King's concubines bears him a son. She believes that the only reason they are still alive is that the new wives and concubines don't have sons yet.

The latest wife is pregnant again, and the due date is fast approaching. Judging from the shape of her belly, Jumo fears that it's a boy this time. She starts gathering essentials for travel. It's easy for her to do because she is currently isolated from the palace and all the activities in the palace. On the night of delivery, word spreads fast throughout the kingdom — *or what was left of it* — that it is a boy!

That night, Jumo gathers her children and flees the capital under cover of darkness. They ride through the night to her kingdom of origin — the Kongo now under Belgian rule.

The next morning, well-wishers come to the palace to greet the newborn son. As people troop in to congratulate the King and new Queen Taraji for their new son they must pass by the shady podium near the palace gate, pay homage to Nyoka, and congratulate her for her new grandson. Nyoka has positioned herself by the entrance in colorful apparel. Surrounded by sycophants, she boasts of how the wicked witch Jumo put a hex on the royal family, preventing the birth of sons, so that her son Kinyonga becomes the next King, and she rules the kingdom through her son with no personality of his own.

It is typical of Nyoka to accuse you of the very thing she is guilty of. In her delusion, Nyoka believes others don't see the hypocrisy. She takes the lie further, claiming that she countered Jumo's witchcraft with strong, powerful prayers, and now a son is born, and Jumo has fled in shame. One would think that this occasion was more about her than the child. Nyoka is good at that — turning every occasion into the "Nyoka show." If she sees the sun rise at dawn, she will claim that she created the sun and made it rise that morning. Then scan the room for admiration and praise from her minions. Woe betides anyone whose face reveals a hint of disbelief.

It takes another woman to cut the controlling strings a domineering female has over a manipulated man. Ika's new docile wife Taraji (Meaning Hope) is equally manipulative but less abrasive in her delivery. Especially now that she has secured her position in the palace by giving the King a son, she plans to eliminate Nyoka's stranglehold in the palace. In her mind, she's living up to the meaning of her name – Hope.

Several months later, Nyoka and Ika get into an argument. Ika is fed up with Nyoka's antics. She slaps him in the heat of the argument. Ika warns her that will be the last time she ever contradicts him. She is banished from the palace, and if she ever comes near him again, he will lock her up. His threat is loud and clear.

"I am the King, not you," he orders that she lives in a hut outside the palace compound.

Nyoka is shocked that Ika dares stand up to her. A few chiefs tell Ika that it is long overdue. He has been perceived as a weak King by the kingdom and their neighbors for quite some time.

The new docile wife is not so docile after all. She is an expert in subtle manipulation and uses Ika's office and physical strength to gain her independence from Nyoka. She has been boosting Ika's confidence for some time, quietly stoking the flames each time Nyoka speaks to him roughly. Taraji is very pretty and likes colorful apparel. She prides herself as a fashion designer and now has the King attending public functions like the annual festival in matching clothes. The Talakawa, the common people are impressed by the King's new image and a new Queen.

From her little hut outside the palace, Nyoka notices that Taraji gets all the accolades and gifts. Nyoka can't stand seeing anyone else happy, especially if she believes she should be the one getting all that attention. One day she meets the cloth trader that Taraji goes to and sells him the best-looking material ever seen. The new Yam festival is fast approaching, and Nyoka knows that Taraji would soon come looking for something nice for herself, the King and the new Prince, named Acheampong. Things go as planned and Taraji buys it from the trader and has him fashion nice clothes for herself, Acheampong and Ika.

A few weeks later, smallpox shows up in the Palace. Nyoka had figured out that the girl was the source of Ika's newfound bravery. She visited her hometown and purchased very colorful imported cloth, then took it to a witchdoctor who tainted it with smallpox spores. Her younger brother Bishop Mathew had immunized her and the Wayo royal family many years ago, so she did not get infected.

The tailor was one of those who received the mark of God from Bishop as a teen when he was part of the entourage that followed Awat back home in the hopes of getting a Wagombe girl at Mathew's church. Fortunately, he did not follow them to the Baptismal castle. He is also immune to smallpox.

Ika and Taraji never got the inoculation and are now dying from the disease.

Jumo and her children were in the Kongo kingdom, while all this went on in the palace and were unaffected. Nyoka spreads a rumor that the Orishas punished Ika and the young wife because they insulted her.

Most people dread Nyoka and believe she has supernatural powers. The baby boy dies, then the mother, and finally Ika. Upon Ika's death, the elders call Jumo and her sons to return to the kingdom — the kingdom cannot be left without a king. Nyoka would have liked to usurp the throne for herself, but tradition won't let her. She is a woman of foreign birth and not a descendant of the Great Ikwunga. The kingmakers select Ika's son Kinyonga in the absence of anyone else.

Power leaves no vacuum. If the one in office fails to use his or her authority, others will fill the vacuum and push their own agenda in the weak leader's name. If things go well, they profit. If they go badly, the weak leader gets the blame. Kinyonga's weakness created a power vacuum exploited, manipulated, and filled by Nyoka and her minion chiefs. They systematically alienate him from the truth and anyone that can tell him the truth. Even the new Kasuku is one of them – Ayilara, Ika's drinking buddy.

Around the same time back in Brazil, Macati has convinced Waggy and several Quilombolas to return to Africa with him. They ride on carts to the docks that night and board the ship with Macati and Armstrong. Those who chose not to return, ride back to the Quilombo. All the while, the cart driver is tied to a tree near the sawmill. On the way back, the returning Quilombolas force him to drive them to his own house and say to him.

"Now we know where you live. If the authorities attack us, we will return to destroy you and your household."

"I didn't see anything," he says

"That is what you say now. Ever wondered how we are prepared for an attack long in advance? Or how we know what route the government troops are taking to reach us? The same sources will let us know if and when you talk. Then no one in your household will see or talk ever again." They make their threats very clear.

"I swear, I won't talk." His lips quiver in terror.

"Your choice, you decide what happens to your family, you, not us."

Russ retreats into the darkness and rides back to the Quilombo.

Macati and the Kapora escapees from the Quilombo and his pirate crew go to the deserted island and load the weapons unto the ship.

They know that the escaped American slaves were moved to Nova Scotia and then to Freetown. Macati and his crew sail east to Freetown.

Chapter Forty-Six

Victory Belongs To Those Who Profit

Freetown Sierra Leone is a rapidly growing town peopled by diverse groups including veterans from the American War of Independence and their descendants. New arrivals from the War of 1812 dubbed the second War of Independence, which turned out to be a fight for freedom to the Africans who fought on the British side, for this is the genesis of their true independence.

To the U.S. and British governments, a stalemate as neither side gained nor lost new territory to the other. It also marked the genesis of the U.S. recognition as a regional power in the international community for taking on the new world power without foreign assistance. They now had free reign to expand their territory in the new world without hindrance from any of the still-standing European powers.

To the American Indians, the war was a total loss. It took their leader Tecumseh and eliminated their sole supplier of modern weapons to stave off the expansionist nation to their east. Not represented in the Treaty of Ghents, the request to return the territories of Ohio, Michigan, and Indiana to the Indians did not make it to the final version of the signed treaty ending the War of 1812. Soon their territory would be encroached upon, and they would eventually be pushed unto reservations.

The struggle to shake off the yolk of an oppressor is paid in pain and blood. The victory celebrations are short-lived because the struggle for "Swarāj" demands even greater sacrifices. A price must be paid in exchange for self-governance. Though free from their American overlords, the newly liberated slaves had to support themselves in a new country where they had no jobs or land to cultivate or the basic necessities of life like food. The indigenous population would not surrender their ancestral lands just as no modern person would give up their home or means of livelihood to refugees from a war-torn country — no matter how much you sympathize with their plight. Hunger and disease set in, and soon, the new arrivals start getting restless. The British colonial administrators had no land or the money to purchase new land. They could not force the indigenous population from their land. The 500 Cudjoe town Maroons were an effective defense force but were not enough to evict the aboriginal people. When you find yourself in a deep hole, you have two choices; die waiting for God to save you or use your God-given talents to climb you out of that hole.

The settlers did three instead, they prayed, climbed, and cried at the same time. The result:

They used local timber to build "modern" furniture and American-style buildings, several of which stand to this day. The demand for modern furniture and American-style buildings rises amongst the colonial administrators and the rich local elites. The Krio soon became the sole building contractors of schools, administrative buildings, and churches in Sierra Leone and across British West Africa. Later they would build ports, railways, and roads. The building experience gained in America and building the Halifax Citadel would yield dividends for generations in Africa. Middlemen traders took goods from the sea to the hinterlands and exchanged them for raw materials like rubber and precious stones to be sold to Europeans on the coast. Freetown rises from a shanty town of refugees to a modern metropolis of its time. Young Mark witnesses the transformation and develops an interest in western education. Young Halima spends a lot of time in the clinic with aunt Daisey formerly known a Crazy Daisy. Nursing the sick back to good health comes naturally to her.

Author's note:

In the absence of an English word to capture this point's essence, I use the Hindi word Swaraj. The closest English translation is independence or self-rule. It is not just the freedom from external oppressors, or the breaking of shackles placed on you by external exploiters but freedom from those things that control you from within; which means you are economically self-sufficient and need not beg for food. The principle works on the individual level and the national level, for nations are made of individuals.

Not all who returned were former slaves. Freedmen like Edward Jones, the first black graduate of Amherst College in Massachusetts and the second black man in the U.S. to earn a college degree, had difficulty securing meaningful employment. Jones was too dark skinned to pass for white at a time when racial discrimination in employment was standard practice in the United States of America. He lands in Sierra Leone in 1822 and helps establish the first western university on the continent — the Fourah Bay College in Freetown Sierra Leone. He would become its first black vice principal, and the Fourah Bay College would become a prominent center of learning with students from across the region. Graduates of the College would lead the movement for the independence movement in several countries.

Graduates include:

- Archdeacon Samuel Ajayi Crowther: Freed captive of a slave ship who became the first black Anglican Archbishop in the world. He translated the Kings James Version Bible into Yoruba — the second time the Bible was translated into an African language. The first translation was the Coptic Bible, which predates the King James Version by a thousand years.
- J. E Casey Hayford: First African Novelist in English, Attorney, and an early advocate of education and African self-rule.
- Henry Rawlingson Carr: First African inspector of schools, first African assistant secretary of native affairs. He had a personal library

of 18,000 books available to anyone interested in furthering their education.

- President William Tubman of Liberia: A descendant of American slaves who became President and turned his nation into a maritime economy with the largest fleet of ships in the world. His portrait is on their currency.
- Herbert Macaulay: Started the push for independence in Nigeria. His portrait is on their currency.

The settlers' success in Freetown gave impetus to the American Colonial Society ACS in the U.S. and their push for a colony of freed slaves in Africa. While the motive and arguments given differed, Paul Cuffee's dream of bringing shiploads of blacks back to Africa was realized in 1822. An exodus of 6000 every year poured into the continent, and by 1836, an additional 8000 came from Brazil. Many of the Brazilian returnees knew where they originated from and settled there. Several Nago descendants returned to Yorubaland were called the Agudas. They were named after the kingdom's section after the King of Lagos (Eko) gave it to them to settle. Those who settled in other parts of West Africa are called 'Tabom People' — a term that's gradually fading away as the Tabom inter-marry with the local population. The language lost, and the only thing left identifying their Brazilian roots are their Portuguese last names and Portuguese-style buildings in Lagos.

Chapter Forty-Seven

The Return Home

Macati stands at the forward deck of his ship as it approaches the natural deep harbor of Sierra Leone. It's like déjà vu to him. White and fluffy clouds cover the tops of the mountains. The ocean waves are calm with the morning sun shining from the east. He squints on getting a first view of Sierra Leone.

"It's going to be a good day." Waggy's voice comes from behind him to the left.

"I have seen this before," says Macati.

"Is it from the dream you told me about years ago?" Waggy asks.

"What dream?" Macati finds the question odd.

"You were standing on a ship heading towards Africa — a town surrounded by mountains, but the mountains were not shaped like the head of a male lion like the one surrounding the Kapora capital."

"Ah yes, I remember." He smiles.

It comes back to Macati in a flash, "This is it!"

"The guide said that Awat, my children and my mother are over there waiting for me under a cotton tree. You have the memory of an elephant. You never forget!" He exclaims.

"True. I also remember you said the guide was standing by your right shoulder. That is why I stood by your left," Waggy confirms.

Macati turns to the right, "Yes, yes, I remember."

"You said the guide was God." Waggy adds.

"Yes." Macati nods, looking up to the heavens.

"I asked what He looks like, and you didn't answer. So now I came up to you quietly to see if He is here standing by you now. And more importantly, to find out what He says happens next."

"To your first question, He looked and sounded like my father Zaki." He answers.

"Are you saying your father is God?" Waggy is puzzled.

"No. He can take up any shape He wants. He appeared to me in the shape of the one person I know and trusted all my life."

"I thought that was me," Waggy feigns disappointment.

"You don't know the future." Macati turns to face him.

"And He does?" Waggy questions him.

"Not Zaki, but as a child, I thought he knew everything - past present and future. So, in his image, God came knowing that I'll pay attention and obey without questioning. If He came looking like you, I would argue back and forth with you." He made his point.

"And I'm always right, but you are too stubborn to admit it." Waggy thumps his chest.

"Delusion of grandeur," Macati sneers.

"Do you not always come back to my point?" Waggy smiles.

"Only sometimes. I just remembered something in the vision. He showed me a large cotton tree where I would give thanksgiving prayers. And the time that Awat, my children, and mother will join me in prayer. My children will inform me that they want to study the white man's ways." Macati further adds.

"Huh? To become like the barbarians who enslaved us?" Waggy's voice reveals his shock.

"My thoughts exactly. Do you see why He had to come in the form of one I wouldn't argue with? I was going to argue but I'm glad I didn't because He would have stopped showing me what is to come. As per your objection, He said that I should let them if I want the Kapora to regain their standing amongst other races of the world."

"What else did He say about the future?" Waggy is curious.

"We will raise an army and regain the throne. When done, He will make a better covenant with me than our Orishas made with the great Ikwunga."

"And you will?" Waggy raises a brow.

"Yes, He speaks to me regularly, and ever since we got to Brazil He has not been wrong. Unlike you, hit or miss."

"I never miss. I just let you win sometimes so you don't cry."

At the ship dock at the Freetown harbor; Macati disembarks and starts walking inland uphill. Members of his crew troop behind him. As they walk, crowds gather along the road leading into town. First a trickle then a large crowd forms on both sides of the road. It's as though a thousand eyes are watching them, each with a hundred questions.

Where did you come from? What is your story?

As they approach the large cotton tree, Trelawny Maroon police officers strain to keep the surging crowd back. Old man Greg and Greg Jr. stand by the tree. Old man Greg has become the designated welcome officer for new arrivals. Macati and his men scan the crowd looking for familiar faces, failing to see the broad smile of two familiar faces before them until one of them makes a sudden bolt into the crowd.

"Isn't that Greg running away?" Says Chuck Mike.

They all turn to watch young Greg running through the crowd towards a cluster of houses.

"*A na m asị gị nnọọ,*" says old man Greg beaming from ear to ear, to say you are welcome in Igbo.

Chuck Mike (Chukwu Emeka) recognizes him from the abandoned recruitment camp.

"He has gone to fetch your family," Old man Greg continues speaking, looking directly at Macati.

"They have waited and prayed for a long time. Your mother, Awat, and the children," he goes on to explain that the anti-slavery squadron intercepted Halima's ship. She, Uzaza, and several other Kapora are now residents of Freetown.

"Where are they?" Macati can't hide his excitement.

Old man Greg points in the direction young Greg ran. Macati turns to leave when he notices Awat running towards the old cotton tree. Young Mark strains to catch up; he has never seen his mother run so fast. Hali walks with Halima and Uzaza towards the tree.

The family reunites, and joy fills the air.

A few days later, Macati announces that he is planning to return to Kapora. Mark informs him that he wants to attend Fourah Bay College to major in Economics. To everyone's surprise, Macati agrees. He goes on further to say an educated Mark would help move the kingdom into modernity. Mark modifies his position and decides to go with Macati to see the kingdom but plans to return to Sierra Leone in time for the fall semester.

Chapter Forty-Eight

Nyoka Gets News Of Macati

The burly African Sergeant Major of the British West African regiment, rushes into the royal compound, huffing and puffing, he heads straight to Nyoka's building. A breathless, skinny, and short man in traditional royal servant garbs struggles to keep up with him. Captain Ferguson, of the British West African regiment walks behind them casually.

"What is the hurry?" Nyoka asks, noticing the sense of urgency.

"We have to gather the warriors to fight Macati," the burly Sergeant Major responds.

"Macati?" Nyoka jumps to her feet.

"He should be enslaved far across the seas or dead from overwork and oppression by now. I heard male slaves barely see their fortieth birthday, and when they do, they are physically and mentally damaged. Are you sure of what you are saying? Maybe it's an imposter trying to incite a rebellion and usurp the throne." Nyoka suggests.

She is in doubt, and refuses to believe what she is hearing, as Macati's freedom and return to the kingdom would disrupt her reign behind the throne.

"My sources are reliable, your Highness. Macati returned with hundreds of armed men on ships. With their modern weapons, they overran the Wayo slave fort from where he was shipped out. They overpowered the guards, took their weapons, and even broke into the local armory and gathered more weapons. One of the guards escaped to tell the story to your nephew, King, Maniwayo."

He responds, saying everything she was desperate not to hear.

"Good, then my nephew should send his army to crush him before he gets to our border." She paces the compound up and down, thinking of her options.

"It happened so fast that by the time Maniwayo mustered his forces, Macati and his troops had disappeared just as quickly as they arrived. We don't know where they are. However, Maniwayo thinks they are coming here; that is why he sent a swift horseman to warn you."

Bemoi the Sergeant Major who now goes by the name "Samanja" points at the short and skinny man beside him.

"Tell me more," says Nyoka as she folds her arms.

Samanja starts to speak, but Nyoka moves her hand in a dismissive wave.

"Please, please, please I beg." She hisses.

"Not you, the little man," she points at Maniwayo's messenger.

"It was a predawn attack. Several landed on the docks with small boats from ships moored in the open sea and gagged the sentry that happened to be awake at the time. By the time the other guards realized what was going on, their ships had pulled in, and they were all over the place, hundreds of them and even more pouring out of the ships and light boats fully armed. It's like they knew the fort's layout and soon had either captured or killed most of the guards. They forced one of the guards to take them to the slave dungeon and released all the Peças down there. The Kapora amongst them have joined Macati."

His vivid description has Nyoka on edge, as she bites her tongue.

"How do you know there were Kapora captives amongst the Peças?"

"Because they hailed Macati as their liberator and identified one of the dungeon officers at the port, as the one who receives all your political prisoners for sale into slavery. He begged for mercy, but they showed him none."

"What did they do to him?" Nyoka is visibly worried.

"They tied him up and cut his ear off piece by piece, forcing him to eat it and recite this phrase." He pauses for effect.

"Those who won't hear will feel." He says.

"What does that mean?" Ferguson asks.

"The Peça who force-fed the jailer is a Kapora warrior chief who spoke against your regime; He said that you and your cohorts have been warned severally, yet you refuse to hear the words of reason, wisdom, or the cries of your people, so now you will feel great pain. That's part of the message they want him to recite to you and Kinyonga, son of Ika. They let him live without ears so he can come to give you the message from Macati."

"What's the rest of the message?" Nyoka says, nervously tapping her foot.

"Surrender or die."

There is silence for a few seconds.

"Where is he now?" Ferguson asks.

"Who?"

"The Kapora jailer without ears, fool! Who else would I be talking about?"

Nyoka almost slaps Maniwayo's messenger.

"Two days journey behind me, your Highness. Maniwayo put him on an old, slow horse, knowing Macati will follow him at a non-visible distance behind. Maniwayo figures that Macati won't attack until the man delivers the message. That is why he sent me ahead on a swift horse, so you ready yourselves for war before he arrives with Macati, and his men close behind."

"Why not attack without warning?" Ferguson asks.

"In Kapora culture, that would be a dishonorable victory," Samanja replies.

"Never heard that one before," Ferguson quips.

Samanja replies in a sheepish tone, conscious of Ferguson's contempt of African belief systems.

"The Orishas and His ancestors, especially the great Ikwunga, demand that you openly declare war before you attack anyone. Sneaky attacks without a declaration of war will bring terrible punishment even if you win the war; like one who swallows a porcupine whole, that victory will be fraught with agony until it is atoned with blood – your blood or that of your firstborn son. Plus there would always be one in your lineage mentally tormented by the spirits of those who died in that war."

While in Kapora culture, the torment of hearing voices and seeing things is interpreted as the voices of the eguns of the wrongfully terminated by you or your ancestors, in the Western world, this mental health condition is recognized as schizophrenia.

Ferguson ponders for a minute, while Nyoka responds with disgust.

"Go quick, inform that foolish boy Kinyonga. I'm coming now, but first, I must send for the head of the cavalry. Let them ride and destroy Macati on his long march from the coast. Catch them while tired and disorganized."

"What about the dishonorable victory?" Samanja asks.

"Nonsense!" She responds in a hiss and claps her hands to indicate that her mind was settled regarding this matter.

"That's Kapora culture. I am Wayo. We strike when the enemy is weak and tired. Besides, this will serve as our answer to the ultimatum he sent that we are yet to receive officially. He doesn't know that we know he is coming and therefore will have his guard down."

Feeling embarrassed by his perceived cowardice in Nyoka and Ferguson's eyes, he feigns bravado.

"I'll go by myself." He insists.

"No!" Nyoka promptly responds.

"You are not a cavalryman. Besides, I need you and everyone I trust close to the throne. Those who mean nothing to me can die fighting Macati while he's still far off." She orders.

"So, it's the same group of warriors you send to trouble spots that you will send to fight Macati?" Samanja smiles.

Nyoka nods.

"Correct, besides they are battle-hardened from all those conflicts. They should destroy Macati or die in the process. Thanks to their stupid warrior code, they won't run or surrender but die first, inflicting heavy casualties upon our enemy. I will send spies within their ranks to get word back to us as the battle unfolds. Samanja, send for the Cavalry commander to meet us at the throne room."

"And you!" Nyoka points at the weary messenger.

"Come with me."

Chapter Forty-Nine

On The War Path

"I still believe that we should have destroyed the Wayo capital instead of sneaking out and running north to cover our tracks." Brathwaite, the Trelawny Maroon leader, says to Macati as they rest by the riverbank after an all-night march.

"We want to preserve as much of our ammunition for the main battle ahead of us; therefore, the decision is not to engage with every enemy, and or their allies we meet on the way, but rather avoid them. Once we capture the Kapora capital and most of its army intact, word of our swift and decisive victory will spread fast to all surrounding kingdoms that the true descendant, the great Ikwunga, is back on the throne and has the full backing of the Orishas and ancestors to assert their mandate. The Wayo, being self-serving opportunists, will not fight but seek peace and trade deals with the new regime. Besides, attacking the kingdom without a formal declaration of war would bring us dishonorable victory," Macati responds.

"Orishas and ancestors?" Waggy laughs.

"I thought you were a Christian?" He folds his arms.

"Yes, but they don't know that, and most of the population hold onto traditional beliefs. Being the direct descendant of the great Ikwunga is the only legal claim I have to the throne; otherwise, anyone has the right to claim it, thereby making ours a republic."

"How expedient," Waggy chuckles.

"Every monarch in the world does the same. Either claim to be a descendant of their god, a great priest, a prophet of that God, or some mythical figure that everyone holds in reverence, including the

Christian ones, even though Jesus had no children. I hear the King of France claimed to be the descendant of Jesus and Mary Magdalene." He justifies himself.

"Ha, that didn't stop his people from cutting off his head." Waggy smirks.

"Ehn now, the ear that refuses to listen to advice will join the head when it is chopped off. He refused to listen to the cries of his people while they suffered; eating cakes while the masses couldn't afford bread. On top of which he was perceived weak, allowing upstarts to exploit his vulnerability."

"Performance is the only real legitimacy to the throne — performance for the people, power, and one's willingness to use that power if threatened."

"That's where the perception of spiritual authority comes in; that the gods and our ancestors will smite anyone who usurps the throne; our victory must look ordained from above. The elimination of the usurpers must be decisive and exemplary to anyone who should consider attempting to overthrow or oppose my authority."

"By performance, you mean economic improvement, correct?"

Waggy seeks clarification.

"Yes." Macati nods.

"And how do you plan to undo the damage Nyoka, and her puppets did to the economy?"

Waggy is keen to understand if this will be even feasible.

"Simple, remove all her corrupt officials and eliminate the taxes they imposed on freeborn." Macati explains.

"Isn't that the arrangement they made with the British?"

"You are right. *They* arranged with the British, not *us*. The Kapora in my regime are not British subjects and partakers of the protectorate agreement. Therefore, we owe them no tributes or taxes as they would like to call it." He makes it clear.

"Remember the Kapora chief we freed from the castle? He said that the British have an officer assigned to the palace. When word of our arrival gets to the city, he will send a message to the headquarters for reinforcement. So, we will be fighting both the Kapora army loyal to Nyoḳa and the British colonial army."

"That will happen if the British get the message. That's why I sent a detachment of horsemen and several the freed Kapora Peças to lay an ambush on the road between Kapora and the British headquarters. They will recognize the royal messengers and capture them, preferably alive, to extract information about the enemy from them. By the time the British hear of the overthrow, it will be too late for them to do anything. Besides, they have no one else to hand over to if they wanted to get rid of us." Macati says.

"Why can't the British overthrow and rule directly?" Braithwaite the Cudjoe town maroon asks.

"Where in tropical Africa have you seen them do that?" Macati responds. They lack manpower, and they die of tropical diseases. That's why they send Scotts to lead African enlisted men to overthrow African kings. This brings me to my next point. Armstrong is going to talk to them on our behalf as soon as we secure the throne. He will offer them trade in rubber, palm oil, and cocoa with the new government. That's what they want, and we can become rich in this trade. Land appropriated from Nyoka's collaborators and Obijinall's family will be used for this very purpose."

"Are you going after Obijinall's people too?" Waggy is surprised.

"Of course, they started the whole thing. To let them live is like letting baby snakes live in your house after killing the mother. Sooner or later, they will grow to bite you. Survivors of the ruling house must be impoverished permanently."

Macati's mercy had met its end.

"How do you intend to do that?" Waggy feels uneasy about this.

"Render them landless. In an agro-based economy, such people are doomed to work for others forever, making just enough to feed for the day. They won't have time to plan revenge or work their way up. People may pity the poor, but they don't respect them enough to fight under their command. If anything, they will use them as cannon fodder in their battle for enrichment."

Chapter Fifty

Kill Him

In the Kapora throne room, Nyoka orders the chief cavalry officer to ride out, seek and destroy Macati. She condescendingly speaks to him, and he turns to the King for a response — out of traditional respect for the throne.

But Nyoka yells, "What do you need his approval for? Move moron!"

The Cavalry officer rushes out of the palace, hoping no one heard Nyoka talk to him like a fool. He gathers ten thousand men on horseback, and they head to the coast to make it on time before sunrise.

Macati and his troops leave the forests and enter a vast plain — the plain slopes upward to the north and east. To the far north is a ridge, and to the east, another. There is dust rising from the other side of the northern ridge, and Macati orders four horsemen to gallop at full speed to the top of the ridge to identify what is approaching. Rising dust could mean one of two things, and both are bad: a large number of hoofs in fast motion — it could be a stampeding herd of large animals like buffalos or an advancing cavalry.

Macati notices light dust rising from the ridge to the east. He orders everyone to immediately head back into the forest and take up a hasty defensive position. If there was any doubt as to who was approaching earlier, the second set of dust covering a wide area confirms that it's not animals stampeding but human beings. A cloud of light dust spreading over a wide area is a sign of running infantry, especially in the dry season. This is the time of the year many African Kingdoms prefer to fight.

Macati knows that you incur heavy casualties fighting your way up a hill, especially if your first contact with the enemy is cavalry galloping downhill towards you. Cavalry is useless when forced to fight in a forest with thick undergrowth. That's why he told his men to go into the woods.

Macati and his men take up positions from behind tree trunks and the top of trees. On the top of a mound, small artillery pieces are mounted to take down large numbers of enemy cavalrymen and infantry before they make it halfway down the plain.

Macati's horsemen barely make it to the top of the hill when the Kapora Cavalry arrives. They fill up the top of the ridge then stop. The four men see the formidable force and turn around immediately. They drive their horses at full speed back towards the forest. The Cavalry comes after them at full charge. Halfway down the plain, the leader raises his shield as a sign for the troops to stop. They stop, and the leader turns to the east.

The top of the east ridge is lined with Parapouls. They caused the light dust that Macati identified as running infantry. The Kapora Cavalry chief knows that he did not invite the Wagombe to join him in the battle against Macati. It looks like he has charged into a trap. Macati's army in the forest on one side, and his in-laws — the Wagombe — on his eastern flank, with the sun behind them.

He is in an awful position. With the sun shining at him, he and his men will not be able to see the arrows coming in from the east because the sun will shine on their eyes. If he must attack the Wagombe, he will have to fight uphill; he can't charge into the forest either — his horses are useless in the forest. They would have to fight hand to hand. He doesn't know how many warriors are with Macati, but he can estimate about ten thousand Wagombe on the ridge.

Defeat is inevitable if he proceeds. The only way out is back the same way he came, and that is if Macati's troops haven't blocked off that route already.

He turns around and is confronted by six officers from within his ranks — they order him to drop his weapon or die. He drops his gun to the ground.

The six mutineers' leader trots towards the forest with his fist up and clenched as a sign to the men to stand fast. He drops his rifle and removes his headdress as a sign to Macati that he wants to talk first to offer terms.

After surrendering to Obijinall twenty-seven years ago, Macati will not yield to anyone else again. Macati turns to the ridge in the east with his telescope and identifies the warriors there —they are Wagombe. He has not contacted them himself and is unsure if they have come to fight him or come to welcome him and Awat. It's possible that Nyoka arranged the overthrow of Awat's family from leadership and replaced them with stooges. Now the stooge has ordered the tall Wagombe to attack him.

The leader of the mutineers approaches the forest shouting something and shaking his fist.

"He is shaking his fist at us," Ferdinand says.

"Is he swearing at us?"

"No," replies Macati.

To westerners, shaking your fist is a sign of rage, but to Africans, it's a sign of praise. Now, if he opened his palm out wide showing all the five fingers, then he is calling you a bastard. In essence, your mother is a prostitute, and your father could be any of the five men she slept with the day you were conceived, and if he shows you ten fingers, then it's ten unknown men. The appropriate response to is to beat up the man who's insulting your mother.

"What is he saying?" Ferdinand is puzzled.

"Macati! Son of Zaki! May your reign be long!" The man shouts.

"We have come to welcome our King back to his kingdom. Macati son of Zaki, I greet you." He bows out of respect.

Waggy recognizes the mutiny leader and yells out of his fighting position, and says, "I have a tail."

The man jumps off his horse and runs to Waggy with tears in his eyes and a quaky voice.

"Anywhere I go, he goes also. Anything I say, he says also."

The leader of the six mutineers who disarmed the Cavalry commander is Waggy's baby brother Kwabena, now fully grown.

The Cavalry men cheer as the long-lost brothers hug and weep for joy.

Macati steps out of the forest. The cavalrymen get off their horses and lay prostrate in respect to Macati. The five other warrior chiefs bring the Cavalry commander to Macati and force him to his knees. He begs for mercy, stating he was acting on orders from the throne, not on his own volition.

Macati says they should tie him to a tree; for the time being, he will decide what to do with him later.

The six war chiefs explain that Kapora Cavalry had grown tired of the Nyoka regime and are happy to establish Macati on the throne in the hopes of returning the kingdom to its former glory. Many of the young men were not yet born when Macati and Waggy were captured. However, their stories were well known in every household.

Soon the Kapora returnees are laughing and talking with their long-lost brothers and cousins.

Jabu jumps on a horse and takes off in full gallop to the east ridge. Makuei and several Wagombe men follow suit. Mark joins them. As they approach the ridge, veteran Parapouls on the ridge shout for joy.

Old Makuak came with them riding on a donkey; his eyes are deemed but mind full of wisdom as he ages. Young Parapouls bring Jabu and Makuei to him.

"I thought I would not live to see this day," says the old man.

"How is my sister?" He asks.

"She is on a ship with Halima, Awat, and your granddaughter. Most of the women stayed behind while the men are heading up to Kapora. Aunt Nandi, Awat, and her daughter will join us after regaining the throne, and the war is over."

"Awat has a daughter? Does she sing chiki chiki wawa?"

"She is too old to sing chiki chiki wawa." A young man with an American accent says in Wagombe, mispronouncing a few words.

"Huh? What did he say?"

Makuak places his hand on his ear, straining to hear.

Makuei laughs, "That is your grandson Mark trying to speak our language."

"My grandson?!" Makuak hobbles forward in the direction of the young man's voice. Young Mark grabs him in a tight hug.

"I never dreamed that I would one day hug my grandson from Awat. Now I can die with a smile." He smiles.

"No, you won't; you have to be around to teach us the way of the ancients," Makuei replies.

"How did you know that we were here?" He asks.

"Jumo sent one of her sons to warn us that you had arrived, and Nyoka had sent the Cavalry to destroy you. I did not save you the last time. I certainly was not going to fail you this time. So, we gathered all the Parapouls and ran here to save you."

"I thought her son was King." Makuei wonders.

"One son is King under Nyoka's thumb. Jumo did this with the belief that Macati is the true King and will look upon this act with favor and spare her son Kinyonga."

"I'm certain Macati will spare him," replies Jabu.

That day, what should have been a war of three armies becomes a festival of joy and reunification in the plains that were supposed to be a battleground. The Wagombe supply train arrives that evening with cattle for the impromptu festival of reunification that is being held. Stories of the ordeal in America and stories of the various kingdoms' demise on the continent are exchanged that day.

Amid the celebration, a lone cavalryman mounts his horse and steals away unnoticed by the festive crowd. Nyoka planted spies within the army to keep her informed of the activities of her war chiefs — and this is one of them.

Chapter Fifty-One

The Enemy Approaches

"Treason! Treason," Nyoka shrieks as she is informed that Kwabena led a mutiny against the Cavalry commander and joined Macati and his brother Wagi. The Wagombe have aligned with Macati. Now Macati is marching on their capital with three armies. His own troops of returnees, the Wagombe and the Kapora Cavalry . The spy quickly slips out of the room as Nyoka flies into a rage. Nyoka is known to lash out at anyone in sight when stressed, including allies. She will blame then curse and strike them in rage. Luckily, some see it coming and disappear until the crisis is over.

Rather than see that it's her they are running from, and not the crisis itself, Nyoka plays the victim, claiming that they abandoned her in the middle of a situation. But Nyoka's wrath on her allies is often worse than the perils of the crisis itself.

"Weak fool! It's all your fault!" She yells at Ika's chubby son, Kinyonga.

"If the army respected you, they would remain loyal to you rather than join that usurper." She kisses her teeth.

"I didn't mistreat the Cavalry; you did," Kinyonga puts up a paltry defense.

Rather than admit the part she played in bringing on this crisis, Nyoka goes on the offensive. First, she mimics his stammer and makes gestures of a mentally retarded spastic.

"I didn't offend the Cacacaaaalvary… Moron, rather than think of how to fight the usurper, you make ridiculous excuses for your failure as King and leader of great men."

"What do you want from me?" He raises his hands up.

The young King looks flustered and confused.

"Think moron! Think! Why don't you send messengers to the Mani Kongo, your cousin to send us troops? Or are you too stupid to think of such? *Ehn ehn?* Answer me moron!"

Jumo walks in and puts Nyoka's nonsense to an end.

"That's enough." She steps in.

"Who invited you?" Nyoka sneers.

"I said that's enough," Jumo responds in a steely voice.

"You alienated my children from their family on the Kongo side, and now you want the same cousins you alienated to come to fight and die for you?"

She couldn't believe this woman.

"Oh, I see, the mother hippo has come to defend her retarded baby…"

Jumo's fist connects with Nyoka's jaw before she completes the sentence, and a loud thud is heard as Nyoka loses her balance, knocking over ornaments and royal artefacts in the room. Thirty years of verbal and psychological abuse are packed in that punch. The punch spins Nyoka around, and she sprawls out across the floor. There is silence for a second as the guards watch in shock.

Jumo walks over and picks up Nyoka's staff, "I said enough."

Nyoka struggles to get up, as her hand stretches out for support. She curses Jumo showing her all five fingers. Jumo swings the staff slamming it into Nyoka's leg just above the knee. Her leg buckles inwards.

"I said enough."

"Stupid guards!" Nyoka shrieks.

"You stand there doing nothing while this animal attacks me?"

Jumo whacks her again, "I said enough."

The guards rush to stop the fight, but Kinyonga raises his hand.

The King orders them to stay put. "She said enough," the young King says to Nyoka.

Jumo pummels Nyoka then the King orders the guards to tie her hands. Nyoka's worst fears are fast becoming a reality. Kinyonga summons the courage to express his true feelings and takes revenge for past offenses done to him and his mother by his wicked and selfish grandmother.

"We have had enough of you. Today, we will strip you naked and drag you through the town while the people you have oppressed for so long laugh at your wrinkled buttocks. We will take you to the city gate and offer you as a welcome present to Macati and those you sold into slavery. We will have a public trial where you must answer for all the pain you have caused others, and then they will put your eyes out and set you to wander alone in Ewa Ufot, the evil forest."

Jumo yanks her to her feet and starts dragging her to the backyard to be tethered to an ox that will drag her around town.

Kinyonga continues speaking his true feelings towards Nyoka.

"You should feel at home amongst the wicked spirits in the evil forest. When you meet death in the jaws of a wild animal or from hunger, your Egun will remain in limbo with the other wicked Eguns in the evil forest for all eternity."

Samanja and Ferguson come in and stop them.

"You can't do that to your grandmother," says Samanja.

"Why not?" The King replies.

"I am the King, am I not?" He challenges Samanja.

"Yes, you are, for now. You are also the son of Ika, a beneficiary of Macati's sale into slavery. We should be working on a defense strategy, not fighting ourselves. I hear he has artillery and hundreds of hardened war veterans eager to destroy you and the entire lineage of Ika. Handing them your grandmother won't satisfy their bloodlust." Samanja draws the attention away from Nyoka.

Nyoka shouts from between the two guards dragging her out.

"He has a point! Macati will kill you slowly! Halima will see to it that none of my descendants live ever to attack her children again."

Jumo stops to ponder for a moment.

"You evil witch, back to sender! I never had a problem with Halima! She won't touch my children." She argues.

Nyoka snickers, "That was before Halima herself and young Ikwunga were sold into slavery while you and him…" she looks at the king and pauses for her point to sink in "…did nothing to stop it. Now you, son of Ika, sit on the throne as King? In Halima and Macati's eyes, your inaction and ascension to the throne make you complicit beneficiaries in their misfortune and your continued existence a threat. We shall all die!" Nyoka lets out an evil cackle.

"We have no cavalry and barely enough men to slow down their march on the city," Captain Ferguson changes the subject.

"I have sent a message to the colonial office; they can send out a detachment of his Majesty King George's army to defend the city. Her nephew, the King of Wayo Kingdom, is friendly with the governor-general and could send warriors alongside them. Her wellbeing is more important now than ever," he says, referring to Nyoka.

Jumo looks at her son and says, "Confine her to her house with no access to the throne room."

She turns to Nyoka and says, "You no longer run things in this kingdom effective immediately. Later, I will deal with you. We've had enough of you and your antics."

Nyoka's evil smile frustrates her even more.

"I think we should send a delegation out to negotiate peace with the on-coming army," says Ferguson.

"Why?" Samanja asks with a quake in his voice.

"We can fortify the city walls and shoot them as they approach." He argues.

Ferguson responds, "Those walls offer no protection against artillery. Without walls, you stand a chance of escape. With them, you are locked in while the bombs drop from above. We will be dead in one hour of bombardment. I fought alongside the Blue Jackets in the war of 1812; they never lost a battle against units better armed and better trained in modern warfare than you. A peace settlement gives enough time for reinforcements to arrive from the colonial regiment and maybe the Wayos."

"Who can we send?" Ferguson asks, looking at Samanja.

"Not me," Samanja responds.

"Macati hates me." He makes it clear, knowing his own fate.

Jumo cuts in, "Send Mama Waggy. I can impress upon her to save our kingdom from the fury of her sons. Macati holds her in high esteem; he will listen to her."

The young King stands up, "What about me?"

"A peaceful handover will be part of the negotiations," Jumo responds with a reassuring look in her eyes.

"What of those involved in his sale to slavery?" Samanja asks.

"You can pin it all on Nyoka," Jumo responds.

"She is known for coercing and manipulating people to do her wicked work for her. If Macati and the returnees could embrace Kwabena, and not kill the head of Nyoka's cavalry, they can deal leniently with others used and manipulated by Nyoka. I will go with the delegation, if need be," Jumo responds in an even tone.

Her years of suffering and smiling at those she detests make it easy for her to hide her disdain for Samanja and her suspicion of his role in enslaving Macati.

Chief Ayilara enters the throne room as they speak.

"I heard the good news."

The smell of palm wine oozes out of his mouth as he speaks.

"Which news?" Samanja turns, startled at the statement.

"That you finally stood up to Nyoka and kicked her out of the throne room.

Finally, Kapora has a sovereign."

Through drunken glazed eyes, he steals glances at the young King and Jumo for signs of his sycophancy's positive impact.

"We are just talking about handing power over to Macati," says Kinyonga.

"Why would you do that?" The Chief is visibly flustered.

"We do so willingly, or he takes it by force," The young King responds.

"Then we fight, oh King!" Chief Ayilara stumbles into a fighting stance.

"The Kapora Cavalry and Wagombe's have joined him, and they are advancing," the young King responds.

"Ah, my King, what shall we do? I am with you."

The realization of fast-approaching doom has a sobering effect on the old drunkard. His posture changes, as he quickly sobers up.

"*Sycophant!*" Jumo thinks to herself but instead says something else.

"Why not come with us to negotiate a peaceful handover to Macati and persuade him to let bygones be bygones for the sake of peace and progress for our people and great nation?"

"What does the King say to that?" Ayilara asks.

"I think it's the only option we have. As an elder of this Kingdom, will you save our people?"

"Yes, yes, anything you ask of me," responds Chief Ayilara.

His mind is racing through the palm wine-induced fog in his head to determine if there's any possibility of Macati knowing of his role in Ika's ascension to the throne —they were drinking buddies. He can argue that he was distrusted and kept out of the loop until after the fact because the conspirators didn't trust him when he drank. The title of Kasuku was thrust upon him after Uzaza's sudden disappearance, and now he must prove himself worthy of the King's loyalty.

While those with noble titles and ties to the throne debate on what their next move will be, Macati is already on his way, with every ounce of strength in his veins to seize all power from those seated on his rightfully inherited throne.

Chapter Fifty-Two

"When Criminals Become Judges"

Ola Rotimi

Macati and his newly formed alliance approach the Kapora capital city gates. From a distance, he observes the dilapidated structure.

"These walls cannot stop a drunk fly, much less an approaching army," Macati laments to Waggy riding by his side.

"Oh, how our people have fallen from glory into the gutter. I have no desire to fight them but rather help them." Macati shakes his head.

"You may not need to fight them," Waggy responds by pointing to the tops of the tottering walls where the turrets once stood. Instead of archers raining down arrows on the approaching army, hundreds of women and children gather to watch the approaching army.

They shout in unison, "Welcome home!"

They are all bearing the flags of Kapora and palm fronds, cheering.

"Where are the men"? Macati asks, scanning his perimeter.

"Is this a trap?" He stretches his hand out and the troops behind him stop their advance.

The city gate opens, and several people from the city come out in their best clothes to greet them. The royal drums sound, and there is a sudden hush.

The elders of the land come through the gates. Amongst them, is Waggy's mother, who can barely contain herself. Waggy breaks military formation and runs up to her with tears in his eyes. Mama Waggy recognizes him from a distance and rushes forward as fast as her aged legs can carry her. They weep for joy as they hug and unite after years of being apart.

Close behind him are Ferdinand, Marcelina, and Orlando, his Sambo children from Brazil. They are eager to see their grandmother. Marcelina, the only female in the group, trained as a nurse in Sierra Leone and came along as an army medic.

The truth is she is so attached to her dad, who still calls her by her baby pet name "Yaya" and would go anywhere he went, even if it was a dangerous military mission.

The elders' approach Macati and greet him, "We come in peace."

They bow in respect.

"Our Lord, our people have seen many perils since your capture and sale into slavery. Would you inflict on us more trouble with your army?" Mama Waggy asks.

"I've heard your wailings far, far away. I've seen our people sold like cattle and reduced to the beast of burdens in faraway lands. I have come not to bring you more trouble, but to recover what has been stolen from me and restore to our people their dignity and prosperity that was stolen," Macati replies.

There's a smile on Mama Waggy's face, as the young boy she saw growing up is now a great man, ready to lead his people and restore everything that was lost and left in ruins in the wicked hands of Nyoka.

"Good words," replies Ayilara, leader of the group.

"The young King has sent us to request that you spare his life and that of his household." He speaks up.

"If you found a snake in your house, would you allow it to live in peace?" Macati replies.

There is silence, as the crowd looks at Ayilara for an answer.

"The house of Ika and the descendants of Nyoka are Pombeiros. They sold our people to slavery, brought our great civilization to ruin, collaborated in the looting of our natural and human resources, and destroyed our environment. All for what? For personal gain and to perpetuate their prominent positions as VIPs of waste and decay! Just like the snake in your house, they would do what comes naturally to them. Slither around with the forked tongues full of lies, doublespeak, and venom. At the slightest opportunity they get, they will strike with their venomous fangs, bringing death to you and your household. Just as you can't turn a snake into a harmless earthworm, you can't change a Pombeiros into a productive member of the community."

"You draw a hard line, leaving no room for compromise. The young King is offering you his crown and total support. You too, give something for the sake of peace," the elder replies.

"An enemy offers you poison in a cup and says, 'let's drink to peace.' Do you reject it, or do you drink it to not appear rude in the eyes of those around? That is the choice you are asking me to make, elders." Macati looks deep into their eyes, as if he can see the inner depths of their hearts and souls.

The elders stand silent. Ayilara moves his walking stick from his right hand to the left. Ferguson sees the sign and quietly signals the troops to take battle formation. The city gate closes, and the women and children on the wall disappear. In their stead, riflemen appear.

"Is this the peace you were offering?" Macati shouts out loud.

He raises his rifle, and artillery guns appear on the ridge above the town.

"This is not what we agreed!" Waggy's mother shouts at Ayilara, feeling betrayed.

"The young King is as much a victim in all this. He needs reassurance that he and his household will not be punished twice. First by Nyoka and now by Macati," Ayilara replies.

"Then a fair trial is in order. Let him state his case and be exonerated of all charges instead of this underhanded maneuver he just did with the white man and riflemen."

She turns to Macati, "When swarms of grasshoppers fight each other, the crows gather for a feast. The artillery guns on the ridge ensure only one thing — the destruction of the Kingdom you claim to love and the death of those who see you as their savior from oppression, backwardness, and poverty. Those who benefit from the carnage are the same foreigners who profited from our enslavement and exploitation. What then is the difference between you and the Pombeiros you hate so much?"

"What then do you propose?" Uzaza steps forward.

Chief Ayilara is taken aback at the sight of Uzaza, he almost chokes on his saliva. Uzaza fixes his gaze on him.

"A trial of reconciliation and an opportunity for everyone to express their grievances," Mama Waggy responds.

"Who will be the judge?" Uzaza asks, giving Ayilara a stern look.

"The elders of the land, just, just like in the old days," the parrot feathers on Ayilara's hat shake as he nods his head.

"You want us to believe that justice is best served when criminals become judges?" There is an edge in Uzaza's voice.

Ayilara turns and hobbles away fast in the direction of the city gate. Macati raises his rifle to shoot.

"What are you doing?" Uzaza demands.

"I will shoot him in the back like the coward that he is. Is that not the spy within the ranks of warriors who betrayed my father? The same one who gained land, property, and your title as Kasuku under Nyoka," Macati responds.

"It is him," Uzaza replies.

"He is also the one who arranged for my capture, your mother, and Ikwunga. Killing him with a single shot is no punishment for the pain and suffering he has caused. We will have the trial in which he must answer for everything he has done. He and everyone responsible will be given the traditional treatment given to thieves. They must return everything stolen, before they are stripped naked, publicly humiliated, and banished from the kingdom with nothing but a loincloth. That is the worst type of punishment you can give a vain and greedy person — public humiliation and poverty. Then we put out their greedy eyes, so they never look on other people's things covetously — as is the customary punishment for covetous and greedy people."

"But he is getting away!" Macati protests, wanting blood.

"Let him run," Uzaza reaches for Macati's rifle and points it to the ground.

"He can't get too far: we will get him. Between now and when he is captured, his mind will suffer great turmoil and run many scenarios on the type of punishment coming his way. The more pressing issue at hand is how to regain the throne without destroying the kingdom and the innocent people within its walls."

"I have a plan for that," Mama Waggy replies.

"You and your armies will pull away from the city. I will get the King to abdicate the throne. When he does, you will be crowned King and you can decree the trial of the wicked," Mama Waggy turns and calls for the townspeople to follow her.

But Waggy blocks her exit.

"Mama, you are an elderly widow, what can an old woman do against soldiers with guns? Let us with arms, strength and military skills handle this!"

"Those who underestimate little people have not spent the night with a mosquito," replies Mama Waggy.

The tiny female Anopheles mosquito is the biggest killer in the world killing on average a million people every year, more than the casualties of America's longest war.

She stops and glares at him with the "Angry mama look" that stops an errant child in his tracks.

She repeats herself slowly. "Those who underestimate little people have not spent the night with a mosquito. Now watch and see what an old woman can do."

Mama Waggy waves him aside with her arm and walks away. She stops and turns to Macati. There is a spark of hope in her eyes, as she looks at him.

"Five days! Give me five days. And if Kinyonga, son of Ika does not flee the capital, abdicating the throne for you, then you can use your muscle, weapons and military skills you learned in *Amrika*"

She points at the guns, horsemen and artillery pieces.

Chapter Fifty-Three

War Has Come.

Ogun, war has come. Bullets and gunpowder, Adelu sends me as challenge to a fight. Bullets and gunpowder. It is well.

Kurunmi by Ola Rotimi

Four days later

Captain Ferguson scans the terrain from the top of the city wall. He is certain Macati, and his army are out there ready to attack. With his telescope, he sees movement on the top of a nearby hill. It confirms his greatest fear. Within Macati's ranks are soldiers that have fought in the War of 1812, the Malê revolt in Brazil, Cudjoe Town Maroons, and pirates skilled with cannons, artillery, and modern warfare. He observes a lot of activity at the peak of the highest hill. He adjusts the focus of his telescope and zeroes in on the activity of these groups of men. His heart races when he realizes what they are mounting on the hilltops.

Congreve Rockets! Congreve rockets, the predecessor of the modern-day missile, were the deadliest weapon on earth in the 1800s. They are capable of hitting a target two miles away; a weapon most western powers sought. But the British — the sole world power at the time — guarded its secret technology the way modern world powers protect nuclear weapon technology.

"How did these Africans get this weapon? No European power, especially the British would give colored people the latest military technology," he thinks. The officer knew that he and his troops would be wiped out in minutes if those rockets were fired. He is aware of the carnage these things caused in the Anglo-Mysore war, its devastation of Napoleonic forces in the Battle of Waterloo and the Americans in the War of 1812.

Historical backdrop:

Tipu Sultan of the Mysore Kingdom in present-day India/Pakistan deployed Mysorean Rockets against the British during the Anglo-Mysore wars, causing heavy casualties. Colonel Arthur Wellesley lost Sultanpet Tope's battle after he and his men suffered a bombardment of Mysorean rockets. Wellesley survived the defeat and lived to fight another day.

Like Africa, the British conquest of the Indian subcontinent was only possible with the complicity of other Indian leaders. Wellesley forged a coalition with several Indian kingdoms and attacked Tipu with a force of over 50,000 men of which, only 4000 were European (less than 10%). Betrayed by one of his own, Tipu was killed in the battle of Srirangapatnam, and the British took several of his Mysorean Rockets back to England. They were studied by Sir William Congreve, who modified and named the weapon after himself — Congreve Rockets. Wellesley's successful subjugation of India with the help of Indian turn coats accelerated his career from Colonel to General and shortly after that, he acquired the title 'Duke of Wellington'. Recently Sir Arthur Wellesley, Duke of Welllington used this new deadly weapon in the British Arsenal to defeat Napoleon in the Battle of Waterloo. He goes down in history as the man who defeated Napoleon in Waterloo.

After Napoleon's defeat, the British Royal Marines unleashed this new weapon on the Americans in 1814 in the Battle of Bladensburg where the British routed the Americans and resulted in the burning of Washington, D.C., bringing a rapid end to the War of 1812. It's the fairy trails and explosion of these rockets that the U.S. national anthem is referring to in its first stanza: And the rockets' red glare, the bombs bursting in air.

The last four days have seen unusual activity within the city. Rumors spread like wildfire that Macati has terrible weapons on the hills overlooking the city. He will make bombs fall on the city like rain killing everyone and everything they land on. Those who wish not to die as collateral damage can leave the city and join Macati. Ferguson himself got wind of this rumor and ordered that all entry points to the city be blocked. He ordered extra guards for the cattle gate near Mama Waggy's hut. He hopes this will buy him time, so the messenger he sent to the colonial headquarters returns with reinforcements. They won't be back for the next two weeks even if they rode at full gallop and the colonial authorities sent the support immediately. Keeping the civilians within the city walls could buy him time while he figures out how to defend the city. He has few warriors and no horsemen, that he can't try to storm the rocket launchers on the hill; they will be blown away before they make it halfway up the hill on foot.

Unknown to him is that Macati anticipated messengers would be sent to the colonial headquarters for reinforcement. Ferguson's messengers were captured two days ago. There would be no British reinforcements.

Ferguson's thoughts are interrupted when one of the palace guards runs to him screaming, "Master, master. The King needs you now! They are about to attack the palace."

"How is that possible? The wall has not been breached, and no one has approached the city yet," he thinks to himself.

He races to the palace and sees the guards standing on the palace wall. The palace walls are in much better shape than the city wall. The city wall, like everything else in the kingdom has not been maintained for over twenty years.

However, the King's palace and the chief's houses like Ayilara and Samanja's houses are well maintained, with imported luxuries uncommon and inaccessible to the average citizen.

Ferguson barely makes it throught the gate when chief Ayilara accosts him.

"Where have you been?! They are coming."

Behind Ayilara are other lacky chiefs, and their families who've come to seek refuge in the safest place in the city, the palace.

"Where are they, and where did they come from?" Ferguson demands. Before anyone could give him a response, he hears drumming and female voices chanting in the distance but not the sounds of war from men.

Ayilara points to the top of the wall. Ferguson runs up to the top of the wall and asks one of the armed guards to point him to the approaching enemy. The guard obliges. Ferguson sees a large hostile crowd gathered in the distance near the market. He orders the guards to come to the western wall and lock and load their weapons. There is a clatter of swords rattling in their sabers as the guards run to their firing positions on the palace wall.

As the guards take up position along the tops of the western wall, Ferguson looks through his telescope at the approaching throng of people to assess their strength. It's as though all the women in the city have gathered by the marketplace known as "Kings Market." Some are holding makeshift weapons, farm implements, and pestles for pounding yam. They are chanting something in Kapora. Ferguson notices there is not a single man in the group.

"What are they saying?" He asks his Sergeant Major, the burly African soldier.

Sergeant Major is often mispronounced as Samanja by the locals, and anyone with that rank is called by his title and not by his name.

A Samanja is the highest rank an African can achieve in the colonial army. Commissioned officers are white, while the non-commissioned officers and infantry boys that make the bulk of the fighting forces are African.

Our elders say, "If the cockroach wants to rule over chickens, it must hire an ox for a bodyguard." The largest, loudest, and most aggressive African is usually elevated to the rank of "Samanja." He barks out the white man's command to the black infantry boys and keeps them all in formation. He is also instrumental in enforcing the white man's law in the land. That is how a foreign minority population rules a large indigenous population.

Everybody likes to feel like a little god and Bemoi relishes the position and the power bestowed on him by the colonial masters. He burnt his kinky hair straight with a hot comb and combed it to the side with a part in the middle, then grew a large mustache and curled it up on both sides to look like a white colonial master. If he could bleach his skin white, he would, but bleaching creams were not yet invented in the 1840s, so an iron stretching comb would do for now.

Woe betides anyone who calls him by his traditional name Bemoi. You salute, stand at attention, and address him by his proper title, "Samanja Sir! I beg to report, Sir!" Then he would permit you to speak. This rule applies to everyone, military and civilian alike: everyone except the white officers.

Because the mangrove tree lives in the river, that does not make it a crocodile. So, it is in the lives of men. Because Bemoi stretches his hair to look like a white officer, talks like them, and overzealously suppresses his people at their behest, that does not make him one of them. As a matter of fact, white officers do not include him in their social gatherings.

At such meetings, they mock, calling him Captain Gorilla, behind his back. Whenever they give him an order, they would say, "Make the apes obey," to which Samanja would repeat to his subordinates as "Aai Show Bay!"— due to his mother tongue interference — to which the African infantry boys would give the traditional response, "Aai!" then they go into a call and response cadence:

"Aai Show Bay!— Aai .... Apes obey! — Yes
"Aai Show Bay!"— Aai .... Apes Obey! — Yes
Forward March... Forward March!
Lefu Rete, Lefu Rete .... Left Right, left Right

Samanja noticed the fear in Ferguson's eyes when he asked the question, referring to the large gathering of women with farming implements and pestles.

Samanja feels a surge of self-importance as the vulnerable Ferguson turns to him for assistance. He translates for him.

"Kinyonga, son of Ika, you have brought great shame to your ancestors. Kinyonga, son of Ika, you have brought great pain to your people.

Kinyonga, son of Ika, you have brought our great kingdom to its knees for the sake of greed.

Kinyonga, son of Ika, you have reduced a proud people to beggars.

Kinyonga, son of Ika, the great Ikwunga reject you.

Kinyonga, son of Ika, may the Eguns of our departed great ones reject you.

Kinyonga son of Ika, your people reject you.

Kinyonga, son of Ika, abdicate and run to those with whom you fed fat on your people's sorrows."

The chanting gets louder as more women join the mob. They start advancing towards the palace at a walking pace, chanting their King's rejection and abdication demands.

Captain Ferguson makes a quick mental calculation. There are over ten thousand of them. His men don't have up to two thousand rounds of ammunition, and even if every bullet hit its mark, there would be at least eight thousand more women that would attack the palace.

He calls for the artillery gun in the palace compound. He decides he would have the guards fire an artillery shell into the middle of the gathered crowd. The loud explosion and death of so many at once will force them all to flee, and the riflemen on the wall will take out anyone else still standing.

Samanja barks the command to the palace guards, "Aai, SHOW BAY!"

"AAAI!" The guards respond.

He orders them into formation atop the wall and the artillery gun is rolled into place. The women keep walking towards the palace gate,

"*Hold your fire!*" Ferguson commands.

He wants the women to get within the effective firing range of the rifles before firing the first artillery round. After it explodes, taking out a large section of the crowd, the riflemen will shoot at whoever is still standing. Every bullet must count.

Mama Waggy leads the women towards the gate, walking as fast as her aged legs can carry her.

"Ready!" Yells Ferguson.

"*Ton dih sapliclap!*" Samanja yells.

His mother tongue interference makes him mispronounce, "Turn the safety clip." The safety clip, also known as the safety catch or decocker, is a device on firearms that prevent discharge if the trigger is pulled accidentally.

There is a clicking sound from the riflemen turning their safety clips from safe to fire. The artillery round is loaded into the gun.

"*In the name of His Royal Majesty, the King, I order you to stop!*" Ferguson yells at the approaching crowd, and Samanja translates the order into Kapora.

Mama Waggy and the women in the front of the line yell back.

"*That usurper is your King, not ours. Macati is our King!*"

"AAAI!!" The crowd behind her hail.

Ferguson turns to the artillerymen, "HIGH ANGLE ELEVATION!"

Samanja hesitates to repeat the order but gives it anyway. The artillerymen raise the guns at an angle so that when fired, the shell goes high then drops into the middle of the crowd from above, causing the most carnage to the approaching crowd.

"Make each shot count," he says to Samanja who in turn barks out the command to the palace guards.

Mama Waggy and the women keep moving forward, chanting their renunciation of King Kinyonga, son of Ika.

"FIRE!" Ferguson's face is beet red.

There is no response from the artillerymen. Not a single shot is fired by the artillerymen or the infantry. He turns to the palace guards, red-faced.

"I SAID FIRE! ARE YOU DEAF OR SOMETHING?"

The women continue their advance on the palace.

"THAT'S A DIRECT ORDER.... FIRE!"

The shrill in his voice reveals near panic as he yells at Samanja.

"Master, they will not shoot at the crowd. Not even into the air to scare them lest a stray bullet hit one of the women by accident."

Sweat pours down Samanja's face as he explains why the guards won't shoot at the advancing crowd.

Mama Waggy had organized this march against the palace. At the front of the crowd are the mothers, daughters, and pregnant wives of the palace guards. The next row were the sisters, aunts, and female family members of the guards. The guards will not fire their weapons lest they kill their mother, daughters, or pregnant wife.

Next to Mama Waggy is Jumo, mother of the King. She agreed to join the rebellion on the condition that her son's life is spared. Ferguson and Samanja at Nyoka's behest have made him a prisoner in his own palace. Nyoka is in full control but can't coronate herself because she is of foreign birth. However, with Kinyonga as her prisoner on the throne, she can rule with Ferguson and Samanja as her executioners. Nyoka can be tried and punished. If Ika was alive, he would have joined them, for he mistreated her and never protected her from Nyoka.

Her beef is with Nyoka. Mothers and wives of the palace guards joined the march, they want their sons and husbands to be spared when they overrun the palace. This march on the palace is what Mama Waggy had in mind when she said, "*Those who underestimate little people have not spent the night with a mosquito.*"

The crowd gets to the gate and starts hitting it with hoes, machetes, and pestles. Ferguson runs to the artillery gun to fire it himself, but the palace guards point their weapons at him. One of them, with a lion's mane armband, approaches the officer and points the gun at his head.

Ferguson raises his hands in surrender. The man motions him to back away from the artillery gun. Ferguson complies. Another guard with a leopard's skin armband approaches and removes the pistol from his belt.

"Master, master," the Sergeant Major calls frantically.

"They will kill you first before they let you kill their mothers. Tell the King to run. We can protect him if he gets out of the palace through the back door in the wall. We can escape the city through the fisherman's gate to the south and get away by boat; I know the river well. I traversed the river with my father many years before."

The palace gate creaks as pressure mounts on it. There is a loud yell outside. The young men in the city arrive with the trunk of a tree. They use it as a battering ram against the gate. The crowd cheers at the sound of the tree trunk slamming the gate — it shudders. Ferguson knows that the gate won't last ten more minutes. He runs into the throne room and finds the young King standing there.

"We have to get out of here," Ferguson says.

"Weakling!" Nyoka retorts.

"Do you want to run without a fight?"

"The palace guards refused to shoot at their mothers, pregnant wives, and daughters," he replies.

"SHOOT THEM YOURSELF!" Nyoka shrieks, wanting to take matters into her own hands.

"They will kill me first; they already took my pistol and would have killed me had Samanja here not intervened."

Samanja points at Ayilara and Nyoka.

"The people are more interested in you than with him," he says, referring to Kinyonga, then turns to the young King.

"Your mother is among them. I think she has negotiated your pardon. However, I recommend you escape lest an overzealous person in the crowd decides to visit you for the sins of your father,

Ika, for the fortune reversals he brought them. The benefits of which you and some of his descendants continue to enjoy to this day."

"TRAITOR! WHOSE SIDE ARE YOU ON?" Nyoka tries to slap him.

Samanja docks backward from the slap.

"Your side, and always been. If Macati gets me, he will do worse to me than anyone else in this palace. Remember, it was me who lured him into Obijinall's trap. Then returned with Buta to lie about his death."

"Then act like it!" Nyoka's eyes dart around the room like a cornered rat seeking an escape route.

"I am. Escaping to the Wayo Kingdom is our only chance. We can return with reinforcement from the capital," Samanja replies.

There is another loud bang on the gate.

The young King takes off. Nyoka and the lackey chiefs follow him out of the palace's back door. Samanja and Ferguson follow suit. A few loyal palace guards run out behind them.

They slip through the back door and head to the fisherman's gate by the river. They pile unto fishing canoes tied to stakes on the bank of the river. In the distance behind, they hear a loud shout of triumph.

The palace gate gave way, and thousands of women joined by men in the city pour into the palace ground by the thousands.

The palace guards stand aside and let the crowd through. The crowd rushes through the palace, looking for the Samanja, Nyoka, the lackey chiefs, and Ferguson. Soon they realize that Nyoka, the King, Ferguson, and Samanja have escaped through the back door. Some of the frenzied crowd start looting the place for jewelry and clothes. Mama Waggy goes to the guard with the lion's skin armband and speaks with him. The guard orders the men to close the gate. The guards help Mama Waggy mount a crate then he shoots into the air to get the crowd's attention. The crowd hail at the site of their leader, Mama Waggy.

"People of Kapora, we came to rid ourselves of thieves, oppressors, Pombeiros, usurpers, and to usher in the legitimate King of our great kingdom."

"YES, wise one!" They shout.

Mama Waggy smiles and says, "Do you kill a wild animal that has been ravaging your flock only to become an animal yourself?"

"Nooo!" The crowd shouts.

Mama Waggy nods, acknowledging their response, then continues.

"You have gotten rid of those who robbed us. Why have some of you turned into robbers?"

The crowd goes silent. Members of the mob push a man with stolen clothes to the front. His eyes widen in shame, as he is exposed in front of the crowd.

"They… they luuluu… looted us… sss-so, I'm lu-lu-lu looting them back," the man stammers.

Some in the crowd agree with him.

Mama Waggy turns to him then makes eye contact with several of those who agreed with him as she speaks.

"Have you not heard the proverb, 'stolen goods bring misfortune?' Some of the things that you carried are sacred objects from the ancients. They bring curses on who so ever removes them from the home of the great Ikwunga. These curses follow you and your descendants. So, while you think you are robbing Nyoka, you might also be robbing yourself and your descendants," she raises her hand.

"Everyone here bear witness; neither myself nor my household has taken a thing from here. Those who wish to bring curses unto themselves, and their descendants do so to their own peril. I have done my duty as an elder to caution you. I go now to bring back the legitimate ruler of this Kingdom. If you are in this cause for the good of our people, follow me."

She motions the guard to open the gate and walks out of the palace grounds. The crowd follows her, cheering, singing, and dancing. The looting stops, and those who took gold objects and statuettes run back in to replace them from where they were taken.

Chapter Fifty-Four

I Paddle Here, I Paddle There. Yet My Canoe Stands Still.

Kurunmi - Ola Rotimi

Faster! Faster!" Nyoka yells at the few loyal guards that left with her as they paddle the canoe downstream. The canoe hits something and can move no further. The two other canoes carrying Ferguson and his loyal men catch up and stall. One of the guards looks at the canoe's front and notices a thick rope across the river just beneath the boats' waterline. They act as a barrier, preventing the boats from moving further downstream.

A loud bang arises from the bank of the river. They all turn in the direction of the bang. A voice comes from the opposite bank, "Surrender now or die."

Ferguson realizes they are easy targets for Macati and his men on both sides of the river. They cannot move forward. Paddling against the currents is both tedious and futile. Jumping into the river would make them food for crocodiles.

They raise their hands in surrender.

In desperation, Nyoka tries to grab a rifle, but Samanja blocks her.

"Do you want to get us all killed?"

"Death is better than being captured by that bastard! The son of Halima will never rule over me!" Nyoka spits.

"If death is your choice, then you can jump overboard, so that you meet him in the jaws of a crocodile. I want to live," Samanja points at the curious crocodile approaching the canoe.

"FOOOOOOL! Macati will kill you slowly for what you did to him."

Nyoka exclaims, knowing her destined fate.

"I will negotiate with him."

"IDIOT! What do you have to negotiate with? ME? Do you want to blame me for all this?" Nyoka tries to push him overboard.

He grabs her hands and pushes her down. She turns to the loyal guards paddling the canoe.

"YOU SIT THERE DOING NOTHING WHILE THIS INGRATE ATTACKS ME! AFTER ALL I HAVE DONE FOR YOU, THIS IS HOW YOU REPAY ME?"

"I am not using you to negotiate. I plan to tell him that the colonial army will revenge the deaths of its officers, and his kingdom will be reduced to ashes if he harms us." He reminds her of the agreed plan.

"He has a point," Says one of the guards.

"Cowards all of you. Fight or die fighting." She kisses her teeth.

"We don't have a chance." They all agree.

"Why are you doing this to meeee!"

Nyoka starts rocking the canoe to capsize it.

"WHAT ARE YOU DOING?" Ferguson yells.

"WE SHALL ALL DIE!" Nyoka threatens them, rocking from side to side.

Samanja tackles her and pins her to the bottom of the boat.

"AAARGH! TREASON! TREASON!" Nyoka trashes around to no avail.

"Paddle to the bank." Samanja orders the men.

The guards turn the canoes and row to the bank of the river. When they get to the bank, the palace guards hand over their weapons to Macati's men.

They have a trial and the traditional punishment for thieves meted unto them – they must be instantly impoverished, stripped naked, blinded then booed out of the kingdom to live out their lives in Ewa Ufot.

Macati assumes the throne and Halima installed as Queen mother. Waggy is his Kasuku. Kinyonga is allowed to go into exile in the Kongo as per the negotiations between Jumo and Mama Waggy. Armstrong negotiates trade agreements between the British colonial administrators and the Kapora.

In the absence of anyone else, they must recognize Macati as King. All property appropriated by Nyoka, and her stooges are returned to their owners. Macati moves on the Jinaali with overwhelming force and installs a loyal chief over them. All land belonging to the house of Obijinaal is appropriated for cash crop plantations to generate income for the kingdom. When a king has good councilors, his reign is peaceful. Macati grafted in several Blue Coats from the U.S., Taboms from Brazil, and Cudjoe town Maroons into the grand council. They will leverage their experience in the diaspora to modernize the Kingdom.

Ferdinand and Macati Jr. and young Halima return to Freetown to attend Fourah Bay College. Macati knows the value of western education will bring to the Kingdom.

As our elders say, *a tree cannot stand without roots.*

A people cannot stand without the knowledge of their roots, so it's important therefore that we tell our children our own stories lest they remain untold by those who profit from our ignorance and servitude.

The End

Made in the USA
Middletown, DE
24 May 2024

54601268R00221